I0600345

Fractured Existence

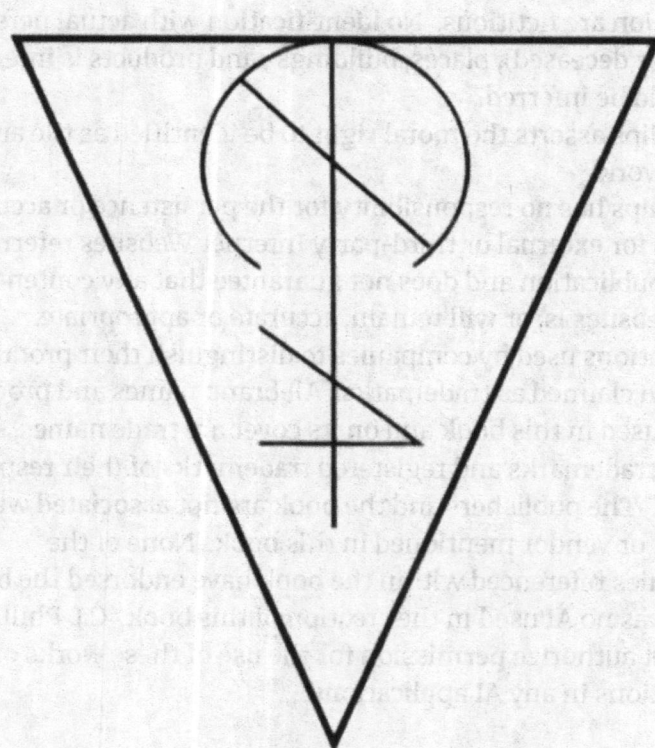

C.J. Phillips

Trigger Warnings

- Retold Rape
- Retold insinuation of child molestation
- Retold childhood abuse
- Buckets of emotional trauma
- PTSD
- IED - Intermittent Explosive Disorder
- Stalking
- Attempted Kidnapping
- Extreme Violent Situations
- Murder
- Severe Anxiety Attacks
- Ectopic Pregnancy
- Loss of Child
- Multiple Sexual Situations
    - M/F/F
    - Dildos with Human Names
    - Fellatio
    - Anilingus
    - Cunnilingus
    - Anal Sex
    - Asphyxiation
    - Begging
    - Double Penetration
    - Edge Play
    - Face Fucking
    - Delicious Brattiness

This one is for those that have waited to be tortured by a rock god. Get it girl. Let him ride your demons into the night. Make him beg for it.

PLAYLIST

Rain - Sleep Token

Yesterday - The Beatles

The Night Does Not Belong To God - Sleep Token

Hate Me - Blue October

Shelter-from the room below - Sleep Token

Just Pretend - Bad Omens

Neon Grave - Dayseeker

IF IT DOESN'T HURT - NOTHING MORE

Is It Really You? - Sleep Token

Zombie - Yungblud

Black - Pearl Jam

Hold Me Now - Caskets

God Is A Weapon - Falling In Reverse, Marilyn Manson

Cold (but I'm still here) - Evans Blue

Little Girl Gone - Chinchilla

Drag Me Under - Sleep Token

All I Wanted - Paramore

Gods - Sleep Token

The Grey - Bad Omens

Caramel - Sleep Token

The Ghost of You - My Chemical Romance
Jaws - Sleep Token
Concrete Jungle - Bad Omens
Calcutta - Sleep Token

Edge
Rain - Sleep Token

From the moment Lily told me that Susie was going to be showing up at the beach house, I felt my stomach muscles harden and my brain turn to mush. That day at the brownstone when we had gone to see Lily, Susie rounded the corner from the living room and I fell instantly. She was perfect.

Red hair, personality just as fiery. These bright green eyes that honestly reminded me of the color of uranium glass under a black light. Her porcelain skin martyred with small freckles covering her cheeks and nose. I still don't know how her slim build can hold such a personality captive.

When she leaned over the railing of the stairway to yell up at Gideon, I could see the muscles flex in her bare legs. The lines in her shoulders were taut like she was trying to hold something back. She shouts, "I was lying then, I'm not now!" then turns back to Matthew and I with a look on her face of pure annoyance mixed with sadness.

She obviously did not like the situation that was going on between Gideon and Lily. I can't say that I blame her, Gideon royally fucked up. But in his defense, he never expected Lily to love him as much as she already did. He would never have hurt her intentionally.

We sat in the living room all just staring at each other while Gideon tore the house apart looking for Lily. But she was already gone. He stepped up behind Susie and asked where Lily had run to but of course Susie couldn't answer that. It wasn't her secret to tell. Gideon wasn't able to see it but I watched a silent tear run down her cheek. She didn't even make eye contact with me but I could feel her pain radiating straight through my bones. She obviously loves Lily. More like a sister than a friend.

That was the moment I realized there was something more there than just me staring at a beautiful woman. Seeing that one singular tear run down that perfect alabaster cheek did more to me than almost 29 years of self torture. I actually felt something deeper than what I wear skin deep. Seeing her sadness affected me, when I thought I was unable to be impacted. She didn't even look at me, but from that moment on she is the only person that I find my mind drifting off to think about. She is the only light in the darkness that fills my head.

And now she is going to be here. At the beach house. With me. As soon as Lily told me, I started to unravel a plan in my head. My initial thought was how much fun this was going to be. Flirting with her, teasing her a bit. See how fiery she can really be. But now that she is going to be here any minute, I can't stop pacing around the room. I have probably looked out the window a dozen times in the last half hour. Basically, I am annoying the hell out of myself.

I hear Lily and Gideon talking about something but I don't really have the time or patience to pay any attention to them. Where the fuck is she? Seriously, it doesn't take that long to get here from the airport. I try to calm my brain down but it is too late for that, I am in full blown hyperfixation mode. I continue to pace as Lily steps up to Matthew asking some other completely mundane question.

I part the curtains again, annoying myself even more with the incessant sidewalk checks when I hear Lily say the name Susie. I immediately turn around and perk to attention. I listen as Lily tells Matthew that Susie has a crush on him. HIM? What the fuck? No. No. No.

Matthew smiles back at Lily, "Really? The redhead right? She is pretty fucking hot. Not gonna lie. And she has a thing for me? That *is* interesting." Before he can even bat an eye, I am lurching around Lily, pointing my finger in his face, "I called fucking dibs dude. Not Fucking Cool."

Matthew grins from ear to ear as he puts his hands up in surrender. He knows I called dibs. I called it the day at the brownstone. He told me then she was fair fucking game. I will fucking end him if he ruins this for me. I turn to Lily as she smiles, "Nope, she told me with her own two lips that she and I quote 'thinks Apollo is fucking hot'." I turn back to Matthew, letting a deep rasp roll from the back of my throat as I poke him in the chest, "I will fucking end you."

I am glaring down at him as he smiles back at me when I hear the voice that has been echoing in my dreams for months now, "Did I miss something?"

I feel my eyes blow wide as I slowly raise my head to see Susie standing behind the chair Matthew is sitting in. The light is radiating from behind her as she perches there in a light blue ribbed tank top and short little white cut off shorts. Her hair is pulled up into a tight ponytail with her long red curls dancing across her shoulder. Her skin is fucking glowing as she turns those verdant eyes towards me with a slight smile on her face.

I feel my body start to harden from toes to fingertips as I take her in slowly. She is just as stunning as the first day I saw her. I slow my gaze down as I see two pert little nipples saying hello to me through the tank top and I silently thank Lily for having the a/c turned on right now. I feel my pulse quicken as I continue to raise my gaze back up to those emerald eyes. Something about this woman stuns me every single time I see her.

3

I shake myself out of the brain fog I am currently experiencing and step up towards her, "Hello. I am Edge. Er, Dionysus. Do you need help with your bags or anything?" I sound like a fucking toddler trying to become teacher's pet but I don't care. I would do anything to keep her eyes on me a moment longer. I watch Susie's eyes darken just a bit when I speak to her and I could have sworn I heard a soft moan leave her lips. I can feel a groan growing in my own chest in response.

She smiles widely back at me, "No, thank you. I am good." She gives me a slight side nod of her head and then turns her attention back towards Lily. She gives her a devious grin, "I am going to go put these in my room." She turns to go upstairs when Lily waves at her, pulling her attention back towards the sitting room, "Well, you are going to have to pick a different room this time."

Susie screws up a confused glance towards Lily. I look at her as well, not understanding what she is talking about when I notice that both Gideon and Matthew are smiling cheekily at me. Lily turns towards me, smiling wildly, "Edge has already claimed your normal room. But the one across the hall from him is open. That is actually the only other one put together right now. If you guys don't mind sharing the one bathroom up there."

Of fucking course I would chose the one room that Susie uses every time she visits. I just liked it because it felt like I was in a castle or something. The vibe it gives makes it feel like it is just tucked away from the world. Away from the chaos. I feel my eyes fly wide as I turn back towards Susie, "We can switch rooms. I didn't know that it was your normal room. I have no problem moving my stuff."

I watch as Susie continues to smile at Lily and I could swear I see her wink at her. She slowly turns her gaze towards me then reaches out and places her hand on my arm. I instantly feel chills run up my arm, down my spine and straight to my

4

balls. My breath catches in my chest as she smiles at me, "No, that is fine Edge. You can stay in that room. I will just go across the hall. Thank you for offering though."

I try to calm my nerves as she smiles then slowly removes her hand from my arm. I can still feel the heat from her palm wrapped around my bicep. I can't look away from her. The majestic creature standing in front of me. I don't even notice Matthew is moving until he is standing up next to me, "Hello again Susie. It is nice to actually get to meet you this time. I am Matthew, or Apollo. But please Jesus god, just call me Matthew here."

I turn my glare from Matthew back towards Susie as she starts fluttering her eyelashes at him. I even see her neck start to turn a soft pink color like she is fawning over him even speaking to her.

She places both hands back on the handle of her suitcase as she gives him a sexy little grin, "It is SO nice to meet you formally Matthew. I know we all saw each other at the brownstone but I am *really* glad that I get to really meet everyone this time. We are definitely gonna have some fun."

I watch her fangirl over him for another moment before I feel the roll of anger coursing through my veins. I glance at Matthew just fast enough to see him wink back at her.

I step around her as I feel a growl try to leave my throat. I have to get the fuck away from everyone right now before I make a right ass out of myself. It doesn't help that I am also rock hard from her touching my arm. I don't even glance back down the stairs as I take them two at a time until I am back on the third floor and walking into my room.

I leave the door cracked just enough to basically torture myself. I know she is going to stay down there talking to her crush for hours and I am going to be sitting here staring at my watch counting the seconds until I hear her enter her room.

5

I throw myself back across the bed and carefully readjust my extremely uncomfortable hard on. I stare at the ceiling, counting the fucking seconds in my head when I hear Lily and Susie coming up the steps. I smile as I sit back up, looking at my watch, 48 seconds. Suck on that Matthew. I brace my forearms on my knees then lean towards the door just a bit to try to hear them better.

I hear them crest the top of the stairs then that sweet voice rolls down the hall towards me, "So, are we gonna hit the beach today? It is fucking beautiful outside today. And I brought my new swimsuit. Maybe see if everyone wants to join?"

I feel another low moan leave my throat as I imagine her in a bathing suit, standing knee deep in the ocean. The waves licking around her thighs with her hair flowing through the wind around her. I am instantly hard again.

I hear Lily let out a small laugh as they round into Susie's room. I stand up, stealthily moving to lean closer to the cracked door so I can hear them better. Lily's voice carries across the hall to me, "Yeah, that sounds like a plan. I hope you brought extra sunblock though."

I hear the slide of the handle of Susie's suitcase go down then it sounds like she is lifting it to sit it down somewhere. I can hear the humor in her voice, "Of course I did. Maybe Matthew will help me put some on." I reach out and grab the doorframe as the anger travels down my fucking veins again.

He will not be touching her. I will cut his goddamn hands off and he will never be able to play drums or beat off again. I was not joking when I said I would fucking end him.

I hear her unlatch her suitcase and I glance through the open crack of the door to see her pulling out a tiny little white bikini. There is more fabric on a fucking wash clothe than on the totality of this little bikini she is pulling out of the suitcase. She

6

turns away from me and pulls the tank top over her head and tosses it down on the bed.

I see her bare back in front of me. I am left in awe at the inkwork on display before me. It looks like a large light blue ink blot is splashed across her back with a side image of a woman wearing a colorful floral wreath on her head.

She is holding a goblet in her hands. Her long blonde hair wraps around her body to cover her bare skin. Below it in calligraphy it looks like it says the words, "Queen of Cups". My eyes travel back up her body and I can see the side swell of her tit as she reaches for the bikini top then pulls it over her head.

I don't even realize that I have the door entirely open as I just stand here, mesmerized by the woman in front of me. I see her turn her head to the side as she smiles down at Lily sitting on the end of the bed, "Will you tie me up?" I feel my legs moving into the room before Lily even has a chance to notice me.

Out of my periphery, I see Lily stop and her jaw drop. I continue stepping forward until I am leaning into Susie's bare back, whispering in her ear, "I will." Susie goes stock still as I see Lily start to side step out of the room. She mutters something but all I can focus on is Susie. I reach down and grab the two white strings dangling at her sides.

I hold my breath as my fingers skim her bare skin. Then I run my fingertips across her back to tie the two strings into a knot in the middle. Susie slowly turns and looks from my hands up to my face.

I am a good 5 inches taller than her so her gaze has to climb a bit to reach my eyes. I watch her skin flush across her neck and chest. I smile knowing that I am the one having an effect on her. Not fucking Matthew but me.

Susie finally meets my eye and smiles back at me, "Thank you, Edge."

I smile back down at her, "Happy to help. Do you need me to tie anything else up?"

Susie lets a deep chuckle leave her throat as she looks at my lips and smiles, "Not right now. But ask me again in a few hours."

I continue to smile at her as I slowly back out of the bedroom then turn to head back into my room. I turn around to face her as I shut my door and she is smiling right back at me as she slowly shuts her door as well.

I lean my forehead against the door after I have shut it and let out a laugh laced with a heavy sigh. Jesus christ this woman is going to be the death of me. I am going to have a fucking heart attack at the age of 28.

I roll myself around so that my back is now flush up against the door and laugh out into the room before me. I take a few more deep breaths to settle my nerves before I push off the door then find my swim trunks.

I change quickly, making sure I look alright in the mirror before I open the bedroom door then step across the hall. I don't even remember the last time I checked myself in a mirror unless I was about to go on stage.

I smile at Susie's door as I bring my knuckles up and lightly rap on it. Two seconds later it is swinging open and Susie is standing there wearing her scrap of cloth, smiling from ear to ear. I grin back at her, "You ready?" She nods her head as we both turn and start to head down the stairs.

I let her move slowly beside me, happy to make our little alone time last as long as possible. We round the stairs to the second floor and hear someone scream. We both stop and stare at the bedroom door in front of us.

I raise one hand and point at the door as I hear a loud grunt come from behind it. I smile still pointing towards the

8

door, "Well, I guess they are busy then." Susie blurts out a laugh along with me as she sashays her cute little ass over to the door.

She raises her hand to knock again and we both hear Lily scream again. She slowly turns her wide eyes back towards me, letting a devious grin come over her face as we hear Gideon from behind the door, "Fuck Lily. Fuck me."

I smile back at her and take a few steps towards her until I am flush up against her side. I smile as I lean my face into her neck, "Maybe we should just let them finish up before we bother them." I look at her neck before me and I can see a vein pulsing extremely fast.

I pull back and turn my eyes towards hers. She is almost panting, she is breathing so hard. I take a step into her until her back meets the wall behind her. I take my arm and raise it onto the wall beside her head as I lean in close to her again. She doesn't break my stare the entire time.

I raise my left hand and use my fingertips to trail down the side of her face, then her neck before coming to a stop at her collarbone. She lets out a small barely audible moan and I smile while staring at her parted lips.

I grin a bit wider, "Are you enjoying listening to your best friend getting railed behind that door Susie?" Her eyes fly up and meet mine as she grips the sunblock bottle in both hands tightly.

She glances quickly at the door then back at me, "No. That is not it at all." I lean in a bit closer to her so her tits are pushed up against my chest. I hear her breath intake sharply.

I smile back at her as I put my lips to her ear, "Yes, you are. You are getting wet just thinking about someone pinning you to this wall and fucking you senseless. Aren't you?"

I pull my face back from hers to watch the skin down her neck and chest start to turn a crimson red again. She smiles as she steps up into my space, "What if I am? What if I am thinking about someone bending me over that railing behind you and just

9

slamming into me until my knees buckle? Until I can feel them running down my legs. What of it?"

I stare at her dirty little mouth as she whispers her fantasies out to me. It takes all of my fucking strength not to make her wishes come true. I smile back at her, "I am sure Matthew is free. Do you want me to go get him?"

Her eyes narrow at me as she gives me a sly grin, "No, I will let him know for myself *exactly* what I want from him. And I am sure he will be happy to help out."

She steps around me smiling smugly to herself as she raps her knuckles on the door. She turns and stares me right in the eyes, "Gideon! Get off of Lily so we can go down to the beach now please!" I smile at her as she turns and struts her fine ass down the stairs. I roll my neck over my shoulders. Good lord this woman is going to fucking destroy me. I smile after her, hoping that she does.

I follow behind her down the stairs and watch her swing around the furniture then head straight out the back doors. I smile while moving slowly, watching the show. As soon as her feet hit the sand, she is running towards Matthew as he is laying a towel down on the sand while laughing with Simone.

I stand at the top of the stairs as she smiles at me then hands him the bottle of sunscreen then turns her back to him. I smile widely as Mona steps forward and starts to rub down her front while Matthew gets her shoulders and back.

I slowly walk down the steps and casually walk past them, "Better rub that in good Matthew. Don't want our little peach to burn." I continue smiling as I walk straight into the ocean and dive into an oncoming wave. I swim a few strokes then breach the surface, turning around and floating as I watch Susie gingerly walking into the water until it is mid thigh.

I continue to hover in the water as I watch her cup water in her hands and pour it down her body. Thank god I am under water so no one will be able to see the effect she has on me. I start to push myself a bit closer to her until I feel the sand beneath my feet again. I walk towards her but stay far enough back that I am still in the water above my waist.

I continue to tread water as I see Lily barrel into the waves and start splashing Susie like they are in grade school. It is something to see. Lily is always so quiet, so reserved. Like she is afraid of something but she is nervous to admit to anyone what it actually is. Then to go from scared little mouse to this wild woman spraying water at her best friend. I laugh as I watch them play around for a while before Lily turns and catches Gideon's eye then blows him a kiss.

Susie looks at me with a side grin then turns back to Lily, "So, you sounded well taken care of earlier." The little mouse then turns back to Susie and plumes a wave of water at her with her hands. I start chuckling to myself again. These two fight like sisters I swear. Lily then turns her gaze towards me and starts pointing between me and Susie, "It is 100% both of your faults."

I stand up a bit straighter, looking from Susie's laughing face to Lily's accusing glare, "How the fuck is it our fault?"

Lily turns to me and puts her little mousey fists on her little mousey hips, "If you hadn't walked in offering to tie her up then I wouldn't have barrelled down the stairs like a mad woman, ranting about how shit was getting hot and heavy up there!"

I laugh out loud and step up a bit closer to Susie, who is laughing right back at me, "That doesn't explain how that led to you getting laid."

Lily's hands drop back down in the water and she averts her gaze for a minute before blushing and looking up at Susie, "He had to prove to me that we are hotter than you guys."

‖

Susie belts out a laugh loud enough to pull everyone's attention from the beach. Sleeping Simone included. I chuckle and lean in towards Lily while looking across the sand at Gideon, "I am sorry but what?"

Lily looks at me then back over her shoulder at Gideon before smiling, "Don't worry. He made his point. We are definitely hotter."

Susie starts chuckling as I step up to her and place my hands on her hips, pulling her around to face me. I lean in so she can feel the heat of my breath on her neck, "Sounds like shots have been fired, love. We should probably try to catch up soon."

I pull back just in time to see Lily charging back out of the water and towards Gideon. I smile back down into Susie's sparkling eyes, my hands still on her hips. She smiles back and places both of her open palms on my chest. Her eyes meet mine again, "Edge. This is fun and all but I don't know if you can handle all the demons that I carry around with me. There are so many of them, they have their own club."

I lean in closer, pressing her chest into mine, pulling her hips towards my own, "Baby, my demons would bend yours over. And then they would make you fucking beg for more."

2
Susie
Yesterday - The Beatles

Well fuck me then. I am standing knee deep in the ocean on a hot and humid day with fucking cold chills running down my spine. This man. What the hell? I am staring into the eyes of a man that scares the hell out of me and intrigues me all at the same time.

He could fucking destroy me. The thought of it brings a smile to my face and heat to my center because I think I would let him. In a heartbeat.

Edge's eyes move to my lips and he smiles back. The heat coming off his body is sending me into a frenzy. I bring my eyes back to his as he leans in a bit closer, "What is that grin about, love?"

I try to pull back slightly, to get out of his orbit a bit. He is intoxicating. The moment he opened his mouth earlier, I knew I was screwed. Yeah, Matthew is hot but Edge. There is just something about Edge. His eyes are like an indecipherable rune that I can't pull away from. I keep finding myself gravitating towards him, no matter what my brain is actually telling me to do. It's like my body won't listen to it.

As soon as I am able to force myself away from him, I drop my eyes back down to the water. I have to get a grip on myself, "Nothing. Nothing important at least."

He steps closer to me and I nervously take another step back. I look up into his face as he smiles widely at me, his eyes narrowing in on me like a laser, "Peach, are you afraid of me?"

I look back up at him, letting my eyes roam over his muscles, his tattoos, "No. But you should probably be afraid of me. I tend to have a habit of ruining people."

He grins as he lets his fingertips skim the top of the water around us. His voice drops lower, and almost sarcastically he says, "Susie. If that is your worry then you can let it go now. You can't ruin someone who is already destroyed."

My eyes fly back to his. I can see the darkness he is hiding. It is honestly fucking exhilirating. I grin wickedly back at him. I take a few cautious steps towards him. I can feel the heat of his skin close to mine again. I lean in and let my bottom lip graze his clavicle. I hear the breath catch in his throat as I lean my lips towards his ear, "You have no idea what destroyed really is, sir."

I watch his eyes close hard at the word sir. I smile up at him as I watch his brain go into overdrive. His gaze turns back to me as he looks down into my eyes, a heat there that wasn't showing before, "Are you a tease or just a brat?"

I pull back, taking a step backwards in the water, "I guess we will just have to see, won't we?"

I turn and walk back towards the shore slowly, smiling to myself with every step. I grab my towel and lay it out next to Mona's, not giving Edge the satisfaction of me turning around to see if he is still looking. I can feel his eyes on me, I know he is watching my every move.

I lay down flat on my stomach after spreading out the towel then look towards Mona. She pulls her sunglasses down,

14

laughing at Edge in the water then turns to me, "I have never seen him speechless before. I think I am in love with you."

I laugh back at her as I shake my head, "Yeah, he is in way over his head. I don't know if he will really be able to handle me."

Mona grins as she pushes her shades back up her face then lays down on her back, "If he can't, let me know. I am positive that I can."

I smile back at her as I feel another chill run down my spine. I am so incredibly screwed right now. That is all I need. The attention of two of them. One is barely even tolerable, if they both start chasing me I may lose my shit completely.

I roll over and lay my back on the towel. Maybe the sun beating down on me will somehow slap some fucking sense into me. I need a moment to just close my eyes and get a grip on everything that is happening. Every fucking noise around me seems to be amplified. I can hear Lily whispering to Gideon. I hear Matthew chuckling at some joke. The soft snores coming from Simone. Everything.

I am completely encased in this world that is Carnal Decay. I understand now how Lily fell victim so quickly. They are all heart stopping, galvanizing, exhilarating. My blood is pumping so fast through my veins I feel like if one more thing happens that I am going to have a heart attack.

I continue to just lay here with my eyes closed trying to gain some sort of composure. I have only been here a few hours and already I feel like I have been wadded up then tossed around like a paper doll.

A shadow falls over me and I open my eyes to see Edge standing in front of me. There is water running down his chiseled chest and abs. His legs as well with his trunks clinging tightly to his muscular tatted thighs. The sun is shining off the metal from the piercings in his nipples and face. The tattoos seem more alive now that they are covered in water. I can feel my

15

mouth starting to water as my heart rate ticks up. Again, I am so screwed.

I close my eyes, turning my head to the side. I am trying to be as nonchalant as possible, "You're blocking my sun. Can I help you?"

I hear him chuckle, "Doubtful."

I turn my face back towards him and open my eyes again. He is serious. I was just playing around asking a question but he is serious. He honestly doesn't think he can be helped.

Now my interest is seriously piqued. What are these demons he is hiding? What has made him so closed off? I sit up on my elbows watching him as he kicks my feet apart then turns quickly and sits down in front of me. I laugh as I sit up a bit, bending my knees. I stare at his back and the ink that is covering the majority of it.

Most of the art is small little images or musical notes. I hear his breath catch in his throat as I trace a few of them with my fingertips. He puts an arm down on either side of my legs, leaning his weight back into them.

I let my eyes roam down his arms. There is a lot of Sanskrit writing on both of them. I wonder what they all mean. I take a mental note to try to remember to google some of them later. He quickly starts shaking his head back and forth, flinging water in every direction.

Mona lets out yell, "Dick!" She quickly rolls over onto her stomach and I see her entire back is covered in colorful floral ink. It is beautiful. I look across the bodies laid out in the sand. It looks like the majority of everyone is covered in tattoos besides Gideon and Lily.

I turn my gaze back to Edge. He has his head tilted back just enough for me to see his down profile. I reach my hands up and start running my fingers through his wet hair. I see the

16

muscles tense in his biceps and his eyes open, looking up to the sun. I smile as I continue to detangle his locks with my fingers.

After a few moments, he turns, rolling over so he is now laying on his stomach between my open knees. I swallow hard, quickly realizing his face is dangerously close to my center. My heart starts beating a mile a minute as my mind imagines him moving closer. Feeling his breath on me. My skin starts to flush and I want to scoot back a bit but if I do that, he will know he has won. And I can NOT let that happen.

I grin back down at him as he stares up into my eyes, "Yes?"

He doesn't smile back, he just takes in the curves of my body until his eyes reach mine again, "Nothing."

I give him another half smile, trying to play the same coy game as him, "It doesn't seem like nothing. You seem like you want something." I watch his eyes as they roam over my breasts then down my abdomen. I see a smile come over his lips when his eyes land in between my thighs. I try to speak normally, but the words only come out as a rasp, "Do you want something, Edge?"

His eyes come back to mine before he smiles devilishly again, "Oh Peach, I want so many fucking things right now. I don't even know where to start."

I nod my head back at him before scooting back then pulling my legs underneath me so I can stand up. I can feel his eyes on me as I look around, not knowing what to do. Just knowing I need to get away from him, from all of them for a minute.

I quickly turn and walk towards Matthew. I reach down, grabbing my bottle of sunscreen before smiling at Lily, "I am gonna run in real quick. Get a drink."

She nods back at me before she leans back into Gideon as he wraps his arms around her. I am happy for her. I am jealous

17

as shit but I am happy for her. She is so much more unafraid than I am. She put herself back out there. I mean, I kinda pushed her and forced her to do it but she followed through. I smile as I turn towards the house then start to head for the stairs. She is braver than I will ever be.

I move towards the steps quickly. Too scared to turn around to see who is staring at me. If I am really being honest with myself though, I am too scared to turn around to see that no one is staring at me at all. That all of this has just been a game. That I am just a toy he feels like playing with today.

I rush inside, shutting the door quickly behind me. I lean back into the door letting out a deep breath as my eyes survey the room in front of me. The cold glass on my back seems to be helping a bit but I need something more. I need a drink. A stiff fucking drink. Anything to calm my nerves and the impending anxiety attack threatening to take over my mind and heart.

I step over to the bar and pour myself a glass of Dalmore. I quickly drink the entire thing in 3 swigs. I pour another half glass as I hear the door open behind me. My muscles instantly tighten so I sit the bottle back down and without even turning to see who it is. I move stealthily through the sitting room then into the hallway and up the stairs. I just need to be alone. Just for a minute.

I have too many thoughts, too many questions running through my head. It is overwhelming. They are all just screaming at me. I can only pick out single words, no actual phrases. I run up the stairs then round down the hall to take the next flight up to the 3rd floor. I barge into my room, shutting the door swiftly behind me.

I am breathing heavily, unable to really get a grip on my nerves. Of course, my body would pick now of all fucking times to have an anxiety attack. I step over to the dresser on wobbly knees and sit my glass down.

Everything is amplified again. I can hear the creaking of the house. The smell of the fabric softener used on the bedding. The light pouring in the window is almost blinding me. My muscles are threatening to lock up on me all together. I lean into the dresser with each hand and drop my head towards the floor just trying to breathe it out. I hear a knock distantly but ignore it as I continue to try to bring my breathing back down to normal.

I instantly crouch down, trying to make myself smaller. Trying to hide from the world, the noises, the voices. My hands are still braced on the dresser but now they look like I am dangling off the side of a cliff and they are barely holding onto the edge.

I continue to take deep breaths, in through my nose, out through my mouth. I can still hear the knocking but I don't fucking want to see anybody right now. I especially don't want anyone to see me freaking the fuck out. I don't even know where this attack came from. It was just too much at once I think. Sensory overload.

I can feel my heart shivering in my chest. I stand up and try to make my way over to the corner of the room behind the door. If anyone looks in, they won't be able to see me here that way. With my vision blurry, I use my hands to follow the lines of the wall until I am finally in the corner. I put my back to the wall and quickly slide down it. Wrapping my arms around my knees as I pull them up close to my face.

I just need 5 fucking minutes of silence. It will go away. I just need the knocking to stop. I need the voices to stop. I don't even hear him when he enters the room. The only reason I even know he is there is because I can feel his presence as he crouches in front of me.

He pulls my chin up to look at his face. I see his lips moving but I don't hear any words. I can feel my eyes floating in

their orbits. Fuck. I know what that means. I try to speak but 2
seconds later the room goes dark.

    When I wake up a few moments later, Edge has pulled me
into his chest and he is laid out on the floor holding me close,
rubbing his hand up and down my spine. I turn my face so my
cheek is pressed into his chest. I can hear his heartbeat steady,
bringing me back down into reality. The smell of the ocean on
him is mixing with another natural musk just rolling off of him.
It is comforting somehow. I decide to just lay here letting him
hold me until I can start to feel my legs again.

    Just fucking great. The one goddamn person I didn't
want to ever see me weak is now fucking holding me to his chest
as I come out of yet another panic attack. This is just wonderful.

    His skin is warm and still just a bit moist from the ocean.
I can still smell the rugged musk of his chest but I am super
focused on his fingertips running up and down my spine and
though it should be comforting, it is making my heart race even
faster. I bring my hands up to his chest and try to push myself
away but his arms just tighten around me. I don't want him this
close. It is too much. I continue to struggle against him but he
just won't let me go. I whisper into the air, "Please, Edge. Please."

    Only then do I feel his arms loosen a bit. I am finally able
to pull away from him. I crawl to the other side of the room on
my hands and knees as fast as my body will allow. I curl up into
the opposite corner and turn my eyes to the ceiling.

    Edge has sat up, bringing his knees up as well just staring
at me. I can feel his eyes cutting into my skin. I just want to be
alone. Why can't he see that?

I continue to stare at the ceiling. The embarrassment of what he just witnessed is hitting me square in the chest, "Can you please just leave me alone?"

I hear him start to move closer to me, "Can't do that love. I am not going to leave you alone in here to black out again."

I let out a long, heavy sigh, "It won't happen again. It is passing now. I just want to be alone."

I can feel him closer to me now. I can feel his warmth along my legs. I look down into his deep blue eyes as they scan the entirety of my face within a second. He finally meets my gaze, "Please, Edge. I just want to be alone."

He blinks, seemingly confused, "Why?"

I look back at him in wonder. Why do I want to be alone? Seriously? What does it fucking matter why? I don't need a reason. But he is in here out of concern, so I try to keep my bitch levels down to a minimum, "I just do. I don't really like people around me when this happens."

He nods his head at me then scoots back a bit, "I will move away but I am not leaving the room until I know for certain that you are okay."

I let out another heavy sigh, looking back to the ceiling, "I am okay. It's not my first rodeo. It will pass and I will be fine again. Until the next one at least."

He lets out a heavy breath into the room around us. His voice sounds concerned but there is something else there as well, "Does this happen often?"

I let out a small steady breath, still unable to meet his eyes, "Enough that I know it will pass soon. Enough that I know that nothing helps."

I hear him sigh again then he stands up. He takes a few steps closer to me and I see him reaching a hand down to me, "Come on. I have an idea. Just let me try this one thing, if it doesn't work I will not bother you about it anymore."

I look from his hand to his face. He is just trying to help I know, but nothing fucking helps. I have been dealing with this shit for years, nothing ever makes it go away. I just have to wait it out and hope for the best. I close my eyes, heaving out another sigh as I take his hand and let him help me to my feet. I don't know why, I just don't want to upset him when he seems so concerned about me. He continues to hold my hand as he pulls me out of the room, across the hall and into his room. He points to the bed, "Sit. Get comfortable."

I look curiously from the bed then back to him, "Sex is definitely not going to help me right now. It may honestly kill me at this point."

I hear him laugh at me before turning back around to face me. His eyes narrow on me though I can still see the smile on his face. His voice though, there is nothing comical in it at all, "If I was trying to fuck you, I wouldn't be so cavalier about it. You will know when I want to fuck you. Now sit down, shut up and get comfortable. Okay?"

I feel my heart start to pick up its pace again. Yep, he is going to kill me. I am going to die. Right here, right now. I take a few steps over the bed and sit down with my legs criss crossed in front of me. *You will know when I want to fuck you.* Jesus fuck, where did this man come from?

He moves in front of me and pulls out an acoustic guitar. I don't know how to tell him that heavy metal probably won't help right now either. But then he starts to strum a few chords and it is enchanting. I watch his fingers move across the strings. His other hand sliding up and down the neck of the guitar. He closes his eyes and turns his face towards the ceiling as I watch him lose himself in the music. I quickly realize he is playing Hey Jude by the Beatles. I smile into the familiarity of it and lean back onto the bed, laying down with my chest pointed towards the ceiling.

22

I let the chords roll over my body. Feeling the blood start to slow in my veins. Well shit. It is working. I smile at the ceiling when I hear the chords to Yesterday start to come across the room. I don't hear the voices screaming at me any more. His songs have seemed to shut them up entirely. I continue to lay here, letting the music wrap around me, holding me until it stops and I am left in complete and utter comfort.

3
Edge
The Night Does Not Belong To God - Sleep Token

I knew what was happening to her as soon as I opened the bedroom door. I would have just kept knocking but I heard something against the wall. Then there was a thump as something hit the floor. I looked around until I saw her cowering in the corner behind the door. She was freaking the fuck out. Not even able to focus her eyes on anything. She was having a goddamn panic attack. I have seen my sister have them dozens of times. I tried to help her the best that I knew. I just couldn't help but wonder what caused it to begin with.

Susie is now spread out across my bed, smiling at the ceiling with her eyes closed as I strum the chords to Yesterday. The song is sad and haunting but it always seems to calm me so I thought I would give it a try with her as well. So far it seems to be working.

I finish the song then sit the guitar down next to me, leaning it against the wall. I stand up and make my way over to the bed, watching her continue to smile at the ceiling. She doesn't even open her eyes as she whispers, "Thank you. That helped a lot actually. I should have known the Beatles would calm me down. I have always loved them."

Proud of myself, I turn and sit down on the edge of the bed next to her. I feel her warm hand wrap around my bicep then she is pulling me back onto the bed with her. I grin at her as I lay on my back and turn my face towards hers. She is still laying there with her eyes closed, face pointed at the ceiling. I scan her profile. Her rosy cheeks. The dimensions of the freckles on her nose as they blend into the alabaster of her skin. She is fucking stunning.

From her full lips, to her sharp jawline. I inhale her deep into my senses, smelling a floral scent rolling off her skin. I smile at her, "I am glad I could help." Her head turns towards me and her neon eyes open towards my own. I can feel my breath catch in my throat, I have never had someone look at me the way that she does. It is like she is looking right through me but seeing everything within me at the same time. I try to give her a soft smile but I know I probably look like I am trying to not swallow her whole.

Her eyes are scanning my face before they come to rest on some sanskrit on my chest. I watch her fingers reach out then feel them as they trace the writing. I hold my breath for fear of moaning out into the room though I can feel the goosebumps as they arise in the wake of her fingertips. She doesn't even lift her eyes up as she asks, "What does it mean?"

I glance down at the tattoo, at her fingers tracing it then look back to her eyes, "Never Again." Her eyes go to my lips as I speak. Her eyes sparkling a bit before looking back up into my stare, "What made you get that?"

I let out a weak breath, "Lots of things." She nods her head to me then looks at her fingers as they trace the letters again. I love that she doesn't push for more. She just accepts what I am saying for face value and doesn't expect some dramatic explanation. I feel her fingers as they roam a bit further up then her palm is on my cheek. She bends her fingers as she runs her fingernails through the short scruff of hair on my jaw and cheek. I watch her face as her eyes move to my lips again. I

25

see her quickly wet her own with her tongue then her soft lips are touching mine.

I immediately go stone still. My eyes slam shut as my mind goes completely blank. I don't know what the hell to do. She gently pushes her lips into mine a bit harder and I bring my hand up to her face. I cup her cheek then move my hand around to the back of her neck. I press her lips harder into mine for just a moment before she pulls back and smiles at me again, "Thank you Edge."

I watch her as she sits up and then moves to the door. She quickly exits out of it and I hear her own bedroom door shut a few seconds later. I let out a frustrated sigh into the room around me. This woman. My god.

I slide my hand into my trunks feeling myself rock hard. I run my thumb on the tip of my dick then drag the bead of precum down my shaft. I close my eyes as I start to slide my hand up and down quickly. I see her green eyes shining back at me. I feel her soft plump lips on mine.

My arm starts to speed up as I see her face in my head. Her lips smiling at me. Her eyes twinkling with danger and desire. That floral scent rolling across her skin. I can still feel the heat from her body being pressed up against mine. The goosebumps that rose up on her neck when I pulled her closer to me. The feeling of her fingers running through the short bristle of my beard, setting my skin on fire.

I feel myself pushing my hips into my own hand as my grip tightens on my dick. Then I hear her voice in my head. Thanking me. The softness of her breath on my lips. My name on her breath. Just the memory of it sets me spinning. I sit up quickly letting myself go. I feel my release hitting my abdomen as I try to contain a moan. My body is riddled with tremors as I continue to pump my dick a few more times at the thought of her lips on mine.

26

I let out a relaxed laugh into the room then stand to find my dirty towel from my shower the night before. I quickly clean myself up then put on some jeans and tshirt before heading back downstairs.

Susie's door is still closed when I enter the hallway. I think about knocking but then think twice about it. She probably needs some time to recover after her panic attack. I smile at the closed door in front of me then head down the stairs barefoot.

Everyone seems to still be outside so I move to the fridge and grab a soda before sitting up on the island so I can see out the window. Simone and Matthew seem to be a bit more cuddly than normal. I smile as I twist the top on my drink and take a long swig of it. Gideon and Lily are out walking hand in hand in the waves lapping up on the beach. Mona is elbow deep into texting someone on her phone.

The smile starts to slip from my face. Everyone has someone. And I am alone. I take another drink, knowing this is the life I have chosen for myself. I can't be mad at them because they are all happy.

Does it suck? Yeah. Is it lonely? Sure. But nobody deserves the shit that I dish out. I slide down off the counter and head back towards the sitting room. Which in turn makes me think of a certain red headed goddess upstairs. I dismiss it fairly quickly though. I don't really think she is wanting anything serious with me anyways. Maybe some fun but I am positive that is all it would be. She is way out of my league.

The light bounces off one of the paintings out in the sunroom catching my attention. There are only a few of them but goddamn if they are not brilliant. Lily truly has a talent. I wish I could create something like this. I step up to the painting of the woman in the cemetery. I reach out tentatively touching the sharp roll and ridges of the paint.

27

I take a small step back, looking at the picture entirely. I immediately think back to the sketchbooks she had brought out last night. She has been through some shit. Her paintings are dark. Darker than her exterior would make you think.

I hear a noise behind me and turn to see Susie making her way over the bar. She is back in a tank top and shorts. Pity, I could spend hours looking at that ink on her back. I quietly move into the sitting room watching her pour herself a glass of whisky. She throws it back, rolling her neck across her shoulders before letting out a loud sigh.

I step up silently behind her and lean in, "Stressed?"

She lets out a blood curdling scream as she turns with wide eyes staring at me. Her scream instantly turns into a laugh as she smacks me in the chest, "Asshole!"

I laugh back at her and take a few steps back to sit on the arm of the couch. She pours herself another glass then moves over to the chair beside me. She is still laughing as she lowers herself into it, taking another drink of her alcohol. She lets a small moan leave her throat before she looks up to me, tipping her glass, "Have you tried the Dalmore?"

I shake my head back at her, scrunching up my face a bit, "Not really a whisky guy."

She sits up handing me her glass, "Humor me, just try one sip of it. I think it will change your mind."

I sigh as I reach out and take the glass. I sniff the liquid first, actually enjoying the scent it is giving off. It almost smells like an aged orange. Not rotted, just musky. I take a small sip of it and the flavors explode on my tongue. I feel my eyes go wide as Susie smiles at me, "Yeah. See, I told you."

I hand the glass back over to her, "That is fucking dangerous. I could drink an entire bottle of that shit. I would be in a coma for a week but it might just fucking be worth it."

She smiles back at me as she takes another long drink from her glass before settling it back against her thigh. She looks around the room, noticing the paintings in the sunroom. She sits the glass down on the coffee table and stands up smiling, "She is painting again?" She looks at me with a hint of excitement in her eyes.

I smile and nod back to her, "Seems so. She has done these few while we were rehearsing. She says everytime she hears us play she gets inspired so we jam, she paints. Win win."

Susie smiles again as she moves into the sunroom to look over the paintings. Her eyes roll over them with so much admiration. She truly is a good friend to Lily. I lean into the door frame, "She is really talented."

Susie turns around still smiling, "She is fucking epic. This is just a taste of what she can do. You should have seen all the ones she had done at the brownstone. They were just mesmerizing. I have stood and literally just watched her for hours. She completely shuts down and there is nothing in the world except for her and the paint. It is inspiring and fucking intimidating if I am being honest."

I grin back as I take a step inside the room beside her, "Yeah, that first night I watched her paint for about a half hour or so before she realized the music had stopped. She looked like a deer in the headlights when she realized we were all just watching her."

Susie lets out a loud cackle at this. I watch her as she shakes her head, grinning wildly, "I know the look. I have seen it hundreds of times. She is always so concerned that people are going to think she is too involved with herself. Like she is being selfish by doing something she loves."

I shake my head at the thought of that. Lily is the furthest thing from selfish. I have never seen her do one selfish thing in all the time we have spent together. The only thing that seems to even be close to selfish was cutting things off with Gideon but that was obviously more of a self preservation issue. Not selfishness.

I look back towards the painting, "She is honestly the least selfish person I think I have ever met in my entire life. She puts too much on herself."

Susie lets out a hoot then moves back towards the couch and picks up her drink before plopping down, "You have no fucking idea."

I follow her into the living room and sit down on the other end of the couch, turning to look at her, "Enlighten me then."

She takes another long drink of whisky before sitting it back on the table and turning towards me. She gazes past me towards the paintings before leaning back into the arm of the couch and bringing her gaze back to me, "Since we were kids, she has always been a bit closed off with new people. Which is why I was shocked as hell that it was her idea to invite all of you here. That is a very un Lily-like thing to do. Don't misunderstand me, I am glad she did it. I have been trying to get those walls knocked down for decades now but I am pretty sure she used the fires of hell when she forged the bricks together."

I let out a small laugh, staring at the couch in front of me. I look towards the back door noticing that the sun will be setting soon. I turn back to Susie, "Is it because of what we saw in the sketchbook?"

Susie instantly tenses, turning to look towards the back door then back towards me, "Yeah. But that is not my story to tell. That is 1000% her. I can't betray her like that."

I nod my head back at her. I admire her dedication to her friendship. Not a lot of people honor the privacy and secrets of others anymore. I lean forward a bit, "I only have one question

30

and then I will never bring the topic up again. The sketch, was it a memory or her imagination?"

I see her shoulders fall just a little bit before she turns to me with darkened eyes, "Memory, unfortunately."

I lean back into the arm of the couch, nodding my head back at her. Jesus fuck! She was only 8 years old when she drew that. I can't believe she had already been through so much before she had even aged to double digits. Seeing a dead body just laid out before her. That is tragic.

I then start to wonder if we are thinking of the same drawing. Maybe Susie has a completely different one in her mind. Or maybe she hasn't even seen the one I am talking about at all. Lily has probably drawn thousands of pictures. I lean forward to ask Susie and as if being summoned, everyone starts to trickle back inside.

I turn and watch Lily with Gideon. I understand now why he seems to be so gentle with her at times. That is not something I have ever really seen from him before. I don't even know if he knows everything or not. He just seems to treat her like she is a bit more fragile than she likes to put on.

Mona comes over and plops down on the couch between me and Susie. She smiles, turning to Susie, "So....bitches or bros?"

Susie lets out a loud laugh, her eyes going wide, "Um, hello to you too Mona."

Mona laughs a bit and sits up to sip on Susie's drink. Susie's eyes meet mine over Mona's back as she is leaned forward and she smiles again, raising one eyebrow at me, "A bit of both, actually."

I am dead. I am dying. My heart is going to fucking stop beating any moment now. Mona lets a soft purr leave her throat as she sits the glass back down and leans back, breaking our eye contact. She turns her head towards me with a devious smile and her eyes darkening a bit, "Let the games begin bitch."

We sit around as a group just chatting and getting to know each other. We order Chinese food and just converse late into the night. Mona has refused to leave her seat between Susie and I all evening. She always has been a cock block but this is just playing dirty now that she thinks there might be a shot for her as well. After a few hours, I say my goodnights and head upstairs.

I am not really that tired but I just have a lot rolling around in my head still. I want to focus on Susie honestly, but I can't get a solid read on her. I don't know if she is seeing anything here between us or not. Don't get me wrong, if she wants to just have a good time, I am fucking down. But I think I may feel a bit more for her than she feels for me. And that has the potential to truly destroy me. Probably in a way I have never been destroyed before. I shake my head, trying to pull her face from my thoughts. I need to get my focus back on the tour. We have one stop left then I can finally go home for a bit. I don't really miss London but I miss my solitude.

I miss the quiet ease of not having anyone or anything to worry about. That is honestly the hardest part of being in this band. I want the experience but I just hate having to be around people to get it.

I step into my room and decide to take a shower before passing out for the night. I grab some shorts then step into the bathroom at the end of the hall. I do love Lily's decorating taste. Everything is so modern here. Clean lines, open shelving. The shower is open on one end with a large glass wall separating it from the vanity and toilet. It is a dream bathroom for most people.

The whole house is that way. I wonder how much she is actually worth? And if she isn't in the mob, how in hell did she get that kind of bankroll? I know her husband died so I am sure she got some kind of life insurance but she has lived this way for a minute. She had all of this long before he died. I turn on the water and strip down quickly.

I grab a towel off the shelf and throw it onto the vanity so it is an easy grab once my shower is done. I turn and step under the hot water, pointing my face into it as it ripples down over my body. I could live in this shower. I run my hands up over my face and through my hair when I hear the door shut behind me. Eyes wide, I look over my shoulder to see a shocked Susie standing inside the bathroom door.

Her eyes are almost as wide as her smile, "Oh my god! I am so sorry. I didn't know you were in here!"

I watch her eyes as they roam down my body. She is checking me out. I smile back at her and turn to face her completely. I see her eyes trail down my body then slowly come back up to my face. I run my hands through my hair again, "You are welcome to join me if you need a shower as well."

Her jaw falls open about a half inch as she laughs and tries to look away. I can see the crimson creeping up her neck. I am learning that is her tell. Just not sure yet if it is because she is embarrassed or turned on.

She smiles as she turns towards the vanity, quickly realizing she can still see me in the reflection then points her face towards the counter, "No. No, I am good. I am so fucking sorry. I should have knocked."

I step out the open end of the shower and approach her, praying to god that I don't slip and land on my ass in the middle of the floor. I lean into her ear, smiling like the devil himself, "Come on. Join me. Or are you too scared?"

I pull back smiling at her as I step back around the glass wall to move beneath the water again. I watch her face as it slowly raises back up in the reflection of the mirror. Her lips have taken a devilish stance on her face.

She turns around to face me as she reaches over and locks the door. I feel my breath catch in my throat. I did not expect her to actually join me. Yeah, I hoped she would call my bluff but watching her shoot her shot has me completely captivated.

I watch her fingers as they unbutton her shorts and then slide her zipper down. She lets the jean shorts fall to the floor at her feet then reaches her arms around both sides of her waist to pull her shirt up over her head. I watch her as she raises that shirt exposing her delicate flesh to me. I see her small little strawberry nipples already pebbled and getting harder by the second. I smile to myself as I feel myself start to thicken at the sight of her.

I let my eyes scour her body, seeing she has another tattoo on the underside of her left breast. It is some kind of writing but it is too small for me to really see what it says.

She brings her arms back down and throws her tank top to the floor as well. She reaches her thumbs down each hip, hooking them into her satin underwear as she slides them down as well showing me that she is bare and smooth. I am going to fucking pass out in this shower. She is going to have to call 911 and cover my naked ass up before they try to resuscitate me.

She continues to grin at me as she steps around the glass wall and moves up close to me. She glances down at my dick then smiles wider with an eyebrow raised as she looks back into my eyes, "I guess you like what you see, huh?"

I am trying to show as much restraint as possible but she is making it damn hard. I raise a hand and place it on her cheek as I smile back into her eyes, "You are stunning."

She pulls her gaze away from my lips to look back in my eyes. She looks shocked at my words. That is bullshit, she

34

knows she is beautiful. She has to. She smiles as she steps around me and under the water.

She turns to face me as she tilts her face back into the water pouring from the ceiling. I see it run down her neck and off her tits in streams. I reach a hand up and place it on her sternum. She looks down at me with the water still pouring over the top of her head.

I watch my hand as it moves down between her breasts to her abdomen. She seems a bit more in tune with my thoughts now that she is under the water with me. She grins as she takes a small step closer to me then reaches out and grips my dick with her hand. I nearly collapse at the feeling of her soft skin on my cock. I let a moan leave my throat as I wrap my other hand around her neck and turn her back to the wall. I push into her, kissing her hard and fast.

I feel her lips smile into mine as I part her lips with my tongue and start exploring. She tastes like vanilla and sin. She continues to stroke my dick in a slow motion as I take my other hand and slide it between her thighs to her pussy.

She lets out a small noise that is somewhere mixed between a moan and a growl. I pull back and watch her facial expressions as I run my finger over her clit slowly. Her eyes are pulled tight as she smiles towards me. I grip her neck a bit tighter, "Look at me."

Susie's eyes fly open and shock is written over her face. I slide my finger down and join it with another as I slide them inside of her. Her mouth falls open slightly as her eyes devour mine. All I can hear is both of us panting as she continues to stroke my dick. Her grip tightens a bit though when I slide my fingers inside of her.

I bring my forehead to hers as I continue to fuck her with my fingers. I look down to see her dainty little hand wrapped around my dick and I almost let loose just at the sight of it. I look

35

back to her eyes and bring my thumb up to hit her clit while I continue to slam my fingers into her.

She speeds up her ministrations on my cock as she smiles into my face then slams her lips back into mine. She is brutal. She is taking whatever she wants and I am letting her. She rotates her hand a bit so with every stroke she is twisting her hand around my dick from base to tip. I continue to kiss her brutally as I feel her starting to clamp down on my fingers.

I break the kiss pulling my face back to look at her as she falls apart under my fingers. I put some pressure on her clit and slam my fingers back inside of her as she lets out a loud moan. I hear her sounds as they reverberate off the shower wall around us. I feel her clamp down on my fingers as she starts pulling on my dick harder than before.

Before I can even think to stop myself, I am shooting cum onto her stomach and the underside of her tits. She continues to smile at me, not saying a word as she rides the palm of my hand while slowly jerking me off some more.

I feel her pussy start to release my fingers. I smile at her as I lean in and kiss her again. Softer this time, but still just as intense as before. I finally pull back as she has her eyes closed, grinning, "So, you do like what you see."

I let out a chuckle as well as I remove my fingers from her tight little cunt and bring them to my lips. She opens her eyes just in time to see me cleaning her juices off my fingers with my tongue.

Her smile drops as she looks at me hungrily with her eyes. I continue to clean off my fingers as she lets go of my dick and quickly turns to be back under the water. I smile at the scene of her suddenly becoming shy. But now I have a full view of her back. I continue to look at her back art until she turns back around and gives me a meek smile, "I am gonna go."

I look back up into her eyes, a bit shocked to be honest, "Why?"

She tilts her head to the side a bit, giving me a confusingly sad grin, "We had our fun. No reason to drag this out." With that, she steps around me and grabs my towel off the vanity. She wraps it around herself, picking up her clothes. She gives me one last parting grin, "See you tomorrow." Then she is gone. And I am alone again. Only this time, I don't want to be. And I have no clue why.

4

Susie
Hate Me - Blue October

I would say that I can't believe I stepped into that shower with Edge but I know me better than that. I had been messing with his head all day, and him with mine. There was no way I was going to back down now. Fuck, I have been eating my Snickers upside down for the last 4 years to pretend it was veins on my tongue. Feral is an understatement. I hurry to make it back to my room and shut the door. Letting out a deep sigh.

I miss Brian. With him there are no attachments. There is no drama. There is nothing but the purpose he serves. Why I named my dildo Brian, I have no idea. But he has been my only relationship going on 4 years now. Ever since Evan.

I wasn't about to stand in that shower and tell Edge that he was the first man to touch me in more than 4 years. One, he would have never believed me and two, no way in hell am I admitting that to anyone but Lily. She is the only person on this planet that I trust. Probably the only person I will ever trust.

Still, I am trying to wrap my head around what I just had the nerve to do. I haven't so much as went on a date in 4 years and I just let that gorgeous fucking specimen of a man throttle me into the shower wall while I rode his hand like it was a roller coaster at Disneyworld. I was afraid there would be some sort of shame to follow my first encounter after Evan. But there isn't.

More like I have been left with the heaviest hollowness I have ever felt in my life.

I throw my clothes on the floor by the window then dry myself off. Slowly, methodically. I need to find a way to get this man out of my head. He thinks he has demons, Ha! My demons are so fucked up they have their own therapists. I pull a large shirt on and find a clean pair of underwear in my suitcase. I quickly pull the damn thing off the comforter letting it slam to the floor then crawl up onto the bed. I let out another sigh as I reach over to the nightstand and turn the light off.

As soon as the room falls dark, I hear the door open. I don't even dare to open my eyes. I hear someone moving at the foot of the bed, "Susie?" Why the fuck did he follow me in here? I thought I had made myself abundantly clear. I let out an aggravated sigh, "Yeah?"

I hear him moving around my side of the bed, tripping over my suitcase on the way, "Fuck, shit. Ow. Sorry. I heard a loud noise. I just wanted to check on you. Make sure you aren't having another attack."

I close my eyes hard, still angry at myself for allowing anyone to see me like that. I turn towards where he is in the dark. I can barely see an outline of him, "Nope. I am fine. It was probably just me sliding my suitcase onto the floor. Thanks for checking on me though."

I blink a few times, it looks like he is reaching out towards me but then pulls his hand back. I see him slowly start to move back to the foot of the bed. He turns again, "If you need me, I will be right across the hall. Good Night Susie."

I blink back frustrated tears, "Good Night Edge."

I watch the shadows as he moves to my door. He stops like he is hesitating again but after a few seconds he steps into the hallway silently closing the door behind him.

39

I let out an exhausted breath. I have this sinking feeling in my stomach that he is going to be a hard one to shake. Mainly because I don't really want to shake him at all. I really actually like him. He is funny and sweet and awkward. He seems to be a bit of a loner which is what makes it hilarious that he seeks out my company at every turn.

But there is something darker there as well. Like he has a whole other side to him that he tries to keep back from the world. I don't know what he is hiding but the mystery is thrilling to try to unfold. It is almost like that saying, darkness attracts darkness. But a large part of me wonders if that is healthy. I know I haven't made a lot of progress the last 4 years but what if he is the wrong decision for me? Or even worse, what if he is the right one?

This damn bed feels so cold and empty. Compared to the feeling I had 10 minutes ago when he was holding me. It has been so long since I allowed anyone to even touch me, let alone hold me. I roll over putting my back towards the door. Trying to calm the storm that is brewing deep within me. 5 minutes later, I am huffing and rolling back over again.

I roll to my back, staring at the ceiling. Fuck this guy. Why am I missing him? Why do I want to call him in here just so he can hold me while I fall asleep? I reach beside me and grab the spare pillow off the bed then shove it onto my face so I can scream into it and nobody will hear.

I throw the pillow back over to the other side of the bed and sit up just a bit, balancing myself on my elbows. I look at the door more anxious than I should be. I know what I have to do if I am going to get a moment's rest. I am going to lay here and hyperfixate on him until I do something about it.

I get up quietly and sneak around my side of the bed. I let out a deep breath then open my bedroom door and slip across the hall. Thirty seconds later, I am opening the door to Edge's bedroom. I turn and slowly close it behind me.

I look towards the bed and Edge is sitting up on his elbows with a look of shock and a sarcastic smile on his face. Of fucking course he is still awake. I give him an honest apology, "I am sorry. I didn't mean to wake you. I truly thought you would already be asleep."

I hear a deep chuckle come from his chest, "Then why did you come in here? If you thought I was already asleep?"

I tiptoe over to the bed and pull the covers back to slide in next to him. I turn away from him and scoot back into his warm body. I close my eyes as I feel him roll over to spoon me. His hand slowly slides from my side to my abdomen. I grin into the dark, "Don't think too much into it. I just didn't want to sleep alone tonight."

I hear him let out another soft laugh then I feel him kiss me on the temple before laying down and settling in behind me. He pulls me from my center, gripping me tightly. I let my hand settle over his arm as his thumb rubs back and forth on my ribs. I fall asleep with a smile on my face and his warm strong arm holding me tight to him.

I jolt awake to the sound of the door closing. I blink my eyes open and see someone moving towards me on the bed. I look up and see that it is Edge in a pair of sweatpants and nothing else. He is smiling and carrying two cups of coffee. I smile back at him as I sit up and scoot to put my back against the headboard.

He hands a mug out to me, "I didn't know if you were a coffee drinker or not but Lily was in the kitchen so she fixed it the way you like it."

I give him another easy smile, "Thank you. That is really nice of you." I hold the mug close to my face and blow on it a few times before taking a drink of it. I let a low moan leave my throat as I smile and pull my legs up in front of me to sit criss-cross.

Edge sits down next to me, smiling at my happiness to the caffeine. He takes a drink of his then lowers the mug, staring into it before looking hesitantly back up at me, "So, why did you come in here last night?"

I feel the smile drop from my face. I am such a fucking idiot. I knew I should have just stayed in my own room. There just always has to be questions. How was I supposed to explain to him that I already have a gravitational pull towards him that I just can't seem to fight? He is going to think I am some kind of fucking obsessed super fan or something. I move my legs over the side of the bed and stand up quickly. I look down into the mug then at the floor, "I'm sorry. I don't know what I was thinking. It won't happen again."

I bring my eyes up to his and quickly look away, "I am gonna go. Please don't read too much into it. Please. I am. I am just gonna go. Thank you again for the coffee." I move across the room to the door as quickly as my legs will allow. I turn the knob and start pulling the door open when I see his hand spread wide across the wood and push the door shut.

I turn and look up into his eyes. I just want to disappear. I am beyond embarrassed. I sigh again, "Please, let me leave."

He brings his hand down from the door and places it on my cheek to turn my face back to his own. He smiles at me gently, "I didn't say there was anything wrong with it. That was actually the best night's sleep that I have gotten in awhile. I was just wondering what brought you in here to begin with, is all."

42

I step out and around his outstretched hand. I look past him for a moment then back towards the door. I am in way over my head and he is just looking for a good time. I hesitantly take in another resistant breath as my chest gets heavy again, "It was a mistake. One I will not be making again. I will see you later." I pull the door open quickly and run across the hall. Shutting my door, finally allowing the tears to flow down my cheeks.

I move towards the dresser and sit my mug down. I have to get a fucking grip on myself. There can never be anything between us. I know that. Even if by some miracle he did see me like that. I just need to do whatever I can to make sure he understands it as well. He is young, but the age difference doesn't really bother me. He just doesn't need some fucked up mental case of a woman in his life. I am sure he has enough stress as it is.

I blow out a deep breath and look up into the mirror. I see a beautiful woman. A beautifully broken woman. Edge deserves someone that is ready to be with him. I am still not ready to really be with someone, physically. I am definitely not ready for any type of relationship. He deserves someone who can love him the way he deserves to be loved. Someone who can actually *show* him what he means to them. Not some hopeless head case like me.

I don't even understand it myself. I am scared to death of being touched but I crave his hands on me. I was trembling with fear when I stepped into that shower with him, but when his eyes met mine I saw more there than I ever saw in Evans. I felt safe. I felt wanted. I felt treasured. I wasn't scared anymore. But as soon as I was out of his orbit, all the old fears came rushing back into me.

I finally shrug the memories from my head then get dressed quickly and grab my coffee mug to head back downstairs. I step out into the hall and see his bedroom door is still shut. I hate that I know he is just a few feet away and I can't touch him. I hate that I feel like I have hurt him, whether it be his feelings or just his pride. I let out another sigh then glide down the stairs to find Lily.

I find her sitting on the back deck looking out over the ocean. I step out the back door and sit down in the chair beside her. We sit in comfortable silence for a few minutes before she turns to me with an unmerciful grin on her face, "So, how are things going with Edge?"

I give her a quick side glare then look back out at the ocean. I watch the waves lightly lapping against the earth below, "There is nothing going on there. You know this."

Lily sits up bringing my attention to her worried face, "Susie, it has been over 4 years. Are you still not ready to try again?"

I give her a soft smile back as I shake my head at her. I let out another sigh, frustrated with myself as much as the situation I have put myself in. I look out over the water again as I sip my coffee. She lets out another hesitant breath and sits back in her chair though I can still feel her gaze on me.

I continue to fixate on the endless blue water in front of me, uninterrupted and tranquil. The surface has a calming effect on me that I didn't expect to find this morning.

I let out an anxious growl as I sit forward and turn to her, "Okay, I want to put myself out there. I want to finally move on from this hell I have been living in but how? How do I do that? No amount of therapy has gotten me any closer. I have smashed every rage room in a 50 mile radius. I have screamed into the depths of hell and cursed the heavens. Nothing seems to work."

Lily leans forward sitting her mug on the ground before her. She moves over and crouches in front of me, putting a hand on each knee and giving me the "You are wonderful and you know it" face that she always gives. I smile into her concern as she whispers, "I know that you want to move on. You deserve somebody that will treat you the way you deserve to be treated. Fuck when you were with Evan, before he lost his fucking mind, the wettest he ever got you was when he would make you cry. You deserve some fucking passion in your life Susie. Just tell Edge, everything."

I shake my head back and forth vigorously. I am not going to relive that trauma with a complete stranger. I can't. He will pity me. That is the last fucking thing that I want. Lily squeezes my knees bringing my gaze back to her, "I know you are afraid. I know that you think he is going to look at you differently. But that is not what is going to happen. If he really respects you, he will understand. And if he is really interested, the past won't matter. I have learned that more than anyone.

"Look at me and Gideon. Sure, he still doesn't know everything but he has been so supportive. So loving. I don't want you to miss out on that because you are afraid of the possibility of it going a different way. You are always telling me that I have to try. That I have to live my life. Now it's your turn Susanna."

I laugh at her use of my full name. She only uses it when she is trying to make a "mom" point. Which seems to be something she does less and less anymore. Maybe that means I am healing and I just don't see it. I look back down into her eyes and nod my head, "Okay. I will talk to him."

Lily smiles victoriously back at me, "Good. Pull him to the side at some point today and just explain your hesitations. I have a good feeling about him, Susie. I really think you two could be amazing."

I chuckle at her again as she stands up and moves back to her seat. I finish off my coffee and stand to take my mug inside. I look in through the glass of the back doors to see Matthew and

Edge sitting in the living room, talking, laughing. I take a deep breath, moving to open the door.

They both look at me falling silent as I step inside and sit my mug down on the island. I look back up but Edge quickly looks away, so as not to catch my gaze. I nod into the air in front of me. I can do this. I am strong. I am capable. I can do this for him. Only for him. I steel my nerves and walk around the island into the sitting area. I calmly step up beside the chair that Edge is sitting in, "Hey, can we go talk somewhere for a minute?"

I watch his eyes as they look past me towards Matthew then go back to his coffee mug in his hands, "I am kinda busy right now. Sorry."

I instantly feel crushed. I finally gain the fucking nerve and strength to talk to someone I feel something for and I am brushed aside. Yeah, I kinda fucking knew that would happen. This is why I don't ever try with anyone. What is the fucking point? Nobody wants someone this fucking broken.

I look at the wall in front of me then glance at Matthew giving him a weak smile. He is staring at me like he expects me to just break apart. I fucking hate pity stares. I look back at the wall quickly, hearing my own voice struggling to stay even, "Yeah. No, that's fine. Sorry to have bothered you."

This is fucking humiliating. I can hear my voice cracking with emotion. I turn to move away and I see Lily standing at the island. I know she can see the pain on my face. Even if no one else can. Her face is all scrunched up like she has seen a puppy with a limp.

I shrug my shoulders at her, knowing damn good and well that everyone in the room can hear me, "I tried. This is why I don't bother." I look back down towards Edge who is still fidgeting with his mug.

I feel a tear run down my cheek and I turn back to Lily, "This was a bad idea. It was too much. I am gonna go. I'm, I'm just gonna go home. I can't be here anymore."

I turn and run upstairs to my bedroom. How can a person who was hollow to begin with feel even more empty? I finally wanted to try with someone and I get rejected. No, not even rejected, completely brushed aside. I am a fucking idiot for thinking he would be different. He just wanted to get a piece and be done with me. And now that I didn't put out, he doesn't have time for me.

I slam my suitcase back down on my bed. Now becoming more angry than hurt. You know what? Fuck him. Fuck him for having this kind of hold over me when I have literally only known him a few days. Fuck me for allowing him to hurt me. How weak am I to allow him to just cast me aside like I am nothing? Like I am unworthy. I am not fucking unworthy. I know I am broken, but god dammit, I really thought for a half a second that he actually wanted me. I really felt something for him and I think that is what pisses me off the most.

I look back towards my bedroom door and growl into the open air between it and me. I stomp over, reaching the door in less than 3 steps. I swing the door open and stomp my way down the stairs. I hear a guitar and drums being played from the dining room. I can feel the anger boiling over like a whistling tea pot. Should I maybe get a grip? Yeah, probably. Am I going to? No, definitely not.

Quickly, I run down the last flight of stairs and hang a quick right into the dining room. I step right up into Edge's space. I see the drumsticks still in Matthews hands as Edge continues to look down at the strings on his guitar.

I don't even bother trying to keep my voice down, "Fuck you Edge!"

47

Edge looks up at me in shock at the tone of my voice and the approach I have decided to take. His mouth parts slightly like he can't believe that little old me would have something like that to say.

I nod my head back at him vigorously, "Yeah, you heard me right Fuck You! Everyone has issues. Everyone has a past. You won't even give me the decency of taking 5 minutes out of your day to listen to me. So Fuck You!"

His eyes are all over my face at the same time. I reach up and angrily wipe the tears away, not entirely sure if they are there out of anger or despair. I look at Matthew quickly then back to Edge, "I am sorry that your precious little ego got hurt because I didn't have sex with you. I am sorry that you feel like less of a fucking man because I walked away. But you don't even care to find out why. Why I am hesitant to begin with.

"Which just solidifies to me that this, whatever this is that you have been playing at the last day was just a ploy to get me into bed then move the fuck on. Which is fine if that is what you normally do. But that is not me. I am done with being used and tossed aside. I am done with assholes like you thinking I am nothing more than a fucking cunt to stick your dick in then leave in the fucking gutter. So Fuck You Edge. Do not for ONE second think that I ever want to fucking speak to you again!"

I turn and march back up the stairs, passing Gideon and Simone on the way. They are just standing at the bottom of the stairs staring at me as I round the corner and start stomping up them. I hear someone running across the hallway then I hear Lily scream into the dining room, "You are a real piece of shit Edge!" Then I hear her footsteps echoing mine up the stairs.

I make it to my room and fall into the center of the floor crying into my open palms. I feel Lily's arms come around me and I begin to cry even harder. Through broken sobs, I am finally able to breathe out a few words, "I just want to go home."

5
Edge
Shelter - Sleep Token

"Fuck You Edge!"

I whip my eyes to Susie's. Her entire face is maroon. She is beyond pissed at me right now. There is something more to it though. Maybe hurt? Embarrassment? I let my eyes wander her face trying to decipher what the hell is actually happening. I watch as tears run down both her cheeks and I instantly feel like a piece of shit, though I have no idea why.

She starts nodding her head back at me like a fucking bobble head, "Yeah, you heard me right Fuck You! Everyone has issues. Everyone has a past. You won't even give me the decency of taking 5 minutes out of your day to listen to me. So Fuck You!"

I keep my eyes on her the entire time. I want to scream an apology back at her. I want to understand where the hell this reaction is coming from. Just because I didn't want to talk to her 5 minutes ago? This seems like a bit of a childish over reaction if I am being honest. I watch her angrily wipe her tears away then she moves in closer to me.

"I am sorry that your precious little ego got hurt because I didn't have sex with you. I am sorry that you feel like less of a fucking man because I walked away. But you don't even care to find out why. Why I am hesitant to begin with.

"Which just solidifies to me that this, whatever this is that you have been playing at the last day was just a ploy to get me into bed then move the fuck on. Which is fine if that is what you normally do. But that is not me. I am done with being used and tossed aside. I am done with assholes like you thinking I am nothing more than a fucking cunt to stick your dick in then leave in the fucking gutter. So Fuck You Edge. Do not for ONE second think that I ever want to fucking speak to you again!"

I watch her as she turns away from me, her hair flying out around her. Then I watch as that gleam of red rounds the corner and starts to run up the stairs. Simone is staring towards me with her eyes wide as Gideon watches Susie run up the stairs.

Lily rounds the corner with daggers in her eyes pointed straight at me, "You are a real piece of shit Edge." I throw my hands out to the sides. I know I am standing here looking like a scolded child but how else am I supposed to react? I don't even know what the fuck is going on!

I feel Gideon's gaze come back to me, "What the fuck did you do?"

I pull the guitar off my shoulders and sit it down in its stand. I turn back around with my arms spread out beside me as I start to pace the room, "Literally fucking nothing. Everything I have tried she has pushed me away. We had a bit of a moment last night. Then afterwards she snuck into my room and slept beside me. I brought her a coffee this morning then she told me it was all a mistake and that it would never happen again, then she left. Like 5 minutes ago, she asked if we could go talk and I told her I was busy. Then she comes down here like a fucking banshee just going off on me."

I take a few steps into the middle of the room, raising my arms again, "She told me not to read too much into it. That it was a mistake and she was done. So I let it die there. I didn't see the point in dragging out the inevitable. She doesn't want me. Fine. I will move on."

I stand in the middle of the room with four sets of eyes just staring at me. I look towards the stairs rerunning her words through my head. It sounds like she has been used before and she was just trying to protect herself from being hurt again. But who fucking said I wanted a one and done anyways? I feel the anger building up deep inside of me. No. She doesn't get to just rip me a new one then slink off and hide. Fuck that.

I round the corner to head up the stairs and Gideon grabs my arm. I look from his hand to his face as he shakes his head at me, "She said she doesn't want to talk to you."

I shake his arm free as I turn back towards the stairs, "She doesn't have to say a fucking word but she is gonna listen." I take the stairs two at a time until I am standing in front of her bedroom door. It is still standing wide open and she is sitting in the center of the room with her face in her hands. Lily is holding her tight as I hear sobbing coming from her palms.

I take a tentative step in, hesitating a bit at the door before clearing my throat. Lily looks at me like she wants to murder me, "Get the fuck out Edge."

I shake my head back at her then stare at the back of Susie's head, "No. She doesn't get to just scream at me and make me feel like shit then just walk away. That is not fucking fair and you know it."

I watch Susie as she starts to stand. Lily backs away, her eyes bouncing between me and Susie like she is watching a tennis match. Susie turns and looks at me, her face streaked with tears. Her eyes are a crimson red and her cheeks are now puffy from crying so hard.

Her eyes narrow in on me then she takes a step towards me, "Fine. Say what you want to say so I can fucking leave."

I look at Lily, hesitantly so she doesn't stab me, "Can we have a minute please?" Lily looks at Susie and I see her give a short nod. She turns back to me, "I will be on the stairs. I swear to god Edge if you hurt her anymore I will fucking end you." I look at Lily in complete shock. It seems like the little mouse has become a lion.

I hear the door shut behind me as I look back at Susie. I take a small tentative step towards her, "You told me not to read into anything. You told me to let you go so I did. I told you I was busy because I didn't see any reason in dragging it all out. You made yourself perfectly fucking clear this morning. You are not interested. There is nothing there. I did not deserve the shit show you just fed me downstairs."

I watch her jaw tick to the right, then she turns, nodding her head as she starts putting her belongings in her suitcase again, "Yup. You're right. I am wrong. I'm sorry. Please leave."

I step up to her and take her forearm in my hand. I just want her to look at me. To talk to me. I want to know why she is so upset right now. I feel her muscles instantly tighten as she recoils, ripping her arm from my grasp. She turns to me in fear and shock, "Don't fucking touch me. Never fucking touch me without my permission."

I put my hands up and step back in my own defense. What the hell? "What the fuck is happening right now Susie? I am so confused. I was trying to get to you to look at me, to talk to me. I don't know what to do. I just want to know what I did wrong. I want to know what I can do to fix this."

She looks back at her suitcase, rubbing her arm where my hand had just been. She throws a few more things in the luggage before turning to me, "I can't be fixed, Edge. I haven't let a man touch me in over 4 years. And when I finally let my walls down, I finally decide to try and take a chance on someone, you were just in it for the game. I am a fucking idiot. I am sorry for embarrassing you downstairs. I will apologize to everyone before I leave. Please just go now. I have to finish packing and call an uber."

I am sorry what? Four years? She has not been touched by anyone in four fucking years? My mind instantly goes back to the shower last night. She let me pin her to the wall and fucking choke her as she rode my hand. That was her first anything in 4 goddamn years? I shake my head, trying to spill some type of understanding into it.

I step closer to her, careful not to touch her, "Why didn't you just tell me that? I would have...I would have been gentler. Also, I never said this was a game. I have tried at every turn to show you that I like you. That I want to get to know you. I tried this morning and you brushed me off. How was I supposed to know anything else?"

She nods again as she closes the top of her luggage and quickly zips it closed. She lets out an anxious sigh towards the bag then picks up another small carry on bag and turns towards the dresser. She starts putting lotions and makeup into the bag. I step up behind her, flat out begging at this point, "Susie. Talk to me, please."

I watch her shoulders sag as she sits the bag down and turns around. Her eyes refuse to meet my gaze though. She just stares at my feet, her voice barely a whisper, "Four years ago, my boyfriend at the time Evan, got fucking wasted on god knows what all and decided to not listen to the word no. He held a knife to me and he just. He just did whatever he wanted to."

I feel my heart sink into the pit of my chest as the anger starts to roll through my veins. Susie's eyes still aren't reaching mine and I do not like this persona that has taken her over. She is not this person. She is not weak. But right now, she looks like she is barely hanging on. I watch her eyes as they seem to search the floor for the words to explain it all to me, "I have not wanted to be touched by a man since then. I reported him. But it was his word against mine. Even though I am the one with the scars. He told them all it was consensual that just got out of hand. Though

53

we both fucking know it wasn't. He was never convicted and is living somewhere in Vermont."

I can feel my heart hammering in my chest hearing the words coming from her mouth. I immediately feel the anger trying to take over. Then it feels like my heart stops beating all together when her eyes come back up and meet mine, "I have not been in a relationship or been with anyone since him. Last night was the first time I have allowed a man to touch me. Last night was the first time I have wanted to touch a man since him. I was scared this morning. I am sorry that I lashed out."

I watch her chest as she heaves out a heavy breath. Like a weight was being lifted off of her. Only then do I realize that I might just be one of the few that actually know this story. I take as step towards her but she averts her eyes again and takes a step towards her suitcase, "I am going to finish packing and then I am going to go the fuck home. I really hope that you find someone and that they are everything you are looking for."

She turns back around and continues to put her things away. I let out another deep breath. I could hear the emotions breaking in her voice when she spoke. She truly believes that she is too broken, too damaged.

I take a small step up towards her, "I don't want you to leave, Peach. I want to fix this. I want to fix us. I want to find that fucking piece of shit and strangle him with my bare hands." I do. I don't think she understands that I would do it. In a heartbeat. I turn around and make sure the door is shut before I pull out my wallet.

I slowly remove a small picture from it, letting out a heavy sigh. I look into the eyes of that little girl staring back at me and let out another hesitant breath. I don't know what else to do. Besides, offer her the same kind of truth as what she just offered me. I reach around her side and place the photo on the

54

dresser in front of Susie. I watch her fingers as they reach out and trace the edges of the photo.

I continue to watch her fingers moving over the picture while still somehow keeping my voice calm, "That is my little sister Ginny. She is 20 now. This picture is from when she was almost 6 years old. I came home one night. From being out doing shit I probably shouldn't have been doing. I was 14 so of course I was out doing stupid shit instead of being home. I heard her crying so I went to her room to find our stepfather on top of her."

Susie whips around, looking at me stunned and wide eyed. I look back at the picture in her hand before turning and pacing the room. I can feel it all coming back to the surface, something that hasn't happened in a long fucking time, "I pulled him off of her. There was so much fucking blood. Susie, I thought she was fucking dead. I thought he had killed her." I feel my own tears slipping out. I haven't talked about this in years. Never down to the details like this. I try to keep that part of my brain bottled up and away from everyone. I turn into a different person when it all rises to the surface.

"I don't even know what happened. I just started beating on him. I broke a lamp over his head. I threw him into the wall. I just kept hitting him, over and over. All I saw was red, I couldn't stop myself. I beat him to the point of him eating through a tube for the rest of his pathetic life. I uh, I did a short stint in a youth offender program. Only like 4 months. I was cleared on self defense since I was a minor. Ginny is better now or at least as well as she can be. She can't ever have children but she was able to get past her insecurities, her fears for the most part. She met a wonderful guy. They are actually engaged."

I feel my chest fluttering with anger and regret, "I should have fucking been there. I should have fucking protected her. I failed her and I will never forgive myself for it. I just...I thought she was dead. I thought he had...it doesn't matter what I thought, she still watched me beat him almost to death."

I don't dare to look at her face. I just continue to stare at the photo in her shaking hand. I know she thinks I am a monster. That I could beat someone almost to death with my bare hands. I let out another reluctant sigh, "I don't talk about this. With anyone. My stepfather had always been an asshole. Normally, he just beat the fuck out of me and leave her alone. But I guess since I wasn't home that night he decided it was her turn."

I reach over and take the photo of Ginny from her hand running my thumb over it lightly before putting it back in my wallet. I slide the wallet back into my pocket and turn to leave the room, still avoiding her eyes, "I am sorry I made you feel like I thought of you like that. It was the exact opposite of what I was trying to get across. I hope that you can get past this. I hope you are able to let someone in because you are an amazing fucking person and you deserve to be happy Susie. You deserve to have someone treat you like a queen honestly. I understand why that someone can't be me. I hope you find some sort of solace. Truly."

I take another step towards the door as I feel her hand wrap around mine. I look down shocked at our entwined fingers and then turn to face her. She is crying again. She gives me a soft smile then steps up to me and wraps her arms around my neck, pulling me in closer to her. I wrap my arms around her back and hold her tight to my chest. I close my eyes tight, praying this is actually happening.

She turns her face to the left so her cheek is pressed firmly into my chest and she just holds me. We stand there in silence for a long moment just holding each other while our admissions float about the room around us. She finally pulls back and looks up into my eyes, bringing her hand to my cheek.

She looks at my lips then smiles before she reaches my eyes again, "I am sorry Edge. You are a good man. A good brother. I am sorry that I let my anger get the better of me. I promise I will not let that happen again. I should have just let it go or talked to you later or something. I shouldn't have just let my anger out like that. I am sorry."

I blink hard as I pull her close to me again. I run my hand down the back of her head, "Gavin. My name is Gavin Edgewood. People started calling me Edge in secondary school and it just kinda stuck."

She pulls back and smiles wider at me, "Susanna Mayfield. My grandma always called me Susie, since I was little. So I just always went by it."

I smile back down at her, staring at her lips, "Susanna. That is a beautiful name."

She smiles back at me as she goes onto her toes and presses a soft kiss to my lips. I bring my hands to her cheeks, not pushing her into me but holding her face close to mine so she can't pull away from me this time. I smile as I pull my lips away from hers and put my forehead on hers.

I hear her let out a soft giggle as she sways back and just stares at me. I take in her face, her expressions. She has freckles on her forehead too. I smile as I run a hand down her face and let it come to a rest at her jaw, "Susanna. I am sorry I blew you off earlier. I was just...I guess you were right. My pride was hurt a bit. But I really think there could be something here. I understand that you have reservations, rightly so. But I can't stop thinking about you. I want you, yes. But more than that I just want to be with you. I just want to spend time with you and get to know you. Can you give me a chance? Just one chance. If I fuck it up, then just cut ties with me. Never speak to me again."

She smiles at me, blinking a few more times before bringing her eyes back to mine, "I would like that very much

57

Gavin. All I ask is that you give me some time. With the physical stuff. It's not because I don't want to. Trust me. I just need to get all this shit right in my head first. I don't want to just jump in and then regret it or you or us. I want to make sure I am totally ready."

I give her another light kiss then pull her back close to me, "Of course. Let's just get to know each other. We may find we annoy the shit out of each other. Who knows."

She lets out another loud laugh and hugs me a bit tighter. I kiss the top of her head and continue to hold her for a few more moments before she smiles up at me, "I need to go talk to Lily before she sets your shit on fire."

I snort out a laugh at her, "Yeah. Please do. I am going to go back downstairs and rehearse a bit."

She smiles at me as she gives me another kiss then walks around me and out of the room. I let out an exhausted breath into the empty space around me. I haven't talked about that night in over a decade. And even then it was only with Ginny. Of course Gideon and Matthew know what happened but we don't talk about it. We don't mention that man. I look at her suitcase laying on the bed then turn towards the open door.

That ex better pray that I never find him. Because I will fucking end him. I don't give a fuck.

Three hours later, Susie is asleep on the couch and I am sitting across from her pretending that I am not watching her the entire time. I have my phone pulled out but let's be honest, my eyes haven't left her since I sat down. I can hear Lily and Mona in the kitchen chattering about something. I am assuming it is food related since Lily is insistent on making us all dinner tonight.

I hear Mona ask Lily where she learned to cook and I can't help the humor bubbling up in me, I don't even look away from my phone as I yell, "They teach it to all the molls in the underground!"

I hear Mona start laughing then I hear Lily yell, "Fuck Off Edge!" I laugh to myself as I continue to peer over my phone at a sleeping Susie. I see her arms moving as her eyes begin to flutter. She must be starting to wake up. I guess all the commotion has stirred her awake. I look towards the kitchen as Simone climbs up onto the island to talk with the others.

I bring my eyes back to Susie as she sits up stretching and yawning. Her hands instantly go to her stomach and she groans, "I'm hungry."

I laugh at her and nod my head towards the kitchen, "I think they are all in there making supper."

She looks over her shoulder quickly then smiles back at me. She walks by me, squeezing my shoulder as she heads into the kitchen and sits on the island next to Simone.

Gideon rounds the bottom of the stairs and sits on the couch across from me. He follows my stare then smiles back at me, "You like her don't you?" I move my eyes to his and give him a quick nod.

I turn my phone off before sliding it into my pocket. Leaning forward onto my knees with my forearms, I glance from the kitchen back towards Gideon, "I really fucking do. It's weird. I haven't actually wanted to get to know someone in such a long ass time. It's a new feeling." Gideon smiles back at me then leans back on the couch.

I watch the girls all chatting in the kitchen, then they seem to huddle together whispering and shit. I smile back at Gideon, "I think they might be concocting a plan to overthrow the monarchy in there." Gideon laughs and sits forward to look towards the kitchen. He turns back to me with an actual look of concern on his face, "Oh shit. You might be right."

We both stand and quietly make our way into the kitchen to try to hear what they are saying. They are all huddled together in a tight circle though, whispering in hushed tones. I put my hands on the island and lean forward, "Are we having fun in here ladies?"

All four of them stand at attention and slowly turn back to see Gideon and I standing here looking at them. They are obviously up to no good. I let my eyes scan them until they get to Susie and I notice she has that crimson running up her neck again. I stand up a bit straighter. Oh shit, they are definitely up to no good.

I glance back over to see Simone slapping Lily in the leg, neither of them able to make fucking eye contact with us. Susie bursts out laughing and runs from the room, launching herself onto the couch as she continues to scream laughter into a pillow. I see Mona out of the corner of my eye step around the island and up to Gideon with a devious smile on her face, "I have to go change my panties...Daddy."

Gideon's jaw drops as I turn back to the two women left in front of me, losing their shit with laughter. I look over my shoulder and see Mona slowly walking from the room still fanning herself with her hand. I turn back to Lily, "What are you vixens in here going on about?"

Lily giggles, looking at Simone, "Nothing. Nothing. We are just making dinner." I eye them both suspiciously, knowing there is something else at play here. Gideon looks around Lily with his eyes going wide, "Is that Gnocchi? God Damn I love Gnocchi. Please babe you have to let me have first dibs."

Both girls start laughing so hard they collapse into a heap onto each other on the floor. Gideon looks at me, "What the fuck is happening right now?"

I hear Susie laughing and clapping loudly from the couch and I smile, "Nothing good I can tell you that right now."

I glance back at the female dogpile going on in the kitchen floor then turn and move towards the couch. I lean over the back of it and see a laughing, crying Susie holding a pillow tight to her chest. I reach down and brush her thigh with my hand, "What has gotten into you girls?"

Susie lets out another loud cackle as she starts shaking her head back and forth. I laugh down at her, "Come on chuckles. Let's go outside. Get you some air." She laughs as she reaches out and takes my outstretched hand. We quickly walk past everyone and out onto the back deck.

She is still holding her side from laughing so hard. I smile over at her as she leans against the railing while still facing me, "I really don't want to know, do I?"

She starts shaking her head back and forth while still trying not to burst out laughing again. She leans forward putting her hands on her knees, taking deep breaths in through her nose and out through her mouth. I give her another grin as I walk in front of her and sit down in a lounge chair.

She finally starts to pull herself together a few minutes later. She can actually look at me and make eye contact now without losing her shit. She looks me up and down then moves over straddling the chair, putting her legs under the arm rests and sitting down in my lap.

I put my hands on her hips and lean back into the chair, trying to will my dick to stay down. She smiles down at me, "So we really gonna do the damn thing?"

I tilt my head slightly, "By the damn thing you mean?"

67

She laughs again and places her hands on my abdomen, "Ya know. Us. Try to see if there is something here."

I smile up at her and raise my hand to her neck. I rub the side of her throat and her shoulder, "Susie. I really, really like you. I would love to explore this and see if there is anything else. That is not something I say very often so this is all very new to me as well."

She grins and looks down at her hands on my stomach, "I really like you too Edge. I think this could go one of two ways. We either end up happy and together forever, or we completely kill each other. I am hoping for the first but would not be surprised by the last."

I let out a deep laugh, letting my hands drift back down to her hips. I shift her forward a bit further up my lap and she moves her hands to my shoulders. She smiles as she leans forward and gives me a soft kiss. I raise my hand, wrapping it around her neck and holding her close to me. I run my tongue across her bottom lip and she opens for me, letting me explore her mouth. She still tastes like vanilla and it is driving my senses crazy. I feel her nibble on my lower lip and I let a moan escape from the back of my throat as a chill runs up my spine.

I feel her hands slowly move up my chest and wrap around both sides of my neck. I put my other hand on her lower back to pull her closer to me. I let my hand go up her back, fully intending on letting it explore some more when the back door opens beside us.

Susie pulls back, flushed with red lips and looks towards the door. I let out a loud groan and let my head fall back on the chair, closing my eyes. Either supper better be ready or someone better be dead. I peer over at the door seeing Gideon standing there smiling from ear to ear. I roll my hand in the air for him to get on with it, "Can we help you sir?"

62

Gideon lets out a loud laugh as Susie tries to scoot down off my lap. I wrap my arm around her back, keeping her firmly planted in place. Gideon smiles even wider, "Dinner in 5 minutes guys."

He slowly shuts the door and I turn my face back to Susie. She is smiling wildly back at me. She places her hands on my chest again, "To be continued?"

I reach down and grab her ass with my hand that is wrapped around her, making her squeak and jump a bit, "You bet your sweet ass this will be continued."

6
Susie
Just Pretend - Bad Omens

Well, dinner seems to be interesting. Edge has been staring at me like I am dessert all through the meal. Gideon and Matthew seem to have some inner circle secret going on. That just leaves us girls in the dark. And none of us seem to have any clue as to what is actually going through any of the guys' heads.

It is also weird as shit to be sitting here eating dinner while surrounded by their band equipment. It is almost as if we are sitting on a stage somewhere just eating a meal with an orchestra set up around us. They did at least move the table deeper into the room so the far end is where all the instruments are but it is still strange to say the least.

I have caught myself watching Lily a couple of different times. She finally seems happy. I haven't seen her smile as much as I have with Gideon. Yeah, Mark made her happy but Gideon, he just seems to complete her somehow. I would say that I am not jealous but that would be a lie. I want that. I want the completion that is written on her face. I want the relaxed expression she gives Gideon. I want someone to smile back at me the way that Gideon does to her. Like he accepts her for everything that she is, was, and will be.

Edge told me that our earlier communications were to be continued and by the look in his eyes, I think I can confirm that is still how he feels. His eyes look like there is some fire behind them just fueling him forward. He is going to totally destroy me if I decide to actually let him in. I have never been scared of being turned on before. What would that even be called? Scorny? Scaroused? Either way I won't lie, I am kinda liking it.

After dinner I carefully and ninja-like move towards Lily and whisper, "Something is up. I don't know what but I feel a disturbance in the force. These boys are plotting."

Lily laughs outloud at me as she looks around the room behind us, "I completely fucking agree. Shit was weird at dinner. By the way, did Edge think he could actually consume your soul through his eyes while he ate his pasta or was he expecting it to just telepathically happen?"

I let a small snicker out under my breath as I look over my shoulder to make sure Edge has honestly gone out to start a fire in the burn pit. I smile as I turn back to Lily, "He literally had me on the edge of my seat for the entire meal. I couldn't even focus on my food. Flustered doesn't even begin to cover what is going on in these panties right now."

Lily gives another laugh as she continues to load the dishwasher, "Yeah, there is going to be some serious damage done there. Just not sure yet which one of you is going to destroy who."

I clutch my pretend pearls like I am shocked by her prediction, but then roll my eyes and lower my hand, "Yeah, you're right. It's anyone's game at this point."

We finally finish getting the dishes loaded then I decide to help Lily carry out a few bottles of Dalmore and some glasses. I check her stock, "I don't think I have ever seen you this low on whisky before."

Lily laughs back, her eyes scanning the shelves above the wet bar, "Yeah, I ordered some more. Hopefully it will arrive at a decent time. My house sitting girl said she would come over and make sure it gets put away for me if we aren't here."

I nod my head at her as I grab a few more glasses and head on out to the burn pit on the beach. Everyone looks pretty well settled in. There are only 5 chairs though so everything is pretty much taken by the time Lily and I make it to the beach. Lily has no problem curling up on Gideon's lap but I am still a bit hesitant to just throw myself on Edge in public. Hell, I am hesitant to do it in private let alone with all these eyes on me.

I instead walk from person to person filling up their glass until it is just me and Edge left. I can feel his eyes on me as I nervously turn away from him and sit down in front of the chair he is in. I thought that this would be the safest option, but now feeling his hand running through my hair I am thinking I am still in trouble.

Mona lets a toe curling moan leave her throat, making us all turn towards her, "I swear on God, I have never had whisky this good before. I don't think I can drink Jack ever again." I nod along with her as I sip my Dalmore.

I stare into the fire trying to focus on the conversation and not the hand that is now massaging where my neck meets my shoulders. Jesus christ his hands are huge. I mean I kinda already knew that but damn. I need to focus on the conversation but he is making it next to impossible for anything other than him to hold my attention.

I feel Edge shift in his seat as he leans forward towards me just a bit, his hand slipping further down my back, "How much would a bottle of this set me back? I may have to buy some while we are on hiatus."

I instantly start to blink back emotions. I seem to realize too quickly that tonight may be the last time I see him for a long time. This is their last show then he is going home to London for months. Then they have a UK tour before they even come back to the states. It could easily be like 6 months or more before I even get to see him again. For some reason, that has me feeling all sorts of ways. None of them are good.

How are we supposed to get to know each other if we aren't even going to be around each other? I mean I know people make long distance relationships work all the time, but we barely even know each other. I don't know how we are supposed to grow into something if we can't even get the seeds planted. My brain is starting to go into overdrive again. I try to let out short slow breaths but it is getting harder to focus. The last fucking thing I need is to throw myself into another attack.

I look over at Lily seeing the concern and embarrassment start to spread over her face. She hates talking about money. Almost as much as she hates talking about politics or religion. I grin at her stumbling over herself as Edge tips his glass to her, "Just fucking humor me daddy warbucks. How much?"

I belt out a loud laugh, turning to look at Edge then the other faces staring at me from around the fire. I shake my head back and forth, "You all are in for the shit now. You might be asking questions you really don't want answers to."

Gideon's eyebrows cinch together like he is confused by my words. That just confirms to me that Lily has indeed not talked to anyone about her financial situation. I watch her cheeks start to turn pink as she whispers over her glass, "Right around $10,000."

I feel Edge's hand grip around the back of my neck while Gideon almost launches Lily into the fire, he sits up so fast. I let out a series of cackles at everyone's reactions. I don't even hear what everyone thinks of the cost of the whisky. I am too busy laughing loudly to myself at their physical reactions.

I do catch a glimpse of Matthew leaning forward in his chair though, "How in the actual fuck do you have that kind of alcohol budget?"

I keep chuckling to myself under my breath. They are going to shit if they ever see the real number attached to her net worth. I look at Lily who looks like she is a mix between amused and horrified, "They truly have no idea do they?" She instantly gives me the stink eye and starts shaking her head back and forth.

I turn a bit to lean into Edges leg, bringing his hand back up to my neck where he starts rubbing little circles with his fingers. I can hear them talking about the brownstone but I honestly couldn't tell you a word that is being said. I am too focused on his fingertips as they dance across the sensitive skin in the nape of my neck. It is just a small little gesture but it has me all up in my feels and that is not a good place for me to be right now.

I finally cut the connection by leaning forward and grabbing a bottle of Dalmore and filling my glass then Edges as well. When I sit back down on my ass, I lean forward so he doesn't have free access to apparently all of my sensitive buttons. Mona leans forward with a look on her face that says she has no shame, "Just out of natural curiosity. How much did the brownstone sell for?"

I smile as I take a drink, watching a smile crossover Lily's face as well. She looks me dead in the eye when says, "After commission, I got a little over 12 for it."

I glance towards Mona just in time to see her spit her drink back into its glass, "I am sorry bitch, did you just say 12 like 12 million?"

Edge is laughing so hard I can feel it through the sand on the bottoms of my legs. I don't know if I am more amused by him or the baby deer look on Lily's face right now. She was never good with attention so this is just making my year. It is like Christmas and my birthday all rolled into one.

Matthew sits forward again, shaking his head towards her, "God Damn Lily. I don't want to know your net worth, do I?" DING DING DING. There is the magic phrase I have been waiting for. I start laughing loudly, shaking my head back at him, "No, probably not."

Lily's face is completely red now. I continue to laugh as I pull my phone and pull up my notes app. I quickly type in an underestimate of the last time I saw her numbers. I turn the screen towards Edge so he can see the message I have left reading 110 million. His eyes bug out of his head and he grabs my phone, ripping it from my hand and turning it towards Matthew, who in turn chokes on his whisky. I grab my phone back from Edge and shoot Lily a wink as she tries to slink under the skin of Gideon.

In all the commotion, I have turned and now I am back in between Edges knees again and he has a hand on each shoulder. I see his empty glass in the sand beside his chair and smile back at Lily. At least everyone loves her super fancy whisky. I know that makes her happy. Edge leans forward a bit more, "So you are like....rich rich then?"

I let out another loud laugh along with Lily and Simone. Edge reaches down picking up his glass, realizing it is now empty as Lily smiles back, "Yes Edge. I guess you could say I am rich rich."

Edge sits back in his chair a bit, "At least you know she isn't in it for the money, am I right?" My shoulders instantly tighten. That was kinda a shitty comment. Does he think I am only in it for the money since I am not a bagillionaire like Lily? Before I have a chance to think too deeply into it, I hear Mona cackle back, "No, she is in it for that dick."

Everyone starts rolling in laughter again. Everyone except for Gideon. His eyes get darker as he leans in and whispers something into Lily's ear. I am too busy laughing and trying not to look like a gold digger to really hear what they are saying. I pour a bit more whisky in my glass and scoot away from Edge a bit to try to think in peace. I can't focus on anything when he is touching me. He looks over at me like he is concerned but I just smile and look back across the fire.

I finally hear Matthew speaking again, "As much as I would love to talk about Gideon's dick all night, I have another topic I want to approach."

I laugh out loud to myself, turning to Matthew, "Are you sure? It's a pretty nice dick. Just saying." I laugh around the fire until I see Edges eyes on me. He looks pissed. Then I remember, he doesn't know about the facetime call. He thinks I must know first hand that Gideon has a nice dick. I give him a shrug and roll my eyes so that way he can see I am just trying to play it off. It doesn't seem to soften him at all though.

I start to get uncomfortable again so I turn even more in the sand so I am basically now just facing Edge and Matthew instead of leaning straight into him. I can feel his eyes on me again when I hear Gideon say, "We just want to know if you are down for something."

Every female around the fire goes stock still. All of us drop our jaws. You do not have a conversation about dicks and then just lead into a throuple topic without warning. The realization starts to trickle across the guys, starting with Edge who is now laughing like a maniac. I go up on my knees, screaming to the gods, "Yes! Her answer is yes!"

Gideon's jaw drops as he is the last one to figure out what we are all thinking. He scrunches his face up at Lily, "Not fucking that. We aren't asking your for a fucking threesome right here in front of everyone. Jesus God. You fucking females I swear!"

Everyone starts laughing again then Gideon starts to float an idea past Lily about her painting live during their shows. I am happy for her. That they want to include her that way. I look over at Edge and he is smiling at Gideon nodding his head along to the conversation. His gaze turns to me as he gestures me closer but I just grin quickly then look away and stare back into the fire. I am trying to play this all off and not let it show that there are currently about 80 different thoughts tearing me apart on the inside.

I can feel his eyes on me while everyone is talking about how their plan is all going to play out. I want to look at him, but honestly I am afraid to. Every time I look at him I feel this deep aching pain in my chest. Like my soul is calling out to him. But I can't let that happen. We barely know each other and who knows when we are even gonna be able to see each other again. This is a recipe for failure. And I have had enough of that for one lifetime.

He doesn't say anything to me but a few moments later I hear him talking about how great of an idea he thinks it is. I throw back the last of my whisky. Feeling all kinds of ways again. I don't know. I feel heavy. Edge is leaving in a few days for the UK. I am leaving to go back to New York tomorrow. I also don't really want him to think I am only interested in him because he has money. I could honestly give a fuck less about it.

I am not broke by any means, but I am also not Lily. I don't have that stacked of an account at my disposal. They are all still talking about paints and charcoal when I stand up and brush the sand off my shorts and legs. I can feel Edge staring at me but I don't dare look at him. I just don't think this is going to work. And the shit part of it is that I am already falling hard for him.

I smile across the fire at Simone and Mona before turning my back to the situation. I quickly run up the stairs then into the house. I put my glass in the sink then make my way up to my bedroom. I fumble through the door then quickly lock it behind me. I don't even bother to turn the lights on. I just curl up on the bed on top of the comforter staring at the dark wall in front of me.

How am I already feeling this way? I mean, I knew I was immediately attracted to him. When I first touched his arm, I saw the want fall over his face. I knew he felt the same way. But when he told me about his sister, what he had done for her...I instantly fell. He risked his entire life, his entire future just to right the wrong that had been done. Just to protect his little sister. You don't meet a lot of people that would do that anymore. I immediately started to fall for him when he opened his heart to me at that moment. Now, I can't seem to stop falling and I don't have a god damn parachute to save me.

I don't even get up to check who is at the door when I hear someone lightly knocking on it. I know it is Edge. But I am a ghost now. I have to be. I am trying to save us both from heartbreak as I feel a tear roll out of my eye and down to my temple.

7
Edge
Neon Grave - Dayseeker

The guys truly had a great idea incorporating Lily into our gigs. This is going to blow up. I just fucking know it. I can feel it somehow. I am riddled with excitement for what it could mean for all of us but I am also torn with why Susie is acting so weird.

It was like the longer we sat around the fire the more distant she became. Physically and emotionally. I kept trying to move her closer to me but by the time she got up and dusted herself off she couldn't even look me in the eyes. She just ran upstairs and into the house.

We finish finalizing all the plans for the next show and I hurry into the house to seek her out. I know she is holed up in her room. Hiding out from everyone. Hiding from me. I make it to the top floor and see her door firmly shut. I step up to it and rap my knuckles on it a few times but I hear nothing from the other side.

I turn to look inside the open door of my room but she isn't there. The bathroom door is open and the light is off so I know she isn't in there either. I reach down and try the doorknob but the door is locked. I let out a loud sigh and knock on the door a bit harder.

Still there is no answer, no reply from the other side. You wanna play games? Fine, let's play games. I walk across the hall to my room and get my lockpick set out of my suitcase. Someone had to break into the hotel bathrooms when Gideon got so fucking high he couldn't stop throwing up. I couldn't just let him die.

And from my wonderfully normal childhood, lockpicking was something I had learned by the age of 10. I turn back out into the hallway and lower myself to the door knob. A few turns and jimmies of the little metal tools and the door clicks open for me. I slide the tools back into their cover and put the case into my back pocket before I slowly open the door and slip inside.

The room is dark but I can see her laying on the bed facing away from me. Maybe she was just tired or drunk then came in here to pass out. I step into the room and I hear the floor creak under my weight. I see her as she lets out a heavy sigh. I can hear the hesitation in her voice as it cracks out, "Closed doors normally mean the person wants to be left alone."

I step over to her side of the bed and sit down by her feet. I can't really see her face because it is dark but I can hear her. She sounds even more upset than earlier. I reach out and put my hand on her leg and she quickly recoils from my touch. Great! What the fuck have I done now?

I lift my hand back over towards my lap, "Okay. So are you going to tell me what I have done to piss you off this time or do we get to play the same games over again like earlier?"

She sits up and scoots herself towards the headboard, pulling her knees in close to her chest. I can see her face now in the moonlight that is pouring in through the window. She reaches her hands up and wipes tears away from her cheeks. My frustration instantly goes limp.

She wraps her arms around her knees and tilts her head back into the headboard, "We can't do this Edge."

I feel my heart rate pick up again. Now why? I turn towards her, putting a leg up on the bed in front of me, "We can't do what?"

She looks down at me then starts pointing a hand between the two of us, "This. Whatever this is. It will never work. You are leaving. I am leaving. We have two completely different lives to lead. You have your responsibilities and I have mine. I love my job, I refuse to just walk away from it to take time to get to know some guy. You have the band, you can't just walk away from that obviously. We just don't have the time to put in the work it will take to figure this thing out."

Why does it piss me off so much that she just referred to me as some guy? Why did I think I meant more to her than that? I nod my head and look towards the floor, "Yeah. Okay. That's fine. If you don't want to try, then we won't. I just thought there was something here." I stand and put my hands in my pockets before turning to leave.

I hear her take in a rattled breath and I turn back to see her face in her hands as her shoulders shudder in emotion. I turn back around and walk around the bed then right up to her side. I keep my hands in my pockets though, "If you think this isn't going to work, why are you so fucking upset? This is what you want isn't it? It's too much, it's too hard. If anyone should be upset it is me. I have been trying. I have put myself out there time and time again and every single time you end up shooting me down."

Her red rimmed eyes come back and connect with mine. I instantly feel like an asshole. I just need to walk away instead of making shit worse. I pull my hands up in defense, immediately letting my own fucking emotions get in the way, "I get it. It's cool. We are cool. It was nice getting to know you Peach. Hopefully our paths don't cross again. Cause I can't take this shit. It's too much. Have a nice life."

I turn and leave her room, shutting the door loudly behind me. I look towards the stairs and think about going downstairs and drinking an entire bottle of Dalmore but then decide I don't want a 10k hangover. I cross the hall and shut my door. I undress angrily, throwing my clothes on top of my packed bag and slide into bed.

I don't know why she is doing this. It is obvious that she feels something towards me. Is she just scared of it? Or is she scared of me? Does she not understand that I would never hurt her? That I would never be like him?

I lay there staring at the wall until I finally fall asleep hours later. I wake up around 2 am and step out into the hall to go take a piss. I can hear whispering coming from Susie's room. I stare at the closed door for a moment before going to the bathroom and relieving myself.

I step back out into the hallway in nothing but my boxer briefs and her door is opening. I watch Lily step out then turn towards the stairs. Next out comes Susie with her luggage in her hand. I let out a snicker and her attention turns to me. She tilts her head to the side like I shouldn't be surprised that she decided to sneak out in the middle of the night, rather than being an adult and saying goodbye in the morning.

I shake my head at her then step around her and into my room, slamming the door loudly behind me. When am I ever going to be worth someone sticking around? When do I get to matter to someone? I stomp over to the bed and sit down on the side of it, heaving air in and out of my lungs. I hate myself for thinking she was different. She can see what I am and she wants nothing to do with me. I can't blame her, I have always known I was going to end up alone. Nobody wants to fall in love with a monster.

I hear the door open and I glance up quickly to see her stepping in and shutting it quietly behind her. She moves across the room letting the moonlight dance across her porcelain skin. She stops right in front of me, "I thought I would just leave tonight."

76

I nod my head towards my hands that are folded in my lap. She lets out another rattled breath, "I didn't think I could face you in the morning. I thought you wouldn't want to see me. I was trying to do you a solid by not being here when you woke up."

I lift my face to look up into her eyes, "Susie, ever since that day in the brownstone, I have prayed for something to happen that would bring us closer. So I could talk to you, so I could get to know you. It was like this vicious cycle of loneliness was over the moment you smiled at me. So I'm sorry that I am not what you want. I am sorry that I am too broken for you to bother messing with."

I let out another loud sigh as I look back down at my hands then nod towards the door with my chin, "You were right. This won't work. You should go. I don't want to see you."

I see her take a small step back in a jerking motion. I look back up at her and she is crying again, "I never said I didn't want you. I never said that you were too broken. I am the fucking broken one, Gavin. Me. And these past few days have fucking done something to me okay? I don't want to leave you. I don't want to ever be anywhere but where you are. But that is not possible. Not right now at least. I was just trying to save myself from a worse heartbreak than I am already dealing with."

She blinks heavy as more tears fall, her face lowering towards the floor, "Because this fucking hurts. So fucking much right now. I don't think I could survive walking away from you if I was to let myself fall for you like my heart is begging me to. I don't think I would survive you Edge. I'm sorry."

She turns to leave and I reach up and grab her hand, halting her immediately. She turns back towards me as I stand up and look into her shimmering eyes, "You think you could fall for me?"

77

She lets out a shuddered breath and shrugs her shoulders, "I am trying really fucking hard not to right now."

I stand in front of her and place my hands on her cheeks. Stroking them with my thumbs as I watch her eyes wander my face before landing back on mine. Selfishly, I pull her towards me, kissing her hard and fast. I feel the surprise in her, I feel her tense but I need her close to me right now.

I have never been with someone that actually had real feelings for me before. Actual things, beyond the physical. I am overwhelmed with gratitude and excitement and fear. Slowly, I feel her hands on my sides as they slowly move to my back then she is pulling me in closer to her. She slides her tongue along my lips and then we are getting lost in a sea of each other. We are all hands and teeth and panting.

She finally pulls back from me and slides her shirt over her head, letting it hit the floor behind her. I watch as her eyes trace my body then she is slowly pulling my briefs down my legs. I hear my own voice catch in my throat as she looks at me smiling, "Let me do this." I look at her confused as she pushes me back on the bed.

I scoot further up on it as I watch her remove her shorts and underwear then crawl up onto the bed. She is straddling my legs as she wraps her hair up in a hair tie she has on her wrist. I watch her raise up just a bit then she takes two of her fingers and starts to touch herself. I turn to steel instantly.

I watch as her head falls back on her shoulders then she slips those two fingers inside of herself. I am watching her fuck herself and I reach out to stroke my extremely hard dick but then her eyes fully connect with mine. She pulls those fingers out then wraps her hand around my cock. She is so wet she has now coated me in her juices.

I feel my eyes roll up in my head as I let a moan out into the room. I feel her start to stroke me harder then she rolls her thumb over my tip, spreading my precum in with her. I have honestly never had a woman do that before. Never straight from the honey pot like that.

I lean my head forward, opening my eyes just in time to see her lick her lips and lean forward. As soon as I feel her lips running across my head, I get shivers down my spine. I watch her as she starts to take me in deeper. I can feel her tongue running up and down the bottom of my shaft. She turns her eyes towards me and I could swear I see her try to smile. Then she is taking me in, all the way to the base.

As I roll my head back onto my shoulders, you can hear the moan rip from my throat and echo around the room. I can feel myself hitting the back of her throat and she isn't crying or gagging or anything. I have never had anyone be able to do that to me before. I wrap my hand up in her ponytail and watch as I push her mouth up and down my cock.

I feel myself start to build up quickly when I notice she has taken her other hand and she is circling her clit in tight little circles. I feel overwhelmed and astounded at what this woman is doing to me right now. I start thrusting my hips up into her mouth then look down, "Peach, I am gonna cum. Pull back baby. I can't hold out." I can hear my own voice cut short and gaspy.

She takes me all the way to the base again. As soon as I feel myself hit the back of her throat, I let loose inside of her. I growl out into the room as I continue to pump myself into her mouth. I look down and see her fingers working vigorously chasing her own release.

I reach down and pull her up under her arms then roll myself on top of her. Her eyes go wide as I part her with one hand and flick her clit with my tongue. Now it is her turn to moan into the room. I smile as I lick from her entrance straight up to her clit. I circle her clit a few times with my tongue before I flick it again and push two fingers inside of her.

She is gripping the sheets to the point of her knuckles turning white. I pull back smiling, "Watch me peach. Watch me devour your sweet little cunt." Her eyes fall back to mine and I lower back in flicking her clit two more times, sucking it deep into my teeth before I feel her start to clench around my fingers. I push them in further and hook them to find that rough patch that holds a sweet release just waiting to be discovered. She yells out into the room as she grabs my hair in her hands. Using my face like a joystick as I lick and nibble my way to her orgasm.

She cums hard, crying into the darkened room. I continue to thrust my fingers into her until I feel her start to unclench. I pull back smiling at her, knowing she is dripping off my chin. She looks down at me, with hooded eyes. She is completely boneless right now. I can tell just from the look on her face.

I smile as I stand up and walk across the room to get my towel from my shower earlier. I wipe my face then my dick. When I get back to her, I wipe off her thighs and run the towel up her center. She is still so sensitive she practically flinches at the touch of the soft fabric on her clit.

I lay down beside her after tossing the towel to the other side of the room, pulling her in close to me. Her back is to me and I wrap my arms around her. I gently grasp one of her tits in my hand as she giggles into the open room. I smile as I lean into her ear, "I licked it, now it's mine."

She lets out a loud cackle and smacks my arm as I reach down with my other hand and pull the blankets up over us. She isn't going anywhere tonight. And if she thinks she is, she better be prepared for me to follow her. I fall asleep to the feeling of her caressing my forearm. I haven't felt this content, this at peace for as far back as I can remember.

I wake up in the morning to the feeling of her running her fingers through the rough bristle of the beard on my jaw. I smile before I even open my eyes because she is still here. She didn't leave in the middle of the night. I saved us. I somehow pulled us back from the brink of the complete disintegration we were facing last night. I open my eyes and see those flora inspired orbs staring back at me.

I lean forward and give her a light kiss. I can feel her smile into my lips as I open my eyes and pull back, "Good morning." She smiles a bit wider, continuing to rub my jaw, "Do you want to come to New York after your show?"

I lean my head back and look at her a little more deeply. I smile at her, in disbelief. She still wants me. I honestly assumed I was going to wake up and she would have given up on us again. I nod my head at her, afraid to break eye contact, "Yes. I really, really do."

She smiles as she leans in and gives me another kiss. I pull her into me and run my hands up her back. I hold her tight as I roll onto my back and pull her on top of me. Her eyes fly wide and she squeaks out a noise between my lips.

I smile wider as she pulls back, looking down at me. Her eyes are scanning my face, "I will catch the first flight out of Savannah as soon as the show is over." She grins wider, "Sweet."

I kiss her again before allowing her to uncurl from me. She sits up on the side of the bed, stretching her arms high above her. I trace the face of the woman tattooed on her back as she looks over her shoulder grinning at me. I continue to trace the large blue pool behind the woman, "Why the Queen of Cups?"

Susie turns towards me so I can see the profile of her naked form sitting before me. I almost forget what question I asked. She grins back at me, "Do you know your tarot at all?"

I shake my head back at her, "No. Simone yes, Mona probably. Me, not at all." She smiles as she leans over, grabbing her shirt and pulling it over her head. She then stands up and slips her underwear and shorts back on. She smiles at me as she zips them up, "Look into it later. You might understand me a bit more."

I sit up and slide over to the edge of the bed. Her eyes roam down my body, settling on my morning gift to the world before her eyes shoot back up to mine. I smile devilishly as I stand in front of her and pull her closer to me. I am hugging her tightly when I hear knuckles rap on the door then it flies open to a wide eyed Simone.

She instantly covers her eyes with her hand, "Ew...Ew...My Eyes! My Eyes!" She reaches over and slams the door shut after she walks back through it.

Susie lets out a loud cackle as she pulls away from me, "You better put some clothes on and quit showing your ass to all the ladies."

I smile as I lean in and kiss her again before slowly pulling back, "Yes ma'am." She smiles devilishly back at me.

Ten minutes later, we are dressed and back downstairs. I have already booked a flight on my phone and numbers have been exchanged. She is saying her goodbyes to everyone, well more Lily than anyone else. She gets to me and I see her eyes start to pool a bit. I smile as I pull her close to me, "Two days. I will be back with you in less than two days. We can make it that long." I feel her nod her head at me then she pulls back. A weak smile on her face. I don't know who I am trying to convince, her or me. I cup her cheeks and pull her into a deep kiss. Something to hold her over until we see each other again.

I pull back and reluctantly let her go. She grabs her luggage and steps out the front door still looking sadly back at me before the door closes behind her. I look around the room at everyone staring back at me. They are all watching me like they are waiting for me to break down or something. An overwhelming urge comes over me and before I know what I am even doing I am throwing the front door open then running down the front stoop.

Susie hears me coming and turns around surprised as I wrap her up in my arms again and kiss her deeply, passionately, with everything that I have. I feel her hands wrap around my neck as she holds me tightly back. I pull my lips from hers and put my forehead to hers, "Don't forget about me."

She pulls back staring into my eyes intently, "I could never forget you. Not even if I tried." I nod back at her as I give her another quick kiss and follow her to the uber. I shut her door after she is inside and watch the car pull away. I already feel hollow.

I turn and head back into the house and upstairs to my room to pack up everything. We will be leaving for Savannah soon. I sit on the bed and feel the urge to put something to paper. I don't know if it is thoughts or questions or what but I just need to write it all down so I can try to make sense of it.

I grab some scrap paper from the desk and a pen then just start scribbling. The words just flow out of me. I have never written anything on my own before. Sure Gideon and I have both co-written a few songs but nothing truly on my own. I pull back looking at what I have just put into words. It is my love song to her. I rearrange some of the lines until it seems to be perfect. I smile down at the ramblings of a crazed man.

"In the shadows where whispers bend,
I will build a sanctuary for your soul to mend

Beneath the weight of the night's embrace
I will provide solace in our secret place

Fingers trace the veins of your weary skin

I will hold back the shadows that contain the sin

Mending with each heartbeat, scars of the past
Ours is an empire that will forever last

In your stillness, my promise remains
I will shelter your heart from the pouring rain

Let the tides rise, let the tempest call,
I am your provider, in my arms you will never fall

In this realm where the lost can find their home
You'll never wander, you'll never be alone"

I fold the paper up, smiling as I slide it into my pocket. I can already hear the beat of the song playing in my head. I imagine playing it close to the bridge, possibly even going palm mute at one point. It is not meant to be loud. It is meant to be felt. Gideon is going to fucking love this.

I pass the lyrics off to him while we are heading to Savannah. He and Simone are elbow deep into them by the time we get there. Gideon has already roped Matthew into it as well. It is definitely something we are going to work on for the next album. It makes me happy to think that I am going to have that little part of her with me while we are on tour.

Everyone kind of scatters to the wind when we get to the hotel. Gideon and Lily are getting her mentally prepared for the task at hand tomorrow. She is going to kill it. We all know she is going to kill it. She just needs to tell herself that. I just don't think believes in herself as much as we do. She has become a part of us. She has brought so much joy and peace to Gideon, I can't imagine them not being together. They are literally soul mates.

I trudge up to my room, which is right across the hall from Matthew. I step inside, sitting down all of my stuff. I meander over to the bed and fall back onto it staring at the ceiling. My phone buzzes in my pocket so I pull it out seeing a message from Susie. I smile as I read that she has made it back home safe and sound. I send her a quick picture of me laid out on the hotel bed with the words, 'I wish you were here' then hit send.

Two minutes later, I get a text back. It is a picture of her, naked about to step into the shower. All I can see is her face in the phone and then her back down to her waist from the reflection in the mirror. I can just barely see the top of her ass but she has a grin from ear to ear with the message of 'I hate showering alone now. I have so much more fun with you.'

I groan again as I sit up staring at the photo a bit harder, at the tattoo on her back. I smile as I type out, 'Don't worry we will be conserving water again very very soon.'

I swipe out of my messages and pull up a webpage. I type Queen of Cups Tarot into the search engine. I am not disappointed in what I find. It says The Queen of Cups is meant to remind us to treat ourselves and others with compassion and sympathy. She encourages us to embrace our emotions and express them honestly, authentically.

I smile as I close out of the screen. I am so falling for this girl. I mess around on my guitar for a few hours before having a quick bite to eat with Matthew then calling it a night. Tomorrow night is the show then I am taking a midnight flight to New York.

I smile as I think about how she is going to have to kick me out to ever get me to leave.

8
Susie
If It Doesn't Hurt - Nothing More

Yeah, I am pouting, walking through the airport towards the line of taxis waiting outside. Yes, I am also aware that I look like a toddler that just got denied an animal cookie. No, I don't fucking care that people are looking at me like I might be having a mental episode.

I don't want to be in New York. I want to be in Savannah. I want to be there with Edge, watching the show. I want to see Lily being a fucking rock star on stage. Or would that be a rock painter? Rock drawing person? Is there even a name for what she is doing? I huff out to myself, if there is I don't know what it would be.

Dammit, why didn't I take a few more days off work? Oh yeah, because I love my job and I don't expect anybody to be able to function without me there. Even though they are fucking fine. I still think nope, they will need me. There could be some kind of emergency and everything starts burning to the ground. And if I am not there to put out the fire then who will?

I lug my bags out the sliding doors and walk up to the first taxi. I throw my bags into the cab and slide in, not even looking at the driver and mumble, "414 East 52nd Street please."

I see the driver throw his hand up in response then turn on his meter. I watch the city fly by me as I think back to the last few days in Nag's Head. I am still scared shitless of opening up to someone again. Giving into someone again. But after Edge told me about his childhood, about his sister, something within me changed.

He is one of the good ones. I keep telling myself that but it is still hard to open up after being closed off for so long. I tilt my head, placing my temple on the car window and watch the streets as we buzz by. I need to figure my shit out. I don't want to screw this up before it even has a chance to start.

A half hour later, I am lugging my suitcase and carry on into my apartment. I drag my feet and my luggage up the stairs to the bedroom and throw everything down on the bed. I need coffee and a shower. But it is currently almost 10pm, so a shower and a cup of hot tea it shall be. I have to be at work by 8 in the morning and then Edge will be here at like 2 am. So I can probably get a little sleep in before he gets here.

Who am I trying to kid? I will be pacing these floors until I hear a knock on the door. I quickly unpack, throwing all my dirty clothes in the hamper then shuffle to the bathroom to put away my makeup. I look at myself in the vanity and let out another sad huff as I put my hair up in a messy bun on top of my head.

Every single time I blink, I see his blue eyes shining back at me. I smell the soft aroma of worn leather. I smile at myself as I pull my phone out of my pocket. I pull up Edge in my phone and send a quick text, "Made it home, safely. About to call it a night soon." I sit the phone down on the counter and reach into the shower to turn the water on. I quickly strip down, throwing my clothes into the hamper when I hear my phone go off.

I look down to see a message from Edge and giggle like a fucking school girl as I open the message to see him sprawled out on his back in the middle of a bed. The text reads, "I wish you were here." I smile into the phone then look up into the mirror. I turn and step towards the shower. I turn the camera on

88

my phone to face view and take a quick picture, sending it back with the message, "I hate showering alone now. I have so much more fun with you."

I laugh to myself as I put the phone back down on the counter and grab myself a towel from the shelf. The phone immediately dings again and I smile at the shower. I can do this. I can not answer right away. I can leave a bit to mystery.

No I can't. I immediately give in and turn around to grab my phone. If I was sitting right now, I would literally be kicking my feet. He instantly answers back with, "Don't worry we will be conserving water again very very soon." I laugh to myself as I sit the phone down then step into the shower. I will make it. He will be here tomorrow and we will have some time together, just us. To really get to know each other.

I let my mind wander to places that are dangerous. I want to feel the weight of him inside me. I want to let myself go to the nature of whatever beast he is hiding in the shadows of his eyes. I bathe as fast as humanly possible and then jump out to check my phone again but there are no new messages. I feel my giddiness drop a bit. It's okay. I will see him tomorrow. After I get dressed for bed, I fall into a restless sleep but hear my phone ringing at some point in the middle of the night. I roll over and look at the clock knowing damn good and well it is Lily calling me. This is her witching hour. I smile as I answer the call without even looking, "What did he do this time?"

Lily lets out a giggle on the other end of the line, "Nothing. Nothing is wrong. I just couldn't sleep. Did I wake you?"

I smile into the room as I scoot up on the bed and give her the same lie I give her every time she calls at 2 a.m., "No, I was up reading."

I hear her sigh on the other end of the phone. I look across the room and out the window. The city is still wide awake around me. I smile as I ask, "If everything is so great then why do you sound so distant right now?"

I can almost hear her smiling, "I am not distant, I am just kinda caught up."

I nod towards the window a few times before rolling over towards the night stand, "He loves you. He is *in* love with you. He is perfect for you and you are perfect for him. Do not let your brain get in the way."

She lets out another half sigh, half laugh, "Yeah. I know." I can hear her moving around, probably getting comfortable in some random hotel chair, "He is everything Susie. It makes me physically hurt when I think about how much I love him. I can't ever be without him. He has healed me in so many ways I will never be able to repay him. I don't even think he would let me try honestly.

"He just, he sees me. He sees through all the bullshit I put into my everyday exterior. It's like he just looks past it and sees the real me that is hiding behind the curtain."

I blink heavily into the void of the room. I know she is scared shitless of letting herself love somebody. Letting herself *fall* in love with somebody. I can't blame her, I know her past. I would be fucked up over it all too. I lean into my pillow a bit more, "So, do you think this is something you want to go forward with. Build a future on?"

I can hear her voice hitch in her throat a bit and I know she is crying but I can hear the happiness in her tone as well, "No, I would. I would marry him tomorrow. I would have a million of his babies. I would adopt 700 dogs and start a chinchilla rescue if he wanted. I don't care. I am done hiding and running. I am his, ya know?"

I let out a loud laugh into the room, "Thank god! Finally! Do you know how many years I have waited for this moment? I am so fucking happy for you Lily. Gideon is a lucky mother fucker now you go and remind him of that every god damn moment for the rest of his life. I love you babe."

Lily laughs back at me, "I love you too Susie. I will call you tomorrow and let you know how it goes." I nod into the phone as I hear her disconnect on the other end. I smile into the shadows in the room, completely happy for her and only 28% jealous. Okay maybe 38%.

Morning comes faster than my body wants to allow. It is 6 am and I don't want to get out of bed. But I have to. The sooner I get my day going, the sooner it will be over. Which in turn means the sooner Edge will be here. That alone puts enough of a smile on my face to get me moving. I throw the covers off and sling my legs over the side. Rubbing my face with my hands. Time to pretend to be a grown up.

I step into the bathroom and put on my normal make up and put my hair into a tight bun on the back of my head. I step back into the bedroom, moving slowly towards my closet. I dress in a blue pinstripe pencil dress and pull out a pair of Jimmy Choo's that Lily gifted me after the funeral. I do not give a fuck that they were her funeral shoes. They are black leather works of art and I am doing the world a favor by wearing them proudly.

I look at my watch, I still have 45 minutes to get to work. That gives me plenty of time to stop for a coffee on the way. It is only a 4 block walk. I smile to myself as I grab my purse and briefcase then move to head out the front door. I smile though, thinking about Edge. He has never seen me all done up for work before. I wonder what he would think of this side of me. I put my stuff back down and step back up to my full length mirror. I smile into my reflection as I take a quick picture then send a good morning message with it.

I make my way down to my favorite coffee house, Penny Lane and order my regular then head back out into the street. I hear my phone ding and look down to see a message from Edge. I grin as I step to the side out of the foot traffic and quickly open the message.

I chuckle out loud making people turn their heads towards me as I read, "That's it. I am quitting the band and moving to New York. Also, if I don't text in the next half hour I am busy. Taking care of some business."

I smile widely as I send a quick reply, "Squeeze it twice for me." I laugh loudly to myself as I turn the screen off and slide my phone into the side of my briefcase.

I spend the majority of my day either checking my phone or zoning out looking out the window. I am completely useless today. I knew I was going to be completely useless but I don't care. I am here in body even if my spirit is in Savannah. Thank god nothing of any real type of crisis happened. I would have been fucking useless. Unless it had anything to do with a certain alternative metal band I would have not have been able to help.

I end up giving into temptation and slip out of work an hour early. I smile into my phone as I take another selfie sending it to Edge with the message, "Finally it's over. I can go home and lay around naked until the riff raff arrives."

I giggle to myself as I make my way home. I decide to order some Italian food and carb out so maybe I will get some sleep before he arrives in the middle of the night. I check my phone around 7 to see a message waiting for me. I open it to see a picture of Dionysus, mask and all. I can see a smirk on his face even under the cover of the mask and paint. There is only a short message but the point is made perfectly, "I will be there soon."

The chills that roll down my spine at him in full gear is something I have literally never felt before. I was definitely right when I thought I was scaroused. Because right now, I am fucking terrified and I am loving every second of it.

I curl up onto the couch in a pair of barely there cotton shorts and a tank top. I turn on a netflix movie and just stare at the tv. Not even really taking anything in. Instead of paying attention to the show, I check my phone every 5 minutes. At this rate, he will never be here. I turn the volume up on the phone and sit it face down on the table far away from me and then end up falling asleep on the couch.

I am suddenly ripped from sleep when I hear my phone ringing. I fly up off the couch and lunge across the table, hitting the corner with my knee. I am screaming out choice four letter words as I hit the answer button. I can hear Edge laughing on the other end, "You gonna open this door or do I need to beat it down?"

My eyes fly towards my front door as I quickly hobble towards it. I don't even hesitate to unlock the door then sling it open wide to see Edge standing there holding his phone and bag smiling from ear to ear. I smile widely back at him, "You're really here?"

He steps in the door, slamming it shut behind him, dropping everything on the floor around us. He wraps his hands around the sides of my face and slams his mouth into mine. I utterly melt under him. I have never had anyone kiss me the way that Edge does. He makes all the dark romance reads come to life. When he kisses me it feels like everything else around me just melts away. All the tension, fear and loneliness just disappears.

I wrap my arms around his neck as he continues to attack me with his lips. It feels more like it has been months, not just

93

hours since I last saw him. I eventually pull back, gulping in as much air as I can. I smile at him, "Yeah, you are definitely here."

He chuckles back at me as he leans his forehead into mine, "I have missed you so fucking much." I can feel his thumb run down my chin and across my jaw. I look up into his eyes. Yup, I am screwed. He has me. There is no saving me after tonight.

I take a small step back, "Let's take your stuff upstairs." He looks around the room realizing it is just a sitting room and a small bathroom off to the side. His eyes look all around then sees a staircase around the corner, "Where the hell is your kitchen?"

I chuckle at him and point towards the stairs, "Up there with the master bedroom and bath. This is just like my living room." He looks around again, nodding his head in approval as he picks up his stuff. I hadn't even noticed until now that he has his guitar strapped to his back. I smile wondering if he will serenade me again while he is here. I hurriedly make my way upstairs and point towards the bedroom, "You can put your stuff in there. If you want. Or if you are more comfortable downstairs that is fine too. Whatever works best for you."

He rolls his eyes and smiles at me as he walks past me then puts his stuff down to the side of the bed. I grin back as he takes his hoodie off and throws it over the chair in the corner. He steps back out into the dining area as he pulls his sleeves up on his arms. He looks me up and down then his eyes go wide, "What the hell did you do to your leg? You're bleeding!"

I look down to see a small stream of blood running from my knee to my ankle. I laugh as I limp into the bathroom, "Well sir. It is entirely your fault actually." He steps into the bathroom behind me. He quickly turns me around then sits me on the vanity, "First aid kit?"

I smile back at him sweetly, "Yes, I love their music." He huffs and frowns at me as I point to a cabinet behind the door.

94

He grabs the small box and walks back over. He sits it down on the counter beside me as he surveys my knee then pulls out an alcohol wipe to clean my leg. He makes a pinched face at me, "This might hurt. I'm sorry."

I smile at him as I feel the sting of the alcohol in my cut. Yeah it hurts but seeing him coming to my rescue makes it bearable. He looks back up at me to probably judge my pain scale, "So, how exactly is this my fault?"

I laugh again watching him pull out a bandage and putting it over my cut, "Well, when you called I had fallen asleep on the couch. I jumped up to grab my phone and banged my knee on the corner of the coffee table."

He nods back at me as he throws away the trash from the bandage and wipe, "So what I am hearing is that I should have picked the lock and surprised you in your sleep."

It was not a question. It was a statement. It was also about 18 different dark fantasies of mine brought to life. He is staring into me sharply and I can't even seem to put an expression on my face. He moves in between my knees and wraps a hand around my back, pulling me closer to him on the counter.

I gasp as I put my hands on his chest, "You did break into my room the other night. I thought I was half crazy because I knew I locked the door."

He smiles as his eyes trail down to my lips then back to my eyes, "Just one of my many, many talents."

I wrap my arms around his neck smiling, "Oh? What else is there?"

He gives me a devilish grin as he wraps both arms around me, picking me up and carrying me back into the bedroom. He tosses me onto the bed, leaving me a giggling heap. He kicks his shoes off and then his shirt is coming over the top of his head. I feel my heart rate pick up as I watch him peel his jeans off and slide them down his legs. He kicks them to the other side of the room then crawls from the end of the bed up to meet my lips with his. I lean back into the pillows as I taste him exploring my mouth.

He finally pulls back for a breath and I reach beneath us and tuck my legs under the blanket. He follows suit then pulls me close to him. He smiles as he runs a finger down the side of my face, tracing my cheekbone then my lips. He smiles at me again, "I am not going to pressure you for anything more than you are ready to give. When you are ready to move forward, all you have to do is say the word. I can wait forever if I have to."

I pull my face back, surprised, staring at him. I blink rapidly, "You would do that?"

He brings his eyes back to me with a look of confusion, "Of course I would. I'm not him. I am not going to force you to do something you don't want."

I am taken aback by his abruptness again. I look him in his eyes as I put my hand on his cheek, "I know you are not him. There is nothing to compare. You are a thousand times the man he was. I am just surprised that you are *so* okay with waiting until I am ready."

He nods his head at me as he leans his forehead into mine, stroking my thigh and the back of my head with each hand, "I am sorry. I didn't mean for that to sound how it came out. And thank you for what you said. No one has ever treated me like I was really worth anything besides maybe a good time. I am not really sure how to act in a relationship where there are real feelings at play. And Peach, you are worth the wait."

I pull back and look into his eyes and then to his lips. I lean forward and give him a deep kiss. Putting everything unsaid into the power behind it. I finally pull back and his eyes are still shut but he is smiling at me. I snuggle into him after

96

reaching over and turning the light off. He wraps an arm around me tightly and whispers, "Good Night." into the darkness.

I take a deep hesitant breath as I dance my fingers across the skin on his chest, "I am going to fall for you. I am going to let myself fall for you. Please don't hurt me." I keep my eyes shut tight but I can feel him staring at me.

His arm around me pulls a little tighter, "I will get it so right. I promise. I can give you everything you want. We will be happy. I swear it, baby."

I feel a happy tear run down my face as I dig my cheek into his neck a bit further. I smile into the night, "Good Night babe." He squeezes me again and I am falling asleep in his arms.

We are awakened way too early by Edge's phone going off. I look at the clock reading 8:45, not super early but still not enough sleep to be happy with. I watch Edge as he rubs his eyes with one hand and uses his other thumb to answer the call. I look over his shoulder to see the phone panning around the room at all the smiling faces.

Edge lets out a loud yawn while stretching his arm out behind my shoulders to pull me in closer to his chest, "What is going on? We are trying to sleep over here."

Lily is waving at me with a big cheesy smile which becomes so infectious that I have to wave obnoxiously back at her. Edge gives me a chuckle as he goes back to watching the screen.

Lily gives me another quick glance then smiles around the room before her, "As I was saying. I have thoughts. I was thinking maybe like an abandoned factory or something outdoors with ruins. I was also thinking at some point wearing the masks and using it promotionally. Every seemed to go fucking crazy about it at the arena. I figured the news has probably already hit the wires about me anyway so why not?"

Edge and I look at each other confused while Gideon whispers something in Lily's ear. He turns to me, "Any clue what she is rattling on about?" I shrug back at him as we both turn back towards the screen.

Edge sits us up towards the phone a bit closer, "This is great and all but what the fuck are we talking about?"

I watch Gideon as he smiles and pulls Lily closer to him, "Lily and I are getting married."

I feel my feet go numb and the breath rush out of my lungs. I don't know if I want to scream, cry or piss myself. Edge smiles widely at me then back to the screen, "Nice man. You finally got her to lock it down huh?"

I am still hearing nothing but a roaring ocean in my head. I have probably blinked 80 times in 20 seconds. Gideon smiles around the room then comes back to the facetime call, "Why is it so hard to believe that she asked me?"

I completely lose my shit. I am screaming so loud the neighbors probably think I am being murdered. I try to grab the phone but it fumbles around both of our hands before getting thrown off the bed completely and landing on the floor. I scramble over the blankets, still screaming, as I grab the phone and bring it back to my face, "Are you fucking kidding me right now? Lily?? Oh my god! Did you really propose?"

Edge is laughing uncontrollably behind me, since I am draped across his lap with the top half of my body hanging off the side of the bed. He wraps his hands around my waist and hauls me back up to the top of the bed as I grip his phone like a lifeline. I am grinning like a crazy person as Lily nods her head back to me.

Edge lets out another snort, "Well fuck me then."

I let out another loud squeal, making Edge shove his fingers in his ears and look at me like I am insane. I grin wildly at the phone, "You ARE calling me later and giving me a play by play!"

Lily grins back at me, "Yes, Mom. I promise."

I start blowing kisses at the phone, "I love you!!!!" Edge reaches over to take the phone from my hands and I start screeching again. He quickly hits the disconnect button and looks at me smirking, "So I take it you are happy then?"

I turn back towards him and wrap my arms around his neck, while slamming my lips into his. His arms instantly wrap around me and hold me as I continue to assault his mouth. I finally pull back and take a deep breath then smile widely again, "I am fricken ecstatic!"

9
Edge
Is It Really You? - Sleep Token, Loathe

Susie has been losing her mind for the last 5 minutes. It would be comical if it wasn't borderline crazy person behavior. She sits on my lap peppering my face in wild kisses, that part I am not upset about. I think I like happy Susie. She is usually pretty comical and sarcastic. But happy Susie has no idea how to control the emotions running through her. Which makes me wonder, what would sexed up Susie act like?

I instantly start to get hard at the images running through my head. I slowly roll her off of me and smile as I get up to go use the facilities. I need to calm down and try to not fuck her within the first 5 hours of me saying we will take our time.

When I step back out into the bedroom, she is already fully dressed for the day and smiling back at me, "Put on some pants. We're going out!" She marches past me into the bathroom to finish getting ready as I laugh back at her.

She is wild and untamed and hilarious. She is everything I have ever wanted in a woman, and also everything I never knew I needed. I can not screw this up. I get dressed quickly and step up behind her in the mirror to watch her applying a light coating of makeup. I scrunch my nose up, "You don't need makeup."

She smiles back at me, "Thank you, but I do. Just a smidge."

I laugh as I watch her applying mascara. She obviously cannot do it without her mouth hanging wide open and holding the opposite eye shut. She looks like a drunken pirate. I pull back and run my hand across her ass, giving her a playful smack as I walk out of the room and into the kitchen.

I step up towards her large picture window and look out at all the people running around the streets. You can almost hear the chaos of the streets through the glass. This city is so overpopulated. Just like back home. Millions of people packed into a tight little container. It is stifling. I need room to stretch, to breathe. I continue to watch the people running around like ants when I hear Susie walk into the kitchen behind me. I turn watching her strut her fine ass in, that floral scent rolling across me. She smiles, "You ready?"

I look at her curiously, "For what?"

She smiles wider as she reaches out her hand, "Time to get a taste of New York." I grin back at her and we wrap our hands together then head downstairs.

We finally make our way out the street. The smells of the city attack me as soon as the air hits my face. The blast of exhaust fumes and street food slap me like an angry lover. I try to adjust my senses to the smells and sounds as we walk a few blocks over to a coffee house. She orders us some coffee and bagels then we find a table to sit at and just enjoy each other's presence.

She smiles over her cup at me, "So, do you only have the one sister?"

I grin back at her nodding my head. I quickly chew the bite of blueberry bagel before clearing my throat, "Yep, just me and her. Mom never remarried, I think she was kinda scared after everything happened with Kelvin. That was my step dad. She felt so much guilt after all of that happened. She was upset for a long time until we finally convinced her that it wasn't her fault. She had no way to know what he was really like. I sure as hell never told her. I was just happy seeing her happy. I didn't want to ruin that with my stories of him being an asshole."

She reaches her hand out and strokes mine. I can hear the sincerity rolling from her voice, "You are a good man, Gavin. Don't let what wasn't said weigh on you. You were just a kid."

I look at her in amazement. Out of all that was just said, her concern lands squarely on my chest. I can feel some sort of something making my chest tight. I cannot believe the amount of empathy that this woman is able to convey with just a look. Just one smile from her and my demons try to hide away from the positivity. I can just be me. This is going to take some getting used to.

I smile back over my bagel at her, "So, what are our plans for the day?"

She grins back at me, "What do you want to do? It is one hundred percent up to you." I look around outside, not really knowing where to start. There is so much to do and see but honestly I would rather just spend time with her.

She smiles as she throws back the last of her coffee then crumples up the paper wrapper of her bagel, "No worries. I think I know just the place."

We throw our trash away and step back out onto the street. Susie grabs my hand then walks to the curb throwing her hand in the air to signal a taxi driver. I look at her suspiciously but decide to play along. Let's see how well she actually knows me. 30 minutes later we are stopping in front of a windowed storefront. She pulls me from the cab and I realize we are standing in front of a vintage guitar shoppe.

I instantly turn into a toddler at Christmas. Yeah, she knows me well enough. She grins at my shock as she continues to drag me towards the store. As soon as we walk in, I see the walls are lined with guitars of all shapes and sizes. The wood grains vary from deep mahogany to light maples. The distinct scent of aged wood mixed with hints of old leather and metal fills the air. I close my eyes and breathe in deep.

It has been a long, long time since I have visited a vintage shoppe like this. I turn to her smiling then give her a quick kiss on the lips before I am running to a wall scouring all the acoustic guitars. I hear someone gently strumming a guitar over in the corner and smile to myself at the familiarity of touching a new instrument for the first time.

You have to have the right connection with the instrument. Just like in life with other people, it isn't easy to find the right one. You are in a relationship with the guitar. It becomes an extension of yourself, of your essence.

I walk through the shoppe taking in the collection on the walls. I immediately stop in my tracks when I see a 1947 Gibson small body Sunburst hanging on the wall. She is a thing of beauty. I step up to her and gently run my fingers over the strings. I can feel the years of use and love etched into the worn fretboard. The air around me feels full, almost heavy even from the weight of the history from just this one instrument.

I turn and smile at Susie. She seems completely content just watching me acting a fool in this moment. I immediately walk up to the counter and ask for permission to strum a few chords. It is like kismet. Me and this guitar were meant to meet. She is coming home with me. I might even name her Susanna.

A half hour later and 6 grand dropped we are stepping back outside to find a cab back home. I don't want to walk around with this guitar strapped to my back. I don't trust people. At all.

It is already mid day when we make it back to her place. She smiles at me and makes up some bullshit about needing to check some work email. We both know it is her way of telling me it is okay to play around with my new toy. She meanders over to the couch and opens up a laptop. I grin at her as I sit down at the other end of the couch, tweaking and tuning my new baby. It isn't long and I am filling her spacious sitting room with music.

Susie at some point shuts the laptop and just lays back into the couch. I see a smile on her face and her eyes are closed as she just listens to me play. She looks so at peace right now. It doesn't take long and I can tell she has drifted off to sleep. I continue to play for a while before I realize it is getting close to supper time.

I put my new toy away reluctantly and go upstairs to find something to cook for dinner. I quickly realize that she doesn't eat at home much. There are like 3 things in her fridge. I smile again as I turn around to go back downstairs and I see her standing at the top of the staircase.

She slowly moves up to me and leans in for a kiss. I accept her into my orbit and hold on tight as she sets me spinning. Every single time her lips hit mine, I am a man lost at sea. And she is my rescue. I reach down behind her thighs and pick her up. She smiles into my mouth as she wraps her legs around me tightly. I walk us into the bedroom and sit down on the edge of the bed.

She continues to kiss me with full abandon. I immediately start pulling layers off of her. I just want to see her body. I want to run my fingers across her bare skin. I want to draw shapes with her freckles. I need to feel her heat on me.

She pulls back long enough to stand up and shed all of her clothing. I quickly pull my shirt up and over my head. She puts her hand on my chest and pushes me back flush onto the bed. I smile as I willingly collapse in front of her. She smiles again as she reaches down and unbuttons my jeans then pulls the zipper down agonizingly slow. She is definitely going to be the death of me.

104

I help her out by pushing my jeans and boxers down my thighs. She looks like an animal about to be uncaged as she slides them the rest of the way off. I am now laying before her, completely fucking hard and at her mercy. She leans over, placing her hands on my thighs then looks up at me, "Let me just do this at my own pace. I want to try something."

I blink back at her, "Are you sure? You don't have to."

She smiles back at me and tilts her head to the left, "I will never know unless I test the waters. Just be patient with me."

I rub my hands up her forearms and give her another smile, "Always baby. Always."

Susie slowly starts to climb up my body. I can feel her heat just inches away from my very painful erection. She leans in, pressing her soft lips against me then starts to trail kisses down my cheek and to my neck. I wrap my hands loosely around her back as she kisses up to my ear, taking one of the many rings in my earlobe into her mouth and tugging gently. I let a moan leave my throat as she moves back to my mouth.

She pulls back just far enough to look in my eyes. I can still feel her breath on my face as she places her wet center down on my dick. I feel a shudder run through her body. I try to watch her closely, gauge how she is doing. She smiles as she starts to rub herself on my dick. I feel my eyes roll up into my head as my hands lower to her ass. I grip her tightly as she continues to rub her wet pussy up and down me.

She has her face into my neck now and is moaning so deep it is making my own throat vibrate. She slips forward just a bit and I almost slide inside of her. I grip her tight and move her back down. Her eyes come to meet mine as I smile at her, "Not yet." Her eyes search my face as she smiles and continues to slide herself up and down my dick.

Susie sits back, adding the pressure of her body as she continues to grind her pussy against me. Her hips start moving erratically. I smile up at her, knowing I am going to make her cum without even being inside her. I move my hands up to her tits, letting them rest heavy in my palms before squeezing them.

She lets out a soft moan as I pinch her nipples between my fingers. I watch as her hands slowly move down her body then come to rest on my abs. She starts sliding across me faster and I feel my own release starting to build within me. I bring my hands back down to her waist and slide her faster up and down my length.

Susie lets her head fall back and I can feel the pressure of her clenching without even being inside her. I roll her underneath of me as she starts to cum and pin her under my weight now. I continue to slide up and down her until I feel myself about to let go. I lean up a bit, gripping my dick tight in one hand and then start slapping her clit with the head of my cock. Her eyes fly wide towards me, "Fuck! Edge!!" I growl my release as it hits her stomach.

She still has her back arched up off the bed as I finish spreading my seed across her abdomen. She smiles into the air around us as she comes back down onto the bed. I smile back down at her and lean in for a kiss. She smiles into my lips when they find her own. I finally pull back then find a towel to clean us both up. We fall asleep holding each other again, tightly like we never want to let go.

The next morning, I decide to let her sleep in a bit. She doesn't hear me when I slip out of the bedroom and head downstairs to play on my guitar a bit longer. It is after noon when she finally makes her appearance. She is wearing a silk robe and nothing else. I feel a growl leave my throat as I stand up to meet her at the bottom of the stairs.

She smiles into my eyes as she wraps her arms around my neck. I nuzzle my face into the soft spot where her neck meets her shoulder and leave a small kiss there. She sighs as she pulls back, "I am starving. Do you want me to order some food in?"

I smile as I nod at her, "Something authentic to New York. I want to try something new."

She smiles as she saunters away to find her phone. An hour later there is a knock at the door. She grins at me as she comes back with a pizza box. We make a little table set up at the coffee table and enjoy our pizza.

She leans onto the table with her elbows as she holds a slice of pizza in both hands, "So, when did you learn to play guitar?"

I smile back at her as I take a large bite, then sit down my own slice. I wipe my mouth with a napkin, "I started playing when I was like 12 or 13. Honestly, I only started to play to piss my parents off. Mom and my stepdad that is. My real dad took off right after my little sister was born. Last I heard, he is living in Scotland somewhere."

She nods her head at me, then starts rolling her hand at me to continue as she takes another bite of her food. I smile across the table, "So after a while, I started to figure out that I wasn't half bad. Then Gideon taught me how to read sheet music, how to pull it all together. I would mainly just play in my room or in Matthew's garage. After a bit, they kinda talked me into coming out of my shell."

She smiles at me again as she sits her pizza down, wiping the crumbs from her fingers. I grin across the table at her, "What about you? What were you like when you were younger?"

Susie lets her eyes go wide before she rolls them to the ceiling. She lets out this noise somewhere between a groan and a laugh, "I was, well, what's the word I am looking for? Eccentric maybe?"

I sit my food down, nodding at her excitedly, "Continue? I need examples."

She laughs as she grabs her soda and takes a large drink. She sighs as she sits the cup back down, "I got into a lot of fights. With boys. I was also constantly finding wounded animals and nursing them back to health, in the garage, without my grandma's permission. I met Lily when I was 14. Then high school was mainly about making sure she lived her life to the fullest. After that was college, I was your typical stupid college kid. Then afterwards I tried to find a job that would actually accept a Liberal Arts degree with a minor in sociology. Not as easy to find as you would think."

I laugh at her as she continues, "Then I fell into working. Especially after grandma died. She was kinda the glue that held me together, so after she was gone Lily became that glue. The rest is just kinda history."

I watch her closely as she starts to clean up our mess from dinner. I can imagine her being a little fiery 9 year old beating the hell out of some boy that had been torturing her or anyone for that matter. I could honestly see her standing up for anyone, she just carries that type of empathy around with her wherever she goes.

I smile after her, "So was that piece of shit the only other real relationship you have been in?"

She glances at me over her shoulder, giving me a smile but I can see the distance in her eyes. Maybe I shouldn't have brought him up. I continue to watch her as she turns back towards me, nodding her head, "Yeah, basically. We were together for a few years. Before him, I had casually dated but I

108

was more concerned with my career at the time. I didn't want any distractions."

I nod my head back at her in response, "I have never really been in a real relationship. I mean I have gone on dates, hooked up here and there but never anything serious. Even in secondaries, the girls kinda looked at me like I was some sort of devil in disguise or something. Which was fine with me, none of them interested me anyways."

Susie walks back towards me, leaning down to give me a soft kiss, "Their loss is my gain."

I smile into her lips as I kiss her back. She stands back up and finishes cleaning up the table. I watch her movements, slow and calculated. I feel like she is just waiting for the other shoe to drop or something. I can tell there is still so much of herself that she is keeping from me. And I hate that. I want to see every side of her, not just the ones she thinks I want to see.

After a while, we decide to go upstairs to the bedroom and watch some netflix. She puts on some show about a bunch of singles living in some way over the top house on an island somewhere.

I am not even paying attention to whatever the show is about. We have laid here for hours just holding each other. I am just way too aware of her skin on my own. I start placing small kisses down her neck and she rolls her body towards my own. I smile into her lips when I feel her hand slide down into the front of my sweats.

I let out a moan into the room around us as she continues to stroke my cock, then she kisses me fiercely. I can feel her everywhere at once. She has enveloped me completely, mind, body and soul.

I hear my phone ringing from the floor below. I don't even open my eyes, "Ignore it. Please don't stop."

I hear a small giggle leave her throat as she continues. But then just a few seconds later, we hear her phone ringing. I growl into the fucking luck of it. We finally have some time to just us this weekend and people keep being persistent bitches at every turn. She sits up straight on top of me. She reaches over to the nightstand and picks up her phone. I keep my hands on her hips, gliding her back and forth on me as she smiles and answers the phone, "Someone either better be dead or thoroughly fucked right now."

I smile into the room as she continues to push her weight down on me. Then she goes still. I hear her voice catch in her throat and I open my eyes to see the color completely drained from her face. I sit up quickly in front of her, "What's wrong Susanna?"

I see a tear roll down her cheek, "Yeah, I am still here. No, yeah. We will be on the next plane. Thank you for calling me. Seriously, Simone. Thank you." She hangs up the phone just blinking into the wall.

She lets out a heavy sigh and scoots back off of me. I sit up closer to the edge of the bed, "Baby, what happened? What's wrong?" It is like she can't even hear me. She is lost in her own mind or something. She sits the phone down and leaves the room. Now roaming dazed into the kitchen. I quickly stand to follow her when I hear her bloodcurdling scream from the next room.

I run from the bedroom to the kitchen and I see her holding a chair from the dining table. I stop in my tracks as I watch her slam the chair into the wall until it falls apart into pieces around her. The splintering sound of the wood breaking apart ricochets off the walls around us. I sprint to her and take her into my arms right as she starts to collapse into a fit of tears and heartache.

I hold her, stroking her hair, "Susie, what the fuck is going on? What has fucking happened? You are scaring me baby."

She pulls back and looks into my eyes as more tears start to fall, "They think Lily just tried to overdose on cocaine. She is asleep right now. They found her in the park about an hour ago."

I feel my eyes fly wide as my jaw drops. I didn't even fucking know she used. I shake my head, confused, "Lily? Lily overdosed on coke? But she doesn't use."

Susie pulls away from me and scoots until her back is against the dining room wall. She lets out another heavy sigh, wiping her face and looking at me, "She hasn't used since high school. She used it as a coping mechanism back then. But apparently her and Gideon, something happened tonight. He told her that he wanted her to leave him. So she tried....."

Susie is beside herself with emotions, rightly so. She is shaking her head and punching herself in the thigh. I scoot over to her, taking her hands in mine, "You are no good to her if you break your own fucking leg. We are going to sit here while you catch your breath. Then we are going to book two flights to London. This is our family. We have to go to them."

Susie's eyes fly up to mine as she wraps her arms around my neck and just starts wailing. I wrap my arms around her back, gently rubbing my fingers up and down her skin. It takes a few long moments but she finally seems to get some of her composure back then leans back into the wall again. I continue to stroke her hand in mine, "What did she need to cope with to begin with? Back in school?"

Susie looks at me and shakes her head, "It's not my business to tell. That is her story."

I nod back at her but then pull her gaze back to me with my finger under her chin, "I get that, but I can't try to help if I

|||

don't know where this is coming from. And I want to help Lily. I don't want to sit back helpless. I promise you right now I will never tell her or anyone else that I know anything."

She continues to shake her head then turns to look out the window, into the dark city on the other side of the glass. She lets out a long breath, "Her mom was really sick when she was little. Like mentally unstable, kind of sick."

I feel my stomach drop, this story isn't going to sit well with me. Did her mother do something to her? As a kid? I instantly start to have flashbacks of Ginny. So small, so broken. I try to push the memories to the back of my head and focus on the issue in front of me but it is nearly impossible. I feel my skin tightening with anger.

Susie turns to me, empathy and sadness written all over her face, "Her mom kinda lost it one night. She killed Lily's sister Nikki right in front of her. Lily was hiding under the kitchen table. She watched her own mother stab her sister to death. She was only 6 years old when it happened."

I fall back onto my ass, completely mortified by what this woman has been through. I shake my head, "I had no idea. I mean I saw the drawing but I never would have guessed it was truly a memory, not just something she drew. Even after you told me it was, I just kinda thought it was an exaggeration. Or that maybe we were thinking of two different drawings."

Susie shakes her head again, wiping the tears from her face, "I wish it wasn't true. She went through years of therapy. At one point, she just stopped talking to people all together because she was exhausted from reliving it over and over. She stopped talking around the age of 8 until we met in high school. She became my sister that day. Not just my best friend. It has been me and her against the world since then."

I lean back up on my knees and pull Susie close to my chest, just holding her as she lets out shuddered breaths, "I can't

12

lose her Gavin. She is all I have. She is my only family. I can't fucking lose her."

I pull her face back and force her gaze to meet mine, "You are not going to lose her. We are going to get her some help. We are going to make sure she stays clean. And I am going to kick Gideons' ass all the way to Asia."

I stand up and reach my hand down to her. She gives me a manufactured smile as she reaches up and allows me to haul her to her feet. She is still shaking so I pull her into another hug, "She is going to be fine. I promise Peach. I will make sure of it." Though I have no idea how.

Susie goes back into the bedroom, pulling a suitcase out of the closet and throwing it on the bed. I quickly start grabbing my stuff and throw everything back into my suitcase.

I watch her as she slowly leaves the room then I hear her pacing around the kitchen talking on the phone, "I am so sorry that this is so last minute but it is a family emergency. I wouldn't just lay all this on you unless it was important." I quickly realize she must be talking to someone she works with.

Then it hits me, I don't even know what she does for a living. I mean judging by the apartment she has done well for herself but still. When everything calms down, I need to remember to ask her.

She comes back into the bedroom then turns to face her closet. I step up behind her and put my hands on her shoulders, "You okay?" She nods as she continues to pull clothes off of hangers, "I am just kinda numb." I kiss the back of her head then move over towards the bed to sit on the corner of it.

She turns back to me with another sad look on her face. Her mouth droops into a frown and she starts crying again. I stand and move to her quickly, "Baby, she is gonna be okay." She chuckles and pulls back from me, "It's not that. I have never been to London. I don't know what to pack."

I laugh along with her as I wipe her frustrated tears from her face. I turn with her and look into her closet. Together, we find about a dozen suitable outfits. Then she grabs some underwear, bras and other essentials until her suitcase is practically bursting at the zipper. She fills her carry on with her makeup and then turns back towards the closet, "Shit! I can't forget my passport!"

I laugh as I pull both of our bags up beside me and I watch her move all her clothes to the side to reveal a hidden safe in the back of her closet. I laugh at her cleverness. She opens it and I catch a quick peek inside, "What all you got in there? Trinkets from all your previous kills?"

Susie turns to me smacking me on the arm then smiles back towards the safe, "Just important paperwork, some cash, just normal safe stuff." I smile as I reach past her and pull out a ring box. I can see the smile in her eyes. I look at her suspiciously again, "Previous engagement or marriage I need to know about?"

She laughs as she takes the ring box from me and opens it towards me. Inside is a beautiful, antique princess cut engagement ring. It is stunning but obviously from a different time. She smiles at it, "This was my grammies. The one who always called me Susie. It is the last thing I have of her. Of any of my family actually." She shuts the lid, putting the box back in the safe before closing the door and spinning the wheel on the front of it.

I run my hand across her neck as she looks back up at me in surprise. I look at her cautiously, "You were serious when you said Lily was the only family you have left?"

She nods and picks up her carry on bag, "My parents died in a car accident before I was even 1. My grandma raised me. No siblings. Just me and her. She passed away a little over 10 years ago. It is just me. Well, me and Lily."

I lean forward and give her another deep kiss before I grab her suitcase as well as mine. She grabs a messenger bag throwing it across her body, then grabs one of my guitars and straps it to her back. That is the hottest thing I have ever seen. My baby, carrying one of my babies. I grin to myself as I grab our suitcases and we rush to the street to our awaiting uber.

10
Susie
Zombie - YUNGBLUD

When I finally get to see Lily almost 2 days later, I don't know if I want to hug her or push her out the fucking window. She is sitting on the couch in their apartment refusing to make eye contact with me. I look at Gideon as I pass by him and throw my bag on the counter. I turn and poke him in the chest with my finger, "I will deal with you later. Asshole."

He drops his chin to his chest then looks back up from me to Edge, letting out an expected sigh, "So glad to see you again too, Susie."

I huff at him as I see Edge slip him a sly grin. I turn sharply walking over to the couch to stand in front of Lily. I start tapping my foot on the hardwood floor with my arms crossed in front of me. She finally pulls her eyes up to meet mine and I melt like an ice cream cone on a hot day. I pour into a puddle in front of her and lay my face across her thighs. Then I am just wailing. I am wailing and screaming and leaving a very noticeable snot puddle on her left leg and I don't care.

I finally pull away and look at her. At her eyes that now match mine. I try to steel my emotions but I know she can read right through them, "You promised me Lily. You promised me that you were done. That you would never do anything to hurt yourself. You fucking swore to me that you would never leave me."

She slides down onto the floor with me and wraps her arms around me, holding me tight and stroking my hair, "I am so sorry Susie. I was just lost for a minute. I regretted it immediately. I promise I will get help. I promise I will find a therapist and I will get my shit in check."

I push her away from me roughly, "Fucking right you will. I am not leaving until I see proof that this shit is getting better. So buckle up baby. You are stuck with me for a bit."

She smiles at me as she pulls me closer, "Then you can just stay through the wedding. There is no reason to rush back."

I pull back from her and point to Gideon, "You still wanna marry this asshat?"

I try to keep my face stern but she can see that I am acting like a brat just to get a rise out of Gideon. She knows all my secrets. She has seen all my plays. She immediately starts laughing as I turn to Gideon smiling, "Just kidding."

He shakes his head at me and looks to Edge, "You are dating this voluntarily?"

Edge smiles back at him pointing at Lily, "You're marrying that voluntarily so why not?"

Gideon rolls his eyes and looks back at me smiling. He walks over and reaches a hand out to me to help me up. He pulls me into a deep, unexpected hug. I take in the natural scent of the ocean that just seems to pour out of him as he whispers, "Thank you for coming. She needs you more than anyone right now." I stroke his back a few times then pull away, looking up into his black eyes, "She is my sister." Gideon nods his head at me as he pulls me back into a hug, allowing me to hide my tears in his chest.

Lily lets out a loud hoot behind me as she stands up and runs past us to hug Edge. I see him whisper something in her ear and she pulls back, nodding and smiling at him. She pulls away and steps back over to the couch, sitting down to get comfortable.

17

I move closer towards her and sit across from her just staring at her. We have always had this thing. We can literally just stare at each other and somehow always know what the other is thinking. She can read my unhinged mind and I can see through her shadows to face her demons for her. I can feel the guys watching us, probably trying to figure out what we are doing. But after a solid 10 minutes of silence and staring I can hear them moving around in the kitchen, deep into some conversation.

She and I look through multiple websites trying to find a therapist that fits her vibes. We pick out a few that we think might work and then we sit back and just talk like old times. About anything and everything. It has only been days since we saw each other but any stranger would think it had been years since we had been near one another.

The guys are sitting at the island facing us but talking amongst themselves. I know Edge is ripping him a new one. And I am kinda loving the energy of it. Lily smiles as she stands up and walks towards the fridge for a drink. She grabs a water bottle out and takes a big drink before nodding her head towards Edge, "So how does this guy compare to Brian?"

I belt out a laugh as I see anger roll across Edge's face. His eyes cut wide to me in shock and annoyance. He wants to know who Brian is. I smile at him devilishly, maybe if he is a good boy I will let him meet Brian later. I turn back to Lily smiling back at her, "There is nothing to compare."

I know that can be taken either way. I also know Edge is super pissed. The tops of his ears have gone beet red. I smile at him sweetly as he looks away from me angrier than I have ever seen before. Maybe it is time for him to be scaroused for once. Or would it be pisorny? There has to be a phrase that is right for this emotion. I will figure it out. We only stay for another hour before we are making our way back to his bungalow.

I have only been here two days and already I feel like I belong here. The aura of this city is doing something to me. Lily was right when she would describe London to me. There is just something about it. There is no other place to compare it to. Edge is quiet the whole way home but I am so lost in my own thoughts and worries about Lily that I don't really seem to notice.

We finally make it home and he holds the door open for me before swiftly walking past me, "I am gonna go practice a bit." And that is it. He is gone. I smile as he walks away. He thinks there is someone else. I let him wallow in his own pity for a few hours before I go into the bedroom and strip down naked.

I reach into my carry on bag and pull out Brian. I hide him behind my back as I walk naked through the house. I get to his guitar room and softly knock on the door. I hear a gruff, "I'm busy." come from behind the door. I smile as I turn the knob and push the door open anyways. His eyes go wide as he starts to devour me with them. I smile up at him, "What's wrong? Are you mad at me?"

He sits the guitar down into its stand before crossing his arms in front of his chest like he is trying to keep his hands to himself. He rolls his eyes letting out a breath and puts his hands on his thighs, "I just. I just thought we had something different. And then I hear that you have been seeing some other dude and it just kinda hit me. I know we never said anything about exclusivity. I just thought it was something unsaid on both sides."

I smile at him as I take a few steps towards him. He watches me from head to toe as I move closer to him. I smile and tilt my head, "Are you jealous of Brian?"

He scoffs at me then looks away when he hears me say his name. I chuckle again as I pull the dildo out from behind me. I smile at him as I stroke Brian, "I mean obviously he isn't nearly as big as you but he has been very, very good to me for the past 4 years. It is hard to just walk away from that."

Seeing the realization crash into his face is the funniest thing I have ever seen in my entire life. I don't know how I am not laughing my ass off right now. His eyes darken and narrow at me, "*That* is Brian? Why the fuck did you name your dildo?"

I stroke him a bit more, making Edge's eyes roll over the movements of my fingers, "Don't listen to him Brian. He is just jealous. He wants me to name his dick too."

Edge laughs as he jumps up from his stool as I scream while trying to run away. He quickly scoops me up and throws me over his shoulder, "You are in so much fucking trouble now." I giggle as he reaches up and smacks my bare ass with his full hand. The giggling instantly stops. The heat that rolls through my body is unlike anything I have ever felt before.

He deposits me with my back on the bed and reaches over to grab Brian from my hand. I smile up at him, "Be gentle. He is sensitive."

Edge laughs at me, tossing Brian back down onto my abdomen. He grins wickedly, "Show me what he can do."

The smile drops from my face. I can feel my cheeks heating up, "I can't do that." He grins back at me, "Why not?"

My face has to be maroon right now. I smile looking away from him, "Cause that's weird."

He grins as he takes off all of his clothes, throwing them around the room. I watch him, my mouth watering at the sight of his perfect form in front of me. He reaches back down and takes Brian from my hand again, "I guess I will just have to see what he can accomplish then."

My eyes go wide as he lays down beside me and starts to rub Brian up and down my center. The anticipation is cruel. I reach up and grab my tit just for some kind of stimulation. I can feel Edge's eyes on me as he leans over and takes my other nipple in his mouth. I let a moan fall from my lips as I arch my chest up into his mouth.

I feel him as he pushes the toy deeper into my core and starts rubbing it up and down my clit. I feel my heart rate tick up and I start panting into the air around us. I look over at him and he is staring at the toy as he starts to move it further south. He looks up into my eyes as he takes it and slowly starts to push it into me. I feel my eyebrows pinch together as my mouth falls open. He is panting right back at me now, "You are fucking beautiful, Peach."

I close my eyes and tilt my head back into the bed a bit further. He continues to slowly push the toy into me until it bottoms out. Then he is slowly, methodically pushing it in and out. I reach down with my left hand and wrap it tightly around his dick. He lets out a hiss as I start to stroke him hard and fast.

He starts to speed up Brian's movements so I match his speed with my hand. I let out a soft moan as I hear him grunting beside me. I look over at him and his eyes move from the toy to my hand as he starts to buck his hips into my fist. I tighten my grip as I feel myself start to clench around the toy.

He lets out a loud moan as he pulls my hand from him then he turns so he is on his knees in front of me. I look up at him as he switches the hand he is using on the toy. He starts to pummel me with Brian as he jerks himself off with the other hand. It is by far one of the sexiest things I have ever seen a man do before. I scream as I feel my orgasm hit me. I am thrusting up towards him as he jerks on his dick harder until he screams my name into the room around us and is depositing himself on my stomach and lower abdomen. I continue to thrust up into the toy as he pulls it from me quickly and starts to devour me.

I scream again as I wrap my fingers up in his hair. He flicks his tongue across my clit and I can feel myself about to fall over the edge again. No pun intended. He flattens his tongue and runs it over my clit pushing in with just enough pressure that I explode around him. I can't hold it back any longer, "God Dammit Gavin. I'm cumming. I am cumming again."

I feel him moan into my clit and I am still reeling from my orgasm. He continues to devour me as I finally start to come down. I wrap my fingers around his head and start to pull him up towards me. His face is finally back to mine and I kiss him roughly as I roll him underneath me.

I am now straddling him and I can feel our sweaty bodies sliding against each other. I want to fuck him so bad. I want to take him into me and never let him go. But I am scared. What if I freak out in the middle of it. What if I freak him out by freaking out? I don't want to ruin what we have now. I finally work up the nerve to pull myself from him and I roll back over onto my back.

I let a sigh out into the room. Edge rolls over towards me and starts circling my nipple with his finger, "I guess Brian isn't so bad after all." I let out a loud laugh around the room as I slap his hand away and stand to get cleaned up. I find a towel and clean myself up then wipe him down as well. He watches me intently as I clean him all over.

I throw the towel across the room and crawl up onto the bed beside him again. I am not going to be able to hold out much longer. Not because he is pressuring me but because my pussy may just pack up her bags and leave me all together if I don't start taking care of her the way she deserves.

My breathing is finally coming back down to normal so I roll onto my stomach and prop my face up at him. Smiling into his eyes, "I really like it here in London."

He grins back at me, "Good. I want you to be comfortable here. I want you to feel at home when you are with me."

Edge rolls towards me, laying on his side as he runs his hand from the back of my knee, up across my ass, then into the small of my back. He repeats this path as he smiles into me,

"What do you think about staying here longer? Or maybe after the wedding I will come back to New York with you for a bit? Before the tour starts."

I smile at him but we both know I am not going to let him do that. I let out a sigh, "You can't come back to New York with me. You have an album to record. Remember?" He nods back at me, staring down at the bed between us.

I let out another breath, "Let's just enjoy our time here. Now. We will figure out our next steps tomorrow. Let's not stress over it now. I want to explore the city. I want to see everything. I want to go to Westminster. I want to see the sites and try the food and meet the people."

He smiles back at me, "We can do that. We gotta be careful though, just like with New York there are quite a few unsavory people out there. I think if we just map out a few places ahead of time we should be good. I will keep you clear of the ruffians."

I laugh at him as I sit up, "Okay, I am American. What exactly do you mean by unsavory ruffians? Cause all I picture in my head is peg legged pirates. With ruffled shirts of course."

Edge lets out another laugh as he leans up on his elbow, "Well of course but no I mean like you know the homeless. There are a lot of rough sleepers around London. We will just make a plan ahead of time."

My heart immediately starts to melt. I hadn't even thought about the amount of people here needing help like that. Like back home. But there are just as many people here as in New York so it makes sense. It instantly makes me feel guilty for not being back home taking care of all the women and children we provide for through the foundation. I glance back at him, "A lot of people then? Is it a lot of women and children?"

He shrugs his shoulders a bit, "Not more of one than the other. I mean it is never fun to see but a lot of them are there

because of their own choices. I would bet the majority of them·
are there because of stupid fucking decisions. I mean it sucks but
it is life. You have to deal with the consequences if you make a
wrong turn somewhere. Idiots never seem to be in short
demand."

     I immediately feel disgusted. He doesn't have an ounce of
empathy in him over the topic. What of those children? What
choice did they have? What about the women who are abused
and running away from life and death situations? I am just
staring at him, shocked at his candor.
     But he is looking at me like nothing just happened. Like
he didn't just minimize these people and their stories, their pain.
I can feel my heart starting to beat erratically in my chest. How
am I supposed to be with someone that can think like that? Feel
that way? I never in a million years would have imagined that he
would be so callous about the topic.
     I can't even look at him right now. My eyes dart across
the room just trying to find something else to focus on. I slide off
the bed finding a shirt on the floor and throw it on real quick. I
don't even look at him as I whisper, "I am going to go get a
drink."
     I basically sprint to the kitchen and grab a bottle of water.
I literally feel nauseous now. This is a hard no for me. This is my
life's work. Helping these people. Helping these women and
children find safety, stability. We aren't all blessed enough to get
a slap on the wrists for our mistakes. Not like him.
     It hits me hard, like a freight train. I can't be here. I have
to go. I have to be away from him to figure out if this is

something I can move past. I can't be with him. Not like this. I have to leave now before I start looking at him differently.

I head back into the bedroom and step over to the window looking out. I let out a shaky breath, "I think I am going to go stay in a hotel until after the wedding. You are busy. You have an album to work on. I don't wanna be in your way."

I hear him moving around behind me then I feel his hands on my biceps. I instantly cringe at him touching me. I am scared at how quickly this is all turning within me. I watch his hands out of the corner of my eye as he lifts them back, "What is wrong? Why are you saying this?"

I turn and look back at him, somehow strong enough not to cry. I can't cry in front of him. Not this time. I shake my head and move over towards my stuff. I grab a pair of pants and slide them on quickly. I start throwing stuff into my suitcase as he steps up beside me again. I can see the pain and confusion in his eyes but I just can't. Not over this. There is no middle ground on this topic with me. And I know if I tell him what bothered me he is going to have a rebuttal. I don't want to hate him. But his words could easily put him into that category really fucking quickly.

Edge tries to turn me towards him, "Susanna. What is wrong?" I shake my head at him as I continue to shove stuff into my bag and zip it shut. I turn around and find my carryon. I start throwing anything I can reach into it, "Nothing. Nothing is wrong. I just, I need to leave."

I hear him pacing behind me, his voice cracking, "Are we going to fast for you? I can slow down. I can cool it. I didn't mean to make you feel pressured."

I let out another shaky breath as I slide my shoes on and grab my suitcase. I throw my carry on over my shoulder and pull my phone out of my purse. I quickly order an uber then look up at his shattered face. I don't want to hurt him. I don't want to break his heart. But he just shattered mine. I need time.

"I just think this is too much right now. I think we just need to put everything on hold. I just can't. I can't be with you right now. I am sorry. I have to go." I practically run past him and through the house. As soon as the door shuts, I start wailing. I run to the curb, just trying not to vomit on his sidewalk.

I am bent over with my hands on my knees just trying to catch my breath. I can't be with someone who can't have any empathy or consideration for those struggling. That kind of callous person does not get to have a part of me, or my heart.

I hear the front door shut and I know he is walking up to me. Luckily, my uber pulls up at that exact moment and I grab my suitcase. I run to the car and throw everything in the back before sliding in. I shut the door, "Please just go. Quickly. Just take me to any at least 4 star hotel please." The car leaves the curb but I don't allow myself to look back. Though I do cry the entire ride to the hotel. I cry through check in. I cry as I lay in my hotel bed. I continue to cry for the next week.

Edge
Black - Pearl Jam

She won't even answer my calls. The wedding is tomorrow and she won't even acknowledge the fractured existence she has left me with. I have tried to find her but Lily didn't even know she wasn't staying with me any longer. I have called, I have texted but she is just gone. She is a ghost. She ripped my heart out when she left that day. I am a hollow shell of a man again.

Worse than before. Because now I have felt love just to have had it taken away. I don't even know what I did wrong. I have thought back over every single moment of our time together and I don't know what I did wrong.

Now I am just left here, sitting in the dark in the middle of the night drinking vodka like it is water. I need to get some sleep. Tomorrow is going to come quickly and I really shouldn't be hung over for Gideon's wedding. I choke out a chuckle, not giving a fuck, as I lift the bottle back to my lips.

Staring at the wall has become the only thing I seem to be good at. Besides getting high and drunk. After the first few days, I tried to just push her to the back of my head. But she is everywhere. Her scent still lingers on the few pieces of clothes she forgot to take. She left some lip gloss laying on the bathroom sink.

I stand and move towards the kitchen. I should probably put something in my stomach besides liquor but when I open the fridge all I see is her favorite Bai water sitting on the shelf. She is fucking everywhere. I cannot escape her.

It feels like a daze as I walk Hera down the aisle. Ares looks stoic and nervous as hell. I step up beside him and Apollo. Trying to keep my eyes on anything except for my past that is about to walk down the aisle towards me. I stare at my feet until I just can't bear it any longer. I can feel her, her presence still pulling on my heart.

Susie is wearing a white satin mask. I can see two ruby red lips smiling at everyone around us. Her hair is all pinned up with a few loose curls rolling down over her shoulders. She is wearing a red satin dress that is hugging her fucking perfectly. I feel a tear roll down my cheek and I quickly turn to my right so I don't have to look at her anymore.

This is a lot more painful than I anticipated. She is fucking stunning and it is gutting me. I didn't even realize I loved her until she was gone. Until she cut me out of her world completely. I let out a slow breath as I try to focus on the ceremony around us. I want to just fucking leave. I want to go somewhere and fucking hide. I don't want anyone to see that I am fucking hollow. That I have been left with nothing but unanswered questions and an empty heart.

I glance over at her as she takes Lily's bouquet. Then again when she smiles and passes her a ring. She looks over at me and I quickly turn my eyes away. I don't want to see her. I don't want to feel this shooting pain through my chest anymore.

As soon as the ceremony is over and we are done taking photos, we follow Gideon and Lily to the limo. Everyone is smiling and hugging. I reach into my coat and pull out a flask, taking a long hard drink of the tequila I poured inside it before leaving the house. I see her look at me and frown. I just smirk at her and tip the flask up again.

128

She looks around quickly and steps over to me, "You shouldn't be drinking right now. It is Gideon's wedding."

I look back her incredulously, letting out a loud laugh, "Like you fucking care. You don't even recognize that I exist. Remember?" I quickly stuff the flask back in my pocket and walk away from her. I hear her sniffle and I almost turn around. Almost. She gave up on me. She doesn't want me. So I don't want her. At least that is what I keep telling myself.

I give Gideon a hug to which he tells us all to meet at the hotel bar in 2 days to really celebrate. Great. Just more time for me to stand around watching the woman I love hate me. I nod at him and turn back to look around the crowd. I see Susie give Lily a hug. She is smiling widely until her eyes reach mine again through the crowd. The smile instantly falls from her face as I try to pull my eyes away from her but I just fucking can't.

She takes a small step towards me like she is going to walk over and say something before she abruptly stops. Her eyes start to jump around to the faces of our family before they fall back on me. My heart clenches in my chest when I see the tears roll out of her eyes and over her mask. She closes her eyes tight before opening them and giving another painted smile to everyone around us. Her eyes reach mine one last time, showing me the emptiness in them. The sadness that she is trying to hold inside those now watery emeralds hidden behind white satin. Susie turns and quickly starts to move further away from me.

She doesn't turn around once. I watch her reach over and throw her flowers into a trash barrel as she continues to stomp across the field. She reaches down and takes her shoes off and tosses them into the field beyond her as she hikes up her dress and literally runs away. I watch her get into a car, then she is moving out of my life again.

I stay drunk for the next two days.

I try to look as presentable as possible before leaving for the hotel. It doesn't matter anyway. There is literally no one there I am wanting to impress. No one who really even gives a damn about me being there besides Gideon. I brush my teeth and hair slowly. I grab my leather jacket as I step out the front door to head to my car. The hotel they are staying at is about a half hour drive from me. I should probably take an uber since I am fully intending to get shitfaced if I have to stare at Susie all night. I guess if worst comes to worst I will just get a room.

I quickly find a parking spot when I arrive. I am walking from the lift when I see Susie walking towards the bar. She is fucking stunning. Wearing a short green dress that flares out at her hips. It looks like it is satin and it holds firm to her sides and chest. Her hair is up again and it looks like she is wearing a single strand of pearls.

I immediately start shaking my head then move towards the front desk to get a room. I am definitely not driving home tonight. After I quickly pay for and take my room key, I head to the bar. I see Gideon immediately and step up beside him to order a scotch on the rocks. He is staring at me like he can see right through me. I try to avoid his gaze but I know he can see me looking towards Susie every 2 seconds.

I can't do this. It was a mistake. I can't be this close to her and not feel the pull to touch her, talk to her. I can't look at my future becoming my past right in front of me. If she would just look at me. Really look at me, she would see this hollow soul pretending to be a man. But she doesn't even care enough about me to check on me. I am just a memory to her. If I am even that much to her. I pick up my glass, glancing her way again as I hear Gideon, "Spill it man."

I quickly look over at him, "What?"

He shakes his head and steps in front of me, blocking my view of Susie and the girls. I let out a heavy sigh as I look into his face. He smiles back at me, "Fucking spill it man. What is happening?"

I roll my shoulders then pop my neck loudly in both directions. I raise my glass to my lips and swallow it in one swig. I slam the glass onto the bar and wipe my mouth. Trying to calm my nerves a bit. I turn back towards Gideon, "I don't know. I don't know what is wrong. We were doing fine. Great even. Then she just closed off. She decided to get a hotel room and hasn't really spoken to me since. Nothing really more than hello or goodbye. I don't know what I fucking did."

Gideon nods his head at me, quickly looking over his shoulder at Susie with her back now turned to us. He turns back to me, "So, you didn't fuck and forget then? You actually think you might want something with her?"

I look back up into his eyes, barely able to pry my gaze from her. I quickly look around the bar then back at Gideon, "We haven't fucked."

Gideons scoffs at me, taking a small step back. He looks at me in confusion, "Like, nothing. Have you tried? Did she shoot you down?"

I huff back at him and wave the bartender over by holding up my glass. He turns to start making me another drink and I look back to Gideon, "I mean we have done...stuff. She gave me head, no gag reflex by the way. And I got her off a few times but we never officially fucked. We were just laying in bed a few days ago talking and she just got up then packed her shit and left. She said it just wasn't going to work. I guess she has plans to go home after this party sometime. I just don't know what the fuck I did."

He looks at me with just as much confusion as I have felt for the last week and half. It has been torture knowing she is here, in this city. So close but still so far away. Gideon reaches out to grab my new drink and hands me the glass, "Okay, here is the plan. We are gonna go somewhere else a little less stuffy. I will keep to you so Lily has a chance to figure out what is what. I will try to find out what is up for you. Yeah?"

I nod and take a drink of my scotch. I just shake my head again as I look back at him, "I don't know what I could have done." I know I sound as defeated as I feel. Gideon leans forward a bit, putting a sympathetic hand on my shoulder, "What were you talking about when she just got up?"

I shrug my shoulders at him, frustrated again, "I don't fucking remember." Gideon rolls his eyes at me. He catches Matthews' attention and waves him over to us. I let out another sigh, great. More pity incoming. He turns back to me as Matthew approaches, "Try to remember. You must have said something that rubbed her the wrong way."

I let out another held breath, lifting my face to the ceiling. Trying to remember everything that was said that day. There has been a lot of alcohol and weed going through my system since then. I bring my face back down, looking between the two of them, "We were talking about all the homeless people around downtown. She made some comment about how she was sad to see a lot of women and kids out there. I told her something like that is just fucking life. Shit happens, or something like that."

I glance at a nodding Gideon then turn to see a huge grin over Matthews face. Then he leans back and just starts howling in laughter. He even sits his drink down on the bar so he doesn't spill it he is laughing so hard. What an asshole! I narrow my

132

gaze at him, "What the fuck are you laughing about man? This isn't really all that fucking funny."

Matthew tries to breathe through the laughter, finally putting a hand on my shoulder, "Have you ever asked her what she does for a living?"

I leave the confusion all over my face, scoffing his hand off my shoulder, "No, I don't think so. I meant to but it just never got brought up. Have you Gideon?"

Gideon shakes his head at us both, just as clueless as me it seems. Matthew smiles widely again, turning towards the girls, "Lily, hey come here for just a second." I watch as she steps up to us beaming. Obviously happier than she has ever been, "Yeah, what's up?"

Matthew starts to chuckle again as he turns his face back to me, "We are just over here talking. What is it that Susie does for a living again? Simone told me but I forgot."

Lily smiles around at all of us, before settling her gaze back on Matthew, "She is the president of a non-profit back in New York." Matthew nods his head again then grins wider while looking at me again, "What kind of non-profit?"

Lily looks confused from me then to Matthew, "For homeless women and children. To get them off the streets and into some sort of shelter. Why?"

I feel the blood drain from my face. I can barely even breathe. Jesus fuck. What have I done? I took her life's work and made shit of it. I try to remember everything that I said that day. My eyes pinch together in regret and pain. I am a moron. I am going to jump off a bridge with no water under it. Tonight. I am done. Gideon looks back to me with even more pity than before, "You are so fucked."

I feel my shoulders drop as I groan towards the floor, "Fuck me. Okay. I have to figure out a way to fix this."

Matthew smiles and starts tapping his watch, "You better move quick she is gonna leave soon."

I look back at him quickly, scared even, "What do you mean?" Matthew shrugs his shoulders at me, "Pretty sure she told Simone she is leaving first thing in the morning."

I stand at attention now. I have to fix this. Right now. Tonight. Gideon turns back to me, "Go get her. Take her somewhere. Fix your shit." I smile back at him and down my drink. I turn back towards the girls, straightening my jacket then I look at at him, "I fucking owe you man."

As I am walking towards my dreams, I hear him reply back, "I will not forget you just said that."

I take a deep breath as I approach the girls. I smile at them all as I step up then turn to Susie. She glances at me then quickly to the floor. I smile around the circle again then turn back to her, "Can I please speak to you outside? Just for a minute?"

She looks up at me, then around all the eyes looking at her waiting for a response. She lets out a seemingly nervous breath, "Yeah. Just a minute though." I nod eagerly as she turns. I put my hand on her lower back as I try to guide her towards the door.

We step outside onto the sidewalk in front of the hotel. I pace about 10 steps before turning to her. She is looking back in the window and I honestly cannot tell if she is crying or pissed. I see the crimson starting to creep up towards her ears as I try to settle my thoughts in my head. I let out another deep breath, "I am a fucking idiot." She turns her eyes at me and tilts her head.

I shake mine back at her, splaying my hands out in front of me, "No. Just let me say this. Then you can walk away and I promise I will never bother you again. I am a fucking idiot. I never even asked you what you do for a living. I had no idea that

134

you spend your days trying to help the people you heard me talking down about. Had I known, I would have been a bit softer about my views on it.

"I know they are not all out there because of bad decisions. I know those kids didn't have a choice in what their parents did or didn't do. I know there are women and men out there just trying to get away from harmful situations. Fuck, I was almost one of them. I could have ended up on the streets just as easily as any of them. I just. I didn't know. And for that I am sorry.

"I am sorry that I opened my mouth and all that bullshit fell out. I am sorry that I am such a fucking horrible person. I am sorry that I can't be what you want. I never wanted or meant to hurt you. I mean fuck, I love you Susie. I love you so much that I don't even know how to breathe let alone function with you gone. I am just so fucking sorry and I will pay for this stupidity every day for the rest of my miserable life."

She finally turns back to me, tears streaming down both sides of her face. She lets out a shudder and turns back towards the window. I take in another deep breath and close my eyes. I will not cry in front of her. I can do this.

I step around her, whispering, "I will never forget our time together. I love you. Goodbye Peach."

I have done everything I can. I put it all out there. She has made her choice and I have to respect it. I pull the door open to the hotel and walk straight past the bar to the lifts. I punch the up arrow and hear the ding as the doors open. Once I am inside, I can cry. I can let loose then. Not a moment before.

I take another deep breath and step inside. Turning, I look at the panel and press the button for the 10th floor. I look up as the doors start to close and I see Susie running full speed at me. She has her shoes in her hands and barely makes it through

135

the doors before they close. I stare at her in shock as she tosses the shoes to the side and throws herself into my arms.

She kisses me hard, hungrily. I wrap one arm around her waist and my other hand into the back of her head as I fall into the wall behind me. She continues to assault my mouth then finally pulls back, "I love you too Gavin. I love you so fucking much and I don't want to lose you. I should have talked to you. But by the time I figured it all out in my head, you seemed to not want me anymore so I let it go."

I put both hands on the side of her face, "You love me? Like for real?"

She smiles as she nods and jumps into my arms, wrapping her legs around me. I hold her close, kissing her deeply as the door dings and slides open. I step out pulling away from her face for just a moment to look up and down the hall to find my room. She continues to kiss and bite at my neck as I carry her down the hall. I finally find my room and slide the key into the slot as I start kissing her fiercely again.

She lowers herself to the floor and starts walking backwards into the room as I step in shutting the door behind me. She reaches behind her and unzips the dress letting it fall to the floor around her feet. I immediately take my coat off and throw it to the floor and pull my shirt over my head.

Susie smiles at me as she pulls a pin out of her hair and it falls all around her shoulders then she reaches down and slides her underwear off. I am already down to my underwear when she walks over to me and pulls my lips hard into hers. She starts to walk backwards as she pulls me with her.

She quickly turns me and pushes me onto the bed. I lay back amazed that this is actually happening. She smiles at me as she reaches down and slides my boxers down my legs, letting me kick them away from us.

She climbs on top of me, smiling as she straddles me. She takes a deep breath as she leans up and grabs my cock at the base then slides down onto it.

Starbursts explode behind my eyes. She tucks her chin into her chest tightly as she lets out a satisfied moan then starts to slide up and down my dick. I hold onto her hips watching her move her way around my body. She finally opens her eyes, smiling at me, "Oh, I am definitely not regretting this."

I smile back at her as I wrap my arms around her back and roll her under me. I look into her eyes deeply, "If it is too much just tell me. I will stop."

She shakes her head back at me, "Don't you fucking dare."

I smile as I push myself further into her and her head falls back into the bed. I can feel her fingernails digging into my back as I continue to push myself in and out of her. She feels like heaven. Like I have literally died and gone to heaven. She is so tight and wet that I feel like she has a chokehold on my dick the entire time.

I smile down at her as I raise her hands above her head, pinning them with one hand as I lean down and take her nipple in my mouth as I continue to spear into her. She lets out another moan and I look at the smile on her face. I slam myself into her harder and she screams into the room, smiling wider.

She is every damn dream I have ever had coming true. I feel myself picking up speed. I can't hold back. Next time, I will take my time with her. Right now, I just need to fucking own her.

I continue to slam myself into her as her eyes fly back open and she looks at me smiling, "Gavin. Just. Please let me know that you're mine." I start pushing into her harder, thrusting until it feels like the bed itself is moving.

I smile into her lips as I kiss her again, "Forever baby. I am forever yours." I lean down further on top of her, bracing myself on both sides of her shoulders as her hands wrap around

137

the back of my head. I look down, watching myself as I shove into her over and over. I hear her gasp and I look up into her eyes. I see a tear roll down her face as she smiles and then I feel her clench hard around me.

"God Dammit it Susie. Fuck, you are so tight." I start slamming into her harder as I feel her break apart around me. I can't hold back any longer. I slam into her once more before I scream her name into the room around us. I continue to thrust into her, filling her with my release. She smiles as she continues to pulsate around my dick. I slam my mouth down on hers as I continue to lose myself in her until I feel her starting to loosen her hold on my dick.

I continue to kiss her until neither of us have any breath left. I finally pull back, hovering over her. I let my eyes search her face for any sign of regret or remorse. She smiles at me, "I love you Edge." My eyes fly back to hers as I smile, "I love you too Peach."

I slowly pull out of her and lay on my back beside her. I can barely fucking breath. I can't believe that just happened. I turn my face to look at her again, "I really am sorry."

She shakes her head, raising one finger towards the ceiling then looks at me smiling, "Rule number one. No apologizing after you have just given me the best orgasm of my life."

I grin back at her, "The best of your life huh? I will just have to make the next one better then." She giggles back at me as she rolls towards me, laying her leg over mine and stroking my chest with her fingers, "Please wait until I can feel my legs again."

I belt a laugh out into the room around us. I reach a hand up and trace her face with my fingers, "I don't want anyone else Susie. Ever. It's you, baby. I hope you know that. I can't lose you. I have been in purgatory for the last 12 days."

12
Susie
Hold Me Now - Caskets

I wasn't strong enough to let him go. Before I even knew what I was doing, I was running through the hotel lobby and flying through the closing doors of an elevator. I love him. I thought I had loved before but I was wrong. This, what we have, this is love. It is raw and it is real. And it is everything I always wanted and dreamed about.

I smile back at him as I continue to let my fingers dance across his skin, "I am not going anywhere. I am going to stay here until you go back on tour. Then I will go home. I am going to find a replacement for me at work and then once that is settled, I am coming to find you. And I am never leaving your side again unless you force me too."

He turns his body towards me, shaking his head at me, "I can't ask that of you Susie. Your work means too much to you."

I put my finger on his lips, shushing him, "You didn't ask me too. I am telling you what I am doing. Not asking if you are okay with it. And you mean more to me than the job. They have had me for a decade. Now it's time for me, for us. Yes, I will still find some way to help out when I can. But right now, we are the most important thing to me. The biggest priority in my life is laying right beside me. I am not walking away from this again. I can't."

Edge leans forward, kissing me on the forehead, "Yes ma'am." I giggle back when we hear a knock on the door. Both of us go wide eyed. Then we smile as we hear Lily, "Open the door assholes, I know you are in there!"

I giggle as I lean forward and grab his shirt off the floor. I slide it over my body and start walking towards the door. I smile wider as I crack it open, seeing Lily leaning into the door frame holding my shoes that I left in the elevator. I grin, feeling my neck starting to heat up as I reach out for the shoes, "Thank you for finding those for me."

Lily pulls them back, playing with me as I huff and reach out again to grab them. I watch Lily's eyes go wide then she spins quickly putting her face into Gideon's chest. I am confused until I feel Edge step up behind me. He reaches his hand up and props the door open as he leans his body into my back. I smile as I reach around feeling his bare ass behind me. I giggle looking back at Lily dying of embarrassment.

I hear Edge chuckle behind me, as he looks at Gideon, "I figured it was only fair. Susie has seen you, so now Lily has seen me." Gideon shakes his head laughing then we see Lily lift one perfect middle finger in the air.

I laugh at her and reach my hand out, wrapping it around hers, "By the way, Brian has been replaced." I see her lift her head up but she refuses to break eye contact with Gideon. I smile at the smirk spreading over Gideon's face as he stares at Lily. She lets out a soft giggle, "It's about fucking time. I would hug you but Edge still isn't wearing pants so I am not turning around."

Edge wraps one arm around my waist to pull me in closer to him, "If that is what you are scared of then I suggest you don't knock on this door for the rest of the night. We are gonna be busy."

I laugh uncontrollably as he pulls me backward, lifting my feet off the floor. He shuts the door abruptly and turns me,

140

putting my back against the wall. I smile up at him as I drop my shoes on the floor then wrap my arms around his neck, "Gonna be busy huh?"

He smiles back down at me as he peels his shirt from my body, "I am not even close to being done with you."

I feel a heat roll down my spine. Edge's eyes are boring into mine, determined and unrelenting. They are narrowed at me with an intense fiery determination. He puts one arm on the wall behind my head as he leans into me. I feel him run his fingers up my side before he covers my breast with his hand. I lean my head back into the wall, letting out a soft moan.

His breathing is low, laced with a dangerous periphery. I can hear myself breathing hard as I open my eyes back to look into his. He lets out a growl as he lowers his lips to mine. My muscles tense involuntarily as I feel a shiver of fear and arousal run through my veins. His mouth is on me within a moment. I wrap my arms around his neck, bringing his body closer to mine.

He is kissing me with a fierceness that I crave. He lifts me up and I wrap my legs around his body. Not a second later, he has me pinned to the wall again. He pulls back, searching my face for something unseen. I smile back at him as I run my fingers through the short bristled hair on his jaw. He smiles as I feel him shift below me then he is sliding back into me.

I feel myself stretching to accommodate him. He is so wide it feels like he could honestly break me in half. I let an anticipated grin come across my face as he pushes further into me. I let out another soft moan as I lean my head forward, putting my forehead to his. He starts to push into me harder and I feel the muscles in my back and abdomen start to tighten.

I hear him chuckle so I open my eyes to see his are closed as well but he is smiling from ear to ear. I lean my head back against the wall and feel him bottoming out inside me. I bite my lip, trying to hold my screams back. I open my eyes again to see

147

him watching my mouth. He starts walking backwards while still holding me firmly.

The bed finally finds the back of his legs and he sits down, still planted deeply within me. He continues to hold me as I roll my hips into his, pushing him deeper than before. He wraps his hands around the back of my shoulders, pushing me further down onto him.

I lean back, "Jesus Gavin." I hear him grunt again and I look back down into his eyes as he continues to throttle me. My hips meeting his own in unison. I put my hands on his chest and push him down flat onto the bed. Once he is laid all the way back I sit straight up so I can feel him hitting the walls inside me.

I continue to ride him as I feel my desire starting to build deep within my stomach. I smile widely as I brace my hands on his chest and start slamming down onto him. I look back down at him and his eyes are closed. He looks completely satiated. I let a devious grin come over my face, watching him try to hold out for me. I continue to grind down on him as I feel it rising quickly within me. "Oh shit. Edge."

I see his eyes slam into mine as he sees my release starting to etch its way across my face. He grabs my hips and starts thrusting up into me harder. I scream around the room as I feel myself clench down on him and the waves of ecstasy start rolling up my spine. I lean down into his mouth, kissing him roughly as I slam my hips into him in short bursts.

Edge wraps his arms around me, pushing himself into me harder than before. I can hear him grunting as I continue to crash into him. My hips are bucking into his wildly as I try to hold onto this feeling just a bit longer. He keeps his lips to mine as he rolls me onto my back, pinning my legs to the bed. He holds my thighs open as he continues to assault me.

He finally pulls back for air and I gulp in as much as I can get while I feel myself convulsing around him still. He tilts his

142

head down until his chin is meeting his chest and he growls loudly out into the room. I feel his growl as it sets loose goosebumps all over my skin. I reach my hands around him and grip his ass on both sides. His eyes come back to mine and I grasp him tighter, my mouth hanging open with need.

He lifts his eyes towards the headboard before closing as he is slamming into me hard and deep. I scream out again, "Edge. Edge, don't stop. I am gonna cum again. Please baby. Please."

His eyes wide, he brings his gaze back to me. I stare at him as I feel another orgasm riddle my body. He yells into the room, "Peach, fuck baby. I am gonna blow." He grunts loudly as he viscously slams into me again and again. I have my nails so deep into his lower back I know I am drawing blood but I don't care.

I cry out and convulse forward as the orgasm hits its peak. I am screaming. He is grunting and thrusting then I feel him swell inside of me as he screams his own release into the room. He continues to pierce the veil into my core until he feels me starting to finally release his cock. We are covered in fevered sweats. Both of our bodies pulsate into the other. He smiles as he brings his mouth back down to mine. He kisses me deep with a mixture of contentment and love behind it.

He pulls back as I smile at him, barely able to keep my eyes open. He slides out of me then scoops me up and deposits me at the top of the bed, then reaches down and pulls the sheet up over my body. I continue to smile at the ceiling, completely boneless and unable to even put words together to form a sentence let alone a thought. He walks around the bed and slides in next to me.

I turn my head towards him, barely able to keep my eyes open. Edge grins back at me and brings his fingers up to trace my jawline from one ear around to the other. I look up into his eyes. He looks at me questionably, "So I probably should have asked this a few hours ago but are you on some kind of birth control?"

I let a snicker leave the back of my throat as I am barely even able to nod my head yes, "Yeah. I have an IUD. Girls best friend." He smiles back at me as he slides his hand across my abdomen, drawing small shapes as he goes.

He looks back up to my face, "How do you feel about kids?" I feel my eyes cut to his quickly. I am feeling much more awake suddenly. I blink hard a few times, "I am not opposed to kids. I just never met anyone I wanted to have them with. Before Evan, there really wasn't anyone significant in my life. Then after him, I didn't even know if I wanted a relationship let alone a kid."

He nods his head back at me, watching my lips as I speak, "Same. I am not opposed but I have never seen myself with anyone serious enough to have that conversation."

I roll towards him as his hand slides across my side and onto my lower back. I reach up and run my hand down his cheek, "Until now?"

Edge brings his eyes back to mine, smiling again, "Are you really mine?"

I lean in kissing him gently before pulling back, "Wild horses Edge. Wild horses."

He smiles again as he pulls me flush against his body. I feel his breath on the side of my face, "Go to sleep baby. We will go home in the morning." I nod my head back to him and let my eyes close.

That night I dream of vast fields stretching out before me, the vibrant greens and yellows of the swaying grass. I see wildflowers dancing in the moonlight. I can smell the sweet scent they carry to me and I feel like I am finally complete. I feel this wholeness take over my soul and I realize I am right where I need to be.

144

I run my hands through the soft blades of grass that are reaching up to my thighs. I can hear the rustle of something behind me and I turn to see Dionysus walking towards me. I stand up straighter, stiffening at his approach. He steps up close to me, placing his hand on my cheek. I search the mask for his eyes but they seem to be closed. He pulls my forehead towards his, whispering, "I am going to burn this world down for you."

I smile into his voice as it travels across my skin, leaving a trail of anticipation in its wake. I let out a soft sigh, "I will give you the matches."

I wake up to the sun shining through the curtains. I feel the bed beside me but it is empty. I sit up onto my elbows and hear water running in the bathroom. I smile at what has become of my life. He is my world now. I have spent so much time working on myself, now it is time to work towards a life with the man that I love.

I throw the sheet off my body then stand up stretching my arms high above my head. I go up to my tiptoes to get a good full body stretch then fall back down to earth with a heavy sigh. It has been a long fucking time since I have felt the familar throb of being this fucking satisfied. I smile at the memory of feeling him inside of me when I hear the water turn off and a shower door open.

I turn and begin to walk to the other side of the room to start finding my clothes. I hear the bathroom door open behind me as I crouch to start picking up my scattered belongings.

I feel him step into my perimeter and I smile as I stand back up in front of him. I turn to face him but then feel his hands on my waist as he keeps my back to him then he starts to push me forward just a bit. I giggle as he walks me up to the small desk on the other side of the room. I feel his hand between my shoulder blades as he applies a small amount of pressure to push me forward.

I smile as I lay my face against the cold grain of the desk. Then there is a sensation of his hand slightly grazing the skin on the outside of my thigh as he follows up to my hip. He grips my hip bone tightly as I spread my legs and close my eyes.

Edge clutches my sides tight when I hear him whimper, "You want me inside you, don't you?" I moan back when I feel him rubbing his dick up and down my center.

I hear him let out a heavy breath, "Arch your back for me." I start to do as I am told as he lets out a small moan, "Yes" as I feel him slide into me slowly. My breath catches in my throat as he slowly works his way in and out of me, inch by gratifying inch. I bring my forearms underneath of me and arch my back up a bit higher. I want to feel him everywhere.

That hand he used to lay me down on the table is now wrapped around my hair, holding me steady as he continues to thrust into me. I place my palms on the desk to brace myself as I push myself back into him.

Edge is punishing, deliberate, intoxicating. I don't care if we ever step foot on grass again as long as he is inside me. He is everything I have ever dreamed of, but also everything I have ever feared. I am telling you, the scarousal is real.

I hear him moan my name into the space around us and I know I am gone. I am losing my damn mind, he has laid claim to it. I no longer possess the capabilities of living alone. I cannot be without him. I slam myself back down onto him harder. Trying to force his brain into the same containment that mine is in.

I want him to only think of me. I want his every breath, his every anything to be about me. I want him to be obsessed. I will happily smile at him like the devil when I lie and tell him he is going too far. There is no too far when it comes to him. I feel my mouth drop open as his hand smacks my ass hard. I am

146

panting and weeping at the same time. I close my eyes begging, "Harder."

I hear him growl behind me, "Hand or dick?" I arch my back a bit more so I can feel him hitting all the walls inside me, "Both baby. Hurt me." He turns my body and drapes me over the back of a chair like I am his jacket or something. I slam my hands into the cushion of the seat as I feel him pull out from me. I glance over my shoulder and watch him stroke himself with one hand while he reaches between my legs with the other. He coats his hand in me then smiles as he pulls that hand back and slaps my ass hard enough that I know it is going to bruise.

I keep my eyes on him as I scream again. His face comes to mine with a delicious gleam in his eyes. He leans into me, rubbing his dick up and down my clit until I am shaking with need. I want him to make me cum so bad. My legs are going to jello soon if he doesn't. I smile back at him as he shoves himself back into me with enough force that the entire chair moves forward a few inches.

I scream at him again as I feel him slide a finger into my ass. He is still pounding into me from behind as I feel him working my other hole enough that he can now place two fingers inside. Everything around me goes dark as I feel myself start to let go to him. I can barely get a full breath out before I am gasping for more air.

It feels like I am shattering around him. He feels it too. I can tell by his movements. He is more erratic, jerking himself in and out of me without any rhythm at all. I scream his name out, gripping the seat of the chair on both sides to the point of making my fingernails bend from the force of it. I feel the pulsation of the waves ricochet through my body as both of his hands are back to my hips and he is spearing himself in and out of me roughly.

Edge growls my name out into the room as I feel him thicken inside me. Not a moment after, I can feel him as he releases himself inside me. I can feel our souls embedding into each other. I start laughing through the panting. I turn my face back over my shoulder and he is staring at me like I am losing my mind. I continue to laugh, "You are fucking heart-stopping."

Edge smiles back at me as he continues to slowly push in and out of me a few more times before I finally allow him to release his hold on me. He stumbles back a few steps, bracing himself on the table with a hand. I stand up and turn on wobbly legs, still smiling at him. I stumble past him and face plant onto the middle of the bed. I hear him laugh out loudly then I feel the pressure of his body as he lays down next to me. I lift my face up just barely enough to see over the comforter and he is smiling at the ceiling with his eyes closed. Living out the ecstasy of the moment.

13
Edge
God Is A Weapon - Falling In Reverse, Marilyn Manson

I don't think Susie quite understands how deep my infatuation for her runs. I want to follow her around like a rottweiler wearing the skin of a golden retriever. I want her to think I am sweet and loving, then I want to ruin her. Ruin her to the point of her never being able to look at another man again. I want her to know for certain that I am the only one that will ever bring her this kind of pleasure. This kind of euphoria.

She is still laying beside me on her stomach. She has her eyes closed but I know she is still awake because she has a big cheesy grin on her face that refuses to drop. I sit up realizing immediately that she has a very large red handprint on her ass that is most likely going to bruise my little peach. I lean over and gently kiss it. She giggles at me again as I turn to her, "I'm sorry love. I didn't mean to leave a mark."

She rolls over giving me a full view of the rest of her beautiful body, "I am completely fine with it. Every time I sit down I want to remember what you just did to me. It was fucking amazing." I smile down at her again, trying to figure out how I got this lucky. Finally, after 28 almost 29 years of torture and pain, I have met another soul just as dark as mine. Someone who matches my wild then ups the ante. I look over at the clock and huff back towards her face. I lean down, giving her a quick kiss, "Check out is in 20 minutes. We gotta get outta here."

I hear a smart little childish whine come from her body as she sits up, shoulders slumped. I laugh at her as she forces herself to get up and start moving. She slides on her underwear then turns to me, "I am NOT wearing those heels. I can barely walk now. I will break my neck in those damn things."

I laugh back at her nodding my head, "It will be okay. I won't let you fall.", as I rise and find my clothes as well. 30 minutes later we are walking towards the front door of the hotel after turning in the key. She groans, looking down at her feet then at the shoes in her hand. She moves to drop them to put them on so she can walk outside. I quickly turn and scoop her up bridal style, listening to a wave of giggles coming out of her chest. I smile down at her as I move us outside and turn right to head to the parking garage.

We make it to my car and I open the passenger side, planting her firmly in the seat. She smiles at me, "Thank you darling." I laugh back at her, "Your welcome pookie." She instantly scrunches up her face at me and starts shaking her head back and forth, "NEVER say that again."

I laugh as I shut her door and make my way around the car. We fly down the city streets. It only takes her about a half hour to pack up her hotel room into her suitcase and then we are back on the road. Headed home. She smiles at me as she holds my hand, jabbering on about something she read in a book last week. I don't care what she wants to talk to me about, she could be reciting the phone book and I wouldn't care. As long as she is here, and she is real.

We pull back up to the house and she jumps out, shoes still in her hand as she runs around the small fence to the front walk. She puts her arms out to her sides and starts spinning in a circle, smiling up at the sky. I grab her suitcase and follow behind her until we make it to the front door. I quickly unlock the door and she runs inside, apologizing to the furniture and coffee maker. Promising to never make them deal with me alone again.

I have never met anyone like her before. She feels so deeply but still wears her heart on her sleeve. I would think she would have it under armed security at all times with the amount of empathy she seems to emit out into the world. I laugh at her antics as I make a silent but solemn vow to be the armor her heart deserves.

She finishes talking to the appliances then follows me into the bedroom. She sits down on the bed, throwing her shoes towards the closet. She watches me as I sit her suitcase down then move over to the dresser and start compressing all of my things over to one side. She stands wrapping her arms around my waist as she steps up beside me, "What cha doing?" I smile at her quickly then move back to finish my work, "You have to have somewhere to keep your stuff, don't you?"

She pulls back giving me a puzzled look. I stand and turn towards her, "If you are going to stay here for a few more weeks then go to New York to tie up loose ends. That means you will be coming back. This is your home now too. I want you to have your own space."

She grins widely at me, taking my face in her hands so she can kiss me fiercely again. I smile at her as I wrap my hands around her as well. I hear my phone ringing from my pocket but I ignore it. I continue to kiss her with full abandonment. That is until we hear someone knocking on the front door. She pulls back from me shaking her head, "We never get a moment's peace. How is a girl supposed to get laid around here?"

I laugh at her as I smack her ass, on the non bruised cheek and turn to head towards the front door. I glance back at her before I round the corner and smile as I see her unloading the contents of her suitcase into the dresser.

I step up the front door, pulling it open to see a smiling Ginny and Michael staring back at me. I know my eyes are wild as I look around and see my mum coming up the walk as well. I grin back at them, "Hey, uh what's going on?" I look down at my sister's hands and she is carrying a casserole dish. I lean in and kiss her on the cheek then my mother as well as she steps up beside Ginny.

Michael snickers at me like he already knows something that I don't. I give him a bit of a side eye then turn back to see Ginny shaking her head.

Ginny smiles back wildly at me, "It's the 12th." I turn my head looking at the calendar on the wall behind the door, seeing a big red circle around the 12th. I close my eyes, smiling. I turn back to her before peeking through one semi closed lid. Michael starts laughing loudly as Ginny bulldozes past me and towards the kitchen, "Mum, he forgot we were coming over. Again!"

Mum steps through the door, pulling me into a hug. I hold her tiny little body in my arms tightly as she pats me on the back. She pulls back smiling at me, "It's okay. He is a busy man. He is allowed to forget sometimes." I give my mum a quick kiss on top of her head as Ginny yells from the kitchen, "Not sometimes, every time!"

I shake Michael's hand as he walks through the door, "I knew not to take her bet. She had a 20 saying you would forget. I don't make bets with that woman. She is a shark." I laugh at him as I slap his shoulder as he walks by. He is not wrong, I wouldn't have taken a bet against her either.

I catch a glimpse of something red and turn to see Susie standing in the door to the hallway. She has changed into a light yellow sundress with her hair still flowing around her shoulders. Her eyes wide, she turns to me and gives me a small grin. I move towards her, placing my hand on her lower back as I scan the room. Mum and Ginny have both gone completely still with their

152

jaws hanging open. I let out a little snicker, "Susie, I would like you to meet my mum, Laura and my sister, Ginny. And this is Ginny's fiance, Michael."

I watch Susie's eyes as they fly between the two women then scan back over to Michael as he walks towards Ginny. I lean into her ear, "I'm so sorry. I forgot they were coming over."

She bats her hand at me, "Nonsense. I am so excited to meet you all." She walks over to my mum, bending down and wrapping her up in a hug. My mother is smiling over her shoulder as she hugs her back.

Next, she rounds the counter into the kitchen, giving Ginny a warm hug as well. She smiles at Michael and as he raises his hand to shake hers she pulls him in for a hug as well. He laughs as he looks over her shoulder at me before she pulls away. She looks around the room smiling, "Hi. My name is Susanna but most people call me Susie. I have heard so many wonderful things about all of you."

Ginny smiles at her then turns to me with astounded eyes, "And we have never heard a thing about you." Michael laughs at her as he puts his hand on her lower back. I flinch at her words, knowing I have not kept in touch with them like I have promised time and time again. Susie smiles towards me as well before turning back to Ginny, putting her hands together as if in prayer, "Give him hell. Please!" Ginny lets out a laugh, pointing at Susie but looking back at me, "Oh, I like her." I nod my head then roll my eyes.

Susie steps up to the counter to see that there is now food and her eyes grow wide. She smiles at everyone, "Let me start the oven to keep this warm and I will set the table and get everything ready for lunch." Ginny smiles genuinely at her, "Thank you Susie." Susie bats her hand at the air, "No problem. I am happy to help." She turns and places the shepherd's pie into the oven and turns it on low.

I see her moving around the kitchen like it is her own back in New York. She is smiling to herself and not even a little bit dazed by my familial intrusion. Michael and Ginny are just staring at her before they start to gravitate towards me.

Mum steps up next to me, "Who is this girl?" I smile as I look towards the kitchen.

I look back down at my mother, "Everything. She is everything." I glance back towards the kitchen watching Susie fluttering around before rubbing the back of my neck and turning back towards my mother, "She uh, she is someone really special to me. I'm sorry I didn't give you any heads up."

Ginny steps up to us as well, throwing another look over her shoulder towards the kitchen. She points a thumb back towards Susie, "Well, this is new. I have literally never seen a woman here before."

I grin back at her, "She is the only one you will ever see here. She uh, she is actually going to be moving in soon."

I feel my mother slap my arm and I look down at her in shock. She scrunches up her face at me, "I swear to God Gavin if you got that poor girl pregnant out of wedlock I will not speak to you for a year." I laugh back at her rubbing my arm with my hand.

Michael is cackling as well. Seeming to enjoy that the spotlight for the male species is on me for once. I smile back at my mother, "She is not pregnant. I promise. Did you have to smack me?"

She nods her head, looking towards the kitchen, "Then why is she moving in? Does she not have a place of her own?" I shake my head at her. I should have known they were going to be suspicious of Susie's intentions. I have not dated anyone with any real swoon worthy qualities.

I watch her move through the kitchen like she has lived here all her life. I smile back towards my mom, "Yes, she has her

154

own place. She is just gonna come live here with me instead. It's really not a huge deal mum."

Michael and Ginny shake their heads at me, watching me watch her. Mum is still huffing to herself as she looks around Ginny to watch Susie as well. Michael turns back around and slaps me on the shoulder, "Well! If you are happy then I am happy. I don't know about them but I am just excited that you found someone to match your...personality? Is that the right word for it?"

I laugh back at him as I fake punch him in the stomach. I look over to see mum staring at me again with her eyes narrowed. I smile back at her as I wrap my arms around her shoulders and pull her in for a tight side hug.

I see Susie as she turns to me with that high wattage grin again, "Okay, table is ready!" We all nod at her and make our way towards the kitchen. Everyone sits down and Susie places the food in the center of the table. One by one she takes everyone's plates and fills them before smiling and handing them back. I watch her in amazement. She is fucking perfect. She finally makes her own plate then sits down beside me. I smile at her as she reaches a hand under the table and rubs my thigh.

I watch my mum as she scrutinizes everything. Her eyes jumping back and forth between us. She takes a bite of food, "So Susie. What is it that you do?" I sigh into my plate, here it is. Let the questioning begin.

Susie smiles back at my mother, "I am actually the president of a non-profit organization back in New York City. We focus on helping underprivileged and homeless women and children. We find them homes, jobs, schools. Anything we can do to help them get their lives back on track."

I look at my mum and her eyes are blown wide. Ginny is smiling from ear to ear. Michael is smiling with his mouth hanging open and his fork hovering in the air. I chuckle to myself as my mum speaks up, "How did you meet Edge then? If you are from New York. From when he was in the states before?"

She takes a bite of food, nodding her head before turning to Ginny, "This is amazing by the way. You have to give me the recipe." She quickly swallows her bite and turns back towards my mum, "No, actually Gideon just married my sister Lily. Well, she isn't my sister by blood but we have been like sisters since we were 14. Anyway, that is how I met Gavin. We all met up at Lily's beach house before their last show in the states. Then Gavin came to stay with me for a few days in New York before we came over here for the wedding."

Mum is nodding her head at Susie. I can see she loves her. She is still just too afraid to let her guard down. She looks between us, "So, are you having sex with my son?" Ginny and I both drop our forks and Susie lets loose a laugh that I have never heard before. Michael is laughing louder than necessary as he pats Ginny on the back trying to keep her from choking to death.

I turn to my mother, "Jesus mum. I am almost 29 years old. I think it is okay for me to have sex." Ginny is still choking on something and trying to wash it down with water.

Susie finally composes herself enough to speak. She sets her forearms on the table, "Yes Laura. I have made love with your son. It is not just sex. I love him, he loves me. We plan on spending the rest of our lives together. He has been a complete gentleman with me for a long time now. He never pressured me or made me feel like it was something that had to be done. He respected my boundaries and my own personal issues with intimacy."

Mum nods her head at her, "Okay, I was just wondering if I needed to worry about any grandbabies soon or not." I look at Ginny and Michael, seeing a flash of pain cross their faces. I notice that Susie must have seen it as well.

156

She gives Ginny a small smile before turning back towards my mum, "We are not planning on having children any time soon. I want to be comfortable here in London first. I want to maybe find a sister organization to work with. Something that is affiliated with my own work back in New York City. I am not saying there will never be children but right now we are just enjoying each other's company. Also, Gavin will be going back on tour soon and I have to go back to New York to tie up loose ends there. That reminds me, I have to find somewhere to either sell or store all my furniture because it will definitely not all fit here."

Mum smiles at her and takes a bite of her food. Ginny leans forward, "What about your family? Are they okay with you moving overseas?"

Susie smiles at me then takes a long drink of water. I smile back at my family, "Susie doesn't have any family. She is an only child. Her parents were killed in a car accident when she was just a baby. She was raised by her grandmother. But she has passed on as well. The only family she has is Lily and now me."

I can feel Susie's eyes on me as I reach over and place my hand over hers. I turn to her seeing her eyes sparkle like she is trying to hold back some sort of emotion. Michael clears his throat again, "So Susie, are you musical as well?"

Susie belts out a loud laugh, "Not even a little bit. I do not have a musical or artistic bone in my body." I smile at her as the conversation finally starts to lighten up and we can sit comfortably finishing our dinner.

After we eat, we all move out to the garden to sit and enjoy the outdoors. Susie is walking barefoot around in the grass humming some tune to herself. Ginny is leaned back in her chair, rubbing her stomach like she ate too much. Michael has already cracked a beer and handed me one as well. Mum snuck inside immediately, probably to do the dishes behind our backs.

157

Ginny smiles towards Susie, "So I have to ask. Are you a natural redhead?"

Susie belts out a laugh but before she can answer I lean forward, "I can vouch yes she is. And she has the temper to prove it."

Ginny lets out a hoot as Susie turns to me and flips me off, "Then quit pissing me off if you're so afraid of it."

Ginny shakes her head back and forth at us both. She smiles towards me as Susie makes her way over and sits down on my thigh. Ginny's eyes jump back and forth between us, "You two really are in love aren't you?" I turn towards Susie and give her a quick kiss before she smiles and turns back towards Ginny.

I feel her arm rub up and down my back, "We really are. I wasn't lying when I said he has been a perfect gentleman. He has been patient and kind and empathic. I am not used to seeing that in men." She turns back towards me and lets out a deep breath. We turn to see my mum walking back out as Susie looks back towards Ginny.

I feel her ball her hand into a fist behind me, "I was sexually assaulted almost 5 years ago. I didn't want to be touched by a man let alone be in a relationship with one. I have been on my own since then and I thought I was completely fine living a life of solitude. Then I met Gavin. And everything changed."

She turns smiling at me, rubbing her fingers in my short beard, "The moment he first spoke to me I knew I was a goner. He was so cute and nervous. But even then he was kind, a gentleman." She turns her gaze towards Ginny, "We kinda tortured each other with teasing for awhile but I think we both quickly realized that we had met our match in each other."

She turns back towards my mother, still smiling, "He never once pressured me into thinking that I had to have sex with him to be in a relationship with him. He told me he loved me before we had even slept together. He is literally everything I have ever dreamed the perfect man would be. I don't know how I got as lucky as I did with him but I am grateful for it every waking moment of every single day."

I look over to see mum and Ginny both speechless. Susie seems to have that effect on people. She starts rubbing my back again then gets up and moves to walk around in the grass again. Mum leans forward and puts her hand on mine. I look up into her clear blue eyes, "Don't fuck this up kid." I laugh along with Ginny.

I shake my head at them both then turn to watch Peach happily walking barefoot through the yard with her hand holding her long skirt up. I turn back to my mum, "I am going to marry this girl." Mum smiles and sits back in her chair, "It's about damn time you settled down. What is she going to do when you are on tour?"

I sit up in the chair a bit, we haven't really cleared everything yet. We are still so new to this. I lean into the table, "I am assuming once she has found a suitable replacement at work and she has her personal stuff taken care of, the apartment and such that she is going to be joining us on tour. At least, I hope she is. I don't think I can be away from her for 2 whole months."

Ginny smiles and looks back out into the yard then stands and moves to the grass beside Susie. They start smiling and talking to each other. I turn back towards my mum, "She is the one mum." She smiles and leans forward to pat my hand, "I like her son. A lot. I would be honored to welcome her into the family. Also, I am proud of you. Being gentle with her. If what she said is true, you did the right thing. Not pushing sex on her."

I let out a sigh, looking out into the garden, "It is true. I wish it wasn't but it is. She has kinda hid in the dark for a long while but now it is time for her to live. I am just honored that she has chosen me to be the one she lives her life with." Mum pats my hand again and we continue to sit in silence long into the afternoon.

Susie continued to talk with Ginny for hours. Everyone was exhausted by the time they finally left. While she took a shower, I noticed that she had unpacked everything. She even found a home for her suitcase in the closet. I stand looking around the room. We are definitely gonna need a bigger place. This was fine for just me but now with her living here as well, we just need more room for everything.

I throw my clothes in the hamper and curl up in bed waiting for her to finish up in the bathroom. I have so many questions to throw at her. She comes walking into the bedroom in nothing but a towel. Her skin is still pink from the hot water and every single question I had 3 minutes ago is completely lost.

I am a lucky motherfucker. I watch her as she continues to dry off then slide on some underwear and a tank top. She turns around realizing that I am staring at her with a smile on my face. She grins back, "Perv." Then bends over and starts to dry her long hair with the towel from the top of her head.

I chuckle at her as she dries it just enough to not be dripping wet. She climbs up onto the bed from the bottom and closes her eyes as soon as her head hits the pillow. I smile at her and lean down to give her a kiss goodnight.

I slide down into the bed next to her. I watch the smile fall from her face as she settles into the pillow beside me. I just take her in, her long red eyelashes, the freckles sprinkling her face. I can imagine our kids being bespeckled with strawberry blonde hair and cute little button noses like her. I continue to scan her face until I hear her whisper, "Are you just gonna stare at me?"

14
Susie
Cold (But I'm Still Here) - Evans Blue

"Are you just gonna stare at me?"

I hear him let out a snicker, "Sorry. I will let you sleep."

I smile back at him. I never told him I wanted to go to sleep. And now that I am laying beside him, it is the last thing I have my mind on. He has awoken something in me. I was alone for so long and now I am not. And I don't want to feel like I still am. I am already dreading leaving for New York. But I am gonna wrap that part of my life up in a nice little bow and move the fuck on.

It is time for me. Finally, I smile as I hear him getting settled in. I open my eyes to see him lying beside me, on his back, eyes closed. I close my eyes and run my hand across his chest. I feel his head turn towards me but I don't open my eyes. I just want to feel him. I can't be this close to him and not reach out and touch him. I let my fingers slide across his nipple piercing and I give it a little flick as I smile, still keeping my eyes closed tight.

I can feel his breath on my face and I smile into it. Then his lips are lightly touching mine. I bring my hand up and wrap it around his neck. He pushes his mouth into me and I feel that feral part of me growing again. I bite his lower lip lightly and he lets out a moan.

Yeah, that's all it takes. I reach down and slide my shirt up over my head. Next, I am sliding out of my underwear. I point to his boxers moving towards him, "Take them off, now."

I raise my eyes to see him staring at me with nothing but lust and need. I can feel him moving his underwear down his legs then he kicks them off the bed. I slide my body over his. He wraps his hands around me, settling on my ass. I slide one leg over him until I am covering his body with mine. I smile as I slide my heat onto him and his eyes roll back in his head.

I lean forward and kiss him as I reach down between us and line him up with my entrance. I slide down onto him forcefully, knocking the air out of him. He lets out another moan as he grasps my hips. I continue to rock my hips into him as he opens his eyes and they narrow on me.

I lean forward and start kissing his chest, nibbling my way up to his neck. I can feel him trying to hold back from thrusting into me. I lean back a bit and wrap my hand around his neck, squeezing just enough to make his eyes fly wide as I start to pound onto him. His hands are so tight on my hips now that he is leaving little white marks on my skin.

I tighten my hold on his neck and lean down closer to him so I am slamming my hips into his in short bursts. I can feel it building in me already. He is frantically thrusting up into me as I smile at him. I lean forward, whispering in his ear, "You are mine. Only mine. If anyone comes near this dick, I swear to you Edge, I will fucking end them."

I pull back just enough to see his eyes wide as he smiles at me. I lean back into him, slamming myself onto him. I feel it about to hit and I grip his throat tight then lean in and bite his neck hard. I hear him panting, "Jesus Christ Susie. I'm gonna cum." I smile as I gently kiss the bite mark then go about an inch lower and bite him again. I feel my orgasm wash over me and I am moaning into his neck.

He holds my hips tight as he continues to thrust up into me. I do one final grip of his neck, seeing him trying to gasp for air as he stares at me. I wait for the timing and when he thrusts into me again I release my hold completely and he screams as he spills into me. I sit straight up on him and continue to spear myself with his cock as he is gripping my thighs tight.

I finally still above him, feeling him still pulsating inside me. I reach around and feel his balls tight against his body. I smile back down into his face, "I own these." He nods his head at me before rolling me onto my back.

I grin back up at him as he forces himself deep into me again. I close my eyes, taking a deep breath. He moves his face close to mine, "This cunt fucking belongs to me Susanna. Tell me. Tell me who it belongs to." I open my eyes back up at him, "You, only you."

Edge slams his lips back into me one last time before he pulls back smiling, "Fucking A it does."

He rolls off of me and I turn on my side, curling up into his body. I place my hand on his chest and he wraps his other arm around me, pulling me in close. I whisper, "I love you" then fall fast asleep.

Three weeks later, I am standing in the center of my apartment trying to figure out where the hell to start. I haven't touched a damn thing yet. I have been avoiding it like the plague honestly. The only thing pushing me forward is the knowledge that the sooner I get this done, the sooner I will be back with Edge.

We spent our last few weeks learning literally every single thing we possibly could about each other. Good and bad. We talked more about his past, his childhood. I never pressured him to tell me more than he was willing to though. Just him opening up as much as he has is enough for me. It shows me how much he trusts me, loves me.

We would spend our days exploring the city. Exploring each other. We also had either dinner or lunch with his family at least once a week. He thought I was going to get tired of them. But he doesn't understand what it is like to not have anyone. He may not have a relationship with his father but his mother and his sister love him fiercely. That is not something I have felt for 10 years. That familial pull.

I look around the room then huff as I grab my laptop and pull it open. I have a few things left to finish up before I can really set into just packing and nothing else. I also have to check to make sure there are no other appointments set up for me in the upcoming weeks. I have interviews starting tomorrow morning for my replacement.

I want to get this done and over with. I am luckily on a month to month lease since I have been here so long so I just have to worry about emptying all this shit out. That makes the process so much easier not having to worry about breaking a lease or subletting the apartment. This place has been good to me but I am ready for a new adventure.

I jump online and find a storage place that will come and take everything big away for you and even put it into storage. I also find a way to have all of my smaller stuff shipped to London. I even reach out to Ginny to make sure that once it is all shipped over it isn't just sitting on the front lawn until we can get there to put it all away.

It is going to cost a small fortune but I don't care. I want it all there when he gets home from the tour. And if I plan this all out right then I may even get to surprise him at a show.

I have already purchased the boxes, tape and bubble wrap. I just have to find the motivation to get started. I turn the radio up blasting Carnal Decay from the speakers. I smile as I hear him playing and that is the kick in the ass I need to get moving.

It almost feels like he is here with me as I start wrapping this life up into neat little packages. It takes me a few hours but I have the kitchen completely packed as well as the living room and the little library nook.

I quickly pass out on the couch, in a heap of exhaustion. I am awakened by my phone ringing around 10 pm though. I instantly smile thinking that it is Lily. I don't even look at the phone as I answer it, "What up bitch?" I hear a deep snicker on the other end of the phone and my eyes fly open.

I hear Edge on the other end of the line, "Is that anyway to say hello to your man?"

I giggle as I sit up and lean into the phone, "I am sorry baby, I thought you were Lily."

He laughs back into the phone, "No. Definitely not Lily. My dick is bigger."

I belt out a laugh. "Don't tell her that, she will fight you." I stare at the floor as I feel the smile start to slide off my face. I let out a heavy sigh, "I miss you."

I hear a heavy sigh in reply, "I miss you too baby." I hear a noise and look at the phone he is trying to now make into a video call. I smile as I accept and the video of him pops onto the screen. I sit up briskly, "Did you just get out of the shower?"

He smiles as he looks down at himself then back to the camera, "Uh Yeah. I was gross after the show."

I groan as my eyes roll back in my head and I plop back down on the couch, "Now my pussy misses you too."

He starts laughing and I look at the video as he climbs into bed and pulls the blankets up over himself. I sit up again leaning into the arm of the couch. He is making a face at me, "What is all that shit behind you?"

I smile as I flip the camera, "Living room, library and kitchen successfully packed." I flip the camera back at me, smiling widely at him, "All that is left is the bathrooms and the bedroom."

He smiles bigger than I have ever seen, "This is really happening isn't it?"

I smile back at him as I start to walk up the stairs. I turn the corner taking in the empty kitchen and dining room, "You better believe your sweet ass it is. You aren't getting rid of me that easily. I think I am going to just put all the big stuff into storage. We can figure it all out before the US tour. The rest of it Ginny is going to meet the delivery at your house and have them put it all in the garage. We should have plenty of time to figure that out before we come back."

He slides down onto his pillow and smiles as he closes his eyes, "Our house Peach. Our house. I can't fucking wait for you to be with me all the time."

I smile back at him, "Me too baby. I start interviewing in the morning for my replacement. Hopefully, it won't take too long to find someone suitable. I have a few good candidates in mind so it should go fairly smoothly."

He nods back at me, then gives me a devious grin, "Why are you not in bed yet?"

I grin back at him, "Because I literally passed out down stairs. I am going to go to bed in a minute."

He lets out a sigh and pushes his bottom lip out, "Fine.....I guess."

I start to move from the kitchen towards the bedroom, "What is wrong with me going to bed? You literally just chastised me for not being there already!"

He winks at me, "I won't be there with you, that is what is wrong."

I laugh at him as I round the corner into my bedroom. I grin mischievously at him, "Well, you may not be here but you can watch me get ready for bed."

He grins into his phone then seems to turn and prop it up on something on the nightstand as he rolls towards the camera. I laugh at him, "What are you propping your phone up on?"

He chuckles, "You don't wanna know. Now take your clothes off."

I laugh back at him. I set my phone up on the dresser so he can see me standing in front of the bed. My hands pause on the hem of my shirt, "Tell me."

He grins from ear to ear, "A bible."

I burst out laughing again while I shake my head at him. I let my eyes meet his in the camera, "Well, might as well give you impure thoughts then."

I hear his breath catch in his throat as I peel my shirt up off of me. He can see my sheer dark green bra underneath, making my skin look even more fair that it normally does. I smile back down into the camera as I let my cotton shorts hit the floor and step out of them to show him the matching underwear to the set.

I lift my fingers around my back to unsnap my bra and I hear him breathy, "You are so fucking beautful."

I look back into the camera and I can see his arm moving just a bit, "Are you doing what I think you are doing?"

He smiles back at me, "Probably. Take that fucking bra off. I wanna see you."

I grin like the devil back at him as I slowly pull the bra and let it fall from my body. I hear him groan and I look back at the camera, watching his eyes trace my body. I hook my thumbs in the sides of my underwear and slowly glide them down my legs.

I stand back up, fully naked in front of the camera and I can see his arm moving faster. I smile at him as I bring my hands up and cup my breasts.

"God dammit. Lay on the bed. I wanna see you." His voice is heavily laced with need. I smile sweetly as I sit down on the end of the bed then use my arms to pull myself up into the center of it. I have one knee propped up as I watch his eyes watching me.

He goes to say something and I let my propped knee fall open onto the bed. He groans deeper, "Fuck me. You look so wet. Touch yourself Peach. I wanna watch you."

His arm starts working harder as I let the smile leave my face and my hand trail down to my center. I swipe one finger over my throbbing clit and let out a small moan. I can hear him making noises on his side but I am too busy with myself to watch him.

I take two fingers and slide them into me. I start thrusting them in and out as another moan comes at me from the phone. I look into his eyes watching me. I start to circle my clit with my other hand and feel my release starting to build.

I smile at him, "Turn the camera. I want to watch you."

He gives me a half grin before turning the camera. I can now see his hard cock in his hand as he strokes it roughly. I watch him as I speed up my hands. He is grunting again and I feel myself about to fall over the edge.

"Fuck Gavin. Your dick is so big. I wish it was inside me right now." He grunts again as I watch his hand grip his cock tighter and he starts to speed up his motions.

"I can't wait to slam into that tight little cunt again. She misses me doesn't she? She wants me to worship her with my tongue doesn't she?" His words cut through me like a knife. He isn't wrong. I want that so bad.

I let out another moan as I feel my release about to hit, "I am gonna cum baby. Fuck." I watch his hand as it speeds up again then I am screaming into the room around me. I hear a roar from the phone and I look back to see him shooting cum all over his abdomen. I clench down so hard on nothing that it almost feels like I am convulsing. I feel my shoulders roll inwards as my orgasm rips through my body.

I continue to push my fingers in and out of me until I feel myself finally coming down. I smile towards the phone as I see him stand and leave the view for a minute. He comes back cleaned up and I see him throw a towel to the other side of the room. He moves the camera back up so I can look back into his eyes.

He can see me, still panting and laying in the middle of my bed with my legs wide open in front of him. He growls again, smiling at me, "This is going to be the longest 8 weeks of my life."

I laugh back at him as I crawl to the edge of the bed and reach over grabbing the phone. I lay back on the pillows and cover myself up. "We are good, baby. It won't be long at all and I will be back there with you. I promise."

I see him nod back at me, obviously exhausted. I smile into the camera, "I love you Edge. I am gonna get some sleep. I have a long day tomorrow."

He smiles back at me, barely opening his eyes, "I love you too baby. Our next show is a few days out but I will still call you tomorrow." I smile into the camera as he closes his eyes again. I hit the button and allow him some sleep. I stare out the window

169

into the bustling city around me. This has been my home for 34 years. That seems like enough.

I spend the next few weeks looking for a replacement and getting everything finalized with storage and shipping. I kinda shot myself in the foot by packing everything that first night. I even had to buy paper plates since my kitchen is already stacked in boxes next to the front door.

Also, interviewing your own replacement is brutal. It takes a few days to really nail it all down but I was right. There are a few candidates that I think would be perfect. I only have one interview left this afternoon, then I can go home and finish packing the bedroom.

I calculate in my head that if I am able to nail down a replacement then that means that I might be able to surprise Edge on tour somewhere. They have like 6 shows left, 2 shows per week. So I should be able to pull it off in maybe 3 shows time.

I was also right about the afternoon candidate. I fell in love with her immediately. She was more than qualified and also had that emphatic side to her that has to come with this job. It is not something I am willing to skimp on. Whoever does this job has to have bleeding heart syndrome for me to even grant them an interview. Before the hour is even up, I have offered her the position and she happily accepted.

I send her to HR to fill out all her paperwork then I finish packing up my office. I pick up my coffee, finishing it quickly then turn around to throw it in the trash. I look out onto the bustling street, all the little ants marching their ways to and fro. I smile until I see a familiar face walking by. My blood runs cold as

I see Evan walking hand in a hand with some blonde girl. She is smiling up at him and he wraps his arm around her.

I feel my legs lock up on me as the screaming in my head gets louder. He looks just like he had 5 years ago when I last saw him. Tall and lean. His blonde hair a strategic mess on his head. He looks like he has continued to take care of himself as well. It is debilitating seeing him out of nowhere. Almost to the point where I question if it is even him at all. I watch them until they are out of view of my office window when I feel the nausea start to roll through me.

I immediately turn and throw up in the trash can. I can feel myself shaking as I try to get a grip on myself. My throat is burning and all I can hear in my head is a steady voice screaming. I start shaking as I realize it is my own voice I am hearing. I throw up again, heaving every last drop of my stomach into the small trash can. I turn and awkwardly fumble through a packed box for some kleenex.

I quickly wipe my mouth and start breathing deeply. I grab my phone and punch Edge's name. I sit, bent at the stomach with my head almost completely between my knees as I listen to the phone ring. He immediately answers but I can't speak. "Hello? Susie, are you there?"

I know he can hear me breathing. I try to say something, anything but it only comes out like a strangled cry. I hit the button for a video call and he can see me, "Oh fuck. It's okay, baby breath. Deep in through your nose, out through your mouth."

I keep my eyes on him as he continues to pace around the arena he is at. I forgot they have a show in a few hours. I shouldn't be bothering him with this shit right now. He is working. I still have my head down between my knees and I feel the tears start to flow.

I am scared shitless but I can't tell him why. He would fly here and kill Evan. He would fuck up the tour and I refuse to do that to the band. Not over my stupid shit. I try to calm my tears but I can't.

Edge keeps his eyes trained on me the entire time. He is being so caring. So calm. I feel like shit that I am making him worry over me right before a fucking show. I don't want his head to be anywhere but where it needs to be when the lights go down.

I try to calm my breathing some more as I hear him on the other end of the phone, "You're gonna be okay baby. Just keep breathing. Deep in and let it out."

I listen to his words but the compassion is only making me want to cry even harder. I have to pull my shit together. I can't let him worry over me. I am being fucking selfish and it has to stop. I can't keep fucking his head up with my bullshit.

I sit up as straight as I can and try to fake my way through it. I smile at the phone and prop up the phone so he can't tell that my hand is still shaking, "Thank you baby. I am better now. I am sorry I bothered you."

I can still hear my voice cracking and shaking but I am just praying it is not coming through on his side. He continues to stare at the screen in concern though so I am not completely convinced that it isn't. He walks behind a curtain, away from the stage, "Do you need me baby? I can be there in no time."

I shake my head viciously at him, "No! Don't you fucking dare. I am just having a moment. It will pass. I shouldn't have called. I shouldn't have bothered you with my shit."

I see him prop the phone up on something then both of his arms are crossed over his chest, "That is fucking bullshit. Don't try that with me Peach. You know I *want* you to call me when this shit happens. I don't want you trying to get through it alone."

I nod my head back at the phone as I take in another deep breath and exhale it slowly, "I know baby. I just hate being a burden on you."

Edge shakes his head back at the phone, "You are not a fucking burden baby. Never. Now tell me what happened. What started this?"

I feel my eyes go a bit wider as my heart clenches in my chest. I don't want to lie to him but I can't tell him the truth. I try to think up something halfway convincing. I swallow hard as I look back at the phone, "I think it is just nerves because I hired someone to replace me today. I still have to train her but it is truly official that I am leaving. I just, I guess it just hit me harder than I thought it was going too."

I watch him as his eyes soften and he nods his head at me, "I know it is rough baby. You can always still change your mind. I won't be mad I promise. We can still find a way to make it work."

I almost start crying harder at him being so complacent and just accepting me for face value. I hate fucking lying to him. I breathe heavily again, "No. That is not what I want. I want to be with you. And it is done. She has already signed the hiring contract. I am going through with this. Don't think I am second guessing my decision. I am not, I just got more emotional than I thought I was going too."

He gives me a soft smile, "I love you so much Peach. You doing all of this for me, for us. I don't think you know how much this means to me."

I feel the guilt rip through my chest again. Luckily though, someone steps up to his side pulling his attention from me for a moment. I wipe the tears away quickly and grab my phone, "You are busy baby and I just had someone walk in. I love you. I will talk to you later after the show." I watch his face turn back towards the phone but before he can say anything I quickly end the call.

       I hate lying to anyone. But this time, it just feels like the most evil and wrong thing I could have ever done. If he ever finds out what just happened, he is going to be livid with me. This is going to have to be one of those moments that I take with me to the grave.

       After I pay the security guard a hundo to walk me home that day, I refuse to leave the apartment alone. I decide it is safer to Zoom train my replacement. I told her I have covid and she shouldn't be around me. I hate lying to anyone but it is better this way.

       It is alot fucking harder than you think to train somebody remotely like this. Luckily, my replacement Megan has been a fucking rock star about it. She has happily worked with me at every turn, from slide shows to videos. I have emailed her at least 500 files and tried to convey to her where all of the hot topics are within the center at the present time. I even go back over the issues of the last 7 years, just to make sure she can sense the patterns if they ever start to arise again.

       Personally though, every single time the doorbell rings or my phone vibrates I jump. I am scared to death that it is Evan. That he is back to hurt me again, or worse finish me. I am fucking terrified that something is going to happen to me. But not because of me, but because of what that would do to Gavin. He would never fucking recover from that. He would blame himself. I know he would.

       Edge has checked on me every single day for the last two weeks. He keeps asking if I have had any more episodes but I just tell him it was the one and it was just the work stress. I am a little worried how easy it has become to lie to him. I hate that I even have to do it to begin with but I know it is for the best.

Finally, just a few days later, I am smiling around my empty apartment. All I have left is a pillow, blanket and a suitcase. It took a little over two weeks but we finished with all the training that poor Megan could handle. I did leave her with my personal information though. I will continue to help her as long as she needs it.

I am relieved to officially be leaving for Brighton tomorrow. I am ready to be back with my family. I need to be close to Lily. Her dreams about Nikki have started again. I need to keep a close eye on her so things don't go sideways again. I need to be with Edge too. The more time I spend away from him the more empty I seem to feel.

I hear my phone ringing around midnight and reach over seeing Edge's name on the screen. I smile as I hit the video button, "Hey baby."

I hear him chuckle, "Why is it so dark in there?" I look around the room, quickly remembering – there are no lamps. I laugh as I shimmy into my pallet a little deeper, "Cause I am sleeping and all the lights are off."

I hear him sigh and I look up at his grinning face, "I am sorry. I shouldn't have woken you. I am sure you have a long day tomorrow. I just fucking miss you like crazy. Is everything still going to plan?"

I roll onto my back, "Yeah, I should have everything wrapped up right as the tour ends." The lies are really starting to eat away at me, but this lie is only to surprise him. He is going to lose his shit and I am here for it.

I let out a loud yawn then hear him chuckle, "Okay babe. Sorry I woke you. I will let you get back to sleep. Call me tomorrow?"

I nod at the phone, "Will do. I love you baby, good night."

I smile into the phone as I hang it up. He is either going to kill me or kidnap me and hold me hostage for a week. I just hope he doesn't catch me in the act. I really really want to surprise him. This is gonna be so much fun.

I have a fitful night's sleep on the hard floor but I don't care. I wake up to my alarm at 5 am. I smile as I stand up and dress in some comfy travel clothes then grab the last of my stuff.

I kept Grammie's ring with me but everything else got shipped over to the house in London. I look at the ring box sitting in my purse and I smile remembering the moment I put it into the box.

Grammie knew her time was coming. Doing me a solid she gave me the ring weeks before she actually passed. There is no way I could have taken it after she was already gone.

Lily and I sat with her those last few days. She told us stories about my grandpa, who I never got to meet. He died from tuberculosis years before I was even thought of.

After she was gone, Lily did everything she possibly could to help keep me in a positive mindset. She was already family to me by that point but it just solidified everything with us. She selflessly helped me through every single step, every single decision.

I apologized to her for months after. That I even needed that kind of help from her. With everything she has gone through, I hate that she felt the need to help me with arrangements for Grammie. But she still did it all, most times with a smile on her face.

I take an anxious breath as I look around the room before me. It is finally done. I do one last walk through of my home for the last 7 years. It feels like the end of an era.

I happily take the elevator downstairs, rolling my suitcase behind me. I drop the keys in the tenants slot with a smile. It is official. I am done here. I am going to England and I am going to spend the rest of my days with the man I love.

I am still grinning as I step out to the street, noticing my uber is already here. The guy jumps out quickly, smiling at me as he walks around and pops the trunk to put my suitcase in. I grin back as I go to open the back door, "Susie?" I feel the fear run down my spine before I even have a chance to turn around.

Evan is standing behind me. I would know that voice anywhere. I try to calm my nerves as I slowly turn to see him standing mid sidewalk. I back up to the car, the handle already being gripped by my hand. I take a deep breath. I try to remind myself that he has no power over me, not anymore. I let the breath out slowly, "What?"

He puts his hands in his pockets and smiles at me, "How are you?" I see the dimples in his cheeks pop out when he smiles. Those dimples used to make me melt. He stays far enough away from me that he can't reach out and touch me but I still feel this intense urge to flee. There is also an extreme roll of anger that washes over me immediately.

I try to keep my voice calm but I know he can read me, "I am great. I am actually about to leave the country. I am moving overseas to move in with my fiancé."

His eyes go wide then he starts to nod, "Yeah, I figured you would have found someone new by now." He is trying to play it cool but I can see the anger in his eyes when I say fiancé. I see the muscles in his shoulders tighten, assuming he is making fists in his jeans pockets with his hands.

I laugh at him and roll my eyes, "What the fuck do you want Evan? There is a restraining order that is still very much fucking valid against you."

He tenses at the words restraining order. He looks lost, almost sad even. If it had been 5 years before, I would have been falling at his feet to fix whatever was apparently broken. He nervously cracks his neck, "I just wanted to tell you that I miss you. And that I still love you."

I laugh loudly into the sidewalk around us. How does he have the fucking nerve to stand here and say that he loves me? After what he fucking did! He never even fucking apologized to me. Never even acknowledged it had happened. I open the door and smile at him before I slide into the seat, "Go to hell."

I lock the door as soon as it shuts and beg the uber driver to go. A half hour later, I am walking through the gates at JFK. I am practically sprinting down the halls even though I am almost an hour early for my flight. I am just scared that he has followed me.

I know as soon as I am on that plane there will be no way for him to get to me. I quickly check in at my terminal then sit in the seat literally right next to the security guard. I pull out my phone and text Lily that I should be there in the next 9 hours or so.

Her and Gideon have it set up that there will be a key waiting for me at the front desk for Edge's room. They will already be at the arena. She will have a backstage pass waiting for me at the front desk as well. I am going to go to his room and get ready then surprise him at the arena.

I scan the crowd for the entirety of my wait. Even though I don't see him, I can feel his eyes still on me somehow. I try to breathe my way out of another panic attack, when my flight is called to boarding. Thank fucking god. I need to get out of this city.

15
Dionysus
CHINCHILLA - Little Girl Gone

I have been trying to get a hold of Susie all day. She has only answered one text and zero phone calls. I even asked Lily what was up with her but she just said she must be busy finishing up with work and the apartment. I know she is right but I just feel like something more has happened.

When she called me having that panic attack, it took everything in me not to just drop this tour on its ass and fly to New York. But honestly, she would have kicked my ass if I did that. And I am more scared of her than anyone else. I just hate feeling like I am letting her down by not being there with her. She needed me and I failed her.

The show finished up about 20 minutes ago. Now I am just sitting in the green room. It is getting harder and harder to get through these shows without Susie here. I still give it everything. I still have an awesome time up there. The excitement beforehand, the anxiety. The gravity of the pull from the fans, it is all still there. But in between each song she is in my head. I wonder where she is, what she is doing. Is she okay? And of course, I am afraid to say anything to anyone because I don't wanna be classified as obsessed. Even though I 100% am.

I now have a very large cup of Dalmore that is getting drained rather quickly. Fans have already started to flock in as well. I just want to get this part over with so I can get back to my room and call Susie again.

I love the music, hell I even love the fans. But this face to face, one on one shit. I can live without it. I was not built to be sociable. Luckily, I don't have to speak. Small talk would literally kill me right now. Per normal, there are a few groupies that seem to show up at almost every show. One has seemed to take a liking to me, even though I have never even given her so much as a head nod. She likes to sit on the arm of my chair and lean over me like she owns me or something.

Susie would annihilate this girl. She should honestly fear for her safety if she tries to show up on the US tour. Though it would be comical to see what Susie would do. That puts another smile on my face as I bring my cup back up to my mouth.

I take a long drink when I hear a voice in front of me, "Do you whore around like this with just the taken men or is it anything with a dick?"

My eyes go wide behind my mask. I see black leather high heel boots that go up to her thighs. A tight little red leather skirt that leads into a sheer corset. The only thing covering her nipples are black x's. I follow the lines of her body up to her face and see those red lips smiling just below a black mask, blocking her face from the rest of the room. But I know it is her. I know that body. I know that voice. I know that red hair.

The groupie beside me stands up, "Who the fuck are you talking to bitch?" Before the groupie can even take another step towards Susie, I am on my feet. I wrap my hands around her jaw on both sides and kiss her deeply. She wraps her arms around me as I back her into the wall and continue to destroy her lips with mine. I don't even care that my body paint is probably rubbing off on her.

I can hear Aphrodite behind me chuckling but I can't pull myself away. Susie is here. She is here in Brighton. With me. I finally let her come up for air. I feel her hands as they run down my back and stop on my ass. She squeezes tight then winks at me, "Did you miss me?"

I laugh out loud as I slam my lips back into hers. Aphrodite walks up nudging my arm to give me some tissues but I don't even look at her as I take them then continue to kiss Susie. Finally, I let her go, then I use the kleenex to clean off the body paint from her face. She smiles as I step away and slowly make my way back over to my seat.

She struts her hot ass over to me then steps around me behind the chair. I feel her lean forward and run her hand down my chest until she reaches my cock and gives it a hard squeeze. I moan and roll my neck to the side so I can see her face. She is smiling at the groupie, "This belongs to me bitch. Remember that."

I hear Ares chuckle as Hestia brings Susie a glass of Dalmore. Hera right beside her. The groupie is still glaring at her as she smiles back, "These are mine too." She sits the glass of whisky on the arm of the chair as she wraps Hera up with one hand, cupping her ass then turning towards Hestia and kisses her intensely.

I am hard as fucking granite right now. Hera smiles as she runs her hand up and down the bare skin on Susie's leg but stares across the chairs at Apollo. She finally pulls away from Hestia then turns back around to the crowd. She wipes her bottom lip off with her thumb as she turns to the rest of the band, "Did you miss me?"

I smile around the room as I lift her drink up over my shoulder. She uses her free hand to squeeze my shoulder then takes the drink and finishes it in one go. Hestia and Hera have already wandered back over to their chairs by this point. Now I am just wondering how many doors in Hestia's mind did Susie just open.

The next 30 minutes go by quickly. The groupie cleared out pretty fast as well. Sorry for her, now that Susie is home she will be with me every single show. Finally, the room starts to thin out and I can breathe again.

After what feels like days, we finally make it back to the hotel. As soon as the door is shut, I am on her. I don't even care about the body paint. I just need her. I need to touch her. I need to feel her hands on me. She smiles at me as I take my mask off then hers as well. I pin her to the wall and start kissing up and down her neck while grinding into her.

I am about 3 seconds away from making her clothes vanish when there is a knock on the door. I pull back growling. I swear to god. I am going to murder whoever is on the other side of that fucking door. Susie smiles at me as gives me another quick kiss then slides under my arm and walks to the door.

I can't see who is standing on the other side but Susie goes completely still. Then she smiles and starts to take a few steps back into the room. Next, I see a smiling Mona as she walks in, eyes completely on Susie. I grin to myself, already knowing where this is going to go. Mona turns to me with a pleading look in her eyes, "Just give me 5 minutes. I need to get her out of my system then I will leave you to it."

Susie looks over her shoulder, smiling a devil's grin and gives me a slight nod. Jesus Christ. I am going to keel over. I smile back at Mona, "The room is yours. Don't mind me over here in the corner completely minding my own business."

Mona gives me another smile and steps up to Susie. She turns her gaze to her then wraps her hand around her neck and crashes her lips into Susie's. As soon as I hear Susie moan, I am harder than I have ever been in my life. I take a few more steps back and sit down in a chair. Trying to calm my racing heart.

That is hard to do when you see two absolutely beautiful women consensually just destroying each other. Susie has her arms wrapped around Mona holding her close to her own body. Mona in turn has her hands everywhere. Gripping Susie's ass, kneading at her breasts, grasping her hair to keep their mouths pressed together.

My dick is painfully pressing into the zipper of my jeans. I just want to slide them down and enjoy the show but I don't want to freak Mona out. I know Susie would be fine with it but Mona, she isn't about men at all. I would never risk our relationship over that shit.

The girls seem to be in their own world though. Like they have completely forgotten there is a grown ass man 10 feet away from them. Susie finally pulls back for a breath and keeps her eyes on Mona as she unzips her boots and kicks them to the side. Then she steps up to Mona and pulls her shirt up over her head.

I almost spontaneously combust when I watch Susie take Mona's tit in her mouth. Mona's head falls back as she moans out into the room. I watch Susie's hands as they wrap around her own top and she slides it up over her head. Mona has already kicked her own shoes off and she is unzipping her tight shorts and pushing them down her thighs.

Susie moves back to Mona's neck and ear. I can see Mona's face over Susie's shoulder as she reaches down and unzips the back of Susie's skirt. Her eyes turn to mine and she smiles, "You can get in on this but you touch her only and we never speak of this again."

Yup. I am dead. My heart has completely stopped. I watch Susie as she turns Mona towards the bed and is kissing her as they slowly move in unison. I am standing now but not really sure where to begin. I don't want to ruin what they have going right now.

Susie pushes Mona down onto the bed. She is laying on her back panting up at Susie. I watch as Susie's hand hooks into either side of Mona's underwear and she slides them down

183

slowly. Painfully slow. I hear another growl leave my throat unintentionally. Susie smiles over her shoulder at me as she slides her own down as well. She is still standing but she spreads her legs then leans forward to take Mona's tit in her mouth again. Mona closes her eyes and grips the back of Susie's head as she starts to kiss and lick down her abdomen.

I take my shirt off then kick my boots to the other side of the room as well. I watch Susie as she parts Mona and slides her tongue from entrance to clit. Mona's back arches up off the bed as Susie continues to devour her. She starts wagging her hips at me as I watch her slide two fingers in and out of Mona while she is nibbling on her clit.

I quickly remove the rest of my clothing and step up to Susie. I line myself up and grip her hips tightly as I ram into her. She lets out a small yelp which in turn makes Mona moan as well. I am trying to go slow to let the girls enjoy their fun, but I have literally never been this turned on in my life. I am just trying not to blow watching them consume each other.

I continue to slam into Susie. Watching the chain reaction I am causing. Mona is biting her bottom lip and I can see Susie's arm as she is working her fingers in and out of Mona's wet little cunt. I close my eyes so I don't end this too soon. But I can't leave them shut. Every little noise that Susie makes, my eyes are open again. Watching her devour Mona while I destroy her from behind.

I am not able to control myself any longer when I feel her start to flutter around my dick. I grip her tight and slam into her again. Whatever she is currently doing to Mona is working out well too. Mona's back arches again and she grips the blankets around her until her knuckles are white. She lets out a scream into the room and I know if she isn't cumming she is pretty fucking close to it.

184

I slam into Susie over and over until I feel her clamp down on me completely and then Mona is screaming Susie's name across the room. It is like a Domino effect. Mona's scream leads to Susie moaning into her cunt. Which in turn leaves me panting 'Peach' into the room around us. The girls start to tremble from their orgasms then I am shuttering as I explode inside Susie. I am shaking from pure adrenaline and need. I continue slamming into Susie as she keeps that vice grip on my dick. Mona is starting to come down from hers, still humming as she keeps Susie's face planted in her cunt.

I start to slow down when I feel Susie releasing my dick. I let out another loud breath into the room as she slides forward and off of me. Her mouth reaches Monas and they embrace in another lustful kiss. I roll my head on my shoulders and move towards the bathroom, "I'm gonna take a shower."

If they hear me, they do not acknowledge it. I smile as I step in the bathroom and look in the mirror. Trying to process what the fuck just happened. This woman is fucking perfect. Every single thing about her. I have finally met my match, in every aspect. I have to lock this down, immediately.

I reach into the shower and turn the water on and continue to breathe heavily into the mirror until I can see the steam coming out around the curtain.

I step in the shower and grab a rag to wash the remaining body paint off my body. It feels like only a few moments pass when the curtain is pulled back just a bit and Susie steps into the shower with me. She is smiling but she won't meet my eye.

I grin at her as I step into her space and put my finger under her chin to bring her eyes to mine. Her cheeks are rosy as I smile and lean down to give her a kiss. She immediately puts a hand up and blocks my lips with wide eyes.

I pull back looking at her confused, "What's wrong?" Her cheeks turn an even brighter shade of red, "I haven't brushed my teeth yet."

I let out a loud laugh, "You do realize I have tasted pussy before right?"

Her eyes close hard and she grins as she shakes her head, "But this is different."

I stare at her hard for a minute, "Are you embarrassed about what just happened?"

She moves her gaze past me, "No, not necessarily embarrassed. I just don't know where your head is right now. I don't want what just happened to come in between us."

I smile at her as I run my hands up and down her arms, "Do you love her?"

Her eyes come back to mine confused. I smile again, "Do you want it to happen again?"

She continues to stare at me confused, shaking her head, "Not necessarily. I mean it was fun but it isn't something I feel like I need all the time. And no, I don't love her. Only you."

I smile at her again and force her to give me a kiss. I pull back smiling, "That's all I need to know then. I enjoyed myself, you enjoyed yourself, Mona got her fix. Sounds like a win/win/win to me."

She smiles widely at me, "So, you're not mad?"

I laugh at her again as I pull her closer, "I just had a threesome with two extremely hot women. Mad is definitely not the word I would use right now."

She laughs at me and slaps me with the back of her hand on my chest. I smile back and continue to clean up. 10 minutes later we are drying off and sliding on some sleeping clothes.

She crawls into bed and settles herself on my chest. She splays one hand widely out and I can feel her smiling as she lets out a loud sigh. I stroke the back of her head then kiss her on her forehead, "This is by far the best night I have had in a long time. And not because of the threesome but because you are here. You suprised the fuck out of me tonight."

I hear her chuckle then she raises her head, sitting her chin on my chest, "Lily helped me get it all set up. Everything is done in New York. I am totally done with that city. I honestly don't care if I ever go back there again."

I watch the expression on her face, a dark shadow falls over her eyes as she talks about New York. I pull back to get a better look at her and realize her eyes won't meet mine again. My heart clenches in my chest tight. A ripple of fear runs down my spine immediately. I sit up, forcing her to sit up as well, "What happened?"

She finally looks at me, pretending to be surprised, "What do you mean? Nothing happened. I just got everything taken care of quicker than expected."

Her voice is shaking. She can't hold my eyes. She is holding something back. I shake my head at her, something is off, "No. There is something more. Something happened. You're lying to me."

She shakes her head hard again, not convincing me at all, "No. No I am not. Nothing happened."

I push myself further from her, feeling a sinking feeling in my stomach. I have never seen this side of her, whatever it is she is doing right now. We don't have secrets. This has to be something serious if she feels she has to lie to me. A thought runs through my brain and fear grips my heart tight, "You are lying. I can see it. Tell me the truth. Is...Is there someone else? Did you meet someone else?"

Her eyes go to mine wildly, "Of course not. You really think that fucking little of me?"

I pull back from her and stand beside the bed, pacing in small steps, "No, I don't think that little of you but you are fucking lying to me right now and I don't know why. I can deal with alot but not fucking lies. What the fuck is going on?"

She slides out of the bed on her side as well. The crimson has come up both sides of her neck again. She has her fists curled at her sides, "You really think that after just a few weeks that I am going to fall into bed with another man? After everything with us? Everything I have been through. You think I am just a whore?"

She shakes her head at me then steps over towards her stuff. She lets out a loud sigh and starts throwing her stuff back into her suitcase. I can see her shoulders shaking and I feel like a complete asshole. I step up behind her, "I don't think you are a whore."

She turns back to me, face covered in tears, "Yes you do. You think something is wrong and that is the first place you jump to. You don't think maybe I am upset that I have left everything behind. You don't even fathom that maybe just maybe I am sad that I left my entire life's work behind. And I did all that for you. So I could be with you. Instead, you just assume I jumped into bed with someone else. That is shit move Edge. Real shit."

She turns back around and starts shoving stuff into her suitcase again. I am getting really fucking tired of watching her pack her shit to leave me. I let out an aggravated sigh, "I didn't ask you to leave everything behind. You did that on your own. You said you wanted it. So what? Now you don't? You are just gonna leave? Where are you gonna go?"

She shrugs her shoulders as she pulls a pair of tennis shoes on, "I don't know. Just somewhere that you aren't."

I let out a laugh, "Great. Just fucking great. So what are you gonna run to Mona or someone else?"

She turns at me with a fire behind her eyes that I have never seen before. Before I even see it coming, she slaps me hard across the face. I stare at her in amazement as she trembles with emotions, "I don't have to fucking run off to anyone Gavin. I was alone when I met you. I can handle being alone again. You are a real piece of shit you know that. I don't need this. I don't need someone trying to own my every fucking thought. And 10 minutes ago, you said you had no issues with what happened tonight but obviously you do or you wouldn't be throwing Mona's name at me right now."

She shakes her head as she turns around and starts to slam the suitcase shut. I am a fucking idiot. Toxic masculinity I think is the term for me right now. I step up behind her quickly, reaching out to touch her arms. She flinches away from me, "Don't fucking touch me."

I feel this rage come over me as I turn her back towards me, "I am sorry. I don't know what I am saying. I don't know what I am thinking. I feel like something is wrong and my brain automatically goes to the worst possible scenario. I am sorry, okay. I don't know what I am doing. I have never been in a relationship. I have never been in love before."

She brings her eyes back to mine, speaking softer now, "Well, you don't accuse someone of just running out on you. And you don't use something you said was completely fine against them. That is not how this works."

I let out another sigh, as I turn and move back to the end of the bed. I sit down putting my head in my hands, "I'm sorry."

I feel her approaching the end of the bed. She pulls my arms up and puts them around her waist. I bring my eyes up to hers and she gives me a slight smile, "You are forgiven. Just don't be a dick again."

I laugh at her as I pull her into my lap and hug her tightly. I inhale the scent of her hair, "I just don't like lies. That is my number one rule breaker. No lies. I can deal with the truth but never lies."

I feel her start to tremble again and I pull back to look at her face, again not able to make eye contact with me. I run a hand down her face, "What is happening right now? What are you hiding?"

She stands and walks around to the head of the bed. She sits down, leaning against the headboard and pulls her knees to her chest. She lays her head to the side to look out the window, "When I called you that day, having the panic attack. I had just thrown up in my work trashcan for 5 minutes. I was upset because I had looked out the window and I saw Evan walking down the sidewalk. I didn't even know he was back from Vermont or wherever the fuck he has been hiding."

I feel a level of rage roll through me that I have only ever felt once before in my life. We all know that didn't end well. I stand, shaking, "You lied to me? Why the fuck didn't you tell me that?"

She turns her eyes to me, "Because I only saw him through a window. He didn't see me. And if I would have told you, you would have dropped the damn tour to come back to New York. I am not going to give him the satisfaction of fucking up my life any more than he already has."

I let out a growl as I grab the hair on the sides of my head. She is right. I would have gone there. I would have hunted him down. Even through her attack she was trying to protect me, protect us.

I move back to the bed and climb up, pulling her close to my chest. I hold her as I rock back and forth, "I am so sorry I wasn't there for you. I am sorry I couldn't help you through it."

She shakes her head and sniffles, "But you did. Yeah, you weren't there to physically help but you were still there. You are the only person that has ever been able to pull me out of an attack. Not even Lily can do that."

190

I continue to hold her close to me and rock her back and forth. She finally lets out a heavy sigh and pushes back from me. She looks me in the eye with an expression I have never seen on her face before. I don't know what emotion she is feeling right now, "There is more."

I blink heavily, "What?"

I hear her take in another rattled breath and I open my eyes to watch her wring her hands then fidget with the blanket, "He was outside of my apartment this morning. I think he was waiting for me. I think he was watching me. He asked what I was doing, I told him I was leaving New York. That I was going overseas to live with my fiancé. He told me that he misses me and loves me. I told him to go to hell then I jumped in my uber and took the fuck off."

I can feel the veins in my neck and temple throbbing angrily. My eyes narrow into slits as I clench my fists so hard that my nails start to dig into my palms. My entire body is now radiating this heat as I imagine myself strangling the life from his body with my bare hands. I can hear my own heart pounding in my ears like a drum as my breathing comes out in harsh, ragged gasps. I struggle to control the urge to scream in rage, frustration.

I look at Susie and she is watching me closely with that strange new expression again. Then it hits me like a tidal wave. She is scared. She is scared of what happened, she is scared of my reaction right now. I take a deep breath to try to calm myself. I pull her close to my chest again and lay back down onto the bed, "You did the right thing. You didn't tell him where you were going. You told him you had moved on. And you left immediately, safely. You did the right thing baby. I am so proud of you."

I hear her let out a stifled cry then she is hugging me fiercely. I continue to stroke her hair and kiss the top of her head.

She is going to have to show me a picture of this guy because if I ever see him out and about I want to know who I am looking at. I want to know this piece of shit if he thinks he is going to approach her ever again.

We lay there holding each other until we both fall asleep.

16
Susie
Drag Me under - Sleep Token

I can't believe I get to wake up next to this man every single day going forward. Last night, when I explained my run in with Evan I thought he was literally going to explode then he flipped the coin, telling me how proud he was of me. I was so afraid of what his reaction was going to be. I am so fucking lucky to have him.

He is still asleep as I lay here watching the sun pour in through the curtains. I watch it as it dances across his face. Gleaming from the piercings in his ear and eyebrow. I study the tattoos down his arm and chest. The sanskrit, the blue waves that roll up his side. I lightly draw an outline of the elegant sanskrit lettering with my finger.

He stirs just a bit but just turns his head towards the window and lets out another small snore. I roll over grabbing my phone, it is not even 8 am yet. I shoot a text to Lily letting her know I am going to the hotel gym if she wants to join. I stand and walk to my suitcase. Pulling on a sports bra and some work out shorts. I grab my sneakers before walking to the desk and leaving a note for Edge. Just in case he wakes up. I don't want him to think I disappeared after our argument last night.

I put the note on his nightstand then make my way to the hallway. It only takes a few minutes to make it down to the gym. I am grateful that it is more than just a treadmill and free weights. They have all the normal machines I like to use.

I start at the ab bench for a few reps then move to the lat pulldown. After a half hour on those, I move to the elliptical machine. I put my air pods in and begin my cardio. I always push myself too far. I should have stopped after 45 minutes but of course I go for a full hour. After I finally slow down, I can barely walk and my thighs are pulsating. I slam back the last of my bottle of water as I turn to see Edge leaned against the mirrored wall just watching me.

I smile as I walk towards him on wobbly legs and throw my water bottle away, "Perv." He laughs as he steps up to me, taking one finger and running it down my neck. I smile at him as his eyes scour my body, "I don't even make you sweat this much."

I laugh at him and start making my way towards the door to leave, "Now you have goals." He laughs back as he swats my ass walking out into the hallway behind me. He walks ahead of me and crouches down, "Hop on, we will go take a shower then find some breakfast." I smile at him as I climb onto his back and he piggy backs me back to the room.

I slowly peel out of my drenched clothes then walk my happy ass towards the bathroom. He is right behind me, I know he is watching my ass as I walk away leaving me smiling into the room around me.

Finally in the shower, I have a rag and I am running the soap all over my extremely sweat infused skin. He is pretending to clean himself but we both know he is only here to watch me bathe. I raise an arm up and I feel his finger run under my left breast. I feel the air still in my chest. I know he can feel the scar that is covered by the tattoo.

As I bring my arm back down, I let out a heavy sigh and look up into his eyes, "That is where Evan held the knife. He left a pretty little nasty and jagged scar."

194

His eyes flash with anger but he just nods his head, looking at his feet, "What does it say? I can't really see the words and I thought you might get a bit freaked out if I just lifted your tit to read it."

I laugh out at him, making him let a small smile slip as well, "beauty behind the pain". He nods his head again then steps up close to me, "Do you want me to find him and throttle him for you?"

I smile back at him as my hands roam down finding his ass and squeezing both cheeks tightly, "Nope. This is the only ass I worry about now."

He smiles again and kisses me. When he pulls back he looks down into my eyes, "If you change your mind, just say the word."

I nod at him as I give him a quick kiss then finish my shower.

Lily has been avoiding me for weeks. Tonight is the last show of the UK tour and the last time she really spoke to me was when she told me about her dreams of Nikki. I just assume she is talking with Gideon about it all but fuck I miss her. Even though she is 5 foot away from me right now it feels like there are miles between us. I hate it when she shuts down like this.

Everyone is already in full gear and paint. I refuse to coat my extremely sensitive skin with the most likely toxic chemicals they are infusing on their own bodies. But I happily wear the mask. The last thing I need is for them to get outed because someone recognizes me.

I am standing stage left watching them all enter the stage from the opposite side from me. They move like a well oiled machine. Everyone knows their marks. They know exactly what the others are going to do without even words being spoken.

195

I watched Edge slowly transform into Dionysus earlier. He just methodically rolled into a different personality. It is wild to watch them all in their alter egos. It is intimidating to be real about it. They all move as one, song after song. I have never seen them live before. I have already caught myself about to cry twice already.

I watch Aphrodite as she is putting the final touches on her piece so I know the show must be ending soon. I watch Ares as he walks to Dionysus and whispers something in his ear before giving him a quick kiss, making the crowd go feral. I smile at them and shake my head.

Ares steps up to the microphone again, taking it in his hands before turning and sending a nod to Apollo then looking towards Dionysus. He turns back to the mic, "Peach". I go stone still. Every muscle in my body goes tight, so tight you could probably bounce a quarter off my ass right now. That is Edge's stupid nickname for me. I turn my eyes back to Dionysus and instead of facing the crowd or Ares he is turned completely towards me.

I let my eyes focus on Dionysus as his fingers start to fly across the fretboard, creating a blur of movement as they expertly navigate the strings. The powerful sound and distorted riffs blare through the speakers, filling my head with a deafening rhythm. Then the drums start to beat in, adding chaos and frenzy to the music. I look at Apollo and watch him just destroying the drums. He is going from standing to sitting to swaying to bouncing on the stool beneath him. I have never seen anyone play live like this before.

The music completely drops off and I turn my eyes back to Dionysus. He lifts his right hand and blows me a kiss before going back to a slow and melodic strum on the strings. I can hear Ares in the background, with that guttural growl he lets out when he is singing something that hits home with him. You can always tell when he is singing with the passion of a scorned soul. I keep my eyes on Dionysus though as the words flow around me. I watch him as he sways, leans to the side, tilts his head at me with that psychotic mask on. I smile as I listen to the words and feel the tears roll down my face.

"In the shadows where whispers bend,
I will build a sanctuary for your soul to mend

Beneath the weight of the night's embrace
I will provide solace in our secret place

Fingers trace the veins of your weary skin
I will hold back the shadows that contain the sin

Mending with each heartbeat, scars of the past
Ours is an empire that will forever last

In your stillness, my promise remains
I will shelter your heart from the pouring rain

Let the tides rise, let the tempest call,
I am your provider, in my arms you will never fall

In this realm where the lost can find their home
You'll never wander, you'll never be alone"

My eyes don't leave Dionysus the entirety of the song. It is fucking brutal, feeling the words that I know he has written for me and not to be able to run on stage and throw myself at his feet. I want to kneel before him, pray to him because he is my world. He is the only God that I will ever bend for.

197

The song ends and he walks towards the back of the stage to set the guitar down in its stand. He turns to me and opens his arms. I let my mouth fall open as I feel someone nudge me from behind. I look over my shoulder to see their manager Lucy pushing me forward with a smile.

I turn back towards him and run full sprint onto the stage. I launch myself into his arms and wrap my legs around him. I kiss him fiercely as the crowd in the arena erupts in cheers. I don't even care that I am kissing him in front of thousands of screaming people. The only people that matter at this moment are me and him. I continue to assault his mouth as his hands settle on my ass.

Eventually, I pull back smiling at him, "I fucking love you so much." I see the smile underneath his mask then realize the entire venue just heard me whisper my love confessions. This asshole is mic'd up.

The crowd is screaming in a frenzy again. I feel my neck turning red as I release my legs from his waist and slide back to my feet. I turn to walk back off stage and he smacks my ass. I smile back at him as I run towards Lucy again.

As soon as I am in the safety of off stage again, I take the kleenex that Lucy is handing me. She smiles at me as I wipe the body paint off my face, "I have never seen him with anyone before. I was afraid he was going to spend his life alone."

I finish wiping the paint off as I smile at her and launch the used tissue into the trash, "Never again. He will never be alone as long as there is a breath in me."

Lucy smiles at me then points towards the back of the stage where we can climb down the stairs and meet the band behind the stage before going to the green room. I see Aphrodite first. I smile at her as I rush up and give her a deep hug. She hugs me back tightly smiling under her mask, "You are so fucked."

I laugh at her, "Don't I know it."

I look over her shoulder and see Dionysus approaching. I smile at her again as I run around her and wrap my arms around my man. I have never been this fucking happy in my life. I can feel his heart beating wildly in his chest. I am sure the adrenaline from the show is still coursing through his veins. That is evident by the massive package he is sporting right now.

I turn back to Lucy and ask for the travel package of tissue she keeps on her. She tosses them to me and I grab Dionysus' hand and start to walk him down the hall towards the green room. I notice a janitor's closet to the right and quickly open the door and push him in. I turn, locking the door before I smile back at him. I can see him smiling as he goes to pull the mask off. I grab it from the bottom pulling it back into place, "Leave it on."

I go to my knees, unbuttoning his leather pants and pulling the zipper down. I feel his hands go to the back of my head as I pull his dick out and take him deep into my throat. He moans out into the room around us. I continue to bob down on him, looking up at his face every few moments. I can feel him getting harder, swelling a bit in my mouth.

He looks down at me and I wink at him. He wraps my hair up in both hands and starts to slam his dick into my throat. It fucking hurts, I can feel the tears rolling down my cheeks but I don't fucking care. I love it. I love the pain. I love the feeling of him using my mouth to take care of his needs. I let a low moan leave my throat and he screams my name releasing himself into my mouth. I continue to suck on him until I have captured every last drop from him. Only then do I pull back and smile up at him.

I stand as he tucks himself back into his pants. I take out a few of the kleenex then clean up my face and mouth. He takes his thumb and rubs it across my swollen bottom lip before pulling me in for a kiss. I smile back knowing he can taste himself on me.

I pull back for air a moment later, sliding the mask back down my face. I take his hand in mine, smiling back at him, "Come on. Let's go play pretend for a bit."

He lets out a chuckle but lets me lead him to the green room. We walk in, way later than everyone else but I don't care. Let them snicker at us. My man had energy to burn and I was too happy to help. I lead him to his seat, pushing him down into it. I step over to the bar and pour us both a drink then walk back to his chair. I hand him his as I step around him and lean into his shoulders like before.

I can see his stalker groupie on the other side of the room but she doesn't dare step forward. It's adorable. She is scared. Honestly, she should be. A few more fans walk past the row of chairs, fawning over the band. I smile as I finish off my whisky, noticing the groupie headed back towards us.

I smile as I lean forward a bit over his shoulder then turn my head to look down the row of chairs containing my closest family and friends. Loudly I ask, "Is it considered an oral fixation if all you want to do is give your man head all the time?"

I smile as I feel Dionysus fighting to hold back his laugh underneath me. Ares is actually vocally laughing at this point, bringing most of the attention over towards him. Aphrodite has her hand over his, squeezing tight with a smile over her face. I know she gets it. I continue to smile down at them, "It's cool, think it over. Let me know later."

I stand back up looking at the groupie as her face turns an alarming shade of red. I smile at her, "Oh I am sorry, were you wanting to talk to them? I will leave you to it." I put my hands on Dionysus shoulders, rubbing them as I tilt my head to the side and smile at her. She turns in a huff and leaves the room. I lean down into his ear, "I am sorry. I know she is a fan but she is just icky and I don't like her."

I hear him let out a chuckle then he turns his mouth to my ear, "It makes me hard as fucking stone when you go territorial over me."

I smile as I try to talk my ovaries down. They are about to climb out of my body and gang rape him right here in the middle of the room.

Two, long ass days later we are back home in London. As grateful as I am to be back home, I am not enjoying the hundreds of boxes waiting for us in the garage. I did not realize I even owned this much shit until I saw it boxed in front of me.

I gladly offer to wait a few days before we even begin to figure out what we are going to do with it all. Edge agrees happily.

On the first day home we just lay in bed all day. Literally doing nothing but holding each other and falling in and out of sleep. Day 2 hits me like a wrecking ball though. I have to do something. I crawl out of bed and change into some work out clothes. Edge watches me intently, "We don't have a gym babe."

I smile over my shoulder at him, "Oh really? I hadn't noticed."

He flips me off and I laugh at him some more as I pull a sports bra on and readjust myself in it, "I am going to go for a run. I need to learn the neighborhood anyway."

He immediately throws the blankets back and starts rooting around in the dresser, "I am going with. Last thing I need is you getting lost and calling me from fucking Westminster or something."

I laugh back at him as I sit on the bed and pull my running shoes on. I take my air pods out of my pocket and slide my phone in. I put the air pods on the table then go to the living room to start doing some stretches to warm up. I hear him step up behind me and feel his hands on my hips while I currently have my hands on the floor in front of me. I smile and look over my shoulder, "Down boy. Recess is later."

He laughs at me then holds open the front door for me to walk out of. We start off on just a light jog. He points out places he thinks might interest me when we leave the neighborhood and start getting into a more commercial area.

We have passed two bakeries, a school and multiple bars before we are even halfway through the run. I want to see it all. I am just trying to soak it all in. Everything in my life is changing so fast but it's exhilarating. We are carving our own path one city block at a time. We end up doing a huge loop and are back on our way home within an hour.

I fucking love it here. I feel like I have been missing out this whole time. We get to a busy intersection and I jog in place while he leans over his knees, trying to heave some air back into his lungs. I laugh at him as I watch the traffic coming to a stop. I look in the first car at the light and stop abruptly. I have never seen the car before but the driver that is eyeing me, eyeing Edge, I have certainly seen him before. "Edge?" I can hear my breath steady though it is still breaking a bit. I don't dare to look away. Edge is still panting, "Yeah babe?"

I don't point. I know he sees me and he knows I see him, "Evan." Edges head jerks up and follows my line of sight towards the sedan stopped at the light. Before I can even grab ahold of him, Edge is running past me, into the intersection. Into oncoming traffic, trying to get to Evan. I hear tires squealing and then I see Evan run the red light and take off down the street.

Edge is walking back towards me, still looking down the street in the direction Evan has gone. How the fuck did he find me in London? I didn't tell him where I was going. How the fuck did he track me? I have all new electronics and my phone is new. I had all of my stuff scanned for air tags before I even left.

I can feel myself getting overwhelmed. I turn to the left and run full speed back to the house. Edge is trailing behind me but not by far. I slam the garage door open. There has to be something in here that he has bugged. That is the only thing that I can think of.

Edge runs up behind me as I start pulling boxes down, "Babe. Peach, calm down. What are you doing?"

I am shaking uncontrollably as I start opening random boxes, "He has to have bugged something to find me. I didn't tell him where I was going. He shouldn't be here, Edge. How the fuck did he find me?"

Edge grabs me and pulls my trembling body into his, "He is not going to get you babe. I promise. If he even thinks about getting close to you I will end him. You hear me?"

I nod my head into his shoulder as I feel the fearful tears start to roll down my face. I try to regulate my breathing but it is really hard to accomplish when you are being stalked by your rapist ex boyfriend. I shudder at the memories of that night. I can't go through that again. I just fucking can't. I barely survived him the first time.

I feel Edge as he runs his hand down my hair, holding me close to him. He finally pulls back then grabs my phone from me. I watch him scroll then he gets to Matthews number and hits send. Two minutes later I hear him, "Hey, it's me. My phone is inside. Could you have security grab the sweep equipment and send them to my place? Yeah, we might have a situation. Just want to make sure before we really freak out about it."

He turns to me nodding, "Yeah. We aren't going anywhere. We will be here waiting." He hangs up the phone and sighs as he turns towards the garage. He claps his hands together loudly, "Okay, we are going to pull out all these boxes so security can do a sweep of them and make sure there is nothing in them. Then we will figure out our next move. Okay?"

I nod my head back at him, happy to have something to focus on for now. We get to work moving all the boxes out and lining the driveway until there is no room left and we have to start setting boxes in the front yard. The entire time I continue to scan the street into our neighborhood. I feel like he is watching me right now.

Half an hour later there are two huge dudes climbing out of an Audi with duffle bags. If I wasn't terrified before, I am now. I pace the entire length of the driveway after they introduce themselves to me and start scanning literally everything.

I barely have any fingernails left. I have chewed them all down so far all that is left is red nubs. Edge steps up to me, "There was nothing babe. They scanned everything twice."

I shake my head at him. They missed something. They had to. There is no way that this is a coincidence.

I turn to Ryan, the bigger of the two guys, "If I bring you inside will you scan the stuff I brought with me in there? Like my suitcase and purse. Just in case there is something in the lining?"

Ryan nods at me then pats Edge on the bicep, "I will take care of her. You guys can put all this back in the garage. We are done with it." Edge nods his head towards him and starts to stack boxes back up. They are making quick work of it before we even make it in the house.

I walk Ryan back to the bedroom, "Okay, my suitcase is in the closet. It has all my purses in it. If you could scan that, I would be super grateful. I will look around here and see if there is anything else that could have been bugged."

I can feel myself still shuddering in fear. Ryan puts his hand on my shoulder and gives me a friendly smile, "It will be fine Peach. We will figure this out."

I smile back at him for his kindness and the nickname that has apparently become a part of me now. I continue to pace the room as I watch him scan all the bags and suitcase. Nothing. There is nothing.

I am shaking my head back and forth as Edge walks in. He moves quickly to me and wraps me up in his arms, "See baby there is nothing. He doesn't know where you are." I nod my head at him but I don't believe a word he is saying. I can just feel it sitting on my chest. He knows exactly where I am. He has always known. He will always know.

Ryan starts walking towards us, running the wand over the top of the dresser for whatever reason when we hear it start to hum then screech. My eyes fly wide as I look at Ryan then Edge. Ryan starts moving things around on the dresser, testing them separately.

Then it hits me. I know exactly what he fucking did. I run to the dresser and pull open the top drawer. I pull my grandmother's ring box out and hold it underneath the wand as it starts screeching around the room. I turn to Edge, "That motherfucker! He knew I would never get rid of this. He had to have done this years ago. How fucking long has he been watching me?"

Edge steps up and takes the box from me. He pulls the ring out running under the wand to no reaction. I let out a sigh of relief as I take the ring and sit it down on the dresser. Edge then takes the box and moves it under the wand, hearing it screech again.

Edge looks to me then to Ryan, "Scan it. Scan it all. The entire fucking house. Call in more people I don't give a fuck. Scan everything!" Ryan nods his head then steps out to go call in backup I guess. Edge turns to me as he pulls the inside cushion of the ring box out. Inside sits a small little round piece of metal. It almost looks like a tiny button.

"I fucking told you. I knew he put something somewhere. He knew I would never leave that behind no matter where I went. That son of a bitch!" I am panting with rage. Who knows how fucking long this psycho has been watching me. Probably this whole fucking time. Feeding on my insecurities and fears. He never pushed to find out where I was going because he knew he would be able to find me. That's why he never came to the airport.

Edge reaches in and grabs the little disc then walks into the bathroom. He wraps it in some toilet paper then flushes it down the toilet. I let out a heavy sigh and move to him, putting my head on his chest, "What am I going to do? I have a fucking psychopath stalking me."

Edge holds me close as he strokes the back of my head. I know he can feel my fear radiating into him. He kisses my temple, "Pack some clothes. We are going to go stay in a hotel. We will have Ryan scan everything we are taking with us. We will even call an uber in case he has chipped my car. I promise you, I will keep you safe. He won't get to you."

I hug him back as I finally allow my fearful tears to shatter me. I shudder and cry into his chest. He holds me the whole time, whispering words of comfort into my ear. He continues to remind me that none of this is my fault, how much he loves me. Just solidifying in my soul that I would walk through the fires of hell for this man.

206

17
Edge
All I Wanted - Paramore

I get us checked into the hotel and make sure they understand the urgency with the security. I don't tell them the entire situation but I give them enough to know that we need to look out for anyone sketchy. That absolutely no one is to know we are here without my authorization specifically. I told them only me, not even Susie. I don't know this guy. How do I know he wouldn't threaten her somehow, make her let him in under duress? I am not playing games with this asshole.

We finally make it to our suite and Susie is just exhausted. I run her a bath then order room service. Afterwards I set to getting us comfortable in our home away from home. She does not know it yet but we are not going back to that house. Ever. I am going to hire somebody to pack up everything and we are moving. Discretely with movers involved. Absolutely no one that we love or associate with will ever be seen at that address again.

If he is watching the house, then I do not want to give him anything to follow. Plus, who knows if the bug really got flushed away. It could be stuck in the pipes under the house or something. I mean more than likely it is damaged from the water but I am not taking any chances when it comes to Susie's safety.

By the time she finishes up in the bath, dinner has already been delivered. She walks out with a towel wrapped around her body and another wrapped around her hair. At least she doesn't look like hammered death anymore. She sits down gratefully with me at the table and starts to eat her pasta. Her eyes roll up in her head as she looks at me, "I love you so much right now."

I laugh at her as I pull my laptop open, then open a search for real estate. I figure now is as good a time as any to let her know my plans. I smile as I turn back to her, fidgeting with my fork, "So, I was thinking."

She groans and looks to the ceiling, "I fucking hate sentences that start with that phrase."

I make a patronizing face at her, "Shut up and eat your food."

She snickers back at me but listens and continues to devour her pasta. I watch her until I am satisfied that she is actually listening to me again, "As I was saying, I was thinking and I think it is time to get a new house. And before you say anything, this is something I had already thought about. Before the fuck weasel showed up. Combined, we just have a lot of stuff. And now that he knows where the house is, I think it is just time to cut ties and find something new. Together, that we both pick out."

She nods her head then does this little neck wobble thing like she is thinking it over in her head, "I mean yeah. That does make sense. What kind of place would you want?"

I smile, excited that she isn't going to fight me on this one, "I would like something a bit further out of the city. Yes, it will suck for the commute into town but for me personally I need room to stretch. If I wanna walk around my backyard in my underwear I don't want to be disturbed, ya know. I want someplace we can grow into."

She nods her head back at me, "I am fine with that. As long as there is a grocery within a half hour drive, I am happy. I would prefer something with a lot of windows though. And maybe a study or library combo would even be nice."

I type in all our requirements then give her a bit of a side eye, "So what price range are we wanting to look at?"

She squints at me, "Depends I guess. How do you want to do this? I am fine with going Dutch. We can 50/50 the hell outta this. Or if you want me to get a mortgage and add you to it so your name is on the property too I am fine with that even."

I smile back at her, "No, I am fine with 50/50. Money just isn't something that we have ever talked about before. I know that you aren't stacked like daddy warbucks but I still don't want you to think you have to put everything you have into this. You tell me what you are comfortable going half with and I will let you know if I can match that."

She laughs out loud at me, covering her now open mouth with her hand, "You are seriously going to keep calling Lily that aren't you?"

I nod back at her, "That is her government name isn't it?"

She shakes her head back at me, "No. I am pretty sure that is not true. And yeah, I may not be as loaded as her but I have my own money. I'm not destitute."

I give her a small side grin, tilting my head at her trying to figure out where this is coming from, "I never assumed you were. I just never brought it up because it doesn't matter to me. Even if you were penniless, I would still want you." She grins wildly at me as she takes another bite of pasta.

Susie then starts to nod as she takes out her phone and pulls something up. She continues to take slow measured bites as she types shit in and scrolls for what feels like hours. Finally, she puts the phone down and tries to look around me at the laptop screen, "I would be comfortable with my half being around 1 or so."

I nod back at her, "That is fine. We could probably find something decent for around 300k. It might be a bit of a fixer upper but I don't mind that. I like putting my own spin on things." I look at her and she is smiling widely at me again. "What?"

She puts her hand on mine, "I meant million babe. I am not insane. I have saved and invested over the years. My job brought in well over 200 grand a year. How do you think I afforded the apartment? The rent there alone was 6k a month."

I drop my jaw, surprised that she has that big of a nest egg that she would be willing to drop on a home for us. I mean I can definitely match her but she has worked her entire adult life for that savings. I just acquired mine over the last year. Sure, we worked our asses off for it but still. It seems too one-sided to me.

I nod at her, astonished by her honestly, "Oh. Okay, well why don't we start low and go high. Let's look around the million mark, so that way it's only 500 each way. Who knows maybe we will find something we both love and want to put our mark on."

She smiles in agreement as we continue to eat and scroll. By the time dinner is done, we have a few houses we want to go to look at. I decide in the morning I will find a realtor and get the ball rolling. I set the food tray out in the hall and walk back in to see Susie already curling up in bed. Red curls splayed all around her on the pillow.

She smiles at me, stretching her hands out in a grabbing motion. I laugh at her as I strip down to my underwear and crawl into bed beside her. I pull her close, realizing she is still naked. I hold her, running my hand up and down her back until I feel her starting to snore. I smile again, kissing the top of her head before falling asleep beside her.

"I still like the second one the most." Susie has not stopped rattling on about the house. We have been looking for over two weeks now. If we are gonna settle on something before the US tour gets rolling, we need to make a decision. What I think is hilarious though is that she is trying to convince me of which house to get, when the entire time I have agreed with her. She just hasn't taken a breath to ask me which I prefer.

I smile at her as we continue to walk hand and hand down the street towards the hotel. We finally decided to get out and get some air tonight. It has been stifling living out of a suitcase. I squeeze her hand, "I am fine with the second one. I liked it too. There is enough room for both of us and my guitars. Plus, it had the most privacy. I would like to maybe have an addition put onto the back of the house though. Maybe get a hot tub or even a small indoor pool installed. A recording studio would be dope too."

She smiles back at me, "I love everything about this story."

I squeeze her hand again as we turn into the hotel, then the lifts to go up to our temporary home. I smile as I turn to her, "Our relationship was saved in an elevator."

She smiles back as she leans in and kisses me, "Seems only fitting that we make our next big decision in an elevator then."

I smile back to her as I hit the emergency stop button on the wall. She glances between it and me in confusion. I smile at her as I get down on one knee and pull her grandmother's ring out of my pocket, "In that case then, how about this? Why not make all of this official. Me and you and a home and a life. Forever?"

If it wasn't completely fucking rude, I would pull out my camera and take a picture of the shocked look on her face right now. She starts shaking her head back and forth with some kind of expression on her face that I have yet to have experienced. I instantly get extremely fucking nervous.

This isn't what she wants. I am rushing it. I nervously look down at the ring then back to her face. I am completely defeated, "No, it's okay. You don't have to say anything. I get it, it's too soon. I just. I don't know, it felt like the perfect time to me. But it's fine. Seriously, we are cool."

I am well aware that I am rambling. I am nervous and I just got fucking rejected by the only person I have ever loved. I reach over to hit the button and slide the ring back into my pocket but she grabs my hand stopping me. I turn to look at her and I see her crying but smiling. I watch her face as she tries to breath through whatever emotion is overtaking her right now.

She brings my hand holding the ring back towards her, "Kneel again."

I smile at her as I get back down on one knee and hold the ring up to her. She lets out another heavy breath, "I never thought that I would find somebody that I wanted to spend the rest of my life with. I thought I was too broken to be loved. I was shaking my head because I am shocked that the heavens have given me a chance at life. At love. I am not saying no, I am saying yes. I want to spend every moment of the rest of my life with you. I want to play house and have a family and spend every single day loving you."

I slide the ring on her finger then stand and wrap her up in my arms. I have never smiled as hard as I do when I kiss her lips. I finally allow us to come up for air and she is smiling at her hand. She looks back up to me, "Grandma would have loved you so much. Thank you for doing this with her ring. It feels like she is here with me right now." I give her another gentle kiss then lean over and hit the button.

The doors open up to our floor and I pick her up bridal style. She starts laughing loudly, yelling at me to put her down. I laugh back as I run to our room and slide the key in the door. She is finally able to slip free of me once we are inside. I laugh at her as I shut the door, making sure it is locked.

She turns back to me, "I do have one request though."

I smile back at her as I step into her bubble and begin the move of getting her closer to the bed, "Anything baby."

She smiles as she continues to take steps backward. She laughs until she feels the bed behind her knees then puts a hand on my chest to stop me from going further, "I want to do it at the new house. I don't want a big production like Gideon and Lily. I know that is what worked for them but I want this to be about us. I just want the band and of course your mom, sister and Michael. Nothing big. Just us with the people we care about the most. Is that okay?"

I slam a kiss into her mouth. She has no idea how happy she has made me. I want the exact same thing. It sucks that we will have to wait until after the tour but I don't care. She is mine. She is going to have my last name. We are going to spend our lives together. That is all that matters. I finally pull back from her, "That is perfect. I am fine with all of it. I can't wait."

Susie smiles up at me as she grabs my shirt and pulls it up over my head. I smile down to her as she traces her fingers over a few of my tattoos. She looks up at me with those glowing orbs, "I want to get a tattoo tomorrow. Do you have a guy here?"

I smile back at her, nodding as I look past her at the clock, "Yeah, he is probably still open. You want me to call him and see if he has time?"

She nods her head smiling at me, "Yes. It won't be a huge one so it shouldn't take more than a few hours tops." I look at her inquisitively, "You already know what you want?"

She nods her head back at me with an enthusiastic smile. "Okay, if you say so. I will call him now. Give me like 2 minutes." I step back from her and do a few laps around the room while I talk to Deacon. He moves a few things around so he can get us in right at 10 am. I tell him how grateful I am then turn around to tell her. She is lying naked in the middle of the bed. She looks like a mythological goddess with that fire red hair fanned out around her. Her alabaster skin glowing against the dark fabric of the comforter.

I step towards her, slowly undressing along the way. I reach the foot of the bed then slowly start to climb up her body. I kiss her thigh, then hip, abdomen and breast. I finally make my way to her lips and I kiss her softly but fiercely. She opens herself to me and I slide in gently. This time is going to be different. I just want to worship her.

I feel her moan into my mouth but I don't pull away. I continue to explore her mouth with my tongue as I pump in and out of her slowly. I can smell the excitement rolling off of her. She smiles into my lips and I am sent spiraling. She is running her hands up and down my back with her fingernails barely dragging my skin. I could stay right here in this moment for the rest of my life.

I feel her slowly start to move her hips to match mine. She nibbles on my lower lip before laying her head back into the pillows. I speed up just barely, just enough to give her a bit more friction. I watch as her mouth opens and I smile at the beauty of her spirit.

I kiss her on the neck then nibble my way up to her ear. I pull back, "Look at me. I want to look in your eyes." Her eyes meet mine and continue to hold strong as I start to speed up my hips some more. She moans again but never breaks eye contact.

I feel her flutter around me and she smiles, "I love you. I love you, for you Gavin. You are my forever." I kiss her fiercely again. I start to slam into her harder. I need to feel her break around me. I need her to feel how much I love her as well. I pull back, still keeping eye contact with her as she shatters around me. I thrust into her one more time before I am falling off the same cliff as her. We hold each other as we fall further and further until we meet again at the bottom. Completely satisfied and happy.

I call our realtor first thing after waking up. We have officially put in an offer. Now we just have to wait to see if they accept it. I don't see why they wouldn't. We ended up offering a little over a million. That is above the asking price so I feel pretty confident about it.

We arrive at Deacons' shop right at 10. She still hasn't shown me the tattoo she wants to get though. We are walking around looking at drawings he has on the walls when she turns to me, "He doesn't know about you right? About the other you?" I smile as I shake my head, "No. He just thinks I am grossly addicted to ink and piercings."

She laughs back at me, "Okay, so then just don't ask me what the tattoo means while he is around. It might give too much away."

I smile down at her curiously, "Why don't you just tell me now then?"

She grins back at me as Deacon calls her back, "Cause it's a surprise. You coming with me?"

I reach out and take her outstretched hand as I follow her back to the ink room. Just being here gives me the bug to want another one, but today is about her. She shows Deacon a picture on her phone. He does a quick trace of it then scans it to make it bigger. She is explaining to him that she wants the outside black but the inside shapes to be a crimson red. I am completely lost as to what she is getting. Then it surprises the hell out of me when she tells him she wants it on her left tit.

I am not the happiest that Deacon is getting a show but it's her body and I am right here with her. Plus, Deacon is a professional. I trust him completely. He gets the drawing lined up before he puts the trace on her skin. It starts above her breast and then comes to a point about an inch above her nipple. She smiles as he starts the gun and gets to work. The closer the outline gets to her nipple the harder she squeezes my hand. I smile back at her and squeeze back.

It doesn't take him anymore than an hour to get through the tattoo. Susie stares at it in her reflection from the mirror before turning back around and leaning back in the chair again. She smiles at Deacon, "Can I have a minute with Edge before you cover it?"

Deacon smiles at us, nodding his head at me before leaving the room, probably to take a smoke break. I move to the other side of the chair to look more closely at the tattoo more closely, "So what is it? You can't take it back now cause it's on your skin, forever."

She laughs back at me as she looks down at it then back up to me, "It is the sigil you use to worship the deity Dionysus. You are supposed to keep it somewhere close to you. So I decided to keep it near my heart."

I feel like I am going to pass out. She just had a part of me tattooed on her body and I didn't even know it. I didn't even know there was a sigil for him. I smile as I look at it. It is an upside down triangle with a semi circle and a line going through it. Closer to the bottom of the triangle is another set of lines drawn at an angle. I have never seen anything like it before. I

216

want to trace it but I will wait until it is fully healed. She is smiling at me, "Is this okay? You aren't mad are you?"

I shake my head, "No baby. I am not mad. I am the furthest thing from mad right now. I didn't think that I could love you anymore but apparently I can. Thank you, Susie. I don't, I just don't even know what to say." I reach out and cup her cheek before I lean down and kiss her.

She is smiling as I pull away from her. She brings her eyes back to mine, "I will always worship you Edge. Forever. This will remind you every time you see it. You are my everything. You are my world."

I take a step back when Deacon enters the room. I am still smiling at this amazing creature before me. I can never show her how much I love her. She keeps topping me every time I try. But it isn't a competition. She is showing me her love just like I show her mine. I am the luckiest bastard that has ever lived.

18
Susie
Gods - Sleep Token

Finally, this bitch is answering my calls again. I have been trying to get ahold of her, like really get ahold of her for over a month. She has been just texting back small answers, never actually accepting a phone call or invitation from me. I was about to hunt her down and kick her ass.

Lily smiles as she holds my hand and we walk down the street. Of course, Edge and Gideon are close behind but still, it feels like old times again. She is smiling again. She is glowing again. That is all I want. To know that she is happy and healthy. That is all I have ever wanted.

I smile as I bump her hip softly, "You are going to be my maid of honor right?"

Lily grins wildly back at me, "Of course I am. You don't even have to ask. I would kick everyone else's asses to have that spot if they even tried to take it."

I laugh back at her as I glance over my shoulder and grin at Edge. He smiles and winks back at me before continuing his conversation with Gideon. I squeeze her hand a bit harder, "I can't believe this is our life. It all just seems fantastical to me. If I hadn't bought that ticket for you, we wouldn't be here with the men we were destined to be with."

Lily sighs as she looks over my shoulder before coming to a stop, "I know. I think about that all the time. If that one song hadn't played on shuffle that night, I may have never heard him sing. I may have never been drawn to him to begin with. It is scary to think about how all of this evolved from just that one simple moment."

I smile at her as the guys step up to us, "Do you wonder if maybe Mark had something to do with it? His spirit kept you awake that night. So you could hear Ares. I mean crazier things have happened."

Gideon and Edge both step up, going silent as they listen to us talk. I smile at a nodding Lily as she looks like she is trying to hold back thankful tears, "Seriously, it was a totally Mark thing to do. That just started the ball rolling. Your painting. Me buying that ticket for you. It was like a domino effect."

Gideon grins widely back at us, "You bought her ticket? For the first show? I knew it wasn't her because when I had the lady look up names of people hers wasn't on there. But I didn't know you so I didn't even think to listen for your name."

I grin back at him then to Edge, "Yeah, she had seen there was a show but they were sold out. Because of some of the functions I had attended before I knew that the ticket box holds tickets. You can pay an astronomical price for them but if you really want it, there is always a way."

Lily and I squeeze hands and start taking a few more steps when I hear Gideon behind us let out a breath, "Well shit...now I really owe her." I smile as I look down at my feet, grateful yet again for everything that has happened.

Lily comes to a stop in front of a storefront. There isn't any advertising for it though. I smiled at her, "Where are we? What is this?"

Gideon steps up beside her, wrapping his arm around her waist smiling, "Think of it as an early wedding gift from us. Come on, we will take you to meet Maura."

I look at Edge, "Who the fuck is Maura?" He just shrugs his shoulders then puts his hand on the small of my back as he guides me through the front door.

I instantly fall in love with the place. It is so fucking calming in here. I hear Edge make some comment about sage and starts rubbing his eye. Gideon starts laughing back at him while nodding his head. A woman maybe 10 years older than me comes around the corner. She walks directly to Lily and takes her into a deep hug, "You faced him didn't you?"

Lily smiles and hugs her again, "I did. He reached out but I ghosted him. I could have never gotten through this without you. You were literally my guiding light through it all." I feel a bit jealous that this complete stranger was her guiding light but I remind myself all that matters is that she is herself again. I try not to snub the woman but it's hard when I see how close she is with Lily. The woman then steps up to Gideon and gives him a hug as well.

She turns to me and Edge as a devious smile comes over her face. She looks back and forth between the two of us, "Oh, this is gonna be fun."

I feel a chill run down my spine but I am not sure if it is from anticipation or fear. She turns back towards Lily, "Are we doing the usual?"

Lily gives me a devious grin back, "Throw the whole book at them. Whatever you can give."

The woman nods her head and turns back to us, "My name is Maura. I am a medium, psychic and apparently a guiding light now." She smiles as she turns to Lily, "I am putting that on my resume, just saying."

I let out a laugh at her, okay maybe she isn't as bad as I thought. She smiles back at me and Edge, "Do you want to do this privately or is out here fine?" I look at Edge and he looks just

220

as shocked and uncomfortable as I do. I grin back at her, "Out here is fine. We don't mind."

She smiles as she walks past us and locks the front door. She pulls down a blind and then moves back to us, "Let's go over here. There is plenty of space." I squeeze Edge's hand as he looks at Gideon like he is going to murder him.

We follow Maura to the other side of the room and sit at a large table. I keep Lily to one side of me and Edge to the other. I have my own girl back in the states but she is nothing like Maura. Something about Maura just screams authentic.

She smiles at us both. She turns to me first, "So, Susie. You are a Leo aren't you?" I smile and nod back at her, "August 3rd."

She grins and nods before turning to Edge, "And Edge, Scorpio?" Edge blushes a bit, "I have no clue what my sign is. My birthday is October 30th." Maura smiles back at him, "Yes, that makes you a Scorpio."

She smiles over both of us. I look skeptically at Lily then back over at Edge. He is fidgeting with his fingers on the table. I reach over and take his hand before turning back to Maura smiling back at her.

She lets out a deep breath, "So you two. You have an extremely eventful relationship going don't you? Edge you are very introverted but in the same breath you crave intimacy. A strong, deep physical and emotional connection. And Susie, you bring the dramatics and passion to the relationship don't you? And when I say drama I mean, red headed feistiness. Am I right?"

I let out a laugh as I nod at her. I look at Edge and even he has a grin on his face while he nods subtly. I look back to Maura and she is grinning back at us.

She picks up a deck of tarot and starts to shuffle them, "You have a tumultuous relationship. Lot's of ups and downs but I believe you have figured out the right easy medium for your relationship. We will ask the cards but I have a feeling about you two. You both are extremely passionate. Susie you are extremely loyal, to the point of even putting him before yourself. You want him to understand just how much you value him and his love.

"Edge, you approached this relationship with an all or nothing mentality from the beginning. You gave your everything to her before she even realized it was being offered up. Didn't you?"

I turn to Edge and see him smiling at me, "Definitely. I knew I was going to fall in love with her the first moment I laid eyes on her." I blink rapidly at him, in shock and admiration.

Gideon leans forward, "I can vouch for this. He called dibs on her the day at the brownstone. She had never even spoken to him before but he called it. He pined after her for forever before they even met."

I look back towards Edge and I see a hint of pink in his cheeks. I smile widely at him then turn back towards Maura, "What else is there?"

Maura smiles back as she cuts the deck one last time then places down three cards. She smiles at us after she lays them out. I lean forward, anxious to see what they are. Maura studies the cards for a moment before looking back up at us, "These cards represent the past, present and future of your relationship. Now they won't tell specifics. They are to be interpreted on a deeper, more personal level. I can tell you what they signify but only the two of you will understand the true meaning behind them."

Edge nods at her, completely entrapped in her every word. I smile at him then turn back to Maura. She taps the first card, "This is your past. This the Five of Wands. Basically what this is saying is that you had a rocky beginning. There were a lot of disagreements, misunderstandings. Which would only be natural with your astrological signs. This is to be expected. It has made you stronger in the end though. The conflict in the beginning allowed you to explore each other on a deeper level. It makes smoothing out the zodiac pulls even easier."

I smile at Lily, giving her a small nod in my agreement with Muara. I turn back as she starts to tap the middle card, "This card represents your present day relationship. This card is the Ten of Cups. People wish their entire lives to see this card. Many never do. This card symbolizes finding divine love. The relationship between you two is forged in the heavens. You were truly meant for each other. I see an extremely long and happiness filled union for you both."

I turn to Edge, "Hear that babe. We are meant for eachother." He smiles back at me with a wink, "I have been telling you that from the beginning." I swat my hand at his bicep then turn back to the third card.

Maura is looking at it intensely, "This one tells a different story though. This is your future. I can't see beyond this card and only the two of you will be able to determine the exact moment that the lightning is striking. This is the Tower. This card signifies an upheaval. Some type of sudden change. There will be chaos and destruction. But you are both strong enough to pull through it. You just have to continue to remember that you are on the same side. You want the same things. Also, that you are destined to be together. Every relationship goes through tests. This will be your biggest. Remember to hold tight to the love you feel for each other right now. Don't let go of it no matter what."

I look at Edge and he seems just as worried as me. He turns to me with a meek smile, "We've got this babe. Wild horses remember?"

I smile at him as I lean over and give him a kiss. I turn back to Maura, "Thank you so much for this. This has been amazing. I truly appreciate you and all your insight." She smiles at us as we all stand to move from the table. Gideon and Lily are walking a few steps ahead of me when Maura places her hand on my shoulder. Edge and I turn around to see a concerned woman standing before us.

She lets out a heavy held breath, "I don't know what but something is going to happen. I don't know when but it will test the very foundation of what you have built." She turns to me and gives me a small grin, "Remember that he loves you. And everything that he does is out of that love for you. He would literally walk through the fires of hell to save you if he could. Hold onto that. Tightly."

I nod back at her, still a bit concerned but I have faith in us. I know that we can get through anything. We already have. Nothing can stop us now.

☿

Lily spends the next few weeks with me, getting the new house set up. Edge has been spending a lot of time in the studio. So if I am not with him, I am with Lily. No one really feels comfortable with me being alone, not knowing where Evan is.

I have put the place together with a little bit of me here, a little bit of him there. It is cozy and welcoming. I am still trying to get used to the laundry being in the kitchen though. That is going to take a minute to really settle in. He has his music room, I have my book nook in an office area. There is a large yard for him to walk around and air out his cheeks if he feels the need. It hasn't happened yet but I am greatly anticipating it. I have a camera ready.

I hear Edge pull into the driveway just minutes after Lily leaves. I drop the unpacking I am doing and rush down the stairs to meet him at the door. He steps in smiling at me barrelling down the stairs. He sits his guitar down right as I leap into his arms, "I have missed you so much today!"

I feel him smile as he nudges his mouth into my neck. He brings his lips to my ear, "I think I missed you more. Since you are the one that sent me a nude and all."

I laugh back at him, pulling back slightly as he starts to walk us up the stairs, "I just wanted to give you some inspiration while you were recording."

He smiles deviously back at me, "Your inspiration led me to spend 20 minutes in the bathroom taking care of an extremely obvious boner."

I laugh as I bring my lips to his. He rounds the top of the stairs and takes me straight into our bedroom. He lays me down before peeling out of his clothes. He slowly removes mine as well, "I have been thinking about this tight little pussy all day."

I let out a soft moan, "Yeah? What are you wanting to do to her?"

He slowly slides my shorts and underwear down as he smiles back at me, "I want to say that I am going to worship her like the goddess she is but someone has had me hard all day from dirty pictures. So right now I am going to fuck her. Hard and fast. And you are going to let me."

I slowly nod my head at him with hooded eyes, "Yes sir."

He growls as he stands back up. He climbs up on the bed between my spread legs. He stares me in the eyes as he slams into me. I feel my back arch up into his chest at the intrusion. "Fuck Gavin. You fucking destroy me every time."

He continues to thrust into me as deep as he can go. I start matching his hips thrust for thrust. He puts his forehead to mine and a few moments later I can feel the trickles of sweat run from his forehead to mine. I smile up at him, "Your dick is so big. Fucking break me baby. I wanna cum on your cock so bad."

He lifts up a bit, just enough to pull my legs up over each shoulder. He continues to slam into me at a new angle. He starts to hit the spot that only his fingers have reached before. I scream his name as I feel myself clamp down on him. He starts thrusting erratically. He is grunting then screaming my name back as I feel him thicken then lose himself inside me. He continues to destroy me for 5 more minutes before lowering my legs and bringing his lips back to mine.

I smile into his kiss. As he pulls back, I whisper, "I love you so fucking much Edge. It physically scares me sometimes. I just feel like something inside me is going to explode and I am going to lose you."

He moves inside me, kissing me again. I feel him start to harden again as he moves slowly, methodically. He pulls back, keeping his eyes on mine, "I would strangle the devil himself for you Susie. I would turn down the heavens if you weren't there with me. I swear to you baby. I will never let you go. Ever."

He continues to push in and out of me until we are completely lost in each other again. I cry at my release. At the perfection of the moment itself.

We arrive in Boston just a few days later. Lily is going to the asylum where her mom was to pick up her last effects. Then she is taking Gideon to meet Nikki. I was supposed to go with her but I agreed that she needed it to be Gideon. He needs to see this side of her as well.

Plus, she is going to tell him about the baby today. I am going to be an aunt. I haven't stopped smiling since she told me yesterday. I find myself crying from time to time. Not in sadness though, in the complete fairy tale that her life has turned into. This child has no idea what it is in for. I am going to be that crazy impulsive aunt that takes it for its first tattoo and lets it stay up to 3 am watching scary movies. We are going to be best friends and I am here for it.

Edge and I decide to spend the day exploring the city. We asked Matthew and Simone if they wanted to join us but apparently they are not on speaking terms right now for whatever reason so we are left to our own devices. We hit Fenway park and the public gardens.

After lunch, I decide to surprise him with our next stop. The look on his face was fucking priceless when he looked up and saw a sign for the Boston Tea Party Museum. I thought he was going to chase me for miles but I ended up giving in after a half a block.

I could spend every moment of every day just giving him hell and then being dealt my punishment. He won't admit it to anyone but I actually think he enjoyed the museum. We spend the rest of the afternoon just walking around hand in hand. Taking in the sites and just being. Not Dionysus, Not Susanna. Just us. Plain normal us.

The next day we leave for the arena early. I hang out with all of them as they prepare for the show. I still think it is not healthy to be covered in that much body paint sometimes twice a week but it is part of their show. I get the necessity of it.

I am excited for the new line up tonight though. Not only will they be performing Peach, but they have about a half dozen other songs that they are going to introduce on this tour. I am just excited to watch Dionysus on stage again. He lives up to his chosen name. When he is on stage he becomes a different person.

Honestly, as soon as the mask slides on the switch is flipped. He becomes sharper, more powerful somehow. Without the mask, he is intimidating but as soon as it slides on, all his rough jagged edges start to shine. He looks at you like he is going to consume your soul. His eyes just glaze over and it is like someone or something he hides deep inside takes over.

I stand stage left, watching them all perform. They are all masters at their trade. Illuminated in strobe lights, perfectly in sync they bring the crowd to their feet. Screaming for more at every turn. I watch Hestia destroying it on the keyboards. She seems to be more comfortable in her own skin recently. We haven't had any more close encounters since that one time, but that is okay. We got our fill of each other and we are still able to be ourselves around each other.

Hera seems to be gravitating towards Apollo on the stage now. She will turn and face him while playing bass. It's as if they are feeding off each other somehow. Which is strange since they apparently have been on/off speaking terms recently. This must be an on day.

Aphrodite of course is still killing it. She refused to listen to any of the new music. She wants to be just as surprised as me. She wants to funnel that music into her art. She is going to make another masterpiece and we all are aware of it. I watch her hands fly over the canvas like a woman possessed. It is hard to keep my attention on the screen of her though when I know that Dionysus is staring me down. I smile towards him, giving him a wink.

Ares flies across the stage. He is everywhere at once. I have never seen him more comfortable in his own skin. It is like everything has finally lined up for him and he can truly be happy. Maybe for the first time in his life. Like there was some battle going on within him before but now, he is five times the performer that he was before. You can just feel the love he has for his craft as it radiates from him.

Dionysus spends the majority of the show facing me or at the very least glancing in my direction. Three times he has run off stage to give me a kiss before the guitar starts back up. I laugh at him every time he runs to me. This night is perfect. We are all here as a family. As a unit. Nothing can break us apart now. We are so much stronger together.

The show finally ends, the crowd still in a frenzy. As the band goes to bow and give their appreciation to the fans, I follow Lucy off the stage. We will meet the band behind the stage and go to the green room together like normal. Lucy is a few feet ahead of me talking on the phone when I see a shadow beside me. My heart slams in my chest when I feel a blade go to my throat.

My eyes widen in fear as my heart instantly starts pounding in my chest. I am trying to fight my way out of this person's grasp but they are too strong. The knife is pressed right against my neck and I am afraid of them cutting me in the struggle.

I am forcefully dragged backwards down into a dimly lit hallway, my feet scraping the floor as I try to gain some sort of balance in the situation. It all happens so fast I don't even have a clear thought to scream. I can hear the sound of a door being pushed open then I am assaulted with the smell of a dumpster and the noises of the city beyond the building.

Whoever is behind me is grunting like crazy as I start to try to fight my way out of their grasp. Then I hear it. That voice I would know anywhere, "You thought you could just get rid of me? You stupid bitch. You belong to me. You fucking know that Susie. You are mine."

I let the fear consume me. But only for 5 seconds. I count to myself as I let myself lose my shit internally. One. I continue to cry and struggle but he just tightens his grasp around me. Two. He turns a corner and I am kicking. Just trying to get some kind of hold on the situation.

Three. I feel Evan's hand as he presses the knife even deeper into my throat. I am afraid to even swallow at this point. He could cut me so easily. Four. I see a dumpster to my right as he drags me backwards down the alley. If I could just grab ahold of it, maybe I could pull myself away from him somehow.

Five. That is all the time I give myself. I am not going to let him take me. I am not going to let him rape me or worse, kill me. I think of Edge living his life alone, without me. Miserable and blaming himself. I will not let this be the end of our story.

I reach out grabbing the bar on the dumpster with my hand. I hold on tight as I use all of my strength to propel myself forward and out of his grasp. I feel the knife as it cuts my neck and I scream loudly, wrapping my hand around my neck.

I pull my fingers back and I see them covered in blood. I don't know how deep the cut goes but I don't think it is too bad. I look up and see the alarm turning to anger on his face. His eyes are wild and everywhere at once. I turn as quickly as I can and start to run back towards the arena. If I can just make it to the door, I will be okay.

I feel his hands as they wrap around my waist. I crane my neck, "EDGE!". I scream as loud as I possibly can. Maybe someone will hear me. Even if it is just a passerby. Evan turns me and hurls me into a brick wall. I feel the back of my head slam into the bricks and starbursts explode behind my eyes.

I shake my head and stumble forward before landing hard on my hip on the ground. I am still seeing double as I look up and see Evan standing over me. I start laughing. Uncontrollably. I don't know why. Maybe I am finally snapping, losing my shit completely.

Evan takes another step towards me. I stop laughing long enough to rasp out, "You are fucking pathetic Evan. You know the only way I would ever fuck you again is if you were to fucking force me, kidnap me. You are fucking worthless. You don't deserve me. You don't deserve any woman."

I instantly feel the sting of the back of his hand across my face. I know I should shut up. I know I am only making everything worse for myself but I just can't stop. I start laughing at him maniacally again. I laugh up until the point when he knees me in the mouth. Hard. I instantly taste blood and wonder if maybe I am going to be spitting out a tooth at any moment.

I turn, grasping the wall as I stand back up on my own two feet. I am unsteady and swaying but I am not just going to lay down and let him finish me off. I see him clearly though when he starts to approach me quickly again. As soon as he is close enough, I grab him by the shoulders and knee him in the dick as hard as I can.

Evan doubles over and I jut to the left to try to get around him. Maybe that was enough to give me a head start. Maybe if I am lucky, I can make it back to Gavin now. I feel his hand on my shoulder as he turns me back around. Then I see his fist coming at my face.

When he makes contact with my right cheek, I feel myself lose control of my body completely. I am flying or maybe just falling. I can't really tell. I just know that when I land with a thud I hear screaming behind me. I look up and see what looks like the devil himself punching Evan wherever his fists can land.

I try scooting back as quickly as I can, which isn't fast at all. I realize too late that it is Dionysus still in gear that is punching Evan. I bring my knees to my chest and wrap my arms around them tightly as I watch Dionysus becoming a completely different person. He grabs Evan by the sides of his head and just starts slamming it into the brick wall I was just up against.

231

I watch him as he slams his head into that wall at least a dozen times. Though after the 5th time, by the amount of blood I see spray out of the back of Evans head, I would be surprised if he is even still alive. Finally, I see Ares and Apollo pulling Dionysus off of Evan. Or what is left of him.

I stare at his broken body laying just feet away from me. He is not moving. He is not blinking. His eyes are just dead orbs staring past me into the alley beyond. Gavin killed him. With his bare fucking hands. And I know I should be scared but I am relieved. I knew he would save me.

19

Dionysus
The Grey - Bad Omens

I am still pumped from the show. It was a massive success for the first stop of our US tour. Everyone lost their fucking minds when they heard the new music. I think this next album is going to be even bigger than the last. You can feel the static energy as it charges from all of us as we leave the stage. We make our way to the back hall, ready for a drink and a moment to relax.

I smile as I pass Lucy, knowing Susie won't be far behind. She never is. I smile up into the hallway and see that it is empty. I turn back around, "Lucy, where is Peach?" She turns to me with a confused look on her face, "She was literally just 2 steps behind me."

I look at Ares and his eyes instantly meet mine, "I will go check stage left, you check the halls." I nod at him quickly and start walking a bit faster down the hallway. I check around every corner, but she is nowhere to be seen. I meet Ares back out in the main hall and he is shaking his head back at me. Where the fuck did she go?

I open the door to the back alley and look down both directions but I don't see anything. My nerves are kicking into overdrive. This isn't like her. She doesn't just disappear without a word. As the door starts to close, I hear a scream off in the distance.

I push the door back open and stare down the dark alleyway. Maybe it was just in my head, then I hear it again but this time I know it is her, "EDGE!" I slam the door open as I start sprinting down the alley. I come across a four way and look down all directions.

I don't even realize that Ares is right beside me as he points to the right, "I will go this way, you go to the left!" I am running before the words even leave his mouth. The anger and fear is coursing so thick through my veins and head I can't even truly put together what could actually be happening right now.

I sprint down the alley, just begging to hear her yell again when I look to the left and see her kneeing somebody in the dick. She moves to run around him but the dude rears back and punches her in the face, sending her flying. It feels like I am watching it in slow motion. Her arms and hair fly out around her as the power from the punch sends her spiraling. I watch the broken mask fly from her face and land on the pavement in front of her falling body.

Before she can even hit the ground, I am running full speed at the guy. I punch him in the stomach, feeling the soft skin of his gut as my fist causes ripples to form. I vaguely hear him screaming in my ear, "SHE IS FUCKING MINE!" as I catch the glint of something shining in his left hand so I grab his arm and start slamming it into the brick wall at his back.

I hear something clang to the ground and I just start swinging. I don't even know where the punches are landing. I get at least a couple hits in before I have my hands wrapped around his head and I am slamming it into the wall behind him. I can't even form words, I am just screaming.

Everything is red around me. I can't see anything but crimson as my eyes coat over and the anger comes forward. I feel someone pulling on my shoulders but I break away and go back towards the pile of flesh now laying in front of me.

234

I kick him in the gut as I feel two sets of hands now, pulling me backwards. I feel myself getting thrown to the ground as I try to catch my breath and figure out what the fuck has just happened. I look to my right and Susie is backed up against a dumpster with her knees pulled tight to her chest. Her mask is laying on the broken concrete just a few feet in front of her. I can see the swelling and bruises already blooming on the right side of her face.

I scramble on my hands and knees to her. But she is in too much shock to even recognize that someone is with her. I pull her close to me and start to rock back and forth. "It's okay baby. I am here. I have you, you're okay."

I look to my right and I see Ares and Apollo standing over Evan. I look back down at the pavement as reality starts to set in. I lost control again. It has been so long since this has happened I didn't even recognize it when it did.

Ares stands and turns to me. He is shaking his head, his eyes everywhere at once, "He's dead." I feel all the blood drain out of me. I start trembling, unable to control myself. I let go of her then turn to the side of the dumpster, dry heaving onto the ground. Susie is crying, rocking back and forth. I look down and she is trembling just as hard as me.

Apollo runs up to me, "Get out of here. I will call the police."

I shake my head back and forth at him, "I am not leaving her like this."

Susie attempts to stand on shaky legs. She holds onto the dumpster as she continues to stare at what is left of Evan in front of her, "Get the fuck out of here Gavin. We will call the police. I will tell them it was self defense. I have a restraining order against him, it will be fine. Just go."

She doesn't even look me in the eyes when she speaks. She is staring at Evan's lifeless body laying on the other side of the alley. I take a step towards her as she looks to Ares, screaming, "Get him the fuck out of here. NOW!"

Ares sprints to me, literally dragging me back down the alley. I look over my shoulder to see her go back down into a crouch. I can hear her agonizing wails echoing all the way down the alley.

Ares finally gets me back inside and sits me on the steps of the stage. He pulls out his phone and makes a phone call. I don't even understand what is happening right now. I am somehow numb. I just literally beat a man to death and all I can think about is how Susie's eyes never reached mine.

I should be out there with her. She needs me. I shouldn't be sitting here while she is out there taking the blame for all of this. I stand and start pacing the hall. I can feel Ares watching my every movement, like he is just waiting for me to take off or lose my shit again.

A few seconds later, he is off the phone and is again dragging me down the hallway. I don't even remember the drive to the hotel. All I know is that everything went black and when the colors started to emerge again I am back in my hotel room.

Lily and Gideon are attempting to get me cleaned up. Lily has a rag and is washing all the bodypaint off of my face, neck and arms. Gideon has a first aid kit and is taping my knuckles. It is like I suddenly awake from a dream and realize that Susie is not here with me, "Where is she?"

Lily's eyes meet mine. Her eyes soften as she looks at me, "She is still at the police station. They had her checked out by EMT's. She is fine. She is gonna have a headache for a minute, probably a concussion but other than that, he didn't hurt her. Just some bruises and superficial cuts. Nothing is broken."

I look towards the window then the nightstand. It is 3 in the morning. I have lost 4 hours. Have I been sitting here the entire time? Why isn't she back yet? I look nervously back at

Lily, "Is she going to jail? I can't let her do that. I won't let her take the fall for me."

Lily is shaking her head back at me. She places a calm hand on my cheek, "She is not going to jail. They are taking her statement. She had all of the information saved in her phone about the restraining order and all the shit he has done in the past. She even told them about London and the bug. They are going to bring her back to the hotel when she is done."

As if being summoned, the hotel door opens. Susie walks in slowly, dumping her shoes, phone and purse on the floor. She doesn't even look at anyone as she steps into the bathroom and turns the shower on. I watch the open door waiting for her to walk back through but she never does.

Lily sits the rag down on the table and runs to the bathroom. She shuts the door behind her and the panic sits in. I have fucked it all up. She wants nothing to do with me. She literally just watched me beat a man to death. I can hear crying coming from the bathroom and I go dark again. I can hear the furniture as it is destroyed around me. If I can lift it, it is being thrown.

Gideon moves back to the other side of the room and just lets me self-destruct. Everything is done. Everything is gone. I can't even get my eyes to focus on one thing at a time. I am gulping air in, gasping for a breath but nothing comes. I stumble and fall to my knees. I feel hands on my face and I look up into two fields of fresh cut grass. She blinks and the rest of her face begins to come into focus.

I see the entire right side of her face now. It is swollen and purple. There are knuckle marks in her temple and upper cheek. Her eye is completely red around the bright green of her iris. She is crying and talking to me but I can't hear any of the words she is saying. All I see is the broken image of the woman I love in front of me.

She is trying to get me to breathe. I watch her lips as they purse as she takes a deep breath in. I try to mimic her actions but I still can't seem to get any air in. I finally hear her voice coming through the fog, "Breath babe. Deep in through your nose. Come on Gavin, breathe for me baby."

I look back up at the destruction on the side of her face and feel myself break. I can't hold the tears back any longer. I am retching with emotions. They can probably hear my wailing all the way down the hallway. She pulls my face into her chest and holds me tight. I reach up and put my arms around her waist and hold her back against me.

I can't believe I let her be broken like this. I can't believe I have failed her, when at every turn I have promised her that I would never let him get to her. I knew he was still fucking out there. I should have been more aware, more diligent. She should have had security on her at all times.

It feels like hours have passed when I hear Susie speaking to someone, "He is okay now guys. We will be fine. Go get some rest. Thank you for taking care of him until I got back." I don't dare to let go of her. Just in case she isn't real, I want to hold onto this mirage a bit longer. I hear Lily's voice in the background, "Are you sure?"

I hear a small chuckle in her chest, "Yes, hun, I am sure. He isn't going to hurt me. We are okay." A few minutes later, I hear the door shut. I pull back from her chest and look around the destruction of the room. This is gonna cost a pretty fucking penny. I look back at her realizing she is only wearing a towel.

I look over the exposed skin of her body. She has bruised hand prints on her biceps and shoulders. There is a small red cut going across the left side of her throat. I go wide eyed as I reach out and run my thumb over it, "He fucking cut you."

I feel her hands wrap around my jaw as she pulls my gaze up to her own, "I am fine Gavin. You saved me. I am fine. He is gone. We don't have to worry about him anymore."

I pull my face from her grasp as I scoot back a few more feet. I feel like I can't control my own thoughts, let alone my body. I start trembling as the anger starts to roll through my veins again. My eyes just keep going from her face to the bruises on her arms, to the cut on her neck. With a shaky breath I tell her, "You need to go. You need to go somewhere that I am not. I don't want to hurt you."

I can feel her as she scoots closer to me. The warmth of her skin as it gets closer to me just ignites something inside of me. The guilt is beginning to become too heavy to bear. I look up into her eyes and they are softly smiling at me, still so empathetic, "You are not going to hurt me. I trust you."

I can feel the anger radiating through my veins. I don't want to lash out at her. I don't want to black out again and hurt her. I shake my head back at her, "No Susie. Leave now. I want you to leave." I look at her and she is shaking her head back at me. Her face is calm, soothing even. I lunge into her face, screaming and spitting, "GET THE FUCK AWAY FROM ME!"

She flinches at me then scoots back, frightened. I watch her as she shakes and scrambles to get back to her feet. She grabs her duffle and runs out the door in nothing but a towel. I lay on my side as I let the darkness take over again. I don't know how long I lay there before I fall asleep, but when I wake up Gideon is sitting on the end of the bed staring at me.

I sit up, cracking my neck. Then the realization of what happened comes crashing back down on me. I bring my knees up and rest my forearms on them, looking at the floor, "I fucking killed him, Gideon."

I hear him somberly from about 4 feet away, "I know."

I shake my head again, trying to get the memories of the night before out of my head. I remember screaming at Susie. Telling her to get away from me. I can still smell the fear in the air. The look on her face as she grabbed her stuff then ran out the door.

I look back to Gideon, "Where is she?"

He lets out a heavy sigh and looks to the door, "We don't know."

I stand up, panic riddling me again, "What do you mean you don't know? She didn't go to your room or get one for herself?"

Gideon shakes his head as he stands and walks towards me. He lets out another deep breath, "She came by this morning and changed her clothes. She told Lily she was leaving and that she would get in touch whenever she figures out her next move."

I shake my head furiously. I grab my phone out of my pocket and hit her number. It doesn't even ring, "You have reached a number that is no longer in service. Goodbye."

I scream into the room around me before finally stilling. She fucking blocked me. I turn back to him, wild eyed, "I have to fucking find her. I can't....Gideon I can't do this. Without her, I can't fucking do any of this."

He steps to me, nodding his head, "Okay. Just sit down. Breath. Let me call Lily. Just try to calm down. We will find her."

I hear him on the phone whispering. I know he is telling her that I am losing my shit yet again because she isn't here. I just want to hold her. I just want to know she is safe, that she is alive. I was so afraid of myself last night I made her leave. I didn't trust my brain. I pushed her away.

I just hope I didn't push her so far away that she never comes back. I feel the tears as they start to pour down my face again. I stand and stumble towards the bar. I grab as many vodka shooters as I can then I crumble to the floor, leaning against the wall.

I crack them open one by one and throw them back. I am about to open bottle 3 when Gideon somehow spawns right in front of me. He rips the bottles from my hands and steps to the other side of the room, "Not happening. You want to be sober when she shows up."

My eyes fly to his, "You found her? She is coming back?"

He shakes his head as he looks out the window, "Lily called her. She is telling her to come back. I don't know that she will but I am going to sit here as long as you need me too. We will wait together."

I stare at the clock on the nightstand for 3 hours. All I can do is replay the look on her face when I screamed at her. When I spit my words into existence. Every time I blink I see her running out the door.

Finally, the hotel door opens and I watch Gideon as he stands. I glance to the left, expecting to see Lily but instead Susie is standing there. She smiles as she gives Gideon a hug. I try to stand, my legs still not completely stable after last night. I begin to straighten my shirt, realizing I am still wearing the clothes I wore when I beat a man to death in an alley.

I immediately start taking my clothes off, throwing them in the trash can. I move wobbly to my suitcase then pull out a clean shirt and jeans. I hear the door shut behind me and I close my eyes. Praying she is still here. I slide some clean clothes on then turn to see her standing 6 feet away from me. She has tears running down both cheeks. I stare at her defeated. I don't recognize the look on her face. I can't tell how she is feeling.

I let out a huff and step to the end of the bed. Sitting down in a panic and leaning forward onto my knees. It isn't 10 seconds later and she is on her knees scooting up close to my body between my legs.

I sit back a bit, looking at her in surprise. I am unable to look at her beautiful face and the destruction he left behind. I turn towards the window with my eyes closed, "I promised you that I would keep you safe and I didn't. He still got to you. I will never forgive myself for failing you."

I feel another tear roll down my cheek as she turns my face to hers. Her eyes are searching mine for something. She lets another indiscernible look roll over her like a mask, "That is bullshit and we both know it."

I let out a long breath as I refuse to accept her words as truth. Her grip on my jaw tightens, bringing my eyes back to hers, "You saved my life. The only reason I have this bruise on my face is because I fought back this time. I fought back because I live for you now. I was not going to let him win. I was not going to let him take me from you. I kneed him in the dick and he punched me. I did this to myself so do not feel like any of it is your fault."

I try to blink back the tears but they continue to fall. I don't even understand the feelings that are rolling through my body right now. I try to speak but no words come out. She gives me a slight grin, "You saved my life, Gavin. I love you so fucking much. I only left last night because I thought you were disgusted with what you had done for me.

"Lily told me that I wasn't allowed to play that game because that is what she did with Gideon and it almost destroyed them. She told me to put on my big girl panties and come home. So I did. I unblocked you but you never called. If you don't want me, I will leave. But only if I hear you say the words."

Something inside me breaks. I pull her face to my chest. Holding her tight as she snuggles her left cheek into my sternum. I stroke her hair, "I fucking killed someone last night Susie. I didn't want to snap and hurt you. Everything was spinning. Everything was red. I wouldn't be able to live with myself if I hurt you."

I feel her smile into my chest, "Yeah. You killed a psychopath last night. A psychopath that was trying to abduct me and do god knows what to me. You saved my fucking life baby."

I release my grasp on her as she pulls back and looks up into my eyes. I tilt my head slightly, "You took the fall for me. You shouldn't have to do that."

She shakes her head at me, I see the crimson starting to build in her neck, "I didn't take the fall for anything. You would have done the same thing for me. We are a team. You would have went to jail for the rest of your fucking life. I can't live without you Gavin. It's not like you are out just killing random people.

"You killed my fucking rapist stalker. Did you really think I wouldn't love you because of that? Of course, I am going to take the credit for it. One, it is empowering as fuck to all those women out there that are afraid for the same reasons. Two, I love you, I am not going to lose you. No matter what."

I stare into her face, ashamed but yet still amazed. I let out a shaky breath, "You're not afraid of me?"

She belts out a laugh, "Why the fuck would I be scared of you?"

I blink back more tears, thinking about the way I spoke to her, "Because of how I treated you. Because of what you saw."

She lets out another laugh and I whip my eyes back to hers. She smiles as she runs her fingers through the short beard on my jawline, "I watched you defend me. I watched you save my life. If he didn't want to get the shit beat out of him, then he shouldn't have touched me. I knew that you would find me.

"I knew that you would save me. I just had to take care of myself until you could get there. And because of how you treated me? You were scared that you were going to hurt me, not because you wanted to but because you were still processing. Why the fuck would that scare me?"

I nod at her again, trying to decipher all of her words. She leans in and gives me a soft kiss before pulling back, "The only thing that scared me was that I thought you didn't want me anymore. Because you *had* to save me."

I shake my head violently back at her, "I would save you a million times more to know you are safe. I will kill anyone that touches you. You are mine. Forever. Right?"

She smiles widely at me again, "Right." She leans in and gives me a deeper kiss than before. I wrap my arms around her back, careful of her bruises. I kiss her back fiercely as I feel more tears roll down my cheeks.

She pulls back for air, giving me a side smile, "Can we go to sleep now? I haven't slept yet. They told me not to in case of the concussion but I think I am fine now. I just want to sleep. We have the room for two more days before we head to D.C."

I smile as I stand and lift her into my arms. I walk around to her side of the bed. I slowly help her out of her pants but leave her in a shirt and her underwear. I strip down as well before I tuck her in then move to the other side and slide in next to her. She scoots her body back into mine and I press mine to hers. We form into a silhouette of exhaustion and acceptance.

20
Susie
Caramel - Sleep Token

"I swear on the love of everything fucking holy. Someone either be thoroughly fucked or dead to be knocking on that god damn door already." I don't even bother to open my eyes. If I open my eyes, I will release the fires of hell on whoever is on the other side of that door.

I feel the bed move. Then I hear grunting and groaning as Edge makes his way to the door. 2 seconds later, I have a little blonde pixie landing beside me and wrapping me in a hug. If it was anyone else, I would have punched them in their face. But I owe Simone a solid after she called and let me know about Lily.

I raise one arm up and zero eyelids as Simone snuggles into my chest making a little purring noise. I smile towards the window, "I am fine. If you think this is bad you should see the other guy."

Simone gasps as I start giggling then I hear Matthew, "Too fucking soon." I am really too tired to give a shit right now.

I kiss her on top of the head, "What time is it?" I feel her roll around then come right back to my arms, "7 pm."

I nod my head and wrap her back up in a hug, "Yeah, I should probably eat and bathe before I pass back out."

I finally allow my eyes to open only to realize, I can only see out of the left one. I freak out for a hot minute then close my eye again, turning towards the room, "The right eye is swollen shut isn't it?"

The next thing I know I have a cool rag placed on it and Edge is rubbing my thigh, "Yeah, babe. I think it is." He still sounds upset. I open my good eye and put my hand on his cheek. I give him a small smile because that is the only painless kind and whisper, "It's not your fault. He got a good shot in, that's all. I am fine."

He nods his head at me again, "I know. But still." I shush him and give a quick kiss before pulling back and sitting up fully in the bed. Every muscle in my body is screaming at me. I see a very hot bath in my future. I would go to the hot tub but I don't wanna scare the women and children with my quasimoto vibes.

I reach over and check my phone seeing 3 missed phone calls. I let out a sigh as I scroll through the numbers, they are all the police department. I look back up at Edge, holding my phone up, "I gotta make a call."

He tilts his head at me then pats my thigh. He moves across the room and throws some sweatpants on before settling against the wall. We haven't told the hotel yet that there is no furniture left in here besides the bed and desk. It was the only two things nailed down that he couldn't throw last night.

I hear the phone ring twice, "Detective Adams." I let out a sigh, "Hello Detective, This is Susanna Mayfield. Sorry I have been sleeping all day. This is the first chance I have had to see you called."

I hear some papers rustling on the other end of the phone, "Yes, Susanna. I was wondering if it would be alright for me to come by. I just have a few more questions."

I let out a sigh, looking around the room, "Yeah Sure. I am staying at the Battery Wharf, room 412. How long should it be before I expect you? I may try to eat some dinner first. I haven't eaten in a few days."

I hear him make some kind of noise, "Oh, I can be there in about 20 minutes actually. We'll just get this done and over with so we can close the folder on it."

I nod towards the window, "Yeah that works"

I hang up the phone and throw it down on the bed in front of me. I let out a heavy sigh and rest my forehead on my hand. I feel a dip in the bed and look up to see Edge looking at me. I give him a fake grin, "More cops are coming by. They want to talk to me again."

He nods his head and stands up. He turns towards Matthew and Simone, "Party is over. Cops are coming to talk to Susie. I will call you guys later. Let you know how she is doing."

Simone nods at him then runs back over to me to give me another hug. I don't know if she realizes it or not but if she keeps acting like a girl we are gonna start treating her like a girl. I think she is secretly a barbie anyways.

I throw the blankets back as they leave for the night. I hobble my tired muscles over to my suitcase and pull out a clean oversized t-shirt to throw on. I don't even care that it looks like I am not wearing pants. Edge sets to putting all the broken furniture to one side of the room. He gives me a half smile, "I should probably tell the hotel about this tonight."

I laugh at him as I hear a knock on the door. I smile back in his direction, "Ya think?" He flips me off as I turn and open the door. Trying to smile, but unable to because of the right side of my face being 10 times its normal size.

Detective Adams flinches when he sees me. I look a lot worse today than I did yesterday. I give him a half grin, "Come on in Detective."

He follows me inside, noticing Edge on the other side of the room trying to keep a lamp standing up on its own. I give him a small laugh as I look back towards the detective. I know all he sees is some bulked out dude covered in tattoos and piercings.

247

I try to hide the growl as I follow his gaze then step directly in his line of sight, "How can I help Detective?"

He brings his gaze back to mine then points to the end of the bed, "Please sit down Susanna. You have to be uncomfortable."

I nod gratefully then sit down on the edge of the bed. I look past the detective and see Edge leaned against the far wall. I motion him over and pat the bed beside me. He walks over, never even attempting to make eye contact with the detective. He sits next to me softly, rubbing a hand over my thigh.

I grin towards the Detective, "Sorry. My manners. This is my fiancé Gavin." Gavin leans forward and shakes the detective's hand, still not making eye contact or saying a word. With his history, he is probably freaking the hell out on the inside. I grab his hand and grip it tight as I turn back to the detective, "You said you have some more questions?"

The detective nods as he continues to take us both in. He pulls out a little notebook from his shirt pocket and crouches in front of us, "Yeah, I was just wondering if you could run the whole night by me again? I just want to make sure we have everything right before we close the lid on this."

I let out another sigh, squeezing Edge's hand to somehow telepathically tell him to keep his mouth shut. I nod at the detective, "Sure. I was walking in the back hallway of the arena. I saw a shadow come at me from the right. I didn't know who it was at first. Then I felt something sharp at my throat, I was just assuming at the time that it was a knife. I was afraid to fight him from that angle because I didn't want him to cut me."

I feel my hand as it runs across the thin line on my neck. I let out another heavy sigh, "I um. He was dragging me backwards so I couldn't really get any footing. He pulled me out into the alley then continued to drag me down and around the corner. I was finally able to grab onto a dumpster as we passed

248

by. I don't think he was expecting me to try to fight back. I didn't the first time. At least not enough."

I feel Edge's hand as he grips my thigh tightly. I look at him giving him a weak grin, rubbing the top of his hand. I can see the pain in his eyes as he just stares at me, listening to me talk. I turn back to the detective, "I , I was able to slip him a bit. I think that is when he cut me. I don't think he was actually meaning to do that. I tried to run but he grabbed me around my waist and threw me into the wall. I was on the ground and I think I might have pissed him off when I started laughing at him."

I can feel Edge staring hard at me now. He doesn't know any of this. No one but the police have heard the story entirely. "I laughed at him and called him pathetic. I told him the only way he could ever have me was to force himself on me. To try and fucking kidnap me. Because he was worthless and he would never deserve the attention of a woman. That is when he slapped me. I started to laugh again and he kneed me in the mouth.

"I was able to get to my feet and when he lunged for me again I kneed him in the dick. Then he punched me." I Vanna White the side of my face for him, "When he came at me again, I kicked him in the dick again. I finally pulled myself up and shoved him into the wall. I got in a few punches when he put his hands around my throat, trying to choke me. And I don't know, I guess it was the adrenaline kicking in. I am not sure. I just kept beating his head into the wall. Just over and over again. I only stopped when my friend Matthew found me out in the alley. He pulled me off of him and called the police."

I turn and look at Edge as I see him breathing heavily through his nose. He knows the last part is a lie. He also knows why I am lying. I grin as I reach a hand to his cheek again, "I am okay baby. I told you. I am fine."

249

The detective turns his gaze to Edge, noticing the bandaged knuckles. He points his ink pen at them, "What happened to your hands?"

Edge meets my eyes then turns back to the detective. Telling him, maybe a bit too sarcastically, "Have you looked around the room? Not a whole lot of furniture left. I kinda lost my shit when I got back to the hotel. I was pissed that she was talking to the police. I was pissed at myself for not protecting her. Pissed that he was able to get to her as easily as he did."

I lay my head on his shoulder and he turns and kisses the top of my head. The detective nods his head and writes something down, "And where were you when all this was happening?"

Edge blinks a few times as I sit up, "I was looking for her. I was still inside though, checking the halls behind the stage. I was hoping she had just ran to the bathroom or was already in the green room."

Detective Adams writes a few more things down while nodding his head. He finally shuts his book then turns back to me, "With the history between you and the deceased, I don't foresee us pressing charges. You had an active restraining order against him. There were also cameras from inside the building, showing everything that you described as he drug you out of the building.

"There were no cameras that far down the alley so we weren't able to see everything. But we do have video of multiple people running through that alley by the side door at one point. I am going to assume it was all of your friends trying to find you. We can't really tell because they are all in some type of costume."

I laugh back at him, "Yeah. I am kinda with the band so that would explain that."

He shrugs his shoulders at me, "I couldn't tell ya. Not really my style of music. But from what we can tell everything you say is completely true. And we have no reason at all not to believe you."

The detective reaches out and takes my hand as he continues to crouch in front of me. I feel Edge stiffen beside me but I don't take my gaze off the Detective, "You were failed by the system the first time Susanna. He should have never been on the streets to begin with. I promise you. I will do everything I can to make this a closed case. You shouldn't be contacted again." He nods his head at me and I feel a tear roll out of my open eye.

I take in a shaky breath and exhale, "Thank you detective. I just want it to all be over. I want to be free." And I do. I have kept myself imprisoned in my own mind, in my own body until I met Edge. I want to be happy. I want to be able to walk down the street and not have to worry about if he is watching me or not.

The detective stands again. Edge is on his feet in a moment, shaking the detective's hand again, "Thank you sir. Seriously. We really appreciate everything you are doing."

Detective Adams grins and pats Edge on the bicep, "Take care of her. She is gonna need you in the coming days."

Edge smiles as he looks back at me quickly then back to the detective, "Wild horses couldn't drag me away."

I let out a light chuckle as I feel another tear fall from my face. Edge walks the detective back towards the door and I plunge back into the comforter around me. I want to go to sleep but I know I need to eat something. And probably bathe.

A moment later, Edge is laying next to me. Pulling me close to his body. I feel him nuzzle the side of my face and I smile towards the ceiling. "You didn't have to lie like that Susie."

I let out a sigh as I run my fingers up and down his forearm, "Yes I did. Or else they never would have believed me. All of it was true though, before the beating his head into a wall part. I fought back this time. He was never going to willingly have me again. I belong to you."

I feel him kiss my cheek again, "I am going to call Matthew, see if he will run and get us some food. Me and you, we are going to take a shower in the meantime."

I nod towards the ceiling. "That sounds good. I want a big fat greasy cheeseburger. With bacon. All the bacon."

He laughs at me as he gets up and calls Matthew. Not 3 minutes later he is pulling me up off the bed to go take a shower. He is being so gentle with me I almost want to smack him for it. But I will save that for like day 3 if he keeps this shit up. I may be bruised but I am not that fragile. I will be okay.

I wobble into the bathroom. I watch him as he turns the hot water on, testing it with his hand first. I look at the mirror, not recognizing the person in front of me. I can't even believe what I am looking at. It honestly looks like I have been hit in the face with a baseball bat or something. I lean in closer, touching where the puffiness is, the bruises. I lightly run my finger over my busted mouth from where he kneed me. I let out a small agonizing whimper as I stand back up.

I know it will heal. I know it will fade and I will be normal again. But honestly, I don't even know who I used to be. I would have never fought back before. I didn't fight back before. I allowed myself to be broken. But even staring into the face of the fighter that I have become, it still feels like I am so weak. Because he was able to hurt me again. He was able to break me one last time.

I glance over to see Edge just staring at me, staring at myself. I wrap my arms around myself trying to pull my shirt up over my head but my muscles are still so sore I let out a small yelp. Edge is at me within a breath. He slowly, gently pulls the shirt up and off of me. He unhooks my bra and pulls it off as well. Next, I feel him sliding my shorts and underwear down my legs.

I turn as he helps me step into the shower. I move around then back myself under the water. Not wanting to feel the sting

252

of the water hitting my face. I just stand there, staring at the water swirling down the drain. Edge is standing in front of me but I think he is afraid to even reach out and touch me. I reach my hands out, gripping his forearms tight.

He brings his arms up and it all finally hits me. All the emotions, all the trauma, all the fear. It rips through my body like lightning. Like something that I cannot contain, can't bottle up any longer. I fall into his arms in tears. He catches me and holds me tight, "I know baby. I know. Just let it out, Peach. I am here."

I feel us sliding down into the tub and then he is just holding me as I lay on his chest, screaming. I can't even get a breath in. I am shaking and utterly wailing. I have been hurt before. I have been broken before. But somehow this is worse. I am devastated. And not for his life being lost. But because he was so broken to begin with. That he was never helped. Never even noticed.

How destroyed does a person have to be to turn into that? I honestly cannot wrap my head around it. I will be okay. I know I will be okay. I will live on and have a family, a life with Gavin. But Evan, he will always be in here. Rattling around in the back of my subconscious. I think that is what scares me most of all.

Edge holds me until the water starts to run cold. We finally stand and turn the water off. I am shivering as he wraps a towel around me and helps me out of the shower. He wraps one around his waist then grabs the last one to towel dry my face and shoulders. His eyes roam my body, I know he has seen all the damage. All the bruises, all the swelling. I look up into his eyes, "Do you think any of it will scar?"

He puts his hand on my cheek and shakes his head, "No baby. You are going to be fine."

I nod my head gently and make my way out into the bedroom. I haven't sat down for 30 seconds when there is a knock on the door. I really hope it is the food so I can just go back to sleep until we have to catch a flight to the next stop on the tour. I hear the door open then knelt in front of me is a wailing Lily.

I smile at her gently as she lightly brushes my face. Her eyes are concentrated on my swollen eye and the bruise covering the entire right side of my face. I watch the tears roll down her face as Gideon steps up behind her. He puts his hands on her shoulders and gives me a solemn nod.

I smile back then look down to Lily again. I pull her close to me and hold her. She is shaking uncontrollably. I sniffle, painfully, "I am okay Lily. He can't hurt me anymore." I feel her nodding her head along with me. She pulls back looking at me again before turning around and grabbing Edge into a hug as well. The shock on his face would be laughable if I could actually laugh right now. She squeezes him tight, "You're not a piece of shit anymore."

I don't care how much it hurts my face, I laugh loudly. I can feel the skin pulling and cracking. Pretty sure that I am tasting blood out of the corner of my mouth but I don't care. Gideon immediately steps up with some kleenex from the night stand and I dab the side of my mouth.

Edge and Lily both turn around concerned and I continue smiling, "There was no way I wasn't laughing at that."

Edge flips me off again and moves to the other side of the room to find us some clothes. He comes over handing Lily a tank top and shorts for me, "Can you help her get dressed? She can't really lift her arms very well."

Lily's eyes fly back towards me and I shrug my shoulders, barely. She nods and turns to Gideon, "Turn around if you want to keep your eyes." I let out another soft chuckle as she starts to get me dressed. I see Edge out of the corner of my eye giving me

254

one more look before walking into the bathroom and shutting the door.

5 long minutes later, I am dressed and sitting under the blankets. Edge is beside me and all of my friends are here. Matthew and Simone got enough food to feed an army. I lean into Edge's side as I watch everyone eating and talking. Every now and again I will catch someone giving me a pity stare but I just flip them off then go back to eating my burger.

I can't even finish half of it and I feel my eyelid getting heavier. Seriously, I could cut fucking diamonds right now it is so heavy. I don't know how long it actually is but after a bit I feel Edge lower me down onto the bed and cover me up. I drift off to sleep. I only barely wake up when I feel him slide in behind me. I roll over and put my face on his chest. I don't even care that it is the bruised and swollen side of my face. I just need to feel him. To know I am really here. That I survived Evan.

The Ghost of You - My Chemical Romance

"Can you just not fight me on this? Please?" I am practically begging her to just chill. Take a few days to continue to heal. She looks at me like I am a walking billboard for crazy. I throw my hands up as she slips her sneakers on.

Susie stands and moves towards me. Her eye still swollen shut, her face now a putrid mixture of like a baby shit green color and a squash with a Barney outline. I don't even know if the hemorrhage in her eye has started to go away. Every few hours, she takes a warm rag to it to keep the crust off.

"I am not missing one fucking show. You can get pissy. You can be overprotective. I don't give a fuck." She smiles as she struts past me to go get her bag and phone. I let out an aggravated sigh as I look at the ceiling.

"You can't even wear a mask. People are gonna recognize you." I turn and face her as she turns back around, narrowing her one good eye at me. She takes her bag off and throws it back down on the table, "Fine. Leave me here then. Don't want to blow your cover."

She turns her back to me and steps up to the window. I want her to be there. Of course, I want her with me but she needs to rest. Her body just went through torture just a few days ago. Just because we are in a new city doesn't mean that she is better.

I watch her as she crosses her arms and turns so her back is fully towards me.

I step up behind her and run my hands up and down her biceps. She shrugs herself out of my clutches and without even turning around I get, "Just go. I don't want you to be late."

I let my hands fall as I stare at the back of her head, "Please don't be mad at me."

She turns and kisses me on the cheek before walking past me, "I'm not. Just go." She continues until she is in the bathroom. She slams the door shut as I start to gather my things to head to the venue. I am left staring at the bathroom door. I wish she could just understand the shit going through my head right now. I am scared. I am honestly lost. Yeah, she is going to be okay but am I? I am still trying to understand how I am just functioning like a normal human being just days after murdering someone.

I knew that I was capable of it. I knew that there was a darkness sitting just beneath the surface but I also thought it was going to remain there. I never expected there to be something more triggering than what had happened in my past. I know if I was strong then as I am now I would have killed my step father that night as well. But I didn't. I had regrets but never this intense form of guilt weighing on my chest with every breath I take.

I let out a sigh as I move towards the hallway, shutting the room door behind me, feeling like I am making a mistake. I should just let her come. But it is too soon. She just needs more time to heal. I watch Gideon and Lily step out of their room with their duffles.

Lily smiles looking past me, "Where is Susie?" I look at Gideon then back down at my feet, "She is gonna sit this one out. She is still healing. She just needs some time."

I hear Lily let out a snicker under her breath, "She needs time or you need time?" I look up to meet her glare but she spins on her heel and continues down the hall.

I look at Gideon, "I can't fucking do anything right. I can't keep her safe. I can't help her heal. I am utterly useless." I feel Gideon's hand on my shoulder as we start moving towards the lift. I turn and look down the hall, wishing I could just stay with her. I just want to keep her safe.

The doors shut and I get into Dionysus mode. I have to. To even attempt to make it through tonight. We get to the arena and go to our dressing rooms. I get changed quickly and then move onto the green room. No one else has made it yet. I grab Ares's bottle of Dalmore and drink an eighth of it down before anyone even shows up.

I feel the muscles in my shoulders finally start to loosen up. By the time we are doing our preshow vodka shot, I am feeling much more relaxed. At least I am able to keep her off my brain for longer than 15 seconds at a time.

The entire show is a haze. I can't even tell you what happened. I am pretty sure I stand in the same spot the entire time. I don't even remember signing the art but I am sure that I did.

I make it back to the green room before anyone else and walk straight to the bar. I grab the entire bottle of Dalmore and sit down in my seat. I can feel Aphrodite's eyes on me as soon as she walks in the room. I throw the bottle back again and just glare at her. She shakes her head at me but I don't care.

I continue to nurse the bottle until I realize way too fucking quickly that it is empty and I have to piss. I try to stand but instead stumble to my right. I feel someone brace me as I start laughing, letting them lead me out into the hall. The bathrooms aren't that far away. I hear somebody giggling and I look down, not even recognizing the person helping me. I laugh again as I continue to stagger down the hallway.

I look up, seeing a hazy outline of someone at the end of the hall. I squint my eyes, is that Susie? All I can see is red hair. I laugh as I fall into the wall again. When I look back down the hallway, they are gone. A few seconds later, Ares is hauling me up to my feet again, "Let's go. You're done."

I laugh at him as he drags me to the alley. I quickly turn away from him and smile into the night sky as I piss against the side of the building. When I finish, Ares spins me and forces me into the back of the SUV. I sit back laughing as he and Aphrodite climb in. Aphrodite looks me square in the eyes, "I spoke too soon. You are still a dick."

I laugh at her as I point in her general direction, "Get in line baby. Everybody hates me anymore."

She rolls her eyes at me as I let my head slam into the door window. I laugh again as I grab the side of my head. I let out a sigh as I settle back into the seat and watch the city fly by outside the window.

Ares pulls me from the car and drags me to the lift. I am laughing at him, I don't know why. It just seems right. I watch Lily as she hits the button for our floor and I turn to face her. I cross my arms on my chest and push my lower lip out like I am pouting right back at her. She doesn't even glance in my direction.

I snub her as the doors open and I stumble out onto the floor in front of us. I lay on my back laughing at the ceiling as Ares reaches down and grips my hand tight, pulling me back to my feet.

I finally stagger down to my room and pull my key out of my wallet. Ares helps me get the door open and I stumble in laughing. I turn around and smack him on the arm, "Thanks brother. I'm good. I am just gonna go to sleep." He looks around the room like he is searching for something as he nods at me.

I kick my shoes off as I hear the door shut behind me. I laugh to myself as I pull my coat off and throw it on the floor as well. I see the bed and I crawl up on it, passing out immediately.

I wake up with a massive fucking headache as the sun shines in through the window. I groan as I try to block the sun from my eyes. I sit up rubbing my temples and look to the other side of the bed but Susie isn't there. I stand up and stumble around the bed to the bathroom but the door is open and the light is off.

I start slapping pockets until I find my phone. "Fuck!" There are dozens of missed calls and video messages. I open my texts, she said she was sorry then nothing. No other texts after that. I open the calls back up and realize they all came after her apology text. That doesn't make any sense. I start scanning the room and I see her bundled up in a little ball on the floor underneath the far side of the table.

I run around the table and try to wake her. She rolls back over towards the wall, "Leave me alone."

I sit back on my ass, "Are you still mad at me about last night?"

She sits up with a blanket wrapped around her shoulders and stares at me. With two open eyes. One is yellow and very obviously still swollen but looking a lot better than yesterday. I smile at her and reach my hand out to touch her face, "Hey you can open your..." She smacks my hand away and looks at me like she fucking hates me.

260

The smile drops from my mouth, "What? What is wrong?" She curls her lips at me, "Don't fucking touch me until you have washed her off of you. And even then, think twice about it."

I rear my head back in confusion, "What are you talking about?"

She laughs at me as she stands pulling the blanket up over her shoulders a bit tighter. She turns to me, "You know. You really had me fooled. The whole not in it for the game. Then the shit with Evan and I really fucking believed this. I thought this all was real. I gave up my entire life for you. I walked away from everything that has ever meant anything to me, for you. Just to be with you."

She pulls the blanket down, showing her chest with marks all over it, like she had scratched herself until she bled, "I got this fucking tattoo to show you how much I fucking worship you. How I will always fucking follow you. To hell if needed."

I step up to her, completely confused and worried. I reach out to touch her and she pulls the blankets back over her shoulders and steps back from me, "Did you have fun last night? I texted you, but I am sure you were working. Which is fine. But then as the time went on, I started to get worried. Then the panic set in. So I had an uber take me to the arena. How is the groupie by the way?"

I stumble back, completely fucking confused by her words, "What are you even talking about right now? What groupie?"

She laughs at me as she throws the blanket off her shoulders, showing me her entire chest is covered in marks, along with her arms. She turns and grabs her sneakers, sliding them on while she shakes her head at me.

I step back towards her, "What fucking groupie Susie?"

261

She stands up smiling at me, it is devastating, seeing a tear falling out of her wounded eye, "The one I saw you with in the hallway last night. You two seemed really happy. Really cozy. I am still amazed she came all the way from the UK to find you but I guess when it's true love, stupid bitches will do anything." She runs her hands down the front of her before giving me a curtsy, "I am fucking proof of that aren't I? I am the queen of stupid bitches."

She turns and walks to the other side of the room. I try to remember what happened the night before, "I don't remember anyone from last night. I remember drinking an entire bottle of Dalmore then trying to find a bathroom. The next thing I know Gideon is helping me into the room and I passed out. I honestly have no idea what you are talking about."

She turns back to me smiling then goes back to putting things in her suitcase, "Convenient. I guess that means it didn't happen then huh?"

I shake my head at her, "Nothing happened with anyone. I don't think I would have been up for performing really well if I had passed out."

She keeps her back turned to me, muttering, "You seemed to be doing fine when I saw you."

I step up beside her feeling the anger start to roll through me, "What exactly did you see? Was I naked rutting around on some bitch or was I just drunk?"

She turns to me, "I needed you Gavin. I just needed to hear your voice. I couldn't fucking handle being alone okay. The silence just got too loud. I tried to call you. I tried to facetime you. You never answered. You never called back. I went to find you and you were with that whore. What am I supposed to think? Huh? What am I supposed to believe?"

262

I turn, still trying to figure out what happened the night before. I sit down in a chair and put my throbbing head in my hands. I let out another sigh, "Nothing happened Susie."

She lets out another chuckle as she turns back to her suitcase, "Yeah, sure."

I stand and march to her, spinning her towards me, "NOTHING FUCKING HAPPENED!" I instantly regret my actions.

Her eyes are blown wide, as wide as they can go at least. She is terrified of me. I see my hands gripping her biceps tight and I hear her whisper, "You're hurting me."

I instantly let her go. I stumble back to the chair as she stands there staring at me dumbfounded. I stand and walk to the other side of the room, "Maybe you should go back home. Go back to London. Maybe we just need to breathe."

I hear a noise from behind me and I know it is her crying. I don't even have the guts to turn around and look at her. I know I am destroying her right now. But it's either destroy her now and get past it or lose her forever because of my temper.

I hear her whisper, "You want me to leave?"

I bring my eyes up to the headboard, "Yes."

I hear her slam her suitcase shut. I flinch at the sound of it. I turn around to see her grab her makeup bag and start to walk towards the bathroom, "I just think we need some space. I don't want to hurt you and I don't know where my head is at anymore."

She continues to walk like she didn't even hear me. I follow her to the bathroom and watch her throwing her stuff into the makeup bag. She turns to walk back out the room, "Get out of my way. Now."

The anger in her voice has seemed to take on its own life. And it fucking hates me. I shake my head at her, "Do you not think we just need a few days to breathe?"

263

Her eyes come up and meet mine. I have never seen her look at me the way she is right now, like she is heartbroken and angry, "I will give you all the time in the world. Get out of my way."

I move to the side and she marches past me. I follow her back to her suitcase, "What then? If you don't think space is good for us then what? What do you want me to do?"

She turns on me, screaming, "LET ME GO!"

My breath catches in my chest as I shake my head, "I can't do that, I won't do that."

She laughs at me again, "You just did."

She turns and throws her make up bag into her suitcase, looking around the room to make sure she grabs every last thing. I move to her and turn her back towards me, "What is so wrong with just some time? Some space?"

She smiles up at me, bringing one hand to my cheek. I feel her fingers run through my beard then her eyes meet mine. There are rivers flowing from both of them, her voice almost a whisper, "I begged you to just leave me alone. I pleaded with you. I told you I was going to fall in love with you. I told you that I didn't think I could survive you. Now I guess we'll get to see if I was right."

I look into her eyes, "I don't want to lose you. I just want us to take a step back and figure out how we can fix us."

She places her hand on my chest, "We were never broken until now. I was mad last night that you left me behind, sure. I was pissed when I saw you with that bitch but if you say you didn't sleep with her then you didn't sleep with her. But instead of just being an adult and figuring this out together your go to is to push me away? Send me back to England? That is it. That is the breaking point. I am not even worth sticking it out for. That is fine. Gavin. I understand. I love you."

264

She turns and grabs her suitcase. I run after her, grabbing the handle from her. She turns back to me rolling her head across her shoulders, "Edge, just let me go. It's what you want. You just fucking told me that. Just let me leave."

I shake my head at her, "I will only let you leave if you promise me that I am coming home to you."

She closes her eyes tight, "I can't lie to you. Even though it's what you want to hear."

I take her suitcase and throw it behind me, "Then you aren't leaving. If you aren't going to be home when I get there then you are staying here so I know where you are."

She shakes her head at me, "So you know where I am? Are you fucking kidding me right now? Which of us is the untrustworthy one here? I was sitting here waiting for you all night while you were out rubbing all over other women. Don't fucking play that card with me Edge. If you loved me, if you even cared about me, why would you send me away? When I fucking need you most? Why would you do this to me?"

I reach out for her and she pulls her hands from my reach. Her eyes fly back to mine, "Goodbye Edge."

She turns and walks out the room. I just stand here in shock. What just fucking happened? I look around the room. She only took her purse. She left her suitcase and everything. I just continue to spin in a circle. I finally get some sense into my head and I run to the door, throwing it open. I will find her wherever she goes. I will swim the fucking ocean if I have to. But instead I come to a complete stop as I see her in the fetal position on the other side of the hallway balling her eyes out.

I run to her and scoop her up in my arms then carry her back into our room. I sit down on the bed with her in my lap, just trying to hold her but she scoots out of my arms. She moves to the floor and crawls as far away from me as she can. I hear another rattled breath as the words come from her chest, "I will leave as soon as I can breathe again. I promise."

I get down on the floor in front of her, "No. Not if it means I will never see you again. That is not what I want. Susie, I have been alone so long I am just used to dealing with shit on my own. I don't know what I was thinking. I seriously just thought hey, she can go home, get a break from me and my crazy and then I will be back and we can just move on.

"I never meant that I didn't want you in my life. I would never say that. I would never want that. I am an idiot okay? I speak before I think, I have a horrible temper obviously, I am a failure at being a boyfriend, fiance, a protector. I am just failing at every turn and I don't know what to do to stop. I just want to stop letting you down."

She is taking deep breaths in through her nose and holding it for a second before letting it out. She does this over and over until her eyes finally meet mine, "When did you fail me? When you brought me out of an attack? Or when you were so patient with me, so gentle? When I met your family? When you saved me from being raped and probably murdered? When you saw all the brokenness in me and you still wanted me? When did you fail me?"

I sit back on my ass, just looking at her. Really seeing her. She only sees the good in me. She looks past the darkness to see what is really lying beneath. She exhales loudly again, "You saved me from myself. You brought me into a world where I can be me. I can be crazy and chaotic. I can laugh again, Edge. I didn't do that for years, not really. I have never felt love, not like I feel for you. No one has ever compared. You are my fucking world and I am just orbiting you. How can you not see that? Why won't you see that?"

I lean towards her, wrapping my hands around the back of her neck and bringing her forehead to me, "I promise I will do better. I will accept this for what it is. I just have to get past these fucking demons telling me that you can do better. That you deserve so much better."

She smiles as she pulls away looking into my eyes, "There is nothing better than you Gavin. I have been everywhere, seen everything. I have never found anything better than you. You calm the storms inside my head. You are the first person I think of when I wake up in the morning, and the last one I think about as I fall asleep. I love you unconditionally.

"Do you have an anger problem? Yeah, probably. But I am not scared of you. I am not scared of us. We can figure this out but only if we are together. Being apart, that never fucking worked for us. We are stronger together."

I nod my head at her as I place my hand gently on her jawline. She leans into my hand, closing her eyes and making a slight purring noise. I grin at her, knowing she is right. I do have a problem, but it won't be fixed by pushing her away.

"So, you stay then. We will figure out something to help me get past all this shit in my head. I don't really know what options there are but I am willing to explore them with you."

She smiles back at me, "We have to quit pushing each other away, Edge. We can't keep hurting each other this way. I was mad, yeah, but I wasn't going to leave. Maybe step in the hall and catch my breath but never leave for good. I promised you that I was here to stay and that is what I fully intend to do."

I stare into her endless eyes, "I am sorry. No more. If we need a breather, then it is 10 feet apart. But still on the same continent. I never meant I wanted you to be gone forever. I just wanted to give you a break from me, my insanity."

I feel her lean into my chest as she splays her hand out wide over my heart, "You are not insane. And even when you are a bit crazy, I like it. It matches my own. Just promise me you will

267

stop trying to push me away. Promise me that we will figure this all out together."

I kiss the top of her head then place my cheek on her crown, "I promise baby. I promise."

22
Susie
Jaws - Sleep Token

This man is going to be the death of me. One minute he is here the next minute he is gone. As I wrap my hands around the back of his neck and bring his mouth to mine, I know he needs help. I know he is lost in the darkness. I just have to stay. I have to stay and refuse to leave. That is what he is used to. He is used to people giving up on him. Not me. I will get him help. I will stay beside him through all of this torture he puts himself through.

I kiss him hard then pull back, "If Gideon says one thing about you flirting with that bitch, I am cutting your balls off and making a necklace out of them."

He lets a loud laugh out into the room before kissing me again. He finally pulls back for a breath, "So are you trying to say you don't want kids?"

I smack him in the chest and pull his chin even with my own, "Are you trying to tell me you fucked up last night?"

He smiles back at me, nodding his head, "Oh, I fucked up. I told you that Dalmore is dangerous. But that is the only mistake I made. I promise you. I honestly don't even think I could get it up for another girl. You have broken me Susie. Little Edge only has eye for you."

I laugh at him as I shake my head back and forth, "Perv."

He laughs along with me as he stands up, reaching a hand back down for me. I take his hand, dropping my bag on the floor.

I feel his hands come down and trace the fingernail marks I left on my chest. I pull my eyes back to his, "I just kept having panic attacks. They wouldn't stop. I was scared to be alone. I didn't even know I did this until this morning. The silence was just so loud, then everything, his voice just kept replaying in my head."

He nods his head at me then brings his lips to a few of the cuts, kissing them gently. Then he is kissing my jaw, my healing cheek, then the outside of my eye. I smile at him as he pulls back, "It will all heal."

I put my hand on his chest, bringing his gaze to mine, "Yes it will."

He nods again as he brings his lips to mine. I kiss him back gently as I feel his hands run up and down my back. I push into his lips a bit harder and he pulls back, "You're still healing."

I don't even open my eyes to look at him, "If you don't fucking kiss me like you love me right now I swear to god Edge. I will make your life a living hell." He snickers as he brings his lips back to mine. Pressing gently again.

I wrap my hand around his neck and hold his mouth to mine as I part his lips with my tongue. I hear a small groan leave his throat as my tongue starts to dance across his own. His hand reaches down and he grips my ass tight. He swiftly picks me up then lays me down on the bed.

He takes my shoes off one at a time before bringing his eyes back to mine, "Are you sure?"

I point to my shorts, "If you don't do your job, I am going to revoke your health benefits."

He laughs as he grips the top of my shorts, "Is that like a nice way to tell me I am going to get fired?"

I smile back at him, "Hey, I still have Brian. Don't tempt me."

He growls again as he yanks my shorts down, causing a gasp to leave my chest. Then I feel my shirt getting yanked up

270

over my head. His lips come down around my nipple as I arch my back pushing my tit further into his mouth. I grip his hair tight as I bite my bottom lip. It feels like it has been months since he touched me like this. I know it hasn't even been a full week but it has been torture.

His eyes come back to mine and I swear they have never been more blue. I smile down at him as he pulls his shirt up over his head then unbuttons his pants, taking them and his boxers down at the same time. I scoot up onto the bed and bend my knees leaving them open for him. He moves up my body like a predator on the Serengeti.

I kiss him hard as he lines up with my entrance and pushes himself inside me. I instantly feel myself stretch around him. I groan into his mouth as he begins to push in and out of me. I lean my head back, closing my eyes, "Jesus Gavin I have missed this."

He pushes into me a bit harder and I look down at him. I can see him holding back. I smile as I wrap one foot around the back of his leg and roll him under me.

He is surprised but puts his hands on my hips as I start to rock onto him. He is watching me closely, "Are you okay?"

I stop moving and lean down close to his face, "If you keep treating me like I am breakable then I am going to break you. Get me?"

He smiles until I reach up and grip his neck tight. He lifts his chin just a bit as I get a better grip on him. I start to push myself down on him in quick short bursts as he lets a moan leave his mouth. I close my eyes and before I know what is happening he is rolling back on top of me.

He grabs both of my hands and pins them to the bed beside my head as I smile back at him, surprised. He kisses me hard then pulls back, "Tap out if it is too much." I look up into his eyes as I see his hand come to wrap around my neck. He

271

squeezes tighter as he starts to push in and out of me. I smile back, never....never will I tap out.

I close my eyes, enjoying the ride. He starts to speed up just a bit and his grip tightens just a fraction. I smile at him as I start to meet him thrust for thrust. I take my hand and wrap it around his, squeezing tighter. His eyes go wide as he continues to throw himself into me. His hand is so tight around my neck that I can barely pull in any air. I feel my mouth open slightly and then I feel myself start to clamp down on him. I am just seconds away from tapping out when he releases his hand and slams into me.

I scream at my release. I have never cum so hard in my life. He continues to slam into me repeatedly until he leans in close to me and wraps his hands around the top of my head. He is using me as leverage to slam himself into me harder each time. I scream out again as I feel it starting to climb deep within me, "Don't stop baby. Please don't stop."

He leans back, bringing his knees underneath him as he lifts my hips from behind and continues to spear deeper and deeper into me. I reach down, digging my fingernails into his forearms as he rolls his head back. Slamming into me over and over. His eyes finally meet mine again and I smile as I feel myself gripping him tight again. His mouth drops open just a bit and he brings his chin back to his chest as he slams into me again until I feel him pulsating in waves inside me. His hands grips the sheets as he screams my name into the room.

I continue to moan as he rides out his waves along with my own. He finally starts to slow down and he smiles down at me as he lowers my hips, "Are you okay?"

I smile as I slowly open my eyes, "Oh yeah. I am good."

He laughs as he leans down kissing me again. He continues to stroke the sides of my head as he pulls back to look into my eyes. I search his face for some sign of anything but all I see is love, adoration. I grin back at him as he slides his legs out from underneath himself then rolls off of me to lay beside me.

I turn scooting my back into him. I feel his arms go around me as he holds me tight to him. I can feel him still half hard behind me. I smile towards the window as I take his hand and move it towards my breast. I close my eyes and smile towards the window as I feel his breath on my neck as he squeezes my tit then rolls my nipple between his fingers.

He lets out a groan as I push my ass down on his cock, making me smile even wider. He moves his hand down in between my thighs, then tries to push them open with his fingers. I look down, watching his fingers as they slip between my legs, finding me still dripping wet for him.

I quickly slip from his grasp and walk over to my carry on. I pull out Brian and turn around smiling at Edge. He chuckles at me as I step back to the bed then slide back down in front of him. I grab his hand and pull it back around to my abdomen, placing Brian in it. I feel his breath as he laughs into my neck. I instantly feel him placing the toy against my clit and sliding it up and down.

I push back on his cock again then he dips the toy a bit lower, hovering right outside my entrance. I slide my hand under his arm and reach between us to grip his hard dick. He moans into my ear again then takes the toy and pushes it inside me slowly.

I close my eyes as I take his dick and place it at the entrance of my ass. I hear his breath intake deeply, "Are you sure?"

I answer him by pushing myself onto him harder. Not hard enough to push him inside, but enough to let him know he has full permission. He pulls Brian out of me, leaving me whimpering as he takes the toy and uses it to spread my juices up the back of me. Making it easier for him to slip inside.

I relax as I feel him slide Brian back inside me, then I feel him grabbing the base of his dick as he slowly starts to push into me. I let out a growl into the room around me. He barely even has his head inside me and I already feel completely full. He is trying to slowly work his way in but I am desperate for more. Desperate for the friction of his movements.

He is still sliding Brian in and out of me as I push myself down onto him further. He lets out a moan, "Goddammit Susie." I smile as I open my eyes and look down to see him sliding the toy into me faster. I lift my eyes back to the window as I feel him starting to kiss my neck and shoulder. I push down on him again and he nips the soft skin where my neck meets my shoulder.

I smile wider as I push down on him further hearing him whisper, "Baby, I am trying to go slow not to hurt you. You are making it very hard to control myself right now."

I smile and look over my shoulder towards him, "Maybe I want you to lose control."

He growls into my ear as he starts to slam Brian in and out of me faster and harder than before. I lean back into him at the same time that he thrusts forward. I can feel him bottom out inside me and it feels like heaven. I turn my head back over my shoulder, "I wanna sit on your lap." He moans into my ear again as he pulls the toy out then wraps his arms around me to roll onto his back. He sits up still inside me. I spread my legs, folding them back around us then use them as leverage to slide him in and out of me. I brace my hands on his thighs as I continue to spear his dick into my ass.

He leans back on his hands and I glance back just in time to see his eyes roll up in his head as it falls back between his shoulders. I reach over and grab Brian then slide him inside of me as well. I am riding Edge and pleasuring myself with Brian when I feel him sit up behind me and reach around grabbing my hand.

I look down watching his hand wrap around mine as he starts slamming Brian inside of me. I scream into the room as I continue to bounce up and down on him. He reaches his other hand around me and starts to circle my clit faster and faster. I can feel myself about to explode all over him.

I let my head fall back between my shoulders as I slam down onto him harder. I can feel him thrusting up into me now. When he puts his mouth back on my neck and I feel him bite down, I lose myself in it all. I clamp down on the toy and his dick at the same time. I hear him grunt behind me, "Fuck Susie. I can't stop, baby I can't stop."

I scream into the room again as I slam back down on him two more times before I feel him swell inside me. He is still pumping the toy inside of me in quick successions when I feel it all building up again. I literally start crying, "Baby, I am gonna cum again. Fuck you are so big. I need it. I need it, baby."

He is circling my clit and slamming the toy into me as I continue to thrust myself back into him. He pinches my clit and I lose all control of my body. My hands grip his thighs tight as I feel myself explode around him. I scream his name as I feel my release gushing out of me. He pulls the toy out of me, throwing it off onto the floor as he takes his fingers and slides them into me instead. He continues to attack my clit and thrust up into me until we can feel the waves passing through both of us.

It is like we are two ships passing in the night. Drawn to each other, destined to crash and tangle into one another for all of eternity. I finally start to come down. I slow down my movements as he lays back down and rolls us back to our sides. I smile as I hear him hiss as he slides out of me.

I fall forward onto my stomach and turn my face towards him. Smiling as he leans in and kisses me. He pulls back to hear me saying, "I can't feel my legs."

He chuckles back at me, "Is that a good thing or a bad thing?"

I laugh back at him, "Right now, that is a very very good thing."

I open my eyes as he brushes the hair out of my face then leans in and gives me another kiss. He rubs his hands down my back a few times before smiling, "Come on. Let's go take a shower."

I nod at him as I try to stand without discomfort. It has been a very, very long time since I have done that with anyone. And certainly never with anyone as big as him. I smile at him with a sideways grin, "I might be sitting funky for a week."

He laughs as he helps me stand then we start to make our way towards the bathroom. I feel his hand caress my ass and I turn to him smiling. He looks into my eyes, "I didn't bruise my peach did I?"

I laugh at him as I smack his hand away, "Your peach is fine babe."

He grins at me as he starts the water and we step inside to get cleaned up. I stand back watching him as I run a wash rag over my body. He is fucking perfect. From his dirty blonde hair, to his pierced nipples then all the way down to his incredibly seducing dick. He smiles at me when he catches me checking him out, "Can I help you ma'am?"

I smile back up into his face, "I am just trying to figure out what I did to get so lucky."

He reaches his hand up and strokes my cheek with his thumb, "I am the lucky one Susie."

23
Edge
Concrete Jungle - Bad Omens

We are finally halfway done with the tour. We only have about 8 more stops and it will finally be over. Then we are taking an extended hiatus. Susie and I will get married. Gideon and Lily will settle in with their incoming family. It is all starting to finally fall into place.

Susie is feeling much better now that she doesn't look like she was smacked in the face with a 2 by 4. She already filed all the paperwork for her fiance visa so as soon as the tour is over we can head home and finally make it all official.

I sometimes wake up thinking that it is all just really a dream. That she isn't real. That none of it is real. But then she hits me with that megawatt smile and I am home again. We have found a regiment that seems to be helping with the anger, the voices. I volunteered to step back from drinking as much as well. I don't know that it was hurting but I damn sure know it wasn't helping either.

Tonight is our last show in New York. We get through tonight and we will move onto another city in a few days. Susie, thankfully has been able to wear a mask again so she has been at every single show. Everything has finally started to fall into place again. I am still trying to get my anger issues under control but I haven't lost it like that last night when I screamed at her.

I have accepted that she loves me for me. Anger and all. But I still need to get some help with it. I have no real idea where to even start looking for help but I know I need it.

I smile at her standing off stage as the show is starting to wrap up. She is also grinning from ear to ear right back at me. We shut the house down, another successful night in the books. I have taken to walking out with Peach after each show. After she was taken from me, I can't just let her walk unprotected. I know he is gone, I killed him. But the thought of her being dragged down that hallway haunts my dreams every fucking night.

Finally reaching the green room, we all step inside then get comfortable with our drinks. The fans start to trickle in and I am again just wishing this part was over. I am fucking exhausted. I just want to go back to the hotel and sleep for a week. Or as long as Peach will let me. I smile as I sip my drink and she rubs my shoulders.

I catch a glimpse of the groupie in the hallway through the line of people. My shoulders instantly tense and I look up behind me to see Susie's eyes on her as well. I can see the red creeping up her neck and I am just praying she is able to keep her rage to herself.

My eyes come back down to the groupie as she steps up smiling at me. Her eyes then go to Susie and she smiles wider as she leans down towards me, "I hate that she is back with you baby. Didn't I take care of you well enough last time?"

My eyes go wide as I try to sit back in my seat a bit further. Susie steps around the side of the chair, her grip still tight on my shoulder, "What the fuck are you talking about bitch?"

The groupie smiles wider as she stands up turning to Susie, "He didn't even seem to remember you when he was balls deep inside me last time. I just assumed he had taken out the trash."

She gives Susie a fake but empathetic smile, "Isn't it just disgusting how men only want one thing?" Susie narrows her eyes at the bitch in front of her, "If it's so disgusting then fucking wash it every once in awhile."

My stomach instantly drops. I turn to look at Ares and he just shakes his head at me. I didn't think I had been with her. He had told me he found me in the hallway with her but we were both fully dressed. There was no way I had time to be with her before he found me. I go to stand up and I see a fist coming from the right.

Susie clocks the groupie in the jaw and she screams as she falls backwards. I grab Susie's arms, holding her back from jumping on the groupie. I can feel her skin and muscles tighten from my grip on her. She leans forward, spitting on the groupie, "You fucking lying cunt. Why can't you just leave us the fuck alone? He is not yours. He will never be yours!"

I continue to try to pull her back as the groupie turns smiling devilishly back at Susie, "That's not what he told me. He told him I made him cum harder than you have ever been able too. He told me I belong to him now."

My throat closes tight as Susie turns to me. The anger in her eyes wild with misunderstanding. I shake my head at her as she pulls herself out of my grasp. She shakes her head at me, "Congratulations on your downgrade, I hope she was worth it."

She turns from me and starts to stomp out of the room. I look down at the groupie as she smiles back up at me. I am completely frozen. Did I sleep with her? I don't even remember seeing her that night. I look at Ares and he shakes his head at me as he stomps over to me. He looks down at the groupie then reaches out a hand to help her back to her feet.

I fall back a few steps not understanding what the hell is happening. The groupie stands back up smiling from me to Ares. Ares lets her hand fall and steps up to her, "I found you in the hall

279

with him 3 minutes after you walked out the door. Fully fucking dressed bitch. There wasn't time for anyone to get balls deep into your raunchy fucking cunt. You need to leave. Now. You are not welcome back either."

I finally feel the air rushing back into my lungs. I am still looking from Ares to the door when he nods towards security. Lucy steps up from in between the two guards, "Party is over everyone. Time to clear the room." The guards start moving towards the doors to open them and usher everyone from the room.

The groupie looks at me and I smile and flip her off as she is turned and ushered from the room by security. Aphrodite runs past me, "I am going to find Susie." I feel my heart tighten in my chest as I fall into step behind her. I am not letting her go. She has to hear the truth from Ares. She has to know nothing fucking happened.

We search the hallways and the bathrooms but she is gone. The longer it takes to find her the more nervous I get. I turn to Aphrodite with her phone to her ear. She looks at me shaking her head as she pulls the phone from her face and hits the end call button. I turn and punch the concrete wall and scream into the empty hall, "FUCK!"

Ares storms past me, "Come on. We are going to go find her." I nod at him as Aphrodite falls into step behind me. I look over my shoulder to see Hera and Hestia dragging Apollo behind them as they try to keep up with us.

She is sitting on the end of the hotel room bed when I step inside. Her suitcase on the floor beside her. I glance around, quickly noting that everything she owns is packed. I step in front of her, taking off my mask and throwing it onto the table before lowering myself to the floor in front of her.

She shakes her head at me then looks past me towards the wall of windows. She lets out a heavy sigh, "I don't believe what she said. I still believe when you told me nothing happened."

I let out a heavy sigh of relief as I put my hands on her thighs. She turns to me, tears rolling down her cheeks, "But I can't do this. I can't keep trying to live through the next day. I want to be excited for the next day with you. Not dreading what the next piece of fucked up shit is going to be."

I lean back onto my heels blinking wildly at her. I look at her bag again then back at her face. She tilts her head to the side a bit. She looks sad, almost heartbroken. I choke out the words, "Are you leaving me?"

She takes in a deep breath, the air shuddering around her twitching chest, "I don't know. I think so."

My heart instantly shatters into a thousand pieces. I shake my head at her, "No. No you can't. I didn't sleep with her. I didn't. You can ask Gideon and Lily. Believe me baby. Please."

She nods her head at me as she takes in another shaky breath, "I believe you. I told you that already. I just don't know how much more of this I can take. Every fucking time I turn around, something else is trying to pull us apart. I am starting to think it is the gods trying to tell us something."

She stands and steps around me, walking to the windows with her arms wrapped around herself. I stand following her, "No, that is bullshit. You know it is bullshit. We are meant to be together. I am yours, you are mine. We are destined, remember? You can't leave me."

She turns around crying again, looking meeker than I have ever seen her, "I don't want to leave you. I don't. I just don't know what else to do. I can't keep living like this."

I step up to her and look down into her face, "Gideon kicked her out. Banned her from the shows. She won't be able to get close to us again. I swear it." I watch her nod her head at me then let out another slow breath.

I put my finger under her chin and pull her face back up to mine, "After this tour, I am going to take a break. We need some time just for us. Without all this chaos around us. We were already planning a hiatus, with the baby coming and everything."

She blinks, scouring my face before giving me a soft smile and nodding her head. She leans into me and wraps her arms around my waist. Finally, I feel like I can breathe again. I grab her back tightly and squeeze her until I hear her let out a laugh, "I can't breath Gavin."

I loosen my grip and smile as I pull back from her a bit. She smiles up at me as I wipe some of the hair out of her face. I smile down at her and give her a kiss as she squeezes me a bit tighter. She lays her head back on my chest and lets out a sigh, "I wanted to stab her in the jugular with a dull pencil."

I let out a laugh as I hug her tighter, "Yeah, that would not have ended well."

She lets out another chuckle as she leans back smiling back up at me again. I kiss her again and hold her as tight as she will allow. I grin into the air around us, "We leave in a few days for a week break. We will be completely alone, except for the band. But at least all the crazies will be gone." She smiles at me again as I pull away and start to get ready for bed.

Susie changes into something more comfortable and a lot more revealing as I take a shower and get ready for bed as well. I keep thinking back over that night, just to make sure my memory isn't playing tricks on me. But Gideon is right, there is no way we fucked. I climb into bed a few minutes later, holding Susie tight to my chest.

I wake up to the sun shining through the window onto Susie's beautiful face beside me. You can't see any lingering marks from the attack thankfully. I reach over and start to play connect the dots with the spots on her face. I see her mouth draw into a smile, "Are you having fun sir?"

I laugh at her as she opens her eyes at me. I lean forward and give her a quick kiss, "What do you want to do today? We don't leave for Nags Head until tomorrow."

She stretches her arms out high above her head as she rolls onto her back. She has started sleeping in the nude. I for one believe it is the best decision she has ever made. She has been getting super hot while she sleeps so instead of sweating to death in the middle of the night she just keeps that heat source tucked into my own.

She sits up then turns to smile back down at me, "I think I have an idea. Come on. Get up. We gotta go find everyone else."

I eye her questionably but do as she says. It isn't 20 minutes later that we are knocking on doors, trying to round up the crew. She refuses to tell anyone where we are going but advises them to wear jeans and no open toed shoes. She could not be more confusing or evasive.

An hour later, we are walking into a building that houses something called a Rage Room. I for one have no idea what we are about to do. I stand back as the people in charge hand us all helmets and jumpers to wear. Lily has decided to sit this one out but is going to be watching everybody through windows.

We are paired up, Me and Susie. Gideon and Mona. Then Simone and Matthew. Susie seems a bit too excited and it is honestly making me a bit nervous. We walk up to a table filled with all kinds of blunt objects. Baseball bats all the way down to golf clubs. Susie turns around smiling at me as she twirls a bat in her hand. The resemblance to Harley Quinn's face is terrifying.

I reach over and grab a sledgehammer, "What am I supposed to do with this?" Susie smiles as the workers walk back up and ask us to sign a waiver. I scan it over, what the actual hell are we doing that we could be physically hurt? I stare wide eyed at Susie as she signs her paper without even reading all the way through it. She turns to me and cocks her head to the side with the bat propped on her shoulder, "Ah, is someone scared?"

I growl at her as I sign my name then put my helmet on. She slaps the visor down on hers and turns into a room. I scan the room quickly noticing there is all kinds of random shit in here. A tv, an old copy machine, dishes, coke bottles, even some old records and vases.

Susie picks up a vase, turning to me, "This is beautiful isn't it?"

I nod at her, "Not really my taste but sure, I guess."

She smiles as she sits it on the corner of the table. She grins madly at me before turning and shattering it with her baseball bat. I jump forward, "What the hell are you doing?"

Susie turns around with a wild gleam in her eye, "It's a rage room baby. You come in here and fuck up shit to get the rage out."

I look around the room at all the different items, "You mean to tell me that I get to just break all of this shit?"

She grins and nods back at me. She quickly reaches down and grabs a glass plate then frisbees it into the wall. She smiles as turns back to me, "Try it. Take something out."

I smile back at her as I line my sledgehammer up and send it into the center of the copy machine. I let out a howl of laughter, "Oh this is bloody brilliant. I should have been doing this years ago!"

She smiles as she runs to another table, "I know, right?" She lines her baseball bat up and swings it at the flat screen tv. It flies onto its back on the floor and she just starts flinging the bat into it. Over her head, down to the tv. Over and over until there is barely anything left. The only worrisome part is when she starts screaming three swings in. This woman has some serious pent up anger.

I take her lead and start swinging the sledgehammer at more and more objects. She sits the bat down and starts slamming porcelain dishes and cups onto the floor in front of her. Every time she throws another one she grunts loudly into the room.

I sit the sledgehammer down and grab her baseball bat. She smiles at me as she turns and watches me completely destroy the copy machine and a printer. I take her lead and start screaming halfway through. I continue to pummel the useless equipment until the bat itself is slamming into the floor. One last swing and the bat breaks in half, splintering long ways down the middle.

I turn to her stunned, "Whoops." She is laughing uncontrollably back at me as she sits a stack of dishes in between us. I grab a plate and frisbee it at the wall, "This is the best idea you have ever had." She laughs loudly at me as we finish out our stack of dishes. We look around the room and quickly realize we have done all the damage we can do.

I am laughing at her as we walk back out the room and I take my helmet off. Lily is standing and staring through a window, smiling from ear to ear. I walk over to see Gideon and Mona taking turns destroying what looks like it used to be maybe a jukebox. I laugh out loud as I shrug out of my jumper. I turn to see Susie looking into a different window and her eyebrows are raised so high they are almost reaching her hair line.

I quickly move over and look through the window to see Matthew and Simone completely wrapped up in each other. Hands and lips everywhere as they stand in the middle of a completely destroyed room. Susie turns to me smiling but pointing through the window, "Pretty sure they are gonna have to pay extra for that."

I laugh out loud as I wrap my arms around her and give her a hard kiss. 5 minutes later everyone is making their way back out into the lobby of the establishment. I give the owners a very hefty tip and vow to return every time I am in town.

As I grab Susie's hand and walk out the front door I yell over my shoulder, "Fuck therapy. This is all the help that I need. Do you think they have one of these in London?"

Susie laughs along with Lily, "I am pretty sure they have these everywhere. I am honestly surprised with your um, anger issues, that you didn't know these existed."

I clutch my pretend pearls, "Yeah, no your right, I should have known. But now that I do there is no going back." I mean it too. I am going to find one of these in every single city we visit. I have not felt this relaxed without booze or sex in a long fucking time. I grip Susie's hand tighter as I veer us all towards a pizza place on the corner.

We all settle into a table and I instantly notice Mona making eyes at someone. I look across the room and see a girl giving her a little side smile back. I start to grin then look to the left of her, instantly recognizing her friend, "Oh, fuck." Susie looks up from the menu, "What?"

I reach over and grab Matthew's hat off his head. I turn to Susie as they both start to object, "Put this on." I shove it down on her head before she can even really object. I hold my hand on top of her head as she tries to pull the hat back off, "What the fuck are you doing? You're smashing my curls!"

I nod my chin in the direction of Mona's new life goal, "See across the room. One glance from her and she is going to recognize your fucking hair. I am pretty sure she has memorized every detail of you that she can."

Susie's eyes scan across the room and I see the realization slam into her face when she sees the groupie sitting at a corner booth. She grabs the hat, tucking her hair up in it, "Fuck, fuck, fuck. Do you think she has seen me?" I shake my head back and forth as Susie slinks down in the seat.

I look at Mona but she is still smiling across the room. I knock my hand on the table, "Earth to Mona?"

She turns to me hesitantly, "Yeah, what's up?"

I frown at her, "Your fucking killing me."

She looks around the table, very obviously the only one left wondering what the hell is happening. I lean forward onto my forearms, "Do you remember that groupie that Susie so casually pissed off multiple times? Mentions of blow jobs and I don't know making out with you after grabbing my dick? Oh yeah then laying her out flat last night?"

Mona laughs out loud as she bobbles her head side to side, "Well yeah. How could I forget?"

I tip my chin towards her new obsession, "Look to the left of your eye candy."

Mona's eyes fly back over to the table then a frown instantly forms on her face, "Shit."

I lean back in my seat, "Yeah, shit."

Mona turns to us frowning, "But she is so cute. She looks like Ruby Rose. I want a girl that looks like Ruby Rose." She crosses her arms across her chest, pouting her lip out, "No fair guys."

I hear Susie let out a breath, "Well, I mean. She doesn't recognize you. Or me thankfully. Maybe you can slip her your number. See if there is anything there?"

Mona rolls her eyes at her, "No, I am not going to jeopardize the band over a piece of ass."

Susie laughs again, "No one is saying jeopardize the band. Maybe see if she wants to meet up for drinks later. Just you two. Get a feel for it all. Who knows? Maybe it might be something."

I wrap my arm around Susie, pulling her close into my side. I give her a quick kiss on the temple before turning back to Mona. I smile wide at her, "You will never know if you are scared of heights if you don't step up to the edge of the cliff."

Mona smiles at me until we hear Matthew knocking his knuckles into the table. I turn looking at him as he looks down quickly, "Incoming." I turn in time to see Ruby Rose walking up to the table with the groupie right behind her. I turn immediately slamming my lips into Susie's to help block her face.

I hear someone chuckling, assuming it is the new girl, too afraid to look back in her direction. "So, hey, I don't know if this is even something you are into but I was wondering if maybe you wanted to get a drink later? Or maybe just meet up and chat?"

I continue to fake kiss Susie just as much as she is me. But we both lean our bodies a bit closer to Mona's side of the table so we can hear her response. I hear her clear her throat, "Yeah. That is definitely something I would be into. Here let me give you my number."

Not 3 minutes later, the new girl and groupie are leaving the restaurant. Susie and I pull away from eachother smiling widely at Mona, "Fuck yeah."

Mona smiles at Susie, watching her take the hat off and throw it back to Matthew, "That was fucking close."

I lean back looking out the window, watching the two girls walking away none the wiser, "Maybe she has given up on me. She does have a pretty nice shiner though. That would deter anyone right?"

Susie shrugs her shoulders, "Hopefully. I just hope our paths never have to cross again. I am trying to not go to jail for murder, not the other way around."

I grin back at her, pulling her closer to me as our food gets sat down in front of us. We all begin to eat our pizza but all of us notice that Mona keeps smiling into her phone as she texts someone.

Susie leans her elbows on the table, "Mona and Ruby sittin in a tree, k-i-s-s-i-n-g." Mona smiles at her and tosses a breadstick at Susie's face. She laughs as she grabs the breadstick and bites the end off of it.

Mona sits her phone face down on the table, smiling around the table at us, "Daija and I are going to get drinks later tonight. Get to know each other a bit better."

I watch Susie as she leans forward, "Fuck yeah!" giving Mona a high five. Lily smiles around the table then sneers at the food. Susie smiles as she leans into her, "Still feeling like food is the enemy?"

Lily rubs her barely even showing stomach, "This child is trying to starve me to death." I laugh out loud, looking at Gideon as he stares down at Lily with worried eyes.

I gain his gaze and smile at him, "It's normal. She will be fine. Eventually, the throwing up will stop. I think after this is the feral stage. Then the last being the 'oh my god get this thing out of me' stage."

Gideon smiles at me as I lean back into my seat. Susie smiles over her shoulder at me, "How do you know about all this?"

I smile at her as I take a large bite of pizza, "I looked up pregnancy symptoms when you started radiating like a furnace and sleeping naked."

Her eyes go wide as she turns to me fully, "You thought I was pregnant?"

I laugh at her as I sit my pizza down, "I am still not convinced you're not actually. But yeah, there for a minute I thought you might be."

She laughs as she leans back then we both glance at Lily who is smiling from ear to ear. I give her a questionable wide eyed stare back, "Why do you look like a jack o lantern right now?"

Lily claps loudly, rubbing her hands together, "Someone is taking a test tonight."

Susie laughs at her as she shakes her head and continues to eat her pizza.

Two hours later, Susie and I are staring at each other dumbfounded in the hotel bathroom. She is shaking her head at me as I continue to look from her eyes down to the positive test in her hands. Well fuck.

24
Susie
Calcutta - Sleep Token

This isn't real. This can't be real. I have an IUD. I can't be fucking pregnant right now. We are just starting to figure all this out. I can't bring a baby into this until I know for a fact that we are okay. That we are good.

I move from the bathroom after sitting the test on the counter. I can't believe this is my life right now. I quietly step up to the window, wrapping my arms around myself as I try to figure out exactly what we are going to do. There is a really strong possibility that the child may be sick or worse, not even viable.

I mean, if it isn't, I will have it. Though I know I am not ready. I will love it because it is an extension of him. I will worship the child's every step, just like I worship his.

The city looks so alive tonight but my head has too many thoughts running through it. Too many worries. I feel Edge as he wraps his arms around my waist. I close my eyes hard, I know he is excited. I know he is happy with this. But he doesn't know the truth behind it. He doesn't know that the odds are stacked against us. This will destroy him.

He sits his chin on my shoulder and I hear him let out a deep exhale, "So I am going to go out on a limb here and guess that you are not nearly as happy about this as I am."

I turn towards him and wrap my arms around his neck, holding his body tight to mine. I shake my head as I feel the tears start to fall, "It's not that baby."

He pulls back and looks me in the eyes, the concern evident on his face, "Then what is Susie? Why are you crying?" He gently wipes a tear away with his thumb as I lean my head into his palm.

I look up at him before pulling away and heaving out another sigh before sitting on the corner of the bed, "There is just a lot that could be wrong right now."

Edge kneels down in front of me, rubbing his hands on my thighs, "What do you mean wrong? I don't understand."

I look up at him again, not wanting to say the words that I know are going to destroy him. I don't want him to worry right along with me but I can't lie to him. I can't hide the truth or hell even my own emotions right now. He deserves to face this with the same knowledge that I have.

His eyes are so innocent right now. He has no idea what we are up against. I steel my nerves as best I can and wrap my hands around his, "You need to be prepared. Just in case things aren't okay."

He shakes his head at me in confusion as his grip tightens on my hands, "What do you mean prepared? You are scaring me babe. What are you talking about?"

I take in another shaky breath and look at our joined hands. I can't look him in the eyes as I destroy this moment for him. I close my eyes, not lifting my face, "There is a very strong possibility that the pregnancy may not stick. Or worse, if it is an ectopic pregnancy, which is very fucking possible because of the IUD. Then, in that case, the baby would never survive anyway."

I feel his grip tighten and his body move back just a bit. I still can't look him in the eyes, "I will call my doctor in the morning. I still have an obgyn here. I will let her know it is an emergency. I am sure she will do some kind of test or something but you just....we both just need to be prepared that this may not end well."

Edge drops to his knees and parts my own so he can scoot up close to me. He pulls me in tight to his body, holding me like I am falling apart. But it isn't me that I am worried about right now. It is him. I will be okay. Yes, it would be painful. To know there was a little piece of him and a little piece of me that would never be allowed to live.

But it isn't like we were planning this. I fully intended to have the IUD conversation with him before we got married so we could plan out this future together. No one likes a surprise, but this surprise comes with serious side effects....complications.

I feel him start to pull back and I still can't seem to face him. Even as he lifts my chin with his fingers, "Look at me baby."

I can't do it. I can't watch him hurt. Just like I can't let him watch me hurt. Not like this. Not about this. I shake my head back at him and he leans in, giving me a soft kiss. I instantly start crying harder. He pulls me in close and holds me as I wail into his shoulder.

Edge continues to stroke my hair and whisper his words of love until I finally start to calm down nearly a half hour later. My eyes are swollen and burning. I can also feel the beginning of a migraine coming on. All from the pressure of crying as hard as I have.

I look up at him, then turn quickly, "I am so sorry. I never dreamed in a million years that this would happen."

He pulls back from me just a bit, "Baby, you haven't done anything wrong. There is absolutely nothing for you to be sorry about. Neither of us expected anything like this to happen right now. It is not your fault Susie. If it isn't meant to be, it isn't meant to be."

I turn away from him and slide up to the pillows. I grab one and hold it close to my body as I lay my head on another. I don't even want to open my eyes. I just want to fall asleep and wake up to all of this being a fucking nightmare.

I feel Edge as he moves behind me and pulls my back in close to him. He just holds me, stroking my arm and my thigh until I finally fall asleep.

The clock on the nightstand says 2:12 am. My eyes fly open though luckily I can't seem to remember what woke me. But then the realization of my world comes crashing back down on me.

I gently move Edge's arm, then slide out from underneath of it. We are both still fully clothed from when we were talking earlier. I grab my phone off the night stand and quietly tip toe into the bathroom. Shutting the door as gently as I can.

I let out a heavy sigh as I hit Lily's name on the screen. It rings twice before I hear her voice, "This is new. Aren't I supposed to be the one to call you this time of night?"

I give her a weak laugh as I crawl into the bathtub and sit down inside, sliding my body down until I am laying in the base of it, "I am kinda freaking out."

I hear her moving around, then whisper something to Gideon. Less than a minute later she finally responds, "Okay. I am alone now. Talk to me babe. What's up?"

I let out another shaky breath as I listen for any noise coming from outside of the bathroom, "I'm pregnant."

I hear a little squeal from the other end of the phone and my heart drops even further. I knew she would be the most excited. Best friends being pregnant together. Our children would grow up like siblings.

I shake my head hard as she giggles out, "Oh my god Susie! I am so fucking excited right now! How far along do you think you are?"

I steady my nerves, once again preparing myself to break someone's heart, "Lily. I still have the IUD. The chances of the baby making it are really fucking slim. I have to call Dr. Kim in the morning. Get an emergency appointment."

I hear the sharp intake of her breath. She doesn't have to say a word but I know she is crying. The pregnancy hormones have her crying literally over anything so I know something this huge is probably destroying her. I listen to the silence a moment longer, "Are you okay Lily?"

She lets out a small laugh and I hear a sniffle follow close behind it, "I should be asking you that. Not the other way around. I completely forgot about the IUD. I know the possibilities are slim but I can't help it. I am excited."

I nod into the open top of the tub, feeling another tear roll from my eye and down my temple, "I know. Just try to keep a straight head about it until we know what is what. I don't want you to get your hopes up so high that it causes you any issues if I am right."

I hear another sniffle, "Okay Susie. I will keep my cool. But if this works out, and the baby is okay. Are you going to keep it?"

I feel a smile cover my face, the first one since I learned the news, "If the baby is healthy and it is not a risk to me, then of course I will keep it. I want nothing more than to start a family with Gavin. Is it a fucked up time? Yeah. But I wouldn't deny our child a chance to live if it is offered to me."

Lily is smiling ear to ear. I can't even see her but I know her well enough to know that she is cheesing right now. I let out another sigh, "I will call you first thing tomorrow and let you know when the appointment is. I think I am going to just spend time with Edge until then. Make sure we are both on the same page."

Lily's voice is chipper again, "Just think positive thoughts sweetie. Stressing over it won't help matters. Just shoot me a text before you go and call me as soon as you find out what is what. I love you Susie."

I smile into the phone as I sit up in the tub, peaking out of the side to find the door thankfully still shut, "I love you too Lil. I will talk to you tomorrow."

I hit the end button and let out another deep sigh. I crawl out of the tub a few minutes later and step out to see Edge laying on the bed in his underwear, staring at me as I gently close the door behind me. I walk around the side of the bed and set an alarm on my phone before stripping down to my own underwear then sliding up close to him.

Edge pulls the sheets up over us as he wraps his arm around my shoulders and kisses me gently on top of my head. I lay my face on his chest and inhale his scent deep into me. Finally, after what feels like days I can feel myself drift off to sleep.

The blaring alarm wakes me up promptly at 7:30 am. I roll over and turn it off before sitting up and stretching my arms and legs. I look over my shoulder and a sleep deprived Edge is staring back at me.

I give him a soft smile before getting up and getting dressed. I take my phone with me everywhere I go, just waiting for 8 am to hit. When it does I immediately call my doctor, explaining the situation. She has them move a few appointments around and lets me know to be there at 10 am. And to wear loose comfortable clothes so they can do an ultrasound.

Edge and I don't speak the entire morning. Not because we are mad, but I think more because fear of the unknown has choked us both. We finally go downstairs and hail a cab.

Dr. Kim is the best fucking doctor in the world. I have seen her for over a decade now. There is no one else I trust more when it comes to my body and the health of it. She is more like a friend at this point. She helped me heal so much after what happened with Evan. She even pointed me in the direction of a therapist that helped me figure it all out in my own mind.

Dr. Kim welcomes me with open arms and a warm hug when I step into the examination room. I pull back and look at Edge and see his eyes going everywhere. It didn't even occur to me until now that he has never seen the inside of one of these offices before. I smile at him then back to Dr. Kim, "This is Edge. My fiance."

Dr. Kim steps around me and shakes his hand, "Hello Edge. It is an honor to meet you."

He nods his head back but is still unable to say anything. I can't say as I blame him. I am pretty much over talking right now as well.

Dr. Kim directs me to sit up on the examination table as she turns and picks up a clipboard, "So do you have any guess as to how far along you might be?"

I shake my head no, but Edge sits up a bit straighter, "I am thinking possibly right around a month. It wasn't long after that when she started feeling like a heater at night when we would go to bed."

I smile over at him, realizing he figured this all out before any of us. He has had a month to mull this over in his brain and I have had less than 24 hours. Dr. Kim continues to write on the clipboard, "Have you had any pain, discomfort or bleeding?"

I shake my head back at her, "No. Nothing like that. I am just really concerned because of the IUD."

Dr. Kim shakes her head and sits down the clipboard. She steps up to the table and gently starts to lower me to lay down, "I won't lie to either one of you. The chances are pretty high that there could be complications. The chance of an ectopic pregnancy with the type of IUD you have is right at 50%. Even if it is not ectopic though, there are other complications that may arise."

I watch her as she turns to Edge, "Has she explained the risks to you?"

He nods his head, "For the most part yes. I did some googling on my own though as well. I didn't want to stress her out with more questions than she was ready for."

I stare at him, feeling another tear trying to leak from my eye. I quickly wipe it away then look towards Dr. Kim, "Let's just find out what we are dealing with and go from there. Yeah?"

Dr. Kim smiles as she pats my shoulder then pulls out the belly jelly and some paper towel. No more than 5 seconds later a nurse wheels in the ultrasound machine and I am staring at Edge.

I don't want to see the screen. The room is instantly filled with noise from inside of me. As much as I don't want to look, I still do. I can't tell what is what though. Thankfully. The only thing I can really recognize is the IUD.

I turn my face back to Dr. Kim and watch her expressions as she runs the wand all over my stomach. After what feels like a lifetime, she removes the wand and starts to wipe off my stomach. I look to Edge then back to her quickly, "Well?"

298

Edge stands up and moves closer to me, taking my hand in his own. Dr. Kim looks from me to Edge then back again, "The pregnancy is not viable. It is ectopic. There is a shot that I will give you today. It will terminate the situation. There is not much more to do beyond that. You were at most 3 weeks along."

I feel my shoulders start to shudder as Edge squeezes my hand tighter. He leans down over me and kisses my forehead, "It's okay baby. It's gonna be okay. We have all the time in the world to start a family. It's okay."

I continue to let the tears roll as he stands back up to face the doctor. It is then that I can see he is utterly crying as well. I have never seen this side of him. He is so broken right now. I turn quickly to the doctor, "Yes, let's do the shot. But also please remove the IUD. I don't want this to happen again. And I want us to be able to start a family as soon as possible. This whole situation has made me realize what I want. What I think we both want."

I look back to Edge and he is smiling but still crying. He nods his head at me, "That is what I want too Susie."

I smile back at him, realizing yet again that I am the luckiest girl in the entire fucking world. I send a quick prayer to whatever god is listening that they heal us from this moment and let us move onto bigger and brighter days.

A Sneak Peek
Of
The next installment

This Side of the Moon

I

Apollo

hate ur f**king self - Kami Kehoe

I guess I just need to learn to accept that I am going to be alone forever. Well, that's not true. I can have my fill of just about anyone that I want, but I am not getting any younger. Everyone around me is getting married and having babies then here I am, 29 years old with nothing or no one to call my own.

I thought for a minute that Simone and I would have something. Something more than just a fuck about. But I should have known better. Simone is not going to settle down. At least not anytime soon and definitely not with me. She made that abundantly clear when she blew me off yet again.

Even when I kissed her in the rage room, I knew that it was useless. There is no point waiting for someone who doesn't want all of you. If they have to pick apart the parts they want and the parts they can do without, they aren't for you. And that is what she does to me, every fucking time. I think things are going well and she slowly starts to remind me of the parts of myself that she doesn't like.

I am not a risk taker. I'm not a golden retriever. I don't follow her around, swooning over her every breath. I get it to an extent. She wants somebody that loves every little bit of her to the point of obsession. But that is not me. I don't feel comfortable stalking my woman like she is prey on the serengeti. I don't think I could be like that with anyone actually. Sure, I would accept her for her. But I don't think I could ever fully be what she wants. She will never accept me for me.

And that is fine. I'll be fine. I am fine. I never really allowed myself to fall for her. There was always some voice in my head telling me to hold back. Not to let her in fully. But I became infatuated with her so quickly. Or maybe it was with the convenience of her.

Possibly there is some romantic part of me that believed that we were meant to be. Because of the band, because we had known each other for so long. But very quickly I learned she only cared about herself, never me, never my pain. I just got caught up in the person I was trying to turn into for her. But that is not love, that is settling.

Settling for someone who doesn't deserve you or your attention. That is not healthy for either party involved. I thought that we were growing but I apparently had a blindfold on. Until it disintegrated and I saw her for what she truly is. Not mine.

Luckily, we have a week in between shows so I can take some time to decompress and just be. That is something I have been seriously lacking. Just some me time. No women, no band, no tour, just me.

I stretch out on the oversized couch in Lily's sitting room at the beach house. I love this fucking house. I love how no one bothers us here. I love that no one knows who we are. It doesn't hurt that this place is big enough for us all to have our own space but close enough that if we want to rehearse we can. Though right now, no one is thinking about music. Lily and Gideon are still in full parental mode. Picking out furniture and names to coordinate with colors. Even though they haven't even closed on a house yet. But they are trying to keep their excitement to themselves for now. Considering what Edge and Susie just went through.

That was fucking rough. Finding out you are pregnant one day then the next being told it wouldn't be viable. I can't imagine the loss that they both feel. But in a selfish way, I am kinda glad it happened the way it did. They weren't ready for a kid yet. Edge still has a lot of shit to work out. He has a lot of demons he needs to get a firm grip on before they are in a spot to start a family.

But who am I to judge? I have never even been in a real relationship. Secondary school doesn't count. That was a lifetime ago. I don't even think I want kids. I mean kids are great but I just can't see myself as a father. I don't think I want to see myself as a father. I am completely content just being Uncle Matthew to all the little brats everyone around me are going to spawn.

I decide I need a drink. Yeah, it's 10 in the morning but I don't give a shit. We have been touring for months already, with 2 more months still to go. If I don't enjoy the time off, is it even really considered relaxing?

I move to the bar in the living room and pour myself a glass of Dalmore. I take in the rich earthy scents of it, smiling at the bottle in my hand. The fact that Lily can't consume it like water right now means I get to have as much as I want. Of course, I will have to slip her some cash if I drink too much. Even though I know she wouldn't accept it, I would still try to find a way.

I take a deep drink as I turn and look around the room. Everyone is off doing their own things this morning apparently. I guess lonely day drinking is all that is on my schedule for today.

I smile to myself as I take another drink. The doorbell rings loudly through the house and I nervously look around the room.

I turn my body and try to see out the back window in case Lily is on the deck. Seeing no one, I turn and sit my glass down on the bar then make my way towards the front door. I look out the window to see Lucy standing there.

I smile, opening the door wide for her, "Lucy! What are you doing here?"

She smiles back at me, small laugh lines coming off her eyes and mouth, "Matthew. Hey! I am sorry to just show up unannounced but I am staying in town. I thought I would just pop by and see how Susie is doing after everything."

I nod my head back at her as I open the door, swinging it wide for her, "Certainly, come on in. I think her and Edge are still upstairs. I can go get them if you want."

She nods her head back to me as she steps into the doorway, bracing her hand on the jam of the door, "That would be great. Hey, my daughter is with me. Is it okay if she comes in too?"

I look around her seeing no one, but this is Lucy. I trust her just as much as I trust the rest of the band. Lucy has been with us since the beginning. She is family. I have heard her talk about her daughters many times but I have never actually met them. All I really know is that they are twins, around 22 or 23. I am actually kinda surprised that they are vacationing together but then I would probably be doing the same thing if my family were close by.

I smile back at her, "Of course it's fine. I will go get them. Just have a seat in the sitting room. I will be back in just a minute."

She grins widely at me as she turns around and starts waving at someone in the car parked in the driveway. I turn and run up the stairs to the third floor.

I put an ear to the door, just to make sure I am not about to see a lot more of Edge than I want to. I smile to myself when I hear him strumming his acoustic. I gently rap on the door with my knuckles. Not 10 seconds later, I see a smiling Susie opening the door.

I raise a hand, "Hey Susie. I don't know if this is a good time or not but Lucy is here."

She looks a bit surprised as she pulls the door open a bit further, turning just a bit so Edge can see us from the chair he is sitting in. He looks just as confused, "What is Lucy doing here? Is something wrong? Did something happen?"

I shake my head at them both as I stuff my hands into my jeans pockets. I have never been the best with words. That is 100% Gideon's department. I shrug my shoulders just a bit, "I think she is here to talk with Susie as well. I think she wants to basically give her apologies, about the situation."

I see Susie's eyes get a bit misty before she smiles and nods her head, "Yeah. That is fine. She is so sweet. Give me just a few minutes and we will be down."

I give her another small smile, "We will be in the sitting room. Oh and I think she said her daughter is with her. Not sure which one though."

Edge smiles as he stands up and puts the guitar in its stand, "So we don't know if it's the rebel or the angel? This could get interesting."

I laugh my agreement, "Yeah, I know. I will see you down there."

I turn and start making my way back down the stairs. I round the bottom of the stairs to see Lucy sitting on the couch. There is another person sitting in the arm chair with her back to me. All I can really see is long curly blonde hair. I smile at Lucy as I make my way back over to the bar, "Would you ladies like a drink? We have the best whisky you could ever dream of drinking. Or I am sure there is some sweet tea or something."

I pick my glass up and take a sip as I hear Lucy, "I will take some sweet tea. I am driving so I really shouldn't drink."

I nod towards the bar as I sit my glass back down. I turn to move towards the kitchen when I hear another soft spoken voice, "I would like to try the whisky. If it's not too much trouble." Her voice is almost a whisper. With a hint of rough gravel to it. Nothing like Lucy at all.

I continue to smile as I move forward to reach into a cabinet for a tall drinking glass, "Sure thing. Let me just get Lucy her tea." I quickly turn to the refrigerator and open the door to pour some tea into the glass. I look around the door but the girl has turned and is looking towards the fireplace. Probably looking at all the artwork Lily has leaned up against the walls.

I shut the refrigerator door and move back towards the couch, "Here you are Miss Lucy." I turn towards her daughter, "I'm sorry I didn't catch your name."

The girl turns to me, pinning me with big beautiful hazel eyes and a wide smile. She is fucking gorgeous. Lucy has been holding out on me. I smile back towards Lucy then at her daughter. She stands and reaches a hand out towards me, "I am so sorry. I have forgotten my manners. My name is Hope."

I smile back at her and I take her outstretched hand in both of mine. From just the one touch of her skin I can feel chills running down my spine. I let my hand linger on hers probably longer than it should, "It is nice to meet you Hope. My name is Matthew."

She nods back at me then her gaze goes to her mother. I could listen to this girl talk all day. She has the softest voice I think I have ever heard. It is a far cry from the females that usually surround me. Lily would be the next closest in line for that honor. I let go of Hope's hand reluctantly then move back

306

towards the bar. I grab another glass then pour both of us some Dalmore.

As I hand her a glass, Edge and Susie appear from around the bottom of the stairs. Lucy immediately sits her glass down on the coffee table then moves around the table to hug Susie. I can see a slow tear roll down Susie's face. I glance at Hope and see she looks almost as uncomfortable as me. Her eyes keep going from her glass to the floor then past me towards the kitchen.

I give her a quick nudge with my elbow, "Let's step out back. Give them a little bit of privacy."

Hope looks at me, eyes sparkling as she smiles and nods her head. I turn and move towards the back door. I graciously open it for Hope then give one last look towards the living room before stepping out onto the back porch.

I shut the door behind me and point towards the patio furniture, "Let's go sit under the umbrella. That sun is scorching today."

Hope follows my hand with her eyes before smiling and moving towards the chairs by the pool. She sits down, smiling out over the property then turning her head towards the ocean. She takes in a deep breath as if breathing in the sea itself. She lets out a small breath, "Is this your house?"

I shake my head as I sip my whisky, "No. I wish but no. This is Lily's house. She is Gideon's wife."

Hope turns back towards me, "I don't think I have met them yet. But they have a beautiful home."

I watch her as she takes her first sip of her drink. Her eyes go wide as she turns towards me pulling the glass from her lips, "Holy crap, that is good!"

I laugh back at her and her little southern twang when she speaks, "It really is. And it should be. You wouldn't believe what Lily pays for it."

She looks nervously from me to the glass then back again. I put up one hand, stopping her thoughts right there, "Don't worry about that. I know what you are thinking. Not only will Lily be offended if we don't drink it, she would be even more angry if we offer to pay for what we consume. Trust me, I have tried."

She lets out another small giggle, "Well, if you insist then." She takes another generous drink and I realize I cannot take my eyes off of her. She seriously could be a fucking model or an actress. Every single detail of her face is gorgeous. From her high cheekbones to her button nose. Her complexion is a warm tan like she spends all her time out in the sun.

I watch her pouty lips as the glass is raised back to them again. I clear my throat and quickly look away. I have to look like a fucking creeper right now. I take a quick drink, "So, Hope. What do you do for a living?"

She smiles and turns slightly towards me, "In all honesty, nothing right now. I had thought about going to college but I just couldn't see myself being happy spending any more time in a classroom than I already have. My sister and I went to a boarding school in England until we were 18. Then we stayed with some family over there for a few years after. We have only been back in the states for a little over a year now."

I smile widely back at her, turning in my chair a bit, "I am from London. All of us are actually. Except for Lily and Susie. They are from New York. Where abouts in England did you go to school?

Hope grins again as she takes another drink, this one a bit larger than the last, "Small world then. We went to Queenswood in London. That's ironic isn't it?"

I nod back at her as I lean forward and sit my now empty glass on the table, "That is. That is. So since school is out of the question, what is it you want to be when you grow up?"

308

Hope tilts her head to the side just a bit before turning and looking out towards the ocean, "I am not really sure. I mean I would like to maybe someday do what my mom does. I am jealous of all the travel she gets to do. But I will admit, it makes it hard to have any type of normal life." She turns to me, giving me a soft smile, "Which I am sure you know all about."

I nod back at her and give her a sympathetic look, "I guess that is partially my fault. Your mom has been our manager for almost 10 years now."

Hope nods and places her almost empty glass on the table beside mine, "Yeah, that sounds about right. We were 14 when we went to Queenswood. Luckily, we were only there for 4 years. Don't get me wrong, it was a wonderful school. It was just hard being away from everything and everyone I had ever known. It was easier for Dai, that is my sister, because she wasn't really attached to anyone in Georgia before we left. She has always been more of a free spirit than me. I had tons of friends that I missed like crazy. Still do sometimes."

I nod at her, "Yeah, I get that. I miss my family like mad when we are touring." A thought instantly flies into my head, "Do you know who we are? The band I mean?"

She shakes her head back towards me, "No. I just know that my mom is your manager. She has always told us she had to sign an NDA or something. She always said it wasn't her business to talk about."

I let out a slow breath and nod back at her. She leans towards me just a bit, "Is it really that big of a secret though? I mean, I don't really pay attention to social media and I also don't watch a lot of tv. Music I know, bands I know but not really by sight. But I have no idea who anyone really is, or what they look like. But I mean if she has to keep it hush hush then it must be a big deal right?"

I smile at her awkwardly, not really knowing what to say. It is not really my place to just word vomit our life story as a band. But at the same time I feel like I have taken a decade of this girl's life away. She deserves some type of answer for that. Some reason to understand why her mom had to do what she did.

As I argue with myself internally, Hope smiles and takes her glass back in her hand. She takes another large drink finishing it off. She waves her hand at me as she sits the glass back down, "Don't worry about it. You don't have to tell me. It is a secret for a reason right?"

I let out a small exhale of relief, "It's not that I don't want to. But it's kind of a whole band decision kind of thing. We don't really let anyone know who we are. Not voluntarily at least."

She laughs, small and breathy, "I mean are you guys like really well known though right? How would people not recognize you out on the streets? It's not like you are Carnal Decay or something right?"

She continues to laugh as I feel the color draining from my face. Well shit. I try to laugh along with her but she can apparently read me better than I think. Her eyes go wide, "Shut up! You are not!"

I smile and lean back in the chair, "Well hell. Cat's out of the bag I guess. I trust you will keep our secret though. You mom will be out of a job if not." I laugh at her reaction, the way her face lights up and eyes go wide.

Hope leans forward in her chair and turns to me completely, "Dai is going to lose her mind if she ever finds out! I won't tell her but seriously she loves you guys. I mean I love you guys too but she had posters on the wall kind of loves you guys. I swear our dorm was half covered in nothing but Carnal Decay pictures and albums. She even has a stuffed doll of Ares. She slept with it every night for 3 years. Which is just fucking weird considering she is a lesbian. But she did and then she also had

310

this tapestry that..." Her eyes come back to mine before going wide then she looks down towards the table, "I am so sorry. I ramble when I get nervous or excited. You have to tell me to shut up, I swear."

I smile as I turn my face towards her again, "I am not going to tell you to shut up. I think it's pretty awesome actually. That she was such a fan before we were even really that well known. But what about you? You didn't have any of our posters up?"

I see a streak of crimson fall across both of her cheeks at the same time. I lean forward in my chair again, "You did, didn't you?"

She shakes her head back and forth, "No. No, I didn't have any posters or anything. But I....nevermind. I can't say it."

Fully fucking intrigued now, I scoot literally to the edge of my chair, "Oh you have to tell me now. I am dying to know!"

She puts her face in her hands while giggling. I reach out and gently take her wrist moving it down towards her legs. Her eyes lock onto my hand wrapped around her wrist and I swear I hear her breath shudder in her chest. She smiles back towards me as I release her wrist and move my hand back. I feel that weird zap of electricity roll down my spine again.

She watches my arm as I move it back over into my own space, "You can't say anything to him. To anyone in the band, I would be mortified. Seriously, but I kind of had a huge crush on someone in the band. But I never really told anyone. I would sit and listen to you guys with her and she would just veg out. Usually high, but I always tried to imagine what he looked like. What he was really like. Behind the mask ya know."

I can feel my heart trying to pound out of my chest. Please god, I have never asked you for anything before. Please let it be me. To think that this perfect woman has been dreaming of me, I could die a happy man. I can see her cheeks starting to turn pink again but I just have to know. I give her a smoldering smile, "Who was it? Which member?"

She smiles back and parts her lips to answer when the back door opens. We both turn and look to see Lucy standing there waving at us, "Thank you Matthew for keeping Hope company while we talked. That was really great of you."

I see Hope stand so I stand up next to her, still smiling towards Lucy, "Your welcome. You are both welcome to stay for a bit if you want. I am sure Gideon and Lily will be down soon. Simone and Mona are in town but should be back soon as well."

Lucy shakes her head at me as I watch Hope step around the table and start walking towards her mother, "No, we have dinner plans but thank you. But there is a street festival going on in town tomorrow. If anyone wants to go, I think we are going after we switch over to our other hotel. We had to change our stay a bit and the hotel I booked couldn't accommodate us."

I don't even think before I speak, "Why don't you both stay here then? There is plenty of room and I know Lily wouldn't mind at all!"

Hope turns towards me smiling brightly before turning back towards her mother, "That sounds like fun mom. Then you wouldn't be stuck with just me. You would have other people to talk to."

Lucy makes a sarcastic face at her, before turning back to me and smiling, "Ask Lily. If it really is okay, just shoot me a text and we will come back after dinner."

I feel excitement rising up in my chest as the two women start to walk back inside. I take a step out into the sun, "Hope, you didn't answer my question. Which member?"

She smiles again shyly as she tucks a strand of hair behind her ear, "Apollo. He is the reason I learned how to play the drums." And with that she is gone and I am left thrumming with emotions under the hot North Carolina sun.

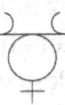

Lily doesn't know it yet but if she doesn't want them staying here I am prepared to go into full toddler mode, flailing arms and screaming. I don't even care that I am a grown ass man. I *will* get my way on this one.

I told myself that I was going to be patient. I was going to let Lily and Gideon come downstairs and get comfortable before asking them. But with each ticking minute on the clock, my nerves are becoming more and more frayed.

20 minutes later, I am banging on their bedroom door. Gideon answers the door, eyes half open and hair going everywhere. I smile at him, "Sexy." He flips me off before turning around, leaving the door open and moving back to the bed to curl back up behind Lily.

Lily opens her eyes and glances at me, "What's up Matthew? Is everything okay?"

I shove my hands back down into my jeans pocket. I know it is my tell that I am nervous but right now I don't care. I have to make this happen. Getting to spend 4 or 5 days with Hope is all I can think about now. I glance nervously towards Gideon, seeing that he can sense that I am on edge. He leans up onto an elbow, "Seriously. What's going on? Did something happen?"

I shake my head, feeling a blush come over my cheeks. Fuck, I feel like a damn teenager asking my parents for permission. This is fucking painful. I let out another sigh, here goes nothing, "So, Lucy just stopped by. She came to see Susie, after losing the baby. She wanted to give them her condolences.

But I also found out that she is staying in town. Apparently, there is something going on with her hotel and she is going to have to switch to another one. I told her she could stay here but she said she would only do it if it was okay with you, Lily."

Lily sits up and leans back into her pillows. She looks to Gideon who shrugs his shoulders and gives her a smile back. She turns back to me, "Yeah, I am okay with it. I love Lucy. She is always welcome."

I let out a heavy sigh of relief before I smile, "Oh and her daughter Hope is with her so she will need a room too. I will go make sure there are two open rooms. Thanks Lily, you're the best!"

I immediately turn and run for the door. Right as my hand reaches the handle I hear Lily, "What do you mean her daughter? I didn't even know she had a kid. I don't know Matthew. The house isn't really kid friendly right now. Maybe we shouldn't give her the green light."

I feel my head fall towards my chest. I knew it wasn't going to be that easy. I give Lily my most charming smile as I turn back around. I can feel Gideon's eyes boring into the side of my head as I continue to walk back towards Lily, "She has two daughters, twins actually. Hope is the only one with her right now. And you don't have to worry about child proofing the house, Hope is like in her early to mid 20's."

I look towards Gideon in time to see a devil's grin fall over his face. Seriously, he looks like a clown living in the sewers right now. He belts out a laugh as he falls onto his back on the mattress. I roll my eyes at his antics before looking back at Lily who is also smiling widely. She swings her legs around then slides off the bed, "Well in that case then. Let's go see what rooms are clean."

I let out another held breath as I put my hands in a praying stance, "Thank you so fucking much Lily. Seriously. You have no idea."

She chuckles as she steps around me before turning back towards Gideon, smiling, "Hope must be something. I have never seen Matthew trip over himself before."

Gideon slides off his side of the bed as he makes his way towards us at the door, "Me neither. It's hilarious."

I flip him off quickly, "You know I can hear you right? Just fuck off with that shit, the both of you."

Lily is laughing as she steps out into the hall, "I think we just have two rooms open. The one next to you and the one Susie stayed in last time. I will go check them, make sure they are still clean. Gideon, you wanna come help?"

He grins at me like a jackal again as he steps around me, "Sure thing babe. Matthew, you wanna call Lucy? Let her know she and her daughter are both welcome."

I give him a quick salute and a smile as I run back down the stairs and step out onto the porch. I walk over and sit down in one of the white rocking chairs and pull out my phone. I quickly send Lucy a text letting her know that Lily said they are both more than welcome.

I sit my phone down on the table and pull my smokes out of my pocket. I light one and sit back in the chair, slowly rocking as the sun starts to set on the horizon. My phone dings and I reach for it quickly. Lucy and Hope will be back here in about an hour. I smile to myself again as a car stops in front of the house.

Mona and Simone climb out with a few bags from what looks like a mall trip. Mona stomps up on the porch steps before noticing me sitting at the far end, "Hey. What are you doing out here?"

I smile back at her as I take another drag off my cigarette, "Just chilling. Lucy and her daughter Hope are going to stay with us here for a few days. I am just out here waiting for them in case they need help with their bags or anything."

Mona's eyes light up. I know how much she loves Lucy. Simone gives me a touch of a side eye though, "I don't think I have ever met her daughters. You said it's just the one though, Hope?"

I nod back at her as I take another drag, "Yeah, not sure where the other one is. They were here earlier and I offered up this place cause they were having hotel issues. Lily said it was fine so they are coming over after dinner."

Mona squeals obviously excited before running into the house. Simone gives me another quizzical stare, "What has you acting all chivalrous?"

I know she is probing for information. She doesn't get to play this game though. She is the one that called everything off with us. We wanted different things. Yeah the sex was fucking phenominal but I have a feeling alot of people feel that way about sex with Simone. I never really felt a deeper, more intimate connection with her though.

I smile back at her, "Nothing wrong with being a gentleman every now and again. Right?"

She nods her head at me as she looks around and back down the road, like she is expecting Lucy and Hope to just be standing there or something. She turns back to me, giving me another half smile, "Just be careful. Don't ruin shit with Lucy because you fuck around with her kid."

I instantly get pissed off. What right does she have to fucking lecture me? I give her a sarcastic smile back, "Nothing to worry about. Hope is a really nice girl, with a conscience. It's a breath of fresh air compared to my last relationship."

I know it is too much as soon as I say it. I instantly regret it when I see the look that falls over her face. She growls back at me, "Fuck you Matthew."

I give her another sarcastic grin, unable to control my own mouth, "You already did that love. Remember? It wasn't enough for you."

She turns from me and stomps inside slamming the door behind her. I hate that this is where we are now. But I will be damned if she is going to think she can just sit back and talk to me like I am the problem. Because I am not. And she fucking knows it.